Colorado Pride

COLORADO PRIDE

JACQUIE GREENFIELD

FIVE STAR
A part of Gale, Cengage Learning

GALE
CENGAGE Learning·

Detroit • New York • San Francisco • New Haven, Conn • Waterville, Maine • London

GALE
CENGAGE Learning⁻

LIBRARY OF CONGRESS CATALOGING-IN-PUBLICATION DATA

Greenfield, Jacquie.
    Colorado pride / Jacquie Greenfield. — 1st ed.
        p. cm. — (Under the Colorado skies ; 3)
    ISBN-13: 978-1-59414-919-1
    ISBN-10: 1-59414-919-4
    1. Colorado—Fiction. I. Title.
PS3607.R4537C665 2010
813'.6—dc22   2010028396

First Edition. First Printing: November 2010.
Published in 2010 in conjunction with Tekno Books.

Printed in the United States of America
1 2 3 4 5 6 7 14 13 12 11 10

DEDICATION

To my husband, Doug, my true life hero and source of inspiration. After more than twenty-six years of marriage, I am wonderfully amazed at how our love continues to flourish and evolve with each stage of our lives. Thank you for taking me on an incredible journey!

To my children, Jacob, Hannah, Adam, and Amanda, I pray that you will all be blessed with your own happily ever after as you enter each new and exciting phase of your lives.

ACKNOWLEDGMENTS

Having the love and support of people with the same passion for the written word is crucial for the continued success of my writing career. My critique partners are not only my professional support system, they are my friends and sisters of my heart. I would not be where I am today without the insight of Diane Palmer, Pamela Nissen, and Roxanne Rustand. Thank you all for the countless hours you've spent poring over each of my manuscripts to ensure that only my best work hits the shelves. You are all truly a blessing, and I am thankful for your continued presence in my life.

Consider it all joy when you encounter various trials, for you know that the testing of your faith produces perseverance.

—James 1:2–4

CHAPTER ONE

Seth Roberts couldn't remember the last time he'd breathed in the pungent aromas of horse manure and hay. Feeding chickens and milking an old dairy cow in subzero Colorado temperatures, just to have something to eat for breakfast, wasn't exactly the kind of memories he chewed on these days.

As he followed his good friend, Jared Garrison, through a newly built horse barn, carefully stepping around fresh mounds of manure, Seth silently wished he'd kept his old leather cowboy boots around. His hand-tooled Italian shoes weren't exactly made for this kind of wear.

Wooden stalls lined both walls on each side of the barn. A different color of horse stood contentedly in each, some chomping on hay, while others slept in the cool spring morning. Eighty-pound bags of oats and feed supplements lay stacked on a pallet in the corner beneath a second-story loft heaped to the ceiling with square bales of hay.

Seth stepped up to the third stall and draped his wrists over the side of the rail, watching as Jared dropped a worn leather satchel on the ground in front of a big, black-and-white paint. "I appreciate you working me in at the last minute to tour me around this morning."

"Not a problem," Jared said, unlatching the stall gate. "My older sister usually does all the tours. She's the head counselor, so I'm not sure what else you need to know."

"Is she around?" Seth rubbed his jaw and glanced down the

aisle. "I don't think I've ever met her."

Jared shook his head. "She left on vacation yesterday morning. Went out to California to watch our youngest sister graduate from medical school. She's supposed to get back next Friday." He pulled out a large plastic syringe from his bag and started filling the vial with some type of thick paste.

Seth cocked his head to the side and read the label on the tube. Looked like Jared was de-worming the mare. "What do you think? Will you be able to fit us into your camp this summer?"

Jared gave a quick nod. "I bumped you to the top of the list. We had a cancellation come in last week. After all you've done to help me get my vet clinic funded and off the ground, I owed you this one."

"Thanks. I can't tell you what a relief that is."

"Glad to help out. As far as some of the basics go, I know each camper is assigned their own horse to care for while they're here, and they're all expected to pull their load of chores every day."

"Chores?" Seth repeated, a little concerned. He flipped through the brochure for the J Bar D Outreach Camp for Kids, suddenly having second thoughts about signing his niece up for this summer day camp. "I thought this program was all about reaching out to the kids. Helping them cope with their problems. After everything Nicole's been through these past few months, I don't think she'll be any too thrilled about scooping horse dung and mucking out stalls."

Jared chuckled. "Believe me, buddy, these horses have a sixth sense when it comes to troubled kids. A summer around these guys, and I guarantee your niece will have a whole new outlook on life."

Seth studied the brochure, contemplating. Growing up in poverty on a rundown farm outside Leadville, he could personally attest to the kind of outlook he'd once had on life. Watching his dad work two jobs only to die of lung cancer in the end, he'd sworn to make something of his life. The moment he'd graduated high school, he'd left home and had never looked back.

Until now.

He kneaded the back of his neck where a spasm of pain shot down between his shoulder blades. His chiropractor attributed his discomfort to all the stress of the past few months since his only sister and her husband had been killed in an automobile accident back in March.

A thick lump formed in his throat. Now that Shelli was gone, he regretted not keeping in closer contact with her over the years.

Jared anchored the mare's head under his arm and quirked Seth a crooked grin. "Better step back a pace. I'd hate to get this stuff snorted all over that Armani suit."

Seth chuckled. "It's Dolce," he corrected with mock offense, following Jared's recommendation to step back and give the mare a little space. He slid a finger under his collar, loosening his tie. "I'm meeting with a realtor from Telluride and some investors at ten. Had to dress to impress."

As a senior account manager at Ferguson and Tate Investments, Seth had been in negotiations for months with a Japanese-based company, Five Seasons Athletics. With the acquisition of a one-hundred-year-old hospital and the surrounding three hundred acres located just east of Colorado Springs, Five Seasons Athletics had plans to demolish the building and put in a high-class golf and country club resort in its place. If he got enough investors in place and funded this project, he had a surefire shot at becoming vice president of Ferguson and Tate's southern division in Dallas. A promotion he could taste, he wanted it so bad.

Jared pushed the syringe into the mare's mouth, squirting the paste down the back of the horse's throat. The horse tossed her head, licking her lips, forcing some of the medicine to ooze out the side of her mouth. As soon as Jared removed the syringe, the mare snorted right on cue, tossing her head, making it abundantly clear she was not enjoying this particular treat.

When it looked safe, Seth reached over and gave the mare a pat on the face. "Looks like your vet skills are coming in handy around here."

Jared slipped the empty syringe into a plastic bag. "I come out about once a week and make my rounds. J.D. would've shown you around himself this morning, but he had to take his wife, Debra, to an OB appointment. She's due in a couple of months, sometime in mid-July. She usually does all the paperwork. They shouldn't be much longer if you want to wait around."

Seth glanced at his watch. "I think I've seen enough, but I appreciate you taking time and giving me the grand tour."

"Uncle Jared! Help!"

A loud whinny and a horse kicking one of the stalls drew both their attentions to the opposite end of the barn. "Uh-oh. Now what?" Jared bolted out of the stall.

"What's going on?" Seth asked, grabbing the gate and swinging it closed.

"I'm not sure," Jared hollered over his shoulder as he hustled toward the sound of the commotion. Another loud thud against the walls and a shrill, high-pitched whinny pierced the air.

Seth raced past several stalls and a small tack room before rounding the corner. He about tripped over a small sprite of a gal with long brown pigtails hanging down her front. She was standing just outside an opened stall where a big black reared up on its hind legs. Jared grabbed a lasso hanging on a wall just outside the stall. When the horse kicked its back legs into the wall, Seth's heart slammed into overdrive as he feared for the safety of the little girl standing so close. He scooped her into his arms and whisked her away several yards across the aisle as Jared tossed the lasso loosely around the horse's neck.

His heart still in his throat, Seth reached down and swept a braided pigtail over the little girl's shoulder, making a quick assessment of her face and arms. "Are you okay, honey? Did you get kicked?"

She tipped her head back and met him with startled big brown eyes, tears brimming her lower lashes. Her bottom lip quivered before she shook her head and pointed toward the entrance of the barn. "Kyle did it," she whispered.

Seth looked up and caught the backside of a young boy darting out into the ranch yard. A big kid from what Seth could tell. Looked about ten.

"Easy, big fella," Jared soothed, holding out his palm, trying to calm the big black. Muscles bunched and visibly quivered as the horse pranced nervously back and forth.

"What happened?" Seth asked, sounding winded. He took in a deep breath trying to calm his own racing heartbeat. Adrenaline still rushed through his veins.

"Looks like the kids spooked Evening Star," Jared said, running a hand over the horse's neck. Once the horse stopped prancing, Jared loosened the lasso and let it slide off the horse. As he coiled the rope into his hand, he turned with narrowed eyes on the little girl.

She pulled back in Seth's arms and ducked behind his head, as if he were going to protect her from Jared. Seth had to contain a grin as he got a better grip on the girl, anchoring his arm beneath the seat of her blue-jean overalls. She couldn't have weighed much more than a bag of puppy food, she was so petite.

He'd known Jared for several years, playing on a summer baseball league together, and lately, helping him get his vet clinic funded and off the ground. Jared would no more swat a fly than harm a little girl, no matter what she might have done.

"Where's Kyle?" Jared asked through gritted teeth. "He knows better than to come in here by himself."

"H-h-he ran that way," the girl said through a tiny trembling voice, pointing to where the boy had run away.

Jared mumbled a low expletive and draped the coiled lasso on the corner post of the stall. "You're both lucky you didn't get trampled on. Are you hurt?" he asked, stepping out and latching the gate.

"N-n-no," she stuttered through a sniffle. "I'm sorry, Uncle Jared."

Jared swept off his cowboy hat and heaved a big sigh, lowering his shoulders. "Awe, Katie, it's not your fault. Looks like I need to have another talk with your brother."

She looked back at Seth, staring deeply into his eyes, her big brown orbs a shiny puddle of chocolate. "Who are you?"

He smiled and had a difficult time deciding whether to put her down yet. She wasn't hurt, but something about the way she looked at him and fiddled with his tie drew him to the little girl. "My name is Seth Roberts. My niece is going to attend your camp this summer. What's your name?"

The little girl hesitantly looked toward Jared as if not sure she should be talking to a stranger. Seth took that as a cue to ease her slowly to the ground.

Jared hunkered down to one knee and opened his arms where she ran into his embrace. "This little munchkin is Katie. She's my niece." He placed a kiss on her forehead. "You scared me to death, young lady. Your mother would never forgive me if something happened to you and your brother while she was gone." He looked over his shoulder toward the opened barn door. "That was her big brother, Kyle."

Seth smiled at the thought of Jared playing babysitter while his sister-in-law went to the doctor. From the sounds of it, a third one was about to make things even more interesting. "Nice to meet you, Katie. I'm sure glad you didn't get hurt. How old are you?"

"Seven." Katie sniffled and started fiddling with one of Jared's snaps on his red-and-blue-plaid Western shirt. "Are you still gonna take us out for pancakes?"

Seth caught Jared's half-grin before he furrowed his brows and touched Katie's chin, forcing her to look up at him. "Do you promise to follow the rules and never ever go into the stalls without an adult with you?"

She nodded with tears filling her eyes again. "I promise."

"Okay, then. Go find Kyle, and wash up. I'm almost finished down here, then we'll head into town."

Her mouth quickly turned into an exuberant smile. The gaps where her two front teeth were missing only made her that much more adorable. "Thanks, Uncle Jared! I'll go tell Kyle." Then she twirled from his arms and galloped all the way out of the barn into the early-morning sunlight.

"Pancakes?" Seth chuckled and rubbed his jaw. "I see you're a sucker for brunettes with big brown eyes."

Jared laughed and stood, brushing hay from his knees. "When it comes to my niece, I'm a sucker for just about anything when she looks at me like that. Sorry about all the ruckus. They know better than to come in here by themselves."

"Don't worry about it. I'm just glad no one got hurt. I remember a time or two when I was their age trying to ride ol' Buckmeister when I thought my pop wouldn't find out. I had to learn with a bruised backside to stay away from the horse, and it wasn't from being bucked off. Shelli and I both had our share of discussions with our dad behind the barn."

Jared chuckled then slid his cowboy hat back on his head, his expression turning serious. "Sorry to hear about your sister, man. It must be tough."

At the mention of his only sister, Shelli, Seth's chest tightened. "More than you can imagine, but it's her daughter I'm concerned with right now. I'm supposed to fly out to LA and pick her up in two weeks. She wanted to stay in California and finish out the school year with her friends, so she's staying with Jerry's folks. She's their only granddaughter, and I think it kind of helped them with the loss of their only son. I really appreciate you getting her into your brother's camp this summer."

"Not a problem." Jared propped an elbow on the steel gate. "I'll have Debra mail you out an application. I don't have a clue as to where she files all that stuff."

"Sounds good. I'll have my secretary fill it out and mail it back as soon as we receive it." Seth strode closer to the stall where the stallion stood chomping on a mound of fresh hay. A small doll was lying on the ground near the horse's feet. He bent and reached between the fence, easing the doll away from the horse. He brushed dirt from the doll's face, which only had one eye and its dark-brown hair stuck out in all different lengths. It looked as though Katie had taken a shot at haircutting. "When did you say the camp starts?"

"In two weeks, the day after Memorial Day. It runs till the end of the summer, the weekend of Labor Day."

The timing certainly worked in Seth's favor. "That should allow me enough time to get a good portion of my negotiations with Five Seasons Athletics under way. Any more delays could cost me my job."

Since his sister's death, he'd had to reschedule numerous meetings and had lost a smaller account to one of his younger colleagues at Ferguson and Tate, which hadn't gone over too well with the senior partners. The conversion of the old hospital grounds into a sophisticated new resort was make or break.

He glanced down at the doll and swallowed. His newfound

role as guardian of his twelve-year-old niece might put a slight kink in his plans. Not only would he be focusing on his job, which would entail a lot of traveling, working long hours, and wining and dining potential investors, he'd have to be dealing with braces, ballet classes, and all that other . . . girl stuff.

A cold sweat broke out above his brow. He handed the tattered doll over to Jared. Was he ready for this? Was he ready for fatherhood?

Jared took the doll. "I'll give my sister a call and give her a heads-up about the last minute enrollment."

"Appreciate it," Seth said giving Jared a firm handshake.

Seth strode out of the barn and headed toward the parking lot. He'd just swung his legs into the driver's seat of his Corvette when his cell phone jingled in his pocket. He tugged it out and immediately recognized the California number. "Hey, Nicki," he answered. "What's up?"

He thought he heard a sniffle. "It's Grandma, Uncle Seth. She's sick."

"Sick? What do you mean? What's wrong?"

"I don't know. You need to come and get me."

Seth gripped his phone tighter. "Is your grandmother there? Can I talk to her?"

"No, she's watching *Wheel of Fortune.*"

He could hear the blare of the TV in the background. "I thought you said she was sick? Where's your grandfather?"

"He's out working in his garage." She lowered her voice as if she didn't want her grandmother to hear the conversation. "I think they just want to get rid of me."

"Do they know you called?"

"Yeah, Grandma's the one who told me to call."

"What about a friend? Can you stay with someone until I get there? Is there anyone I can call?"

"No. I've been staying at Chrissy's house the last two nights.

Please, Uncle Seth." Her voice sounded more urgent. "I don't like it here. Can you come and get me?"

Seth clenched the steering wheel tighter, contemplating his options. He could call a taxi and get her to the airport, putting her on the next flight out of LA, but something about a young girl traveling alone didn't sit well in his gut. The best thing to do would be for him to go out and pick her up himself. One call to his secretary, and he could have all his meetings rescheduled and a flight booked to LA. He might not have a job to come home to, but this was too important. He had to be there for Nicole.

"Hang tight, honey. I'm on my way."

Scrunched into the window seat of a Boeing 727, Heather Garrison Thomas gripped the armrests of seat 9E. Perspiration beaded her upper lip. Her heart pounded so hard she could hear her pulse thrumming between her ears.

Ever since her father was killed in a small plane crash when she was ten, she'd never stepped foot in an aircraft. Now, at twenty-nine, she was stuck on a flight out of the Los Angeles International Airport on an emergency trip back home to Colorado Springs.

The plane took a shallow dive. Her stomach lodged somewhere in her throat. Pressing trembly fingers to her mouth, she forced a heavy swallow. The scents of a woman's perfume and fresh-brewed coffee only worsened Heather's airsickness. Amtrak may have taken her thirty-eight hours to get out to California, where she'd attended her younger sister's graduation from UCLA Medical School, but at least she'd been able to keep her head up and her lunch down the entire trip.

Staring through a small portal window, she found a canvas of brilliant blue sky stretching to the far ends of the universe. But it was the disturbing vista a thousand feet directly below the jet that painted an entirely different picture. Ominous gray and black swirling clouds warned of a powerful thunderstorm brewing over the distant Rocky Mountains. Maybe they were going to fly around the turbulent cells and miss the storm entirely.

A loud ping echoed throughout the plane as the Fasten Seat Belt lights flickered on.

"Attention passengers. For your safety, the pilot has asked that you return to your seats and fasten your safety belts. We will be encountering a bit of turbulence on our descent into the Colorado Springs Airport. Please stow away any loose articles beneath the seat in front of you, or store them in the overhead compartments. We ask that you return your seats and tray tables to the upright position. Thank you."

Heather would've laughed if she weren't about to lose her lunch. Given the direction her life had taken in the last few months, she should've known the plane would nose-dive straight into the eye of the storm.

She tipped her head back and forced a heavy swallow, tightening her hold on the armrest. If she'd learned anything over the years, it was that no matter how turbulent things got at times, she had to hang on tight through the bumpy spots, appreciating every smooth spot along the way.

So far, she'd managed to land on solid ground. She just prayed her brothers had been completely honest with her about a fire that had erupted out at their ranch over the weekend.

Closing her eyes, she regretted ever leaving home in the first place.

"Go and have a good time," her older brother, J.D. and his very pregnant wife, Debra, had urged Heather as they'd dropped her off at the train depot. Their first baby was due at the end of July, and Heather hadn't wanted to impose on them during such a critical time in the pregnancy. But between J.D. and Debra, and their younger brother, Jared, they'd all assured her

21

that her two kids, Kyle and Katie, would be fine with them for a few days.

Three, to be exact.

An emergency phone call at her sister's apartment had jolted Heather out of her brief sabbatical from motherhood. According to J.D., her nine-year-old son, Kyle, had found a box of matches in the kitchen, and like any ordinary kid with a curious nature, had started a stack of newspapers on fire.

J.D. had rushed Kyle to Saint Anthony's Children's Hospital where he was treated for first-degree burns on his hands and arms. Thank God her seven-year-old daughter, Katie, had been outside and was unharmed. And other than minor smoke damage to J.D.'s house, he'd assured Heather that everything was under control, and it was unnecessary for her to fly back early.

She hadn't been convinced.

Not because she didn't believe her brother, but because Kyle wasn't just any ordinary kid. With his mild form of autism, his actions could be unpredictable. The trauma of the fire, coupled with the change in his home environment, could set off a gamut of emotional outbursts.

She had to get home to her kids.

The plane lurched. Her stomach followed. Blood quickly rushed from her head, and she didn't think it was going to flow north anytime soon. She bent over at the waist and propped her head against the seatback in front of her.

"Uncle Seth, I think this lady's, like, totally gonna barf."

Heather cringed. The roiling of her stomach let her know that she, no doubt, was the lady in reference. Hoping to dispel the worries of a young girl sandwiched in the middle seat beside her, Heather rummaged through the tote bag at her feet. "I . . . I'm not going to barf," she said with a shaky voice, trying to convince herself through the power of persuasion. "I'm just looking for a parachute."

A deep throaty chuckle sounded from a man sitting in the aisle seat. A large warm hand covered her shoulder. "Miss? It's all right. There's always a lot of turbulence going over the mountains."

Miss? She hadn't been called Miss in almost ten years.

With the tray table knob jabbing into the top of her head, she slowly turned to face the man whom the girl had referred to as Uncle Seth. She blinked, finding herself mesmerized by the brilliance of a pair of eyes as blue as the Colorado skies in mid-July.

His deeply tanned complexion and thick ebony hair made him appear young, late twenties maybe. She'd been acutely aware of him from the moment he and the girl had boarded at LAX, but other than a polite nod and a brief "Hi," no other exchange had actually taken place, much to Heather's chagrin. He would have been the perfect distraction to keep her mind off the emergency back home and her airsickness

Unfortunately, most of the flight he'd been stooped over his tray table, reading some sort of legal brief. Although the pilot instructed them to stow their things away for safety, this man's briefcase remained opened with several documents stacked neatly inside.

When the plane made another slow dip, she groaned and curled her arms into her stomach. "I used to fly with my father in his Cessna as a kid, but I've never flown in an airliner. Is it always this bumpy?"

He flicked a glance out the window behind her. "We have to fly right through a thunderstorm to get into the landing pattern. The unstable atmosphere is making it a little rougher than normal. We should level out in a few minutes." Then he leaned closer and lowered his voice. "If you think you might need it, there's a bag in the seat pocket in front of you." His eyes held a hint of mischief when he added, "You know, in case you need to barf?"

She caught his ornery half-grin and slowly raised her head, straightening from her hunched position. "Thanks, but I'm going to hang onto my lunch, if possible."

"Ugh, hell-o-o-o," his niece interrupted, giving a loud crack of her gum. "Am I, like, not sitting here?" Drawing her legs away from her uncle, who'd leaned across her legs to talk to Heather, the girl's expression was one of obvious annoyance. Or as her daughter Katie would say, "She didn't want to get his cooties."

With spiked, strawberry blonde hair, purple lip-gloss that matched vibrant purple fingernails, and womanly curves barely noticeable beneath her layered spaghetti-strap T-shirt, the girl looked to be in her early teens. Loud bass music filtered from a set of earphones connected to a compact MP3 player.

Clearing his throat, her uncle made a quick glance at his niece before turning back to Heather. "Are you going to be all right? I know the flight attendant. She could probably bring you some crackers or a soda."

Touched by his concern, she smiled and shook her head. "Thanks, but I should be okay."

"If you change your mind, you know where to find me." He slipped her a barely noticeable wink before he straightened and began arranging his legal papers into a neat pile inside his briefcase. Closing the lid, he clicked the shiny gold clips shut, the Gucci logo emblazoned on the surface of the black leather case indicating very expensive tastes. He wore no ring, Heather had noted right away, but then again, neither had her ex-husband after their first year of marriage.

His niece unfastened her safety belt, peering over the seats toward the front of the plane. "Let me out. I gotta pee." Her knee jostled up and down in an impatient bounce.

"Again?" he whispered, sounding slightly annoyed. "We might hit more turbulence. We'll be at the terminal in under twenty minutes. Can't it wait?"

"Ugh, my eyeballs are floating, already. I drank two whole sodas." The girl scooted to the edge of the seat, blowing a bubble with her gum then sucking it back into her mouth with a loud crack. "Come on. I'll be quick."

Seth hesitated, glancing down the aisle before he flipped his tray table up, securing it into place. Then he leaned slightly into the aisle and shoved the briefcase under the seat in front of him. Grabbing hold of the seat, he stood to his full height, towering over the girl as she slipped by him.

A young red-haired flight attendant met Seth in the aisle and propped her hands on her waist. "You're going to get me fired if you don't keep your niece in her seat." She didn't sound too upset and the broad smile on her face indicated she wasn't too worried about losing her job.

"Sorry, Rita." Seth blew out a heavy sigh, watching his niece slam into the restroom. "It's hard for me to say no to her right now."

"I understand," Rita said with a trace of sympathy in her eyes. "Don't worry. John said we've made it through the worst part of the storm. She should be all right." Then she touched his arm and lowered her voice. "When are we getting together for another pizza party? It's my turn to treat."

Seth covered Rita's hand with his own and laughed. "I don't know if I'm up for another all-nighter. But I'm sure Marty will be all for it. That's all he talked about for weeks."

"Jenny, too," Rita said with a giggle. "She asks about you and Marty every time I see her."

Heather couldn't help but notice Rita wore no ring on her finger, and when Heather met the woman's gaze, she realized she was eavesdropping on what was obviously a personal conversation. She diverted her gaze to her own left hand, rubbing her thumb over her ring finger where a white tan line was the only remnant of where her gold band had been for the past ten years.

The divorce papers were due to arrive any day in the mail, officially ending her marriage to Eric Thomas—ultimately, throwing her headfirst into the singles scene.

She gulped. Single. Even thinking the word made her shudder. Funny how the ring had once made her confident around the opposite sex, but now her finger was bare, making her feel vulnerable.

Using her peripheral vision, she watched how the flight attendant batted her eyelashes, leaning against Seth and touching his arm as she talked. She also laughed at everything he said, revealing a set of stunning white teeth.

Heather ran the tip of her tongue from one corner of her mouth to the other, wetting her lips. It'd been a long time since she'd flirted with a guy. She wasn't even sure if she knew how to do it anymore.

Rita's laugh drew her attention back to the stunning couple in the aisle. "Look me up when you get a chance. I have a few days off next weekend. You've got my number," she added with another laugh, full of invitation.

"I'll check my schedule. You be sure and tell Jenny I miss her hugs."

"I will."

As Rita made her way down the aisle, Seth dragged his fingers through his thick ebony hair and met Heather's gaze. "Mind if I sit there?" He splayed a hand toward the middle seat beside her. "I think my niece has been up and down ten times this trip."

Heather gulped. *Ready or not.*

Fiddling with her gold hoop earring, Heather gave a tentative smile. "Sure. I get the feeling she's not too thrilled about sitting beside me anyway."

"Don't take it personally," he said, easing into the middle seat. "Nicki and I haven't exactly hit it off since I picked her up."

"Ugh, it's Nicole," his niece corrected, quickly returning from the restroom. "I hate Nicki. Sounds like a dog's name or something." She plopped down in the seat beside her uncle. "Got any more gum? This piece tastes like rubber."

He reached into the pocket of his creased, light-tan Dockers, pulling out an opened pack of gum, offering her a piece.

She wrinkled her nose. "Yuck. It's cinnamon."

His jaw muscle ticked as he spoke in a low conciliatory voice. "Sorry. It's all I've got."

Instead of a thank you, the girl rolled her eyes and snatched the whole pack of gum away. Then she slid her headphones over her ears and cranked up the volume on her MP3 till the bass of the music could practically be heard three aisles away.

Muscles bunched at the base of Seth's square jaw as he took in a slow deep breath. Without a word, he reached down and secured his seat belt, giving what seemed like an extra jerk of the strap.

The air surrounding Heather suddenly felt warm. Moisture dotted her upper lip. She puffed a whiff of air up onto her face and gathered the material of her pink cotton blouse between her fingers, fluffing it in and out, trying to circulate the stuffy cabin air.

Seth reached up and opened a vent directly above her head, every contour of his muscular biceps evident through a pressed, wine-colored dress shirt. "See if that helps," he said, looking down at her with concern. "It's pretty warm in here."

She arched her neck, the cool air a welcome relief on her face, though she wasn't sure if the warmth on her skin was from the stuffy cabin, or the fact that she was sitting by one of the sexiest men she'd ever laid eyes on.

God, please don't let me throw up on him.

"Thank you," she barely managed. "That feels much better."

"What kind of plane did your dad fly?" he asked, spreading his knees slightly and wedging his feet under the middle seat in front of him.

She turned and stared out the window, thinking about her father, feeling her face relax into a reminiscent smile. "An old Cessna 172 Skyhawk. We had an airstrip at our ranch north of Colorado Springs. He used to take me down around Canyon City and fly over the Royal Gorge." It'd been almost twenty years, but she remembered it like it was yesterday. "It was so beautiful. Those were some of my best memories with my father."

"I take it you haven't flown for a while?"

She shook her head. "Not since I was ten. He crashed his plane into the side of a mountain and was killed. Guess I've kind of avoided the whole airport scene since then."

"I'm sorry," he murmured, sounding sympathetic. "I'm sure that's got a little to do with your airsickness. We should be on the ground in about twenty minutes. Just hang tight." Then he turned slightly and held out his hand. "I'm Seth Roberts, by the way. As you already heard, this is my niece, Nicole."

Heather gulped, staring down at his outstretched hand. He probably expected her to return the courtesy, which meant accepting his hand and telling him her name. If she ever wanted to get the hang of flirting, she might as well start with the basics. After all, it wasn't like they'd ever see each other after today.

Tentatively slipping her hand into his very capable grip, she smiled. "Heather Thomas."

His fingers curled around hers. "Nice to meet you, Heather. I take it you're from Colorado Springs?"

"Yes, actually. Born and raised on a horse ranch about twenty miles north of there. Couldn't imagine living anywhere else. How about you? Will you be connecting to another flight?" Okay, so now she was just being nosy.

He shook his head. "I've lived in Colorado all my life. Grew up around Leadville and moved to the Springs about five years ago."

Heather's heart rate kicked up a notch at that bit of information. She also realized he still had hold of her hand. Or maybe she still had hold of his. Either way, an odd feeling shot all the way up her arm, landing somewhere in the middle of her chest

As if reading her thoughts, he glanced down and smiled, giving what seemed like an extra squeeze before relinquishing his hold.

She tugged her hand back, cradling it with the other, stunned at the sensations still shooting up her arm. "Is your niece from the Springs, as well?"

Nicole made a low snorting sound. "Hardly."

He shook his head. "She's lived in LA all her life. This is her first trip to Colorado."

"You'll love it," Heather said, speaking to Nicole.

Nicole shook her head and turned away, mumbling, "I'd rather go to the moon."

Seth blew out a heavy sigh. "Nicole, we've talked about this. Please, just give it a chance."

"Whatever." She blew a bubble, sucking it back into her mouth with a loud crack.

Seth's jaw muscles worked as he clenched his mouth closed, obviously a tad irritated with his niece. He started rubbing the back of his neck and rotating his head on his shoulders. The tension between these two was almost palpable.

Heather turned and glanced out the small window, focusing on a giant fixed wing of the aircraft where a row of tiny rivets vibrated along the ailerons. Her eyes widened. Were those little bolts actually supposed to hold this massive jet together? She almost laughed at the irony, but at the moment, the simple act of breathing seemed difficult.

She blew out a heavy breath and looked up at the ceiling where a bright-red emergency exit sign caught her attention. She almost laughed. At thirty-thousand feet, where, exactly, would they be able to go?

The jet took a swift dive, jostling Heather forward. She tightened the grip on the armrest. Clenched her eyes shut, held her breath . . . prayed. She wondered what it had been like right before her father had crashed into the side of the mountain. Was he scared? Had he felt any pain?

"Easy, honey," a low, warm baritone murmured near her ear, followed by a searing warmth covering her hand. "Just a few more minutes. Everything's going to be all right."

She froze. Felt her heart skip a beat. Then wondered if it had actually stopped beating altogether. Over the years, there'd been many times when she'd felt her father's presence beside her, heard his voice whispering reassurances in her ear, telling her that no matter had badly her ex-husband had treated her and her kids, they were going to be all right and that they were never alone.

When she was certain her heart had started beating again, she slowly turned and found herself staring at a man's profile. Though not her father's, he was just as handsome. His eyes were closed. A small scar at the corner of his brow made him that much more real. He had strong, chiseled cheekbones and a square, smooth-shaven jaw. His nose, though in perfect proportion to his face, had a slight bump in the middle, as if it had been broken and had never been properly set. Another scar at the base of his chin had her envisioning him as an outgoing little boy who probably always had scrape marks on both knees as well.

His cuffs were rolled back, revealing a smattering of dark hair on his lean forearms. A shiny gold Rolex watch with a wide masculine band circled his wrist. He had the nicest hands she'd ever seen on a man, too. Long fingers tapered at the ends into buffed square fingernails. And at the moment, one of those strong hands was wrapped securely around hers. Taking in a calming breath, she caught a trace of musk along with hot cinnamon, the scent reminding her of the cinnamon dots her son liked to eat with his ice cream. The sweet thought amazingly brought her comfort.

A gentle brush of his fingers over the backs of her knuckles soothed her unsteady equilibrium. She closed her eyes, reveling in the simple act of holding hands with this total stranger. It'd been a long time since she'd felt protected, wanted . . . loved.

Even before Kyle had been diagnosed with autism six years ago at the age of three, the strain of raising a difficult child had taken a heavy toll on her marriage. Despite what medical experts told them, her ex-husband had always blamed her for their son's problems and rarely showed her any type of affection. Holding hands was something she only did with her kids.

Then she remembered Kyle's burns. Hair raised on the back of her neck. Her heart beat faster. Eric had wanted to institutionalize Kyle from the beginning, insisting he was a danger to Katie. Said he'd get better care and education from professionals. Although there was a good private facility north of Colorado Springs that dealt with children just like Kyle, she'd opted to homeschool him with the daily support of highly skilled therapists and nurses at Saint Anthony's Children's Hospital. There was no way she'd ever send her little boy away. He belonged with her at home, and there was nothing Eric could do to change that.

Or was there?

This fire might be the ammunition he needed to send Kyle to

the institute. Although she'd been awarded full custody of both kids, he'd threatened more than once to take the case back to the courts and sue for custody of Katie.

To add more fuel to the blaze already nipping her in the butt, Saint Anthony's had announced they were officially closing their doors shortly before Christmas. After some kind of an explosion in the boiler room last winter, there were talks of demolition and possibly developing a high-class golf and country club resort in its place. Without Saint Anthony's support she didn't know where she'd turn.

Oh, God. Would he do it?

Would Eric take away her kids?

The plane lurched as it touched down on the runway. As the jet put on its brakes, the roar of the reverse thrusters drowned out all the noise on the plane. When the noise waned and the jet slowed down, Heather braved a peek out the window as the plane taxied toward the terminal. Through a light rain, she was relieved to see the majestic sight of Pikes Peak off in the distance, the snowcapped tips the only white that was left after the spring thaw.

Home sweet home. And solid ground. She breathed a sigh of relief. It would take an act of God to get her to leave Colorado again.

"Everything okay?"

Her heart resuming its normal rhythm, she rolled her head to the side until she was just inches away from an extraordinary pair of dark-blue eyes. *Seth Roberts.* She didn't even know this man, and yet, it felt good holding his hand. It felt right. His warm cinnamon breath fanned her face like a gentle summer breeze. His lips curled into a heart-stopping smile that made her ear lobes tingle.

She reached up and fiddled with one of her gold hoop earrings. "Yeah, I'm fine. Looks like we made it." She hated that her voice sounded breathy and winded.

"Was there ever any doubt?" he said, patting her arm.

She looked down at his hand, suddenly feeling like a child on her first kiddy ride at the fair. Between anxiety over the fire at home, remembering her father's plane crash, and the fact that they'd just flown through a thunderstorm to boot, her panicked reaction during the flight had been perfectly justifiable.

She straightened and tugged her hand from his grip, suddenly realizing just how vulnerable she was to a man's touch. If she didn't want to get hurt again, she had to learn to keep her guard up. She wasn't about to let another man take control of her life.

As the plane came to a complete stop, passengers stood and opened the overhead bins to retrieve their carry-on luggage. Seth ducked from under the overhead compartment and stood, stretching his upper body, his shirt straining against bulging shoulder muscles. She couldn't help but take in the view of his firm derriere, positioned right at her eye level. His tan Dockers accentuated his narrow waistline and muscular thighs.

Yep. It was a darn good thing she'd never see this man after today. Keeping her guard up around him might not be the only thing she'd have to worry about. She tugged her blue-jean skirt down over her knees and wiped her sweaty palms on the denim material.

Reaching into the compartment in front of him, Seth pulled out a pink Barbie tote and attempted to hand it to his niece.

Nicole backed away. "Ugh, like, you don't actually think I'm going to be seen carrying that, Uncle Seth. Barbie's, like, totally juvenile."

His jaw tightened, his eyes narrowing in irritation. "Just take the bag, Nicki—I mean Nicole," he quickly corrected. "All your other stuff is being shipped out next week."

"Fine," she snapped with another huff of irritation, dropping the object of her embarrassment to the floor. Whirling around with her nose stuck in the air, she continued to chomp on her gum.

Seth's nostrils flared as he expelled a long, controlled breath, his fingers kneading the muscles at the base of his neck. Heather wondered just how long his niece would be visiting. Much longer than a couple of weeks, and dear Uncle Seth was going to be in need of some serious chiropractic work.

Reaching down, Heather grabbed her tapestry bag from under the seat, and when the aisle cleared, she scooted out of the seats next to Seth and straightened. She raised her gaze till their eyes met and neither one of them moved. At five-foot-nine, she only came up to this man's chin. The contours of his shoulder muscles bulged through his shirt. She'd never met anyone as big and tall as her brothers, both as broad as barn doors and not an ounce of fat of either one of them.

His lips curled into a lazy grin, crinkling the edges of those incredible blue eyes. "Do you have a suitcase?"

She cleared her throat. "It's the black one in the section behind you, but I can—"

Seth tugged it out. "I can carry it if you'd like."

"No, really. It's not necessary." She took the bag and quickly followed Nicole. As they inched toward the exit of the plane, she held her luggage in front of her to squeeze down the narrow aisle, acutely aware of Seth standing directly behind her. His arm brushed against hers as he grabbed each seat beside her.

The line stopped and he nudged into her backside. "Feeling better?" he asked, his low baritone sounding near her ear.

She craned her neck around, finding a warm smile bearing down on her. She fumbled with her bag and nudged forward. "Yes. Much better. Thanks." She bumped into Nicole and felt a heated blush warm her cheeks. "Oops, sorry."

Nicole spun around and stared up at her, then glared at her

uncle before she gave Heather another cursory scan. "Don't tell me he got to you, too? Figures. My mom warned me about him. I've just never seen him in action before now."

Got to me? Heather gave a quick shake of her head, wanting to explain about her airsickness. "No, you don't understand—"

"Save it," Nicole quipped. "Like I care who he flirts with."

As Nicole whirled around and popped her gum, Seth gave a low groan and whispered from behind. "I'm sorry. You'll have to excuse my niece. She and I are going through a bit of an adjustment period right now."

Heather's face had never burned so incredibly hot. Was Nicole right? Had Seth actually been flirting with her? Looking down at her luggage, she scooted forward. "Don't worry about it. I'm just glad to be home."

Why was she letting herself get carried away by a total stranger's simple act of kindness? The man reeked of money and class, and from the looks of his expensive leather shoes, the shiny Rolex on his wrist, and his leather briefcase with the fancy gold clips, dear Uncle Seth had "Rich Executive" stamped all over him. An exact replica of the man she'd just divorced.

She squared her shoulders, taking in a deep breath to clear her senses. She'd be darned if she'd let herself fall for another self-serving, power-hungry executive, no matter how caring and attentive and gosh-darn sexy he happened to be.

"Do you have a ride home?" Seth asked, breaking into her thoughts. "I'd be glad to drop you somewhere."

CHAPTER TWO

Clenching her carry-on tote, Heather yanked herself back to the real world. A world where she was first and foremost a mother of two wonderful children. Truth be told, the whole idea of being single again scared the bejeebers out of her. She couldn't wait to get home and give both her kids a big hug. "I appreciate the offer, Mr. Roberts, but my brother should be here to pick me up."

"*Mr.* Roberts, huh?" He chuckled, as if using his formal name amused him.

She tried to stay a step ahead of Seth as they strode down the jetway toward the terminal. She spotted her younger brother, Jared, and waved, drawing his attention. Clad in faded blue jeans, scuffed cowboy boots, and a straw Stetson cowboy hat, Jared's grin broadened as he approached. She was surprised when he extended his hand in greeting to Seth, still just a few steps behind her.

"You ol' sly dog," Jared said with a laugh. "What country did you just fly in from?"

Seth shook his head and grabbed Jared's hand in a strong manly grip. "LA, and it wasn't business."

Heather glanced between the two men. "Jared? Do you know Seth?"

"Yep. Played baseball with him a few summers ago. Now he just tells me what to do with my money."

Seth motioned his head toward Nicole. "Jared, this is my

niece I told you about last week. Nicole, this is Doctor Garrison. He's a veterinarian."

Jared tipped his cowboy hat and grinned. "Nice to meet you, Nicole. I'm real sorry to hear about your mom and dad."

Heather watched Nicole, wondering what had happened to her parents.

Nicole merely shrugged her petite shoulders and continued chomping on her gum.

Jared tilted his head and gave Nicole a lopsided grin. "I don't suppose you California girls have ever ridden a horse before?"

Nicole adjusted her Barbie tote over her shoulder and looked around uninterested. "Like, I'd rather go to the beach."

Unfazed, he glanced up at Seth and winked. "Welp, there's no beach, but I've got this feeling by the end of the summer, you'll be the best little cowgirl east of the Rockies."

Nicole rolled her eyes and popped her gum. "Yeah, whatever."

Jared straightened and took Heather's shoulder bag. "You ready to go? I think Debra almost went into early labor this weekend."

Heather blew out a gust of frustration. "I never should have let you guys talk me into leaving in the first place."

"Everything's fine, Heather. I was just kidding. You really didn't need to fly home early." Jared gave a deep sigh and faced Seth. "My sister's convinced the world wouldn't spin if she wasn't here to take care of everything."

Annoyed at Jared's comments, Heather warily looked up and met Seth's gaze, wishing her heart wouldn't flutter every time she did. "Thank you for all your help. I hope I didn't inconvenience you on the flight."

"Not at all," Seth said with a smile.

"Why?" Jared protectively stepped closer, touching her lower back. "Did something happen?"

"No," Heather answered, slipping the strap of her purse over her shoulder. "Just unwarranted hysteria on my part. If you'll excuse me, I need to use the little girl's room before we head out to the ranch."

Seth could only grin as he watched Heather's backside disappear through the restroom door. "You've been holding out on me, Jared. How come you've never told me about your sister before? Is she married?"

Nicole shook her head and gave a loud sigh, mumbling something about him being a rich playboy bachelor just like her mom had told her. After her flirting comment on the plane, he wondered exactly what his sister had told Nicole about him.

Jared arched his brows and hooked a thumb in a belt loop. "Heather's been married since right after high school."

Married? Seth couldn't help but feel a little deflated at that bit of news.

"Her husband left her two years ago, though. The divorce just came final last month. I'm afraid her ex did a real number on her heart."

"Dang, sorry to hear that. She seems like a nice lady." Inwardly, he cringed. As much as he'd like to pursue the long-legged brunette, after last summer's fiasco with his ex-fiancée, Brenda, he'd sworn never to get involved with another divorcée again.

Brenda's ex-husband's constant interference had been a major reason Seth had broken it off with her in the end. To top things off, her three young boys had never really accepted Seth into their lives. He'd been the brunt of practical jokes more times than he could count. Finding dog crap in his shoes had been the final kicker. Last he'd heard, Brenda and her ex-husband had remarried and were expecting another child.

"Can we go already?" Nicole huffed. "I'm like, totally starved."

Seth gripped his briefcase. "In a second. I wanted to thank Jared again for getting you enrolled in his brother's day camp this summer."

"Not a problem," Jared said. "I had Debra put the application in the mail on Friday after we talked. You'll probably get it tomorrow or Tuesday."

"Can I bring Spike?" Nicole pleaded.

"Spike?" Jared arched his brows.

Seth rubbed the pads of his fingers over his eyes and groaned. "Spike is her pet lizard."

"He's an iguana," Nicole corrected, like there was a difference.

"Cool," Jared said with a short laugh. "How big is he?"

"About a foot and a half, nose to tail." Nicole spoke to Jared without any of the sarcasm Seth had come to know.

Jared nodded. "Spike is more than welcome at the ranch. In fact, we could kind of adopt him over the summer. You'll have to take him home on the weekends, but the other kids will love him. How are you set for a tank?"

"Her stuff isn't due to arrive till next week sometime. Until then. . . ." Seth paused, rubbing his chin. "Got any suggestions? I'm not too thrilled with the idea of rolling over and finding Spike in my bed the hard way."

"As a matter of fact, I got a tank sittin' empty at the clinic. I'll drop Heather off at the ranch then bring the tank over with some supplies. Sound good?"

"Thanks, Doctor Garrison," Nicole said, sounding sincere. "Maybe you could take a look at him to make sure he's okay. He's never flown before."

"You got it. I'll even bring my iguana stethoscope." He winked.

That made Nicole smile. Her vibrant green eyes sparkled with the first signs of happiness all day. In that instant, it was as if Seth was staring into his younger sister's eyes. A heavy weight settled deep in his chest, knowing he'd never see Shelli's pretty green eyes or hear her sweet laughter again.

It had been the longest two months in his life since she and her husband had been killed. As executor of their estate, Seth had made numerous trips out to LA, settling all the paperwork and working out the details of his newly appointed role as guardian over his twelve-year-old niece.

After the funeral, Nicole had pleaded with him to let her stay with her paternal grandparents in California so she could finish out the school year and be with her friends a little longer. Hoping to make the transition from California to Colorado a little easier for her, he'd agreed.

Unfortunately, her grandparents hadn't been prepared for such an enormous responsibility at this stage in their lives. And with school almost out for the summer, he'd decided it was best for Nicole to make the move now, two weeks earlier than planned.

Despite the anguished sound in her voice on the phone Friday when she'd begged him to come get her, she'd made it abundantly clear since he'd arrived that she was not happy with the situation. She'd been about as friendly as a trapped badger.

She still hadn't said but two words to him about the events of that fatal night that took her parents' lives, or about her folks in general. His gut told him she was keeping something from him, but until he could get her to trust him, it was like talking to a gum-popping, bubble-blowing brick wall.

He'd loved his sister dearly and wanted to provide the best possible home for her only child, but he had to face facts. He'd been a bachelor living on his own since he'd turned seventeen back in high school. What the hell did he know about raising a young girl, especially one suffering from such a severe emotional loss?

As Nicole wandered away toward the window overlooking the runway, Seth blew out a heavy gust of relief. "Thanks again for getting me into your brother's camp this summer. But I've got another favor to ask. You said the camp doesn't officially open for two more weeks, after the Memorial Day weekend."

"Yeah, most of our counselors are college kids. That's when they show up."

"I don't suppose there's any chance of Nicole getting started earlier? Say, tomorrow?"

Jared sucked air through his teeth as he shook his head, sweeping off his tattered straw cowboy hat. "I don't know, man. That would have to be Heather's call."

"Heather?" Seth repeated, surprised. Then he remembered Seth saying something about his sister being head counselor. "I guess I didn't make the connection." He glanced back down the airport corridor.

"Yeah, she makes most of the decisions when it comes to who gets accepted into the camp."

Seth rubbed his jaw, staring off toward the women's restroom. The idea of dealing with that pretty lady the rest of the summer didn't sound all bad. Although, after her hasty departure, he had this feeling she probably wouldn't be too thrilled about dealing with him.

A little worried, he turned back to Jared. "Think you can talk her into it? I wasn't supposed to pick up Nicole for another two weeks, and I've had meetings set up that can't be rescheduled. If I lose another account to Davison, I may as well kiss my job good-bye."

"You talking about Larry Davison?" Jared asked.

"Yeah. You know him?"

"That guy would scam his own grandmother."

"That's why I can't lose this account. If I can get the investors' signatures by the end of the summer, I'm pretty much guaranteed a promotion to senior VP of the southern region. I could be living the good life in Dallas by my thirtieth birthday."

"Texas, huh?" Jared rubbed his jaw. "Sounds like a pretty big move."

"Yeah, but it all hinges on my meetings with Five Seasons Athletics. I'm supposed to be in Denver by ten in the morning, and after canceling on them Friday to fly out to pick up Nicole, I have to make this meeting. But I also don't want to leave Nicole alone on her first day. What do you think? I know it's last minute, but I'm really in a bind. I'd hoped I could drop off Nicole at the camp. Money's not a problem," he reassured as an afterthought. "I could pay double or whatever you think's reasonable on such a short notice."

Jared took a moment and stared toward the restroom. "Heather was supposed to be in California on vacation this whole week, but since she's home early, she'll probably be out at the ranch anyway. Between J.D., Debra and me, there'll be plenty of people around to help if she needs it." Jared shoved his hat back on his head. "Be out at the ranch by eight. I'll make sure someone's around."

Seth clapped Jared on the back. "Thanks, man, but do me a favor. Maybe you could keep our names out of it for now. Nicole made a few rude comments on the plane. Heather might be more receptive to the idea if she doesn't know it's us yet."

"Don't worry. I'm sure Nicole will come to love Heather before the summer's out."

A thud against Seth's own heart suddenly had him a little worried. Probably just the stress. "I owe you one, big time."

"How 'bout if I take you up on that?" Jared countered with a grin that had Seth taking a step backwards. "What have you got planned for next Friday night?"

Seth made a wary glance toward his niece. "With the way things are going? I haven't gotten past today. Why?"

"How would you like a chance to help raise funds for the local animal shelter? They're holding a black-tie charity dinner and auction where a few of the local celebrities are being auctioned off for dates. And since I provide the shelter with free veterinarian services, they've asked me to join the lineup."

Seth held up a hand. "Don't tell me you want me to parade around in a tux and be auctioned off?"

"I was actually hoping you'd come and bid on one of the bachelorettes, but as one of Colorado's most eligible bachelors, your idea sounds much better. Thanks, buddy," he said, clapping Seth on the shoulders. "I'll call your office and get your bio. Be at the Royal Rock Hotel Friday night by eight."

Glancing around for Nicole, Seth nearly groaned. "I'll try to be there, but I'm not making any promises right now."

"I understand. Just let me know. I'll stop by your penthouse in about an hour." Jared turned and jogged toward the exit.

As Seth waited for the luggage carousel to bring around Nicole's other bag, his cell phone rang. He unclipped his phone from his waist, recognizing his younger brother Marty's cell phone number on the caller ID.

Marty was the youngest of the three Roberts kids, four years younger than Seth. Born with Down syndrome, Marty was only a year old when their mom had died. Pop couldn't handle the responsibility of caring for a special-needs child, so he'd turned Marty over to the state. After Pop died, Seth had taken over custodianship and was the main reason Seth had moved to Colorado Springs after college.

Although he enjoyed talking to his brother several times a week, Seth still couldn't get the anxious feeling out of his gut every time his brother called. Ten years ago, Marty had fallen and had suffered a broken leg at the Pine Tree Family Services Center where he resided. Only nineteen at the time, Seth had still been in college and hadn't owned a cell phone. It had taken almost twenty-four hours before the hospital had been able to locate Seth. From that point on, he'd set up a cell phone plan between himself and his brother so Marty could reach him at any time. Marty also knew how to get hold of Seth's secretary at Ferguson and Tate Investments if for some reason he couldn't get through on Seth's cell. As much travel as he'd been doing lately, he was glad for the reassuring communication with his only brother.

He flipped his phone open and answered, "Hey, buddy. Everything okay?"

"Is Nicki here yet?" Marty's loud voice boomed into the phone.

Seth laughed and held it away a few inches. "Yep. I'm dropping off her stuff at my place, then we'll be over before you have to go to bed. How's that sound?"

"I can't wait. I made her a supwise today. She's going to love it."

"I'm sure she will. We'll see you in a couple of hours. See ya, buddy."

"Okay. Bye, buddy."

Seth heaved out a deep breath and faced Nicole. So, this was it. Next stop . . . home.

He warily approached her from behind and gave her shoulder a gentle squeeze. "You ready to go home?"

She jerked away from his touch. "I don't have a home, remember?" She rolled her eyes in disgust and strode over to where she could pick up the pet taxi.

As many times as he'd seen that look today, he was beginning to wonder if her eyeballs could actually roll out of their sockets.

Yanking off another Barbie suitcase from the luggage carousel, he studied the offending blonde doll on the front. Didn't all girls like Barbie?

Juggling her two suitcases, his duffel bag and his briefcase, he went to the counter and waited with Nicole for Spike to arrive. Nicole's eyes lit up the moment the attendant handed her the cage, cooing at Spike like he was a cuddly little kitten instead of a scaly, spiked lizard. Were those things poisonous?

Spike looked up at him, his beady little eyes and thick tongue almost daring him to come find out. Seth motioned his head toward the exit. "Come on. Let's get out of here."

Shuffling close behind, she followed him toward the long-term parking lot to his yellow Corvette. He clicked his key chain, unlocking the doors, then set their luggage on the ground. He yanked the passenger seat forward, wedging all her luggage in behind. Moving aside, he let Nicole slide onto the seat before settling Spike's pet taxi on her lap.

"What do you think about going out to the Garrison ranch tomorrow?"

She narrowed her eyes and glared up at him. "I'm not going to some stupid camp for babies, Uncle Seth, and you can't make me. You're not my father, and you never will be!"

"Mommy! Mommy! Come quick! Kyle's gonna jump!"

Heather practically leapt out of her well-worn leather cowboy boots. Standing in the supply closet of the J Bar D Outreach Camp for Kids, Heather clutched a clipboard to her chest and turned just as her daughter ran through the office door. "Isn't Kyle helping Uncle J.D. in the barn?"

Katie skidded to a halt, grabbing the sleeve of Heather's blue-denim work shirt. "Yeah, but he's standin' on the edge of the hayloft. Hurry, he's gonna jump!"

Heather cringed, envisioning her nine-year-old son with a broken arm, a shattered leg . . . or worse. After being treated for minor burns from the fire this weekend, another trip to the emergency room was the last thing Kyle needed right now.

With her heart in her throat, she steered her daughter toward the playground. "You run and play on the swings, honey. I'll go check on Kyle."

As Katie galloped toward the playground, Heather ran down the ranch yard around to the side of the barn, glancing up to the second-story hayloft. She blew out a gust of relief to find the door latched and no child splattered on the ground below. J.D. normally kept it locked unless they were loading hay into the loft.

She hurried back around the barn, giving an audible grunt when she ran smack dab into the chest of her big brother. At six-foot-five with biceps that could put any professional steer wrestler to shame, J.D. was anything but soft.

She stepped around the huge cowboy in her path and strode into the barn, glancing up toward the hayloft. "What happened?" she asked, her breathing heavy more from worry than exertion. "Katie said Kyle was in trouble."

Sitting on the edge of the loft with his booted feet dangling below, Kyle rocked back and forth with his hands cupped over his ears, autistic traits he'd displayed since being diagnosed with autism at the age of three. He continued to sway as he chewed on the rim of his favorite purple Colorado Rockies T-shirt. Gauze bandages were wrapped around both hands, leaving only his index fingers free.

J.D. jabbed a pitchfork into the dirt floor of the barn. "Katie shouldn't have bothered you. I've been keeping a close eye on him. There's a whole mound of hay only four feet below him if he decides to jump or accidentally falls. He's jumped higher than that from the swing set."

"We were up most of the night with his hands. I'm sure he's tired."

J.D. mumbled a low curse as he swept off his hat and banged the dust against his jeans. "I know I've said it before, but I can't tell you how sorry I am that this whole thing happened. Debra was in the kitchen when the smoke detectors went off. She thinks he found the matches in the end table in our bedroom. She likes to burn those scented candles."

"I'm not blaming anyone, J.D. Kyle knows not to play with matches. We've talked about the dangers a hundred times. I don't understand what came over him."

"He reminds me of Jared," he said with a hint of a grin. "Remember when he was nine and he set the cat's tail on fire?"

She gave a brittle laugh. "Yeah. The poor little guy hid out in the barn for two weeks. Jared's lucky Dad wasn't alive. He would have skinned his hide and grounded him to the barn right along with the cat."

J.D. gave a low throaty chuckle. "Believe me, after all the chores I had him do, I'm sure he'd have gladly lived in the barn. But, seriously," he said, staring up at Kyle. "I hope you don't think we weren't watching him this weekend. Debra and I love your kids like they were our own. We'd hate to lose your trust over this."

"Oh, J.D.," she said, wrapping her arms around his firm muscular waist. "You haven't lost my trust. I love you guys so much. Let's just be thankful Katie was outside when the fire started and everything turned out okay. This was just one of those hard lessons in life that Kyle had to learn on his own."

J.D. cleared his throat and pulled away, glancing up at Kyle. "Hey, pardner. Why don't you come on down and help me with the horses? You can sit on Evening Star when we're done."

That caught Kyle's attention. Even though he wouldn't look at J.D., his eyes widened and he quit his habitual rocking.

As he scooted away from the edge, J.D. ushered Heather toward the door. "Come on, let's give him some room. He's nine years old, almost stands as high as my chest. What are you feeding him anyway?"

"You're one to talk," she jested, hesitantly leaving Kyle to get down the ladder by himself. "You were bigger than that at his age. I guess he's taking after both his uncles."

She stopped far enough to give Kyle his space, but close enough if he needed her. He climbed down without incident then picked up a barn cat sauntering by, stroking its fur and rubbing it against his face. "Kyle, go on up to the house and see if Auntie Debra has any muffins left. I'll be there in a minute."

Dumping the cat on the ground, Kyle lumbered out of the barn, his growing feet making his long strides awkward and cumbersome.

J.D. picked a piece of straw from her shoulder. "Mom and Brad called. Since Kyle is all right, they're heading up to Seattle to Brad's architect convention. They should be home sometime over Memorial Day weekend."

"I'm glad they decided to stay. To be honest, I was homesick the moment I boarded Amtrak."

"Did you and Megan have a good time while you were there? How was the ceremony?"

"Long, but I'm glad I got to be there for her. I think I took two hundred pictures. I'll download them onto your computer later." With a bittersweet smile, she remembered how proud she'd been of Megan when she'd accepted her diploma in front of a huge auditorium with hundreds of people watching. Taking night courses to attain her behavioral therapist degree, Heather had unceremoniously received her diploma through the mail.

"What about Eric?" J.D. asked. "Have you told him about the fire? I tried his cell phone several times yesterday, but couldn't get through."

Avoiding J.D.'s gaze, she dug the toe of her boot into the dry dusty soil. "I was going to try him this morning, but since Kyle's burns were so minor, and Eric's clear on the other side of the state in Telluride, I didn't want him rushing over and complicating matters. You know how much he hates hospitals."

"No. Just Saint Anthony's," J.D. quipped with a little sarcasm.

"I know. I think he holds them partially responsible for Kyle's autism."

"Eric's an idiot."

"You're preaching to the choir, J.D. But to be honest, the hospital's not the only reason I didn't call him. Kyle's been acting out and misbehaving for the past few months. Even his therapists have been experiencing problems with him. It's as if he's turning back inside himself again. We've come so far, and now I'm afraid he's slipping away." Her voice wobbled and she had to force in a heavy gulp of air.

"What are the chances Kyle knows about Saint Anthony's? Didn't you say one of his therapists was laid off last week? Maybe he heard them talking and he senses something's going to change."

At the reminder of Saint Anthony's closing their doors, Heather's anxiety level jumped up another notch. "I suppose that could be part of the problem. Tracey Watson has been with Kyle ever since we started therapy six years ago. She was one of his favorite teachers."

She rubbed her palms over her arms, a sudden chill of apprehension racing up and down her skin. "How can they do it? How can they just tear down a vitally important asset to this community and build another golf course? If it weren't for Saint Anthony's, Dillan might not be alive today."

Dillan was their thirteen-year-old cousin who'd been born with a defective heart. He'd received a heart transplant three years ago. Now he was an active teenager, participating in team sports at school and involved in rodeoing. All because of Saint Anthony's.

"I don't know where I'm going to turn, J.D. We've worked with some of those doctors and nurses for the last six years. Without their support, I'm afraid it'll only give Eric more reason to try to take my kids away from me."

"Hey," J.D. said, giving her that big-brother-I'm-always-here-for-you grin that always made her smile in return. "There are a lot of good facilities you can turn to for support, and if you'd give yourself half the credit you deserve, you'd see that Kyle has thrived under your care. Everyone, including all the therapists at Saint Anthony's, agree that Kyle has made remarkable progress since you started homeschooling him and Katie. You're doing a great job. Eric's not going to take your kids." He gave her arms a squeeze. "Trust me. Kyle's just going through a normal growing phase like all kids his age. You're being too hard on yourself. Quit worrying."

"I can't help it," she said, crossing her arms over her chest. "Just wait till Debra has her baby. Then we'll see how you handle things."

A proud smile spread across his face. "I still can't believe I'm going to be a father. Every time I see her and feel the life growing inside her, I swear I fall in love with that woman all over again. I just wish Dad could've been here."

"He's here, J.D. Just look around." She splayed her hands out to his thriving ranch. "You've kept his dream alive. He'd be proud."

Located north of Colorado Springs between the rich timbers of the Black Forest and the dry prairies of eastern Colorado, J.D.'s large spread surrounded their mom and stepfather's home. The yellow ranch house at the top of the hill was where all four Garrison kids had been raised. J.D. and his wife, Debra, now owned all the surrounding acreages, living in a big Colonial two-story near Elk Ridge Ravine at the back of his property.

Two years ago, they'd converted a portion of their ranch into a summer day camp for emotionally and physically challenged children and young teens. The facilities were only set up to accommodate twelve daytime campers, forcing them to turn away dozens of applicants every year. But on the flip side, the small enrollment gave each child the individualized attention and support they needed from each counselor to be able to face whatever challenges had been handed to them.

Although she and her two kids lived in a condo in the city, as J.D.'s head counselor, Heather and her kids spent most of their time out here at the ranch. Heather's only stipulation was that the kids who attended needed to be there, either for emotional support and healing, or for encouragement in coping with some sort of a physical challenge. She definitely didn't want their camp to be another daycare drop-off point for parents with a busy schedule.

Jared had just acquired his own veterinarian practice and lived above his clinic in town, but still made it out here several times a week. Megan would be flying home in a couple of weeks before taking up residency at a Denver hospital, and they'd all be together again like old times. Heather couldn't imagine living anywhere else.

Breathing in the rich Rocky Mountain aroma of pine trees and new spring grass, she squinted into the early-morning Colorado sunshine. Pikes Peak glistened off in the distance. The rain showers overnight made everything sparkle with dew. Several dozen broodmares grazed in five large paddocks surrounding a new indoor riding arena. A lighted outdoor roping arena had also been erected where J.D. did most of the training and riding. He'd even constructed a huge playground complete with a swing set and a tree house. A petting zoo had been set up, housing two miniature ponies, a potbellied pig, and several goats; animal contact being highly therapeutic for kids coping with difficult challenges.

J.D. flicked a glance at his watch. "Did Jared tell you about a new camper starting this morning? They should be here any minute."

"Briefly. I was so worried about Kyle last night, I didn't get any details. Just that Jared owed an old friend a favor."

He nodded. "A little girl lost both her parents in a car accident. She's an only child and I guess she's taking it pretty hard."

Remembering how difficult it had been when her father had died, Heather couldn't imagine losing both parents. "We'll have to do all we can to offer her support and let her know she's not alone."

J.D. nodded, wiping his brow with the sleeve of his denim shirt. "Debra has an OB appointment at nine-forty-five. Then we're supposed to head up to Denver to pick up a new saddle. But if you're not up to showing them around this morning, maybe we could reschedule the doctor appoint—"

"Don't you dare," she admonished with a waggle of her finger. "After all you two have gone through to get this baby, I don't want you missing any doctor appointments."

Shortly before they were married, a car accident practically left Debra paralyzed from the waist down. It was a miracle in itself that she was able to walk again, much less get pregnant and carry a baby to term. With only two months to go, it looked like Debra was determined to pull off another miracle. "You take care of that baby. I can handle everything myself."

A low rumble of a car engine drew their attention to the entrance of the J Bar D Outreach Camp for Kids. Shielding her eyes from the early-morning sun, she gazed longingly at a golden-yellow Corvette as it pulled into the parking lot at the top of the hill. Sleek. Sporty. Fast. She loved speed. Feeling the wind in her hair.

When she was younger, her father used to take her out in his restored 1969 Mustang Boss 302. She would read the maps as he drove the winding mountain roads of Colorado. He'd also let her be in charge of all their flight plans whenever they took off for the afternoon to fly. He'd called her his little navigator.

Then she realized the yellow Vette had parked right next to her green minivan. The dusty coating and boxy shape was a steep contrast to the spit-polished shine and sleek lines of the little sports car. Practically speaking, however, without a backseat, there wasn't much room for groceries and backpacks. The yearly insurance premiums alone on the Vette probably cost more than the book price of her minivan with over a hundred thousand miles.

Her ex-husband had always driven something sporty, usually a foreign convertible. But in the entire span of their ten-year marriage, Eric had never let Heather behind the wheel of any of his cars, didn't trust her driving. Although ironically, he'd had no problem letting her chauffeur their kids around in their minivan every day.

The driver of the Corvette slid out from behind the wheel. Dark hair and sunglasses were all she could make out from this distance, but a quick scan of the rest of him in his tailored, navy-blue business suit gave her an eerie sense of déjà vu.

Eric had always dressed impeccably well in Dolce&Gabbana tailored suits. Combine those with his expensive sports cars, and he'd been a babe magnet every time he'd left the house, which had been every night the last two years of their marriage. He'd made it perfectly clear that an up-and-coming business executive couldn't be burdened with the demands of a nagging wife and two whiny kids.

Heather nervously rubbed her thumb over her left ring finger. "From here, he kind of reminds me of Eric."

J.D. shook his head. "Just because he wears a suit and drives a fancy car, doesn't mean he's a bad guy. Now, go on up there and do what you do best: reach out to the little girl." He yanked out a pair of leather work gloves from his back pocket. "I need to finish putting up the hay, and if you want, send Kyle and

Katie back down. They can help me feed the baby goats."

Heather smiled and watched as J.D. yanked a pitchfork from a mound of straw. He and Jared had both been wonderful father figures for her kids. If only all men could be bred from the same Garrison stock. Handsome, honest, trustworthy. They were the only ones she could truly depend on.

Scooping up the yellow tomcat, she stroked its softness as she strode up the hill toward the office. She slowed her pace when she found Kyle crouched down on his knees, peering into what looked like some kind of a fish tank. From the looks of the green lizard-looking animal inside, however, she didn't think it was fish related. Whatever its origin, Kyle seemed to be totally engrossed as he tapped the glass, his nose just inches away from the reptile inside.

"Have you ever seen an iguana before?" Hunched down in a squatting position across from Kyle, the driver of the Vette tried to make conversation with her son. "His name is Spike."

She couldn't see the man's face, but his low baritone voice hit an all-too-familiar chord. She slowed her stride as her heart kicked up a notch.

"Do you like animals?" he asked Kyle.

Kyle didn't answer the man or look him in the eyes, and to a stranger it would probably seem as if Kyle were ignoring him. But the guy didn't seem to be fazed; in fact, it was as if he understood her son's aloofness, asking him simple yes and no questions.

"Would you like to pet Spike?"

Katie's shrill voice sounded from the backyard. "Kyle! Kyle! Let's go pet the horsies!"

With a slight hesitation, Kyle backed away from Spike, and for the briefest of seconds, he actually looked up at the man from the corner of his eyes and said, "Cool." Then he bolted down the ranch yard toward the barn.

Heather's heart swelled with a flicker of hope. Maybe J.D. was right. Kyle was just going through a normal growing phase.

The man gave a low, easy chuckle as he watched Kyle jump over the corral fence. The familiar laugh made her halt in her tracks next to the yellow Corvette. She knew without even seeing his face this was the same man she'd met yesterday on the plane.

Seth Roberts.

Peering down through the passenger window, she found his niece sitting inside the car, confirming what she'd already deduced. Nicole was the little girl who'd lost her parents in a car accident. Her strawberry blonde curls were pulled back in an array of colorful butterfly clips. Her head bobbed up and down as she listened to her MP3 player, the bass of the loud rap music sounding through the headphones. She wore a fluorescent-pink tank top and her pencil-thin legs were covered in what appeared to be brand-new pair of dark-denim capri jeans. A pair of bright-pink flip-flops finished off her stylish ensemble. Her cute and sassy attire was more appropriate for the mall than a horse ranch. Heather made a mental note to keep her out of the barns today.

Clothes, they could remedy. Sorting out emotions after such a catastrophic loss as losing her parents was a whole new ball game. For this girl to learn how to cope and find a way to go on with her life, it was going to take a group effort, including her uncle, whom she assumed was Nicole's newly appointed guardian.

She put a smile on her face and lowered the cat to the ground. "Good morning, Mr. Roberts. Welcome to the J Bar D Outreach Camp for Kids."

Seth stood to his full height, sweeping off his sunglasses and meeting her gaze from just a few feet away. Familiar, piercing blue eyes cut straight through the early-morning sunlight. He was taller than she'd remembered on the plane, exuding a somewhat intimidating aura of power and authority. A pin-striped navy-blue suit fit snuggly across his broad shoulders, the pressed trousers pleated at the waist and hanging loose enough to move freely, yet close-fitting around the thighs to indicate a firm, muscular build. A white starched dress shirt was tucked in where a black leather belt only emphasized his toned, trimmed waistline.

But it was his handsome chiseled face that had been ingrained into her memory. Dark brows arched perfectly over those beautiful blue eyes, a slightly misshaped nose, and how could she forget those lips? Even now, his smile did things to her insides that quite frankly she'd never felt before.

Yesterday, she'd blamed her jittery reaction to him on the turbulence and her anxiety of getting home to her kids. The only thing shaking now was her knees.

Hoping to appear confident, she extended her hand in greeting. "Jared told me we had a new camper starting. He didn't give me the impression it was you and your niece."

"Good morning to you, too, Ace." His lips curled into that unforgettable, heart-stopping smile as he wrapped his fingers around hers. "I must say, you left quite an impression on me." He turned his hand over with hers still snuggled in his grip.

She glanced downward, her eyes widening when she understood what he meant. "Oh, my gosh. Did I do that to you?" Fingernail indentations were still visible below his knuckles where she'd held onto him for dear life as they'd descended into the Colorado Springs Airport.

He patted the back of her hand. "No blood drawn. What about you? How's your stomach? Your color is looking better today. Although, green was a good shade for you."

Knowing her cheeks were probably turning to a deep shade of red, she had to force herself to keep her chin up. "I'm feeling much better, and thank you for all your concern yesterday. Did you meet Debra? She's our administrator in charge of all the paperwork."

"Yes, she's finishing up on the applications and getting release documents ready for me to sign."

"Like, hello-o-o." His niece cracked her gum, giving them both an incredulous expression as she stared up at them from the passenger seat of Seth's Corvette. "Can we, like, get on with this already?"

Realizing their hands were still joined, Heather quickly broke the contact and took a step back, casually tucking her trembly fingers into the hip pockets of her jeans.

Seth pulled the door wide and reached in to slip the headphones off his niece's ears. "Say hello to Ms. Thomas, Nicole. She'll be your counselor this summer."

"Give me a break. She's the only reason we're here." Nicole gave an exaggerated roll of her eyes. "I don't know why you even bothered driving clear out here. I told you a hundred times. I'm not staying at some stupid camp for babies. I stayed alone all the time when Mom and Dad had to work. But, oh-h-h-h," she said, glaring up at her uncle. "I guess you wouldn't know that, seein' as you rarely came to visit us." She popped her gum and shot her uncle a spite-filled glare that could have melted the windshield.

As if that were the end of the discussion, she readjusted her headphones over her ears, pointed her nose toward the driver's-side door, and crossed her arms over her chest.

With his jaw clenched shut, Seth released a heavy gust of air, pacing several feet away from the car. Heather, not sure whom to approach first, followed Seth and spoke in a low voice. "What's going on, Seth?"

He stopped and shoved a hand on his waist. "As you can tell, my niece isn't exactly receptive to this whole idea. In fact, she's not thrilled about moving in with me, period. We haven't exactly been close." He looked over at his niece and rubbed the back of his neck. "I really do hate to leave her right away, but like I explained to Jared, I've got clients flying in from Japan with meetings scheduled the rest of the week."

Meetings? Nicole's whole world had been turned upside down and this guy had the gall to fret about a few business meetings? Keeping her voice civil, Heather squared her shoulders. "Does your company know about your situation? Surely they'll let you have some time off."

"I've already taken several days off for the funeral, and then again when we settled their estate." He gave a short, cynical laugh. "I'm afraid their philosophy is work first, golf second, and family a distant third."

Her spine stiffened and she had to grit her teeth. Throughout her entire marriage to Eric, he'd practically lived at the golf course and country club, leaving her and the kids alone most weekends. Even during the evenings, he'd ditched them in a heartbeat to entertain potential investors in his real-estate deals.

Seth made a swift glance at his Rolex then dragged his fingers through his hair, each strand falling perfectly back into place as if it hadn't even been touched. "Look, Heather, I don't have a lot of options here. Leaving her alone in my penthouse suite on the fifth floor of the Royale isn't exactly an ideal environment for a twelve-year-old little girl."

"I'm not a little girl," Nicole piped up from the car. "I'll be thirteen next month, so I don't need a babysitter. Admit it. The only reason you're dumping me here is because I'm cramping your style. Probably afraid I'm going to touch your stuff or something." She rolled her eyes. "As if."

A muscle in Seth's neck twitched. He narrowed his eyes on Nicole. "As you can see, since I picked her up, she hasn't exactly been Miss Congeniality."

Nicole shot him an I'm-not-thrilled-to-be-with-you-either glare, her gum cracking seeming to have become louder.

Seth arched his brows as if saying, "See? I told you so."

Heather narrowed her gaze, giving him what she'd hoped was a reprimanding glare. "Gee, if I'd just lost my parents and had to move away from all my friends and everything I'd ever known, only to go live with a man I barely knew, I think I'd be a little cranky, too, Mr. Roberts. And to be quite frank, I hardly think rescheduling a few business meetings would mean the end of the world if it meant looking out for the welfare of your niece."

Nicole's mouth gaped open as she switched her gaze between Heather and her uncle, but Nicole didn't say a word. Neither did Seth, for that matter. Good. How many times had Heather wanted to say that very thing to Eric every time some meeting had taken precedence over his family? Maybe she'd made her point with this Seth Roberts, and he'd take his newfound role of parenting more seriously. For Nicole's sake, Heather prayed he would.

Instead of a quick comeback as she'd expected, Seth pinched the bridge of his nose and closed his eyes. For a split second, he actually looked remorseful, and Heather wondered if she'd been too harsh.

He hunkered down in front of his niece, lowering his voice. "Nicole, believe me, I want you to come live with me, and you're definitely not cramping my style. Now, I'll admit, I don't know the first thing about parenting, and it's probably weird moving in with a guy you barely know. But I loved your mom very much. I can't imagine what you must be going through. Please, honey, I want to make this work. Just give me a chance."

Nicole turned away and didn't say anything. She stopped chomping on her gum and her shoulders lowered. Seth had obviously gotten to her. The way Heather's chest felt, he'd tugged at one of her heartstrings as well with his emotional plea.

"Listen, if you really don't want to stay, I'll call my boss right now and cancel. You're far more important to me than a boring business meeting. We'll spend the whole day shopping for some new clothes or something. If you still don't want to come back, maybe I can find one of my neighbors you could stay with for a while, just until you get to know the area. What do you say? I'll do whatever you want."

She gave a small lift of her shoulders and didn't answer, but Heather picked up a slight sniffling sound and her heart grabbed. After she'd lost her father, it had taken weeks before she could talk to anyone. It was pretty clear Nicole was overcome by tears and didn't know what to say, either.

Heather stepped toward the door and rested a hand on Seth's broad shoulder. His muscles tightened under her touch. He was definitely a man who stayed in shape. "Seth, why don't you go into the office and start filling out the paperwork? I'll talk to Nicole and explain how we operate around here. If she still doesn't want to stay, then it would probably be best if you made other arrangements for the summer."

Seth bowed his head between his shoulders, almost looking defeated. With a weary sigh, he shoved a hand on his thigh and stood, staring down at his niece, as if contemplating whether to stay or go.

Taking his elbow, Heather tugged him away from the car and walked him to the office. "Let me talk to her a few minutes. She's just as unsure about this as you are."

As they approached the office door, Seth covered her hand and rubbed his thumb over her wrist. "Contrary to what you believe, Heather, I really am concerned about Nicole. Her welfare is all I've thought about these last few months. But like you said, she hardly knows me. To be quite honest, I don't know the first thing about little girls." He thumped his head with the heel of his hand. "Oops, I mean preteenagers." He slipped Heather a crooked grin that made her insides quiver. He, no doubt, probably had plenty of experience with big girls.

Kyle's loud bellow broke through the stillness of the morning. Heather whirled around and found J.D. carrying her son over his shoulder. Kyle was kicking and hollering at the top of his lungs.

"Uh-oh," Seth said, lowering his voice. "Looks like your brother's got his hands full with that kid."

Heather had barely opened her mouth to inform him exactly who that kid was when a shrill ring of Seth's cell phone left her jaw gaping open. Clueless to his careless remark, Seth casually reached into his jacket and pulled out his phone. "Roberts here." Then he mouthed to Heather, "I'll meet you in a minute."

Without letting her answer, he spoke into the phone. "Hey, Sue. Sorry I missed you last night."

As he turned and walked away for privacy, Heather gritted her teeth. A girlfriend? Did Seth just ditch her to talk to a girlfriend?

She turned around and met J.D. and Kyle, trying to keep her breathing level, not sure if she was irritated with Seth or with herself for letting her attraction to this man consume all her common sense.

She wrapped her palms around her son's face, looking him square in the eye. "Kyle, stop. That's enough."

After a few seconds of struggle, Kyle stopped thrashing. J.D. was able to set him on the ground, keeping a firm grip on his shoulders from behind. "I'm sorry, Heather. He wanted to take Evening Star out into the pasture by himself. When I told him I had to leave, he started throwing a fit. You know he's not ready to ride alone yet."

"I know. It's not your fault." When Kyle's gaze lowered to the ground and his jaw muscles relaxed, Heather took a calming breath and rubbed her palms over his shoulders. "Kyle, you know the rules. Unless you're with an adult, you can't be around the horses by yourself. Now I want you to go into Grandma Kara's house and find a book. I'll be in and read to you and Katie after I show some people around the ranch."

With his hands cupped over his ears, Kyle began to sway back and forth. Not sure he understood, Heather placed a kiss on his forehead. "Go in the house, honey. Auntie Debra's homemade muffins are on the kitchen counter." With that, he pulled away and ran inside the house through the camp office door.

J.D. shook his head. "Kyle's a strong little cuss. How do you handle him all by yourself?"

Afraid to admit even to J.D. that she did, in fact, have her hands full with her son, Heather stood tall and flexed her biceps. "I'm a lot stronger than I look. I've still got a few pounds on him."

J.D. chuckled. "I'm leaving in a few minutes. Are you sure you can handle everything?"

"I'll be fine. Let me know when you're headed back this afternoon. I wanted to take Kyle to Saint Anthony's for an emergency therapy session. After this weekend, I want to make sure he's okay."

"You got it."

As J.D. followed Kyle into the office, Heather found Seth pacing the parking lot, still talking on his cell phone. She took in a deep breath and shoved her hands on her waist.

Little boys she could handle. She had a feeling this big playboy was going to surpass her tolerance level.

CHAPTER THREE

Heather strode toward Nicole and gave her a tentative smile, staring down into the passenger side of the Corvette. "I'm really sorry about your parents. I lost my daddy when I was ten. I bet you miss them."

"Sure, whatever." Nicole bit her vibrant purple fingernails, obviously trying to appear unfazed by her situation.

Heather blew out a heavy breath and stepped closer. "Listen, Nicole, I think we need to start over." She knelt down in a squatting position, interlacing her fingers between her bent knees, bringing herself eye level with Nicole. "I don't know what you've been told about our ranch, but this is definitely not a camp for babies. Most of the kids are between twelve and sixteen. We have a lot of fun and challenging activities planned throughout the summer. But we depend on every camper to help out with chores and making a ranch this size run smoothly. In fact, if you don't think you can handle the responsibilities of caring for horses and making new friends, maybe you should just go back to your uncle's penthouse in the city. I really want you to stay," she assured. "But if you decide you don't want to, we have lots of girls your age who would be thrilled if we had another opening."

Nicole glared out the driver's-side window, her nose pointed in the air. She pursed her lips in a straight line and didn't answer.

"What's it going to be, Nicole? You said yourself, you're not a baby. We aren't going to force you to stay. It's your choice."

Although still hesitant about dealing with her uncle, Heather hoped Nicole would stay. Something about the girl reminded Heather of how she'd been after she'd lost her father. For months, she'd given everyone the silent treatment, taking off on a horse for hours at a time, making everyone worry . . . making everyone miserable. But at least she'd still had her mom and family. This girl had lost everything.

Nicole finally mumbled, "Okay, I'll stay." Tears welled in her eyes, and Heather knew there was a very sensitive young woman inside her haughty exterior.

Relieved she'd decided to stay, Heather tentatively touched her shoulder, hoping Nicole would look at her. "I'm glad. I think you'll find we're pretty decent folks to hang out with, but just like your uncle, you have to give us a chance."

Nicole shrugged away, fiddling with her MP3 player. "I said I'd stay, okay?"

Hoping to get Nicole into a better mood, Heather shoved her hands on her thighs and stood. "Okay, then, let's take a quick tour. You'll even be assigned to a cabin this summer. You'll have to share it with three other girls, but you're welcome to go there for privacy anytime. I want this to be a good experience for you. It's not a prison."

Heather leaned over and gingerly picked up Spike's tank from the ground, holding it at arm's length. Spike backed up, his beady little gray eyes narrowing. "I don't think he likes me," she said, suddenly wary.

Nicole grabbed a yellow backpack from between her feet. "It just takes him a while to get used to you."

"Does he bite?"

"Not usually, but it's not his teeth you need to be worried about. It's his tail. If he gets mad, he'll whip you so hard you'll wish he'd bitten you."

Heather gulped. "Well, then, we'll just have to make sure ol'

Spike here stays happy, won't we, little guy?"

Nicole pulled her thin frame out of the car. She stood all of five feet and couldn't have weighed more than eighty pounds with her backpack. Hopefully, after a summer of working the ranch, she'd get some muscle put on those bones, and with any luck, a smile on her face.

"Follow me. I'll give you the grand tour and tell you a little about the place."

Tagging close behind, Nicole fiddled with the straps of her yellow backpack. "Do I really get to ride a horse?"

Heather smiled. "That's the whole point of staying on a horse ranch, isn't it? But I gotta warn you." She slowed her stride and leaned close, speaking confidentially. "If you've never sat on a horse, your behind might get a little sore after the first day. Think you can handle it?"

Nicole nodded enthusiastically, her eyes filling with light. "Yes, ma'am."

"Whoa. First of all, call me Heather. Everyone around here is pretty friendly. Second of all, you'll get to ride only after you learn all the safety rules and how to groom a horse. That big guy you saw earlier was my older brother, J.D. He owns the ranch and will be your trainer. You'll meet him and his wife, Debra, later."

Heather shortened her strides to match Nicole's as they headed toward one of four cedar-sided cabins. "That boy poking his fingers at Spike's tank was my son, Kyle. He's nine and has a disorder called autism. Have you ever heard of that?"

Nicole shook her head.

"Autism is a disorder that affects some children and adults. It's not an illness. It's more like a learning dysfunction. They have a hard time adjusting to their environments, so sticking to routines and doing things that are familiar are real important to people like Kyle. It may take him a little longer to warm up to you, but once he gets to know you, he's a great kid. I also have a seven-year-old daughter. You'll meet Katie in a few minutes. I have a feeling you three and Spike here will become good friends over the summer."

They stopped in front of a small cabin where Heather gladly handed the tank over to Nicole, then unlocked the door. "This cabin is all ready to go. I still have a few things to do on the boys' cabin, but maybe you can help me out after you get settled in." She pushed the door wide, motioning for Nicole to enter first.

Nicole stepped in, her big green eyes widening. "Wow, this is my room?"

"Yep. Think you'll be able to hang out here with us during the days? There's no TV, but there's a clock radio you can listen to when you want to be alone. There's also a stack of spiral notebooks in the desk. I want you to start writing a little bit every day."

"You mean like a diary?"

"Sort of. You can write anything you want: poems, stories, or just how you're feeling. Sometimes it helps to write those things down. They're private and no one else will read them."

Nicole set the tank on a wooden desk in front of the window. Spike turned toward the sunshine as if ready to lie out for a tan. She dumped her backpack on the bottom bunk of a rustic pine bed covered in a pink-and-white embroidered quilt. Another set of beds were on the opposite wall. Although the campers generally didn't stay overnight, some of the kids needed a place to lie down and take breaks during the day.

Lacy curtains adorned both windows. Several stuffed animals decorated a rocking chair in the corner next to a small nightstand.

"Too bad I can't just live here." Nicole blew out a heavy sigh, slumping onto one of the beds.

Sensing a little homesickness, Heather tried to give her a reassuring smile. "You must miss your old bedroom, huh?"

"Yeah, I guess. Even at Grandma's I had my own TV."

"Do you have your own room at your uncle's place?"

"Hardly. His spare room is crammed with computers and filing cabinets." With a roll of her eyes, she added, "Oh, he offered me his bedroom, but with all his clothes and junk in there, I said I'd rather sleep on the foldout sofa in the living room."

Heather reached over and touched Nicole's shoulder. "I'm really sorry. This must be a difficult time for you, losing your folks then moving away from your friends."

She quickly diverted her gaze to her MP3 player. "Doesn't matter where I live. As soon as I get some money saved up, I'm totally getting out on my own. I don't need a babysitter."

Heather's stomach tightened. The thought of Nicole out on the streets at such a young age made Heather's heart ache.

"Between you and me?" Nicole blew a bubble and sucked it back into her mouth. "I don't think Uncle Seth's any too thrilled about me moving in with him, anyway."

"Why's that, sweetie?"

"From what Mom told me, I guess he's a total playboy. Dates women from all over the world. But if you ask me, he's a real yawner. Since he picked me up, he's like either on his cell phone or typing on his laptop. I swear, he's about as exciting as dried toothpaste."

A knock came at the opened door. "Is this a girl's only club?"

Nicole jerked her head toward the door, mischief flashing in her bright green eyes. Her lips pressed together, suppressing a giggle.

Heather's pulse jumped up a notch when she found Seth gripping the top of the doorframe with his head ducked inside. Only a sliver of sunlight filtered around his broad shoulders. His suit jacket had spread open, revealing muscular thighs straining against his pleated dress trousers. He seemed out of place amongst ruffled curtains and lacy bedspreads.

Picturing this playboy bachelor becoming a father to an almost-teenage girl forced Heather to bite back her own giggle. Did Uncle Seth have the slightest idea what it took to raise a girl just hitting puberty?

At the same time, she couldn't help but worry about Nicole's welfare. Was she planning to run away?

"Please, come in and join us. Nicole and I were just going over some of our routines."

The annoying drone of Seth's cell phone made her skin crawl, feeling like fingernails on a chalkboard.

He held up his finger toward her and took the call, of course. Wouldn't want to keep the caller waiting; their time obviously much more important than hers and Nicole's. He nodded a few times, then said he'd be there, wherever there was, at eight o'clock tonight.

"I'm sorry," he said, slipping his phone into his pocket. "I've got a lot of stuff going on right now. This is nice," he said, looking around the room. "What do you think, Nicole?"

"It doesn't really matter what I think, now does it?" Nicole stood and stepped across the room, adjusting Spike's tank and setting out a container of food.

Heather grabbed hold of the top bunk and met Seth's frustrated gaze. "We don't have a lot of rules, Mr. Roberts, so I'll be brief. I expect Nicole here every morning, Monday through Friday by eight o'clock sharp, and she's to be picked up every night by five-thirty."

"Wait a minute." He ducked the rest of the way inside and straightened, taking one long stride toward her. "There's no way I can be here every day by five-thirty. Six at the very earliest."

Forcing herself to remain grounded, Heather had to tip her

head back to meet his gaze. "I'm sorry, but these are the rules. Now, as far as what she'll need to wear. She'll be working in the barns and corrals, and eventually with all the livestock, so she'll need to wear old jeans, a T-shirt and a long-sleeved shirt. Riding boots if she has them, or a pair of old tennis shoes until she can get a pair."

His mesmerizing blue eyes hadn't even blinked as he listened without interruption. Her face started to feel warm under his intense scrutiny. She gripped the bed tighter, trying to keep her mind focused on Nicole's needs, not on the fluttering sensations in the middle of her stomach. "We'll be outside in the sun most of the day, so she needs to wear some sort of a hat as well as sunscreen. She's welcome to bring a backpack with personal items, books, CDs or tapes, stuff like that, but the main thing is she gets settled into a routine as soon as possible."

He finally blinked, but it was a slow, deliberate movement with his gaze watching her mouth as she spoke. Self-conscious, she touched the tip of her tongue to wet her lips before she added, "We'll provide lunch and an afternoon snack every day, but she needs to have a good breakfast before she arrives."

He raised his gaze from her mouth, looking into her eyes. "I think we can handle that."

"I also expect you to spend at least one hour a week here at the ranch with Nicole. You can either call and schedule your time or show up when it's convenient for you."

He studied her in no particular hurry then looked over at Nicole. "What do you think, Nicki? I mean, Nicole," he quickly corrected. "Do you want to stay? It's up to you."

She gave her trademark shrug and roll of the eyes while examining her purple fingernails. "Whatever," she mumbled.

Heather held out her hand. "Do we have a deal, Mr. Roberts?" She didn't move nor did she even blink.

Seth took Heather's outstretched hand and securely wrapped

his fingers around hers. "Agreed, but I can't guarantee an hour every week, and five-forty-five is the earliest I can make it."

"But—"

"And if I'm late," he added, stepping closer. "I'll pay you ten bucks per minute. Deal?" He squeezed her hand for emphasis.

Heather's pulse doubled under his intense gaze . . . and his touch. Her mouth went dry and she found it hard to speak. She'd almost let Seth's devilishly gorgeous charm intimidate her, but her bitter experience with Eric's lure had left her hardened where men were concerned. Like Eric, Seth obviously thought money could solve all of life's problems. Well, she had news for him. With the kind of settlement she'd received from the divorce, money didn't mean squat to her.

Squaring her shoulders, she narrowed her gaze, fully aware of the heat radiating between them. "Five-thirty, Mr. Roberts. You can arrange your visits through Debra or myself. If you have a problem with the rules, you know the way out."

He flicked a glance at her lips, then back to her eyes before he gave a short laugh. "You drive a hard bargain, Ms. Thomas. I guess we have a deal."

He dropped her hand and turned toward Nicole, who had resumed her slumped position on the edge of the bed. "I'll see you tonight, then." When she didn't answer, Seth hunkered down to Nicole's eye level, resting his elbows on his knees. "Are you sure about this? Maybe I can find a neighbor—"

"Forget it," she snapped. "Anything's better than being stuffed in your stupid building all day long."

Seth's cell phone rang again. He reached down and sent it to voice mail, actually ignoring it. "Try to have some fun, okay, honey? Call me anytime if you need to get a hold of me. You've got all my numbers where I can be reached."

"Fine. Whatever." A sheen of tears filled Nicole's eyes before she turned away.

He started to reach for her hand, but then drew back and shoved to standing, expelling a heavy sigh. He finally nodded to Heather. "Guess I'll see you tonight, then. Let me know if there are any problems."

Heather opened her mouth to speak, but his cell phone rang again. This time he answered after the first ring on his way out of the cabin.

As soon as Seth ducked out the door, Nicole gave a short laugh, her foul mood suddenly replaced with amusement. "That was pretty cool, Heather. I bet he's never had a woman stand up to him like that before."

Even though she was probably right, Heather had to set the record straight. "I take this camp pretty seriously, Nicole, but Seth's not the only one who has to make some adjustments. I know you've been through a lot lately and things probably don't make sense to you right now, but whether you believe it or not, your uncle loves you. He only wants what's best for you."

"Hah! Uncle Seth doesn't love me. He's just stuck with me because no one else wanted me. It's got nothing to do with love."

Heather's heart swelled in compassion for this injured girl. Hearing the concern in his voice and seeing the look in his eyes every time he talked to Nicole, Heather knew Seth's feelings for his niece ran deep. Okay, so his manners needed some polish and he needed to learn how to relate to young girls, but all in all, Heather's gut instinct told her Seth was an all right kind of guy.

She gripped Nicole's shoulders and bent her knees, looking her in the eye. "You have to remember, this is all new to your uncle. He lost his only sister and is hurting, too. You both need some time to adjust and learn how to become a family."

Heather held out her hand in a peace offering. "Tell you what. Let's you and me join forces this summer. Maybe we can break down his macho, power image. If we can find a way to get him to lose that cell phone, there might actually be a pretty sweet guy underneath all those expensive clothes."

Nicole's frown turned into a small grin, her green eyes almost sparkling with a bit of hope. She grabbed hold of Heather's hand. "You know, after the plane ride yesterday, I thought you were some wimpy chick trying to make moves on my uncle."

Heather laughed. "And now?"

Nicole scanned Heather from head to toe. "You're a pretty tough lady. I think my uncle may have just met his match."

Seth slid his cell phone onto the center console of his Vette and stared down at the first cabin on the left. Maybe this Heather Thomas was just the one to break through Nicole's cocky, know-it-all attitude. He reached over his shoulder and strapped on his seat belt, feeling a small smile of satisfaction tug at his lips.

Nicole may have just met her match.

Chomping down on a cinnamon disk, he drove down the long asphalted lane toward the highway, hoping Heather could break through the wall Nicole had built up around herself. He certainly hadn't been able to say or do anything right. Now he wondered if what he could give Nicole would actually be enough. He could never take the place of his sister, and at Nicole's age, there was one thing he knew for sure: she definitely needed a mother figure in her life.

He found himself thinking about the feisty brunette counselor, her confidence and the strength she'd exhibited this morning a stark contrast to the insecure and delicate woman he'd met on the plane yesterday.

Big brown eyes with flecks of gold were by far her number-one asset, with a full set of shiny, heart-shaped lips coming in a close second. Streaks of shimmery strands of spun gold intertwined amongst light-brown hair that hung clear down to her waist, wound together in a thick braid. Like yesterday, she wore no makeup, and her scent . . . all he could smell was an unusual concoction of sweet lilacs mixed with a subtle trace of horses and hay.

The whole earthy, natural thing wasn't usually the type of woman who caught his attention. But when she'd strode up the yard this morning wearing those faded, hip-hugging jeans, a low-scooped T-shirt, and scuffed leather cowboy boots, he'd had a sudden urge to yell, "Yee-haw!"

Shifting into gear, he sped down the highway toward the interstate that would take him north to Denver. Nearing I-25, his cell phone rang. He flipped it open and answered, "Roberts here."

"What time do you meet with Chang Liu?" Joe Ferguson never had been one to sit on a deal long. He liked to work fast and have several irons in the fire at the same time.

"Mr. Liu and his Japanese associates are flying into Denver this morning. We're meeting with their American-based company, Five Seasons Athletics, around ten. Mr. Liu's still hedging, but I've got a feeling after I show him and his team what I've got in mind for the old hospital grounds, we'll be able to sign them on without a hitch."

"Great. I've already got somebody lined up for you to meet. He's got a lot of connections with the State House and should be able to get you a good start on seed money."

Seth sped up on the entrance ramp, checking his mirrors as he merged onto the interstate. "Get in touch with my secretary and set up a meeting for next week. Sue has my schedule."

"We like what we're seeing, Roberts. The board is meeting in two weeks to discuss your promotion. Don't screw this up."

Seth choked out a laugh. "Thanks for the vote of confidence."

"You know what I mean. Did you get your niece all settled in last night?"

"Yeah. I just dropped her off at a children's day camp she'll be attending this summer. I'll have to pick her up by five-thirty every night, but I should still have plenty of time with Mr. Liu this afternoon."

Joe cleared his throat. "If you need to be with your niece, Seth, we could always give this account over to Davison."

Seth gripped the steering wheel and pressed down the accelerator. "No, sir. I've got everything under control. Nicole won't be a problem."

"Listen, my daughter's fourteen and attends an excellent girl's school out east. It might be kind of hard to get your niece into the fall semester at this late date, but I'll have my wife call and get you a referral."

After what Nicole had just lived through, the last thing he wanted to do was ship her off to live with more strangers. "I don't know, Joe. I'll give it some thought. We're still trying to get to know each other." Adding with more conviction, he said, "You don't have to worry about Mr. Liu. I won't let you down."

As he sped past Castle Rock, he flipped his phone shut, thinking about Joe's proposition. Sending Nicole to a prep school next fall hadn't even crossed his mind. Nicole would certainly get the best education money could buy, and she'd be around girls her own age, doing things that a normal teenager would be doing. And if he moved to Dallas, she'd have to make another transition into a new school anyway.

More than anything, Seth wanted Nicole to have the best education and give her the kind of opportunities Pop had never been able to afford for Shelli. Dance lessons, music lessons, anything Nicole wanted, Seth was determined to make sure she never wanted for anything the rest of her life.

Maybe a structured school was what Nicole needed right now. He barely had time to grocery shop, much less keep food stocked in the refrigerator. He realized last night how empty his cupboards were when Nicole had rummaged through the kitchen, slamming each door, only emphasizing that fact. He'd ended up ordering in pizza, which seemed to make her happy.

He'd offered her his bedroom, but she'd absolutely refused to even cross the threshold. He made a mental note to pick up a new bed this weekend and convert the den into a bedroom, giving her some much-needed girl space.

He was just grateful Spike had a home for the summer. The bug-eyed lizard didn't exactly give him a warm, fuzzy feeling. A prep school sounded better and better the more he thought about it.

A worried thought crept into Seth's mind. Do prep schools allow iguanas?

Five-thirty-nine.

Heather strode outside the office of the J Bar D Outreach Camp for Kids. Impatient, she paced the asphalt parking lot, looking for any sign of the yellow Corvette. So far, Seth had driven into the driveway promptly at five-thirty every night this week. Usually, a few minutes late picking up a camper wouldn't make that big a difference to Heather, as long as it didn't become a habit.

But tonight was different. Tonight she had to stop by the seamstress to pick up a dress before they closed at six. Somehow, Jared had wrangled her into another one of his save-the-animal benefits that was being held at the Royal Rock Hotel tonight at eight o'clock.

He'd not only volunteered her to give a speech on behalf of the animal shelter that needed funds, but he'd had the gumption to sign her up to be auctioned off as one of the available bachelorettes!

She loved Jared dearly, but she'd wanted to strangle him when he'd told her about the auction. In the end, though, she'd agreed to go, if only for the good of the shelter. Unfortunately, she wasn't going anywhere until Seth picked up Nicole.

Heather flicked an impatient glance at her watch and tapped the toe of her cowboy boot. Five-fifty-one. Her blood pressure soared off the charts. It didn't matter if Seth would be willing to pay a thousand bucks a minute. Being this late without at least calling was inexcusable.

Standing on the front porch, Heather put two fingers between her lips and whistled. "Kyle and Katie, go get in the van and put on your seat belts. We need to leave as soon as Nicole's uncle gets here."

Heather stormed back into the office and dialed the seamstress, begging her to stay another fifteen minutes. How did she let Jared talk her into this charity auction in the first place? Being auctioned off like a head of cattle? If she hadn't agreed to speak on behalf of the animal shelter, she'd back out right now.

The familiar low rumble of a sports car pulled into the lot. She hung up the phone, locked her desk and grabbed her purse. As she opened the door, she tripped over the threshold and flew face first into a set of chest muscles made of steel.

With an arrogant laugh, Seth set her back, holding firmly to her shoulders. "I've had my share of ladies throwing themselves at me, but frankly, Ms. Thomas, I'm shocked."

She pressed one hand against his chest and tried to push back, but he held firm, giving what he obviously thought was a grin that would make most ladies tremble.

She trembled all right, in downright fury. "It's almost six. You're late."

"Didn't you get my message?"

"Message?"

"I called Debra around five-fifteen. There was an accident on the interstate just north of Castle Rock. Shut down the highway for a good thirty minutes."

"Oh, well, Debra hadn't mentioned anything to me. She and J.D. went into town to pick out some baby furniture. Probably excited and just forgot. You know how pregnant women get. Now, if you'll kindly move away from the door, I need to get home."

Seth's brows arched. "No, I don't know how pregnant women get, and I thought you lived here."

"Nope. This is my folks' place. J.D. owns the rest of the acreage and lives with Debra at the back of the property."

"So, where do you live?"

Pulling away from his clutches, she turned around and jammed the key into the office door lock. "I've got a condo in town. Listen, I really don't have time to talk right now, and if you actually did call, which you can bet I will verify with Debra, I won't charge you for being late."

He gazed at her, staring intently into her eyes. "I get the feeling you don't like me very well. Why is that?"

She took a deep breath and lowered her voice. "Look, I don't know you enough to like or dislike you, but you're coming very close to the latter if you show up this late again. Now, I really have to be going. I'll see you Monday."

Feeling his heated stare on her backside, she climbed behind the wheel of her minivan, waved to Nicole as she met her uncle at the office, then rushed to the seamstress and picked up her dress. By the time she picked up the babysitter and fed the kids, she only had twenty minutes to take a quick shower and get dressed.

Her hair still damp, she swept it into a pile on top of her head, leaving a few long curly tendrils framing her face and neck. Digging out a bag of makeup, she opened a new bottle of foundation that she'd bought for her trip to California, but had never used. After brushing on rouge and a touch of mascara, she rummaged through her jewelry box and held up two neck-laces.

"Which one?" she asked Katie who was busy sniffing all her bottles of perfume.

Her long sandy-brown curls bobbed loosely all around her shoulders. "I like the red one. It matches your dress. Can I wear the glass one?"

Heather laughed and shook her head. "No, honey. It's a diamond. Not glass. Please, you know the rules. No playing with Mommy's jewelry." Heather fastened the teardrop ruby necklace around her throat and slipped the matching earrings through her pierced lobes. She could say one nice thing about Eric. He had good taste in jewelry.

His taste in dresses, on the other hand, ran a bit on the skimpy side. He'd picked this little number out years ago for her to wear to a black-tie dinner and dance. It didn't seem right to go and buy a brand-new dress when this one was hanging in her closet.

Smoothing the formfitting gown over her hips, she gazed at her reflection in the full-length mirror. She'd asked the seamstress to let it out in the bodice, her bust line a full cup size fuller since having the kids. The red, sequined, floor-length dress was held up with only two thin straps. She'd even bought a strapless Wonderbra to give herself a little boost.

It was a wonder all right. She shoved her hands under her breasts, resituating, hoping nothing fell out. Maybe it was too much—or too little. She tipped her head back and almost cried, "Oh, God, what am I doing? I can't sell myself to the highest bidder." It almost sounded illegal.

"You look so pretty, Mommy."

Even though the compliment was a little biased coming from her daughter, it had been so long since Heather had heard that from anyone, she actually felt pretty for a change. She bent over and wrapped her arms clear around Katie's tiny waist and swung her around the bedroom in a circle. "Have I ever told you how much I love being your mommy?"

Katie giggled as she pushed away and jumped to the floor. "Can we watch *The Lion King* after you leave?"

"Sure. I should be home to tuck you into bed. Pick some perfume and spray some on my wrists."

Katie picked Obsession and spritzed both wrists, giggling as she doused herself. "Mmmmmm, now we both smell good."

Checking her lipstick, Heather grabbed her matching red sequined clutch and her notes for the speech. After slipping on her three-inch spiked heels, she kissed her kids and headed out the door. Maybe if she didn't trip down the runway first, some rich millionaire bachelor would bid on her.

Hah! Been there, done that. If she'd learned anything from her failed marriage, it was that money could definitely not buy happiness.

CHAPTER FOUR

Seth tugged at his black bow tie as he jogged across the parking lot of the Royal Rock Hotel. By the time he'd gotten home and had settled Nicole in with Mrs. Swanson and her daughter Maggie, one floor down, he'd barely had time to shower and get into his tux. He was just thankful Nicole had made a new friend in the building. As many times as he'd seen the Swansons in the elevator, he'd never actually spoken to them. Apparently, Maggie and her mom had been living there the past four years.

He slowed his strides and entered through the revolving glass entryway into the hotel lobby. After locating the Lincoln Ballroom, he took a steadying breath and opened the double mahogany doors. Everyone had already been seated around several round tables adorned with elegant place settings and bottles of wine.

He found Jared sitting at a back table and clapped him on the shoulder. "Sorry, I'm late." He spoke in a low voice just over the din of conversation in the room. "I'm never going to get the hang of this parenting stuff. What'd I miss?"

Jared shook his head. "Not much. Just a few speakers. The auction starts in about twenty minutes. They're doing the men first." He scanned the crowded banquet hall. "See any hot prospects?"

Seth slid out a chair and scanned the crowd speculatively. He spotted a tall blonde, maybe forty, eyeing him. She raised her champagne glass and blew him a kiss. He nodded, not sure if he was up for this kind of crowd tonight. Truth be told, he hadn't even dated anyone since his breakup with Brenda. He made a nervous glance toward the exit doors, wondering if it was too late to make an escape.

A round of applause indicated the end of one of the speakers. Seth clapped and recognized John Wilson of Wilson Manufacturing sitting at a nearby table. The company manufactured circuit breakers and had factories all over the country.

John was sitting with his youngest daughter, Jennifer, who was good friends with his brother Marty. Although Jennifer lived with her parents, she did a lot of activities at the Pine Tree Family Services Center.

Seth raised his glass to John and smiled in greeting, then slid a wink to Jennifer. Her grin spread from ear to ear in her round, pudgy face. She giggled and buried her reddened cheeks in her father's arm. She was such a sweetheart.

"Ladies and gentlemen. Our next speaker is the head counselor at the highly respected J Bar D Outreach Camp for Kids. She is a noted public spokeswoman and children's advocate, appearing regularly at area clubs and organizations on behalf of children and families who are learning to cope with childhood diseases and disorders. She's got a huge heart where kids and animals are concerned, and as a sister to one of the town's prominent veterinarians and one of tonight's eligible bachelors, she's agreed to speak on behalf of the animal shelter. She's also joining the lineup as one of our beautiful and talented bachelorettes. So, please, let's give a big round of applause and welcome Heather Thomas."

As the applause filtered around him, Seth could only stare as the tall lady counselor appeared from the side of the stage, gracefully strolling to the podium. Beautiful didn't even begin to describe how Heather looked on stage tonight. Breathtaking. Astonishing. Definitely a far cry from the whole earthy, natural woman he'd actually found himself anxious to be near this past week.

She wore a formfitting, red-sequined dress with nothing but two thin straps holding up the top . . . barely. Her bulky work shirts had certainly concealed some of her more notable assets. He took a long sip of his champagne, and without taking his eyes off her, he leaned over to Jared. "You didn't tell me your sister was going to be here."

Jared gave a proud grin. "Yep, she's even agreed to go up on the auction block. I promised her I'd bail her out if no one bids."

Seth shook his head and laughed. "With that dress? She'll probably pay for half the shelter all by herself."

"I'll tell her you said that. She's kind of got a little self-esteem issue ever since her husband left her."

"You wouldn't know it by looking at her. She's gorgeous." Seth ran a finger under his collar, the room suddenly warming up ten degrees. He'd been trying to muster up the courage to ask her out all week, but had never found an appropriate time, either because of work, or because Nicole had been in the room.

He'd never had problems communicating with women before. Of course, he'd never met anyone like Heather before either. Compassionate. Smart. Level-headed. Athletic. Good with children. Great attributes all rolled into one woman.

Jared had said she was a little vulnerable right now after her divorce. That would certainly explain why she'd been so standoffish toward him this past week. Showing up late to pick up Nicole probably hadn't won him any brownie points either. Even though it wasn't the best timing to get involved with anyone right now, he couldn't deny this incredible attraction he'd felt for her ever since he'd met her on the plane. And the way she looked at him with those big brown eyes, and how her voice quivered ever so slightly every time they'd talked, he couldn't help but feel some kind of a connection with her. Somehow, he had to convince her that not all men were jerks. He had to show her how a beautiful, sensitive, young woman should be treated.

That shouldn't be too hard.

"Good evening. Thank you for coming out this evening to such a worthwhile cause." From onstage, Heather made a slight adjustment, lifting the microphone and giving a confident smile to the audience. "I was born and raised on a horse ranch and have lived around animals all my life. I can't stress enough the vital role animal shelters play, especially in today's society where more and more abandoned animals need homes."

Seth found himself lost in her eyes as she spoke statistics and revealed the amount of money spent on each abandoned or abused animal. Her passion for this cause rang apparent in her plea for donations. Her big brown eyes almost sparkled with enthusiasm.

Or was that just her dress?

He thought she'd looked sexy in the tight denim jeans she'd worn at the ranch. That was nothing compared to this red-sequined number, shimmering under the iridescent glow of the spotlight.

She seemed totally at ease in front of the audience as she told several anecdotes about her brothers. How they'd saved countless abandoned kittens and puppies, or about injured fawns they'd discovered in the forest near their ranch and had nursed back to health. Her admiration for her brothers almost made him a little sad, or maybe it was guilt, knowing how he'd let his own sister and brother down over the years. Since moving to the Springs, he'd been able to visit Marty at Pine Tree quite often, in between travels. But it hadn't been as convenient to see Shelli. And now, unfortunately, there was no way to make it up to her. He just had to make sure he devoted more time to Nicole.

"So, I urge you," Heather pleaded, bringing him out of his remorse. "Dig deep into your hearts, and your pocketbooks. With your help, we can save hundreds of orphaned animals and place them in loving homes and safe environments."

Seth had never realized how desperately these shelters needed funds. Suddenly inspired, he leaned over to Jared. "I need to see someone before the auction begins. I'll meet you behind the stage."

When he stood, Heather stopped speaking right in the middle of a sentence. He smiled and sent her a conspiratorial wink.

She cleared her throat and looked down at the podium. "I, um," she stammered for the first time tonight. "I think I've begged enough for one evening. Without further ado, please welcome back your master of ceremonies, Mr. Maxwell Steele."

With her heart pounding wildly inside her chest, Heather escaped off center stage and slumped behind a curtain. What was Seth Roberts doing here?

She peered through a crack in the curtains and saw him say something to her brother before hurrying out the back doors to the lobby.

Jared. Of course, she should have known.

She stepped away from the curtains and reached into her clutch, pulling out a small compact. She blotted her upper lip and forehead, trying to convince herself it didn't matter. So what if Seth Roberts was here. So what if he was the sexiest, best-looking man in the room. From all appearances, dressed to the nines in a black tux, it looked as though he'd be one of the eligible bachelors up for bid. Maybe she could hide out here all night and avoid him altogether.

"Hey, sis." Jared approached her from behind and placed a

kiss on her cheek. "You were spectacular, as usual. Thanks for doing this tonight. I know you hate to be away from Kyle and Katie."

"No problem," she said, sounding a little breathless after seeing Seth in the audience. She stuffed the compact into her purse.

"Hey." Jared's voice lowered as he turned her around to face him. "What's the matter? You're not nervous are you?" He squeezed her shoulder. "You're absolutely beautiful. You have nothing to worry about. It's me who should be nervous. There's a lot of stiff competition out there."

With trembly fingers, she reached up and straightened Jared's black bow tie. "The way some of those women eyed you when you walked by, I doubt a hunky doctor like yourself will have any problems snagging a date." Wanting to find out the scoop on Seth, she gave the bow tie one last tug. "I saw you talking to Seth Roberts. I didn't realize he was going to be here tonight."

"Yeah. I asked him to join the lineup the day I picked you up from the airport. Good thing, too. Because of him the place sold out in the last week since he'd signed on. He's pretty influential in his elite circle."

Heather arched her brows. "Wow. I had no idea."

The MC summoned all the bachelors up to center stage. She reached up and kissed his cheek. "You're not so bad yourself. I bet there's a lot of bidders out there who want to be in your elite circle."

"Thanks. Keep your fingers crossed." Jared slid his black Stetson cowboy hat over his head and sauntered toward the stage in a slow John Wayne kind of swagger. It was amazing that such a good-looking, warmhearted guy like Jared hadn't been snatched up by now. He'd had a bad relationship several years ago, but now that his clinic was off the ground, maybe he'd find someone and settle down himself with a wife and kids. Maybe this auction was just the ticket.

She peeked through the curtains and watched as the MC auctioned off the first three bachelors. Everyone applauded as the women approached their newly purchased escorts. Only two gorgeous bachelors remained. Jared and Seth. She scanned the crowded banquet room. The bidding began with Jared and escalated clear up to two thousand dollars before the gavel slammed.

A beautiful blonde in a stunning, floor-length, black dress strode forward. She couldn't have been older than twenty-five. Heather's heart swelled as she watched Jared gallantly offer his elbow, leaning over and placing a quick kiss on the woman's cheek. Did he have any idea how charming he could be?

"You're in for a real treat, ladies." The MC walked over next to Seth. "Our last bachelor on the block is noted for his financial advice in magazines such as *Forbes, Financial Times,* and *Gentlemen's Quarterly,* to name a few."

Heather straightened, a little abashed at Seth's stunning accomplishments. She knew he was big in the financial world, but his credentials were remarkable as the MC continued reading his resume. "He stands at six foot, four inches tall and weighs in at two hundred pounds of pure muscle. His hobbies include flying, backpacking, and taking beautiful women out to dinner."

Flying? Was Seth a pilot? She cringed, remembering her plane fiasco last weekend. The bidding began and she found herself riveted to her spot, waiting to see how much someone was willing to pay. She almost wished she could bid. Even though Eric gave more than enough to support her and the kids, she'd put most of that away for their future and wouldn't dream of touching it for something so frivolous.

The bidding escalated quickly, narrowing down to just two bidders. One, unbelievably, was a man. Upper sixties, she guessed. He didn't bat an eye as he continued to increase the amount, leaving only one other lady in the running.

The bid reached clear up to six thousand dollars before the gavel slammed and the man yelled, "Sold to the gentleman in front. Congratulations, Mr. Wilson."

The older gentleman rose and extended his hand toward Seth as he strode down the steps.

Why would a man bid on Seth? Unless he was. . . . Heather placed a hand over her mouth and stared at Seth. Maybe that's why he'd never married.

Seth caught her gaping, but his smile only widened as he extended his hand to a young woman sitting next to the older gentleman bidder.

Heather wanted to crawl into a box. The lady with styled short brown hair and a smile that ran from ear to ear had all the characteristics of a person with Down syndrome.

Seth bowed regally before the woman and held her fingertips. "Hi, Jenny. Are you ready for the best night of your life?"

The young woman named Jenny blushed profusely at Seth's attentions, giggling and hiding her face in the arm of the man who must be her father.

"You are the prettiest girl here tonight," Seth added. "Did you get a new dress?"

"Mommy said it makes me look older." Jenny splayed a hand over her shoulder. "I like the flowers on the sleeves."

"Your mother was right. The pink flowers are my favorite."

The happiness Seth brought to this woman created a well of tears in Heather's eyes. She remembered Seth's conversation with the flight attendant about missing Jenny's hugs. Heather knew without a doubt this was the woman he'd been referring to. Seeing a whole new side to Seth Roberts, she slipped back behind the curtain, feeling a little ashamed for thinking the worst about Seth. She just wanted to sneak out the back door and head home.

The MC came over the microphone and summoned all the bachelorettes up to the "auction block." Several women scurried past Heather, and she found herself being shuffled onto the stage with three stunning blondes in shimmery black dresses, and a fiery redhead in a gold little strapless number. Standing near the back of the pack, she took in a quivery breath and sent up a small prayer of hope that someone would bid.

The women before her sold quickly, the bids amazingly running between three and five thousand dollars each. She hung back, still hoping on the off chance to escape at the last minute. Finally, they called her forward. With trembling knees and a racing heartbeat, she stepped into the spotlight and was greeted by applause.

A young woman walked on stage and handed a note to the MC. He looked over at Heather and smiled. "Well, Ms. Thomas. It seems you have a secret admirer, and a wealthy one at that. An anonymous bid has been placed for ten thousand dollars."

Heather gasped, along with the entire room. "I don't know what to say."

"Well, unless anyone else wants to bid, ten thousand going once, going twice, sold!" The MC slammed his gavel and everyone applauded, cheering loudly.

She scanned the entire room. Jared stood at the back with his date, but he only lifted his shoulders in a shrug. Her eyes locked on Seth's as he stood next to the young woman named Jenny. He only clapped, not giving her any indication that he'd done the bidding.

If Seth hadn't bid on her, who did? And why had he remained anonymous?

Quickly exiting the stage, she grabbed her clutch and kept her head down. Everyone touched her arm, congratulating her as if she'd just won an Oscar. She wanted to go home. This whole auction had made her uncomfortable from the start. But on the bright side, they'd raised almost thirty thousand dollars for the animal shelter.

Jared whistled as Heather approached. "Wow, sis. Someone must have it bad. Have you figured out who it is, yet?"

Nervously biting her bottom lip, she shook her head. "I was hoping you might know. Any ideas?"

"I have my suspicions." He chuckled. "I think I'll let you stew on it for a while." He gently took the lady's hand standing next to him, stared deeply into her sparkling blue eyes and introduced her. "Melanie, this is my sister, Heather Thomas. Heather, this is Melanie Whitewood. She and I went to vet school together."

"Nice to meet you, Melanie. I'd warn you about Jared, but as you probably already know, he's just an all-around sweet guy. I hope you two have fun on your date. Where are you going?"

"Well," Melanie gave a shy glance toward Jared. "I thought a weekend trip into the mountains might be kind of fun."

Jared smiled and nodded. "Sounds perfect."

Heather took this as her cue to leave. "I think I'll let you two get reacquainted. I told the babysitter I'd be home early."

Jared glanced toward the stage where a band was warming up for the dance. "Why don't you stay for a few songs? The babysitter can tuck them in tonight."

She bit her bottom lip, tempted to stay and find out who spent all that money on her. The chicken in her made her shake her head. "No, I really should be getting home. Good night. Have fun."

Heather slid gracefully past Jared and Melanie, who'd snuggled closer together. Thinking about Melanie's idea of a date made Heather shudder. It didn't matter how much her anonymous bidder had paid, she wasn't about to go gallivanting off for a weekend trip with a total stranger and leave Kyle and Katie again. She exited the building and reveled in the cool mountain air. A refreshing breeze brushed the back of her neck, making her shiver. She fumbled in her purse for her keys.

"Leaving so soon?" A familiar low baritone sounded from behind.

Heather gasped and jerked her head around.

With a crooked grin sliding across his smooth-shaven face, Seth remained leaning casually against a stone pillar, his ankles crossed in front of him. The way her heart leapt out of her chest only confirmed her earlier assessment that he was by far the most handsome bachelor on the stage tonight. Of course, she always was a sucker for guys in black tuxes. But something told her that this guy could be wearing a pink kimono, and she'd still drool.

She warily tipped her head to the side and approached him with caution. "Are you in the habit of lurking outside hotels, Mr. Roberts?"

"Only if there are beautiful women in long red dresses coming and going." His smile was far too seductive for her comfort. He shoved away from the wall and met her halfway across the front sidewalk. "You're absolutely breathtaking, by the way. It's no wonder you brought in the highest bid."

"I don't suppose. . . ." She cleared her throat. "I mean, did you?"

His grin broadened, a devilish gleam sparkling in the depths of his deep blue eyes, but he didn't answer.

Embarrassed, she shook her head and stared down at her clutch. The chill she'd felt earlier was now doused with a fiery warmth spreading up her chest to her face. "I'm sorry. It was silly of me to even suggest—"

"What?" He gently touched her chin, forcing her to look up at him. He stood so close he could probably see the beating of her heart. "That someone would offer ten thousand dollars to have the privilege of taking you out?" The backs of his knuckles brushed her cheek as he whisked a strand of hair from her face. "To be honest, I probably should have offered more."

She had to coax her legs to remain standing, her eyes to stay focused on his, and her brains to be unfazed by his nearness. But, oh, Lord, it was her heart she found difficult to control.

He slid his hand into his trouser pocket. "I didn't know you were such a noted public speaker. I'm impressed."

Remembering his long list of accomplishments, hers seemed trite in comparison. "Just local stuff on kids and family relationships." Snapping her fingers in jest, she added, "Gee, why aren't I surprised that you've never heard me speak before?"

"Am I that predictable?"

"Your kind are very predictable, Mr. Roberts."

"My kind, huh?" He chuckled with husky seduction and moved closer, his gaze touching her in places that sent her nerves on fire. His scent of musk and pure man radiated all around her, making her head feel dizzy.

She stayed her ground, clutching her fingers to her purse to keep from trembling.

"So, tell me, Ms. Thomas. Standing so close to such a beautiful woman, what exactly would my kind do in this situation?"

When his gaze lowered to her lips, her breath caught in her throat. A delicious sensation trickled down her spine. She couldn't deny this overwhelming . . . curiosity, for lack of a better word, to feel his full lips on hers. It'd been a long time since she'd felt these female stirrings of attraction for a man. She'd only ever dated Eric, marrying him shortly after high school, and even then, she'd never had these overpowering grown-up sensations take over all her senses.

Predictable or not, she found herself running the tip of her tongue over her lips, letting her eyes flutter closed.

The warmth of his body drew near. His mouth was just a whisper's length from hers. Instead of kissing her, he brushed his cheek against hers, his nose resting just below her earlobe. "As much as I'd like to kiss you right now, I'd hate to prove you right and be too predictable." He breathed deep. "Although, you are quite tempting. Do you always smell this good?"

His breath tickled her skin and she scrunched her shoulder to her neck, her cheek inadvertently pressing against his. Startled at the searing heat coming from the slight contact, she drew apart and opened her eyes, only to find a seductive grin radiating from ear to ear. He'd drawn her into his playboy charisma like a honeybee to a freshly bloomed flower. She only hoped the dimly lit evening masked her embarrassment.

Why was she acting like this? It was obvious he was only teasing her. She didn't come close to the kind of women he was used to dating. Embarrassed, she pulled her keys out of her purse and stepped backwards. "I think we'd better call this evening a night. I'll agree to go out with you because that's the honorable thing to do, but anything beyond dinner is out of the question. Now, it's late and I told the babysitter I'd be home early to tuck the kids into bed."

"Babysitter?" His dark brows arched.

She stared up at his confused expression. "Kyle and Katie? My kids? Hasn't Nicole told you about them?"

He shook his head, like he was in some kind of a bad dream. "No, she's hardly said two words to me the entire week. I thought Kyle and Katie were J.D. and Debra's kids. I didn't even know you had children."

"For a little over nine years now. Katie's seven. Guess you'd better do your homework the next time you go throwing your money around." She tried to play it light, but seeing the shock in his eyes was more than she could bear.

She turned around and hurried toward her minivan, slid the key into the door, then peered over her shoulder. "Hey, maybe you can trade me in for one of the other models who don't come with all the emotional baggage of a family."

When he didn't answer, she opened the door and lowered her shoulders, disappointed in herself for letting the man rob her of all logical thinking. But she was also disappointed in Seth. She'd hoped he wasn't as superficial as she'd pegged him from the beginning. She was almost certain there was a decent guy underneath all that panache and charisma.

She made the mistake of looking at him again and found him watching her, but something had changed in his eyes. Sympathy maybe?

Adjusting her dress, she slid behind the wheel and switched on the ignition. With the door still open, she gave a resigned sigh, disenchantment flooding her soul. For a brief moment, she'd actually felt like a full-fledged desirable woman and had fallen for this man's charm and devastatingly gorgeous smile.

But the fact remained she had two rambunctious children waiting for her at home. Nowhere did a world-traveling, millionaire bachelor fit into the picture of Disney videos and frozen pizzas.

She squared her shoulders and gave him an apologetic smile. "Don't worry. I won't hold you to the date. Just promise you'll still give a donation to the animal shelter. We'll forget this even happened." She closed the door, buckled her seat belt, then heard a tap on her window.

Seth was there, looking entirely too handsome . . . and definitely way out of her league. She pressed the button, lowering the glass.

"For what it's worth," he said, almost looking guilty, "I'm sorry about the remark I made about your son Monday morning. I was way out of line."

She lowered her shoulders. "Don't worry about it. I love him to death, but I have to admit, Kyle can be quite a handful at times. I'm truly sorry for any inconvenience—for tonight, I mean."

"There's been no inconvenience. If anything, knowing you have children only adds to your appeal. From the little I've seen, you're a great mother. That should have been at the top of your credentials in there."

"Thanks," she said looking down at her lap, picking at her manicured red fingernails. "I'm afraid my ex-husband wouldn't exactly see it that way."

"Jared mentioned he moved away from the area. Does he see the kids much? I mean, what kind of custody arrangements do you have? What about child support?"

"I've got sole custody, and when it comes to money, he's right there for the kids, always getting Katie expensive gifts. But he's moved to Telluride and doesn't get back to the Springs too often. Big real-estate mogul. No time for family," she added with a little disgust.

"Telluride, huh?" He slid his fingers through his thick black hair, distracting her from what they'd been discussing.

"Look, Seth, I'm sure you don't have time to hear all about my family life. Compared to your world travels and exciting adventures, my life must seem pretty boring and pathetic."

He perched his forearms on her door and leaned close. "Pathetic, huh? Sounds to me like the lady needs to have a little fun put back into her life."

"I have plenty of fun with my kids," she said, almost sounding too defensive. "I love being a mom and watching my kids grow. I don't need anything or anyone else in my life right now."

"Well, that's to be determined. I shelled out quite a few bucks for the honor of your company. I hope you don't plan on backing out on me."

She met his gaze, his smile melting into hers even deeper than it had before. How could she back out on him now? She had to do this, if only for the benefit of the animal shelter.

He traced his fingertip up her arm to her shoulder then pulled out the pin holding her hair in a bun. The weight of her heavy mass of hair whooshed down over her shoulders in one fell swoop. The silkiness on her skin was exhilarating.

He smiled. "There, much better. If I didn't say it before, you're astonishingly beautiful tonight."

The formality was gone and the gleam in his eyes even more dangerous. He lowered his gaze to her lips, and for a moment, she thought he was actually going to kiss her this time. A shiver prickled her skin, but she doubted it was from the cool night air.

Once again, she really did want him to kiss her, if only to rid her of these ridiculous fantasies of what his kiss would feel like. If he was anything like Eric, it would probably be forced and hard and lacking any real finesse.

"Heather?" His voice was a husky murmur next to her face. God, she loved how he said her name, like a warm summer breeze off the prairie.

She hadn't even realized she'd closed her eyes. When she peeked at him through slitted lids, she answered barely over a whisper. "Hmmm?"

He touched her chin, rubbing his thumb just below her lip. "I'll see you Monday. And when you line up a babysitter for our date, be sure and tell her you'll be late." He tapped the end of her nose. "You definitely won't be home in time to tuck your kids into bed."

CHAPTER FIVE

Tossing a grooming brush in a bucket, Heather led a big, dapple-gray mare into the corral and gave her a swift pat on the rump, sending her through the gate. Nicole and J.D. had just finished an hour-long riding lesson in the arena. But J.D. and Debra had to leave for an interview with a pediatrician for their new baby, and since they were running a little behind, Heather had volunteered to put the horses away.

A quick glance at her watch informed her she still had three hours before her meeting tonight at Saint Anthony's Children's Hospital. She'd organized a control group to discuss the goal of opening a specialized children's learning center, as well as locations for this type of a facility. And, of course, funding. Several of the parents of her support group, along with therapists, nurses, and even some medical doctors who were losing their jobs, agreed to join her at the meeting at seven.

It was Friday of the Memorial Day Holiday, and after tonight, she was looking forward to a nice relaxing weekend at home with just her two kids. Next Tuesday, after the three-day weekend, a rush of new campers was scheduled to arrive for their first week of the summer season. Three new counselors would be starting as well, which would help alleviate some of Heather's workload. Then she could get back into more of a routine with Kyle on his studies.

Since burning himself, she'd let him slide on most of his math and language assignments because of the pain from his burns. The bandages on his fingers had also made it difficult for him to grasp a pencil.

The summer-like weather wasn't helping matters either. Kyle loved to be outside with the horses as much as Heather did. Temperatures were forecast to be in the mid-seventies to upper seventies throughout the holiday weekend and into the first week of June. Without any air movement in the barn, it already felt like the middle of July.

She yanked off her flannel shirt and draped it over a stall fence. Since Nicole was the only camper around, Heather was tempted to change out of her tank top and jeans and get into a pair of comfortable shorts and a bikini top to catch some rays.

Better not. Seth would be out to pick up Nicole soon. Finding Heather in a bikini probably wouldn't appear too professional, which, in retrospect, was exactly how he'd treated her all week. Strictly business. He'd dropped Nicole off by eight every morning and had picked her up promptly by five-thirty each night. He'd been cordial at best when he'd arrived, keeping his visits brief and their conversations even shorter. He hadn't said one word to her about their big date. Probably realized what a mistake he'd made.

Oh, well. Getting involved with him—or any man—was the last thing she should be doing right now. She had to think about her kids and keep focused on what was best for them. After all the emotional trauma of their father moving out and rarely coming to visit, she couldn't let herself get involved with Seth, or with anyone for that matter, only to have him leave in the end.

And Seth would. Maybe not right away, but eventually, he'd come to reality and see how much responsibility came with dating a single parent with two challenging kids, especially when one had autism.

Standing inside the barn, Heather flipped her long braid over her shoulder and peered toward the hayloft where Kyle and Katie were playing cards with Nicole. She had Spike on a leash and they were all sticking their tongues out at one another. Their conversation, of course, centered around whose tongue was the longest. The few times Heather had gotten close, Spike won, hands down.

A low belly laugh made her smile. It was so good to see Kyle open up again. Nicole had learned to communicate with her son in a way she'd never been able to do, which only made Heather question her own parenting skills for the millionth time.

"Kyle! Give it back!" Katie squealed.

"No! Mine!"

Heather hoisted herself up the ladder to the hayloft, her knees making a slight popping sound. "Kyle? What's going on?"

"He won't give me my cards!" Katie yelled, proceeding to stick her tongue out at him. She was definitely in contention with Spike.

"Katie, sticking your tongue out is very unladylike. Kyle? We've talked about sharing. Now give the cards back to Katie."

"No. My cards."

With an exasperated sigh, Heather narrowed her eyes on Kyle. "Do you want to sit in your room all by yourself?"

He threw the cards at Katie and cupped his hands over his ears, rocking back and forth.

Not wanting to get her son all upset, Heather climbed the rest of the way to the top and sat down next to him. "Come on, honey. How about if I play?"

Katie's big brown eyes lit up. "Yeah! I'll deal."

Heather gave Nicole a sideways glance. "As long as Spike stays way over there."

"He won't hurt you. Look, he likes you." Nicole held him up to her face. "Pet him."

Heather squirmed and stroked his back, his scales feeling like a dried alligator. "Okay, that's enough. He can like me over there." She drew her cowboy boots beneath her crossways and watched as Katie dealt everyone five cards. Sorting them into pairs, Heather asked, "Kyle, do you have any three's?"

He gnawed the rim of his T-shirt. "Go fish."

Heather drew a card and studied Nicole. Her moods had been such a pleasant contrast to the angry little girl who'd shown up that first day two short weeks ago. It seemed Kyle and Katie had had a positive effect on her as well.

Of course, Heather would like to think she had a little to do with Nicole's improved disposition. They'd had several good talks, mostly about her mother and some of the things they'd done together, like taking long walks, riding bikes, staying up late talking about school and, of course, boys.

But Nicole had talked about her father only once, saying only that he had been away a lot on business. Heather could certainly empathize with the girl, remembering many long nights waiting for Eric to come home. He usually had liquor on his breath and a strange perfume on his clothes.

Even though Seth had been prompt about picking up his niece every night, Heather couldn't help but wonder what he did the rest of the evening. Did he stay home and spend quality time with Nicole? Or did he ditch her every night and head back out to another meeting—or maybe even a date?

That thought sent Heather's mind to spinning. Now that Nicole was living with him, was he still bringing women to his penthouse? Did he realize how impressionable she was at this age?

Hoping to get some answers, Heather reached over and stroked a wisp of strawberry blonde hair out of Nicole's face. "How are things going between you and your uncle Seth? Has he been working a lot?"

Nicole handed Katie a jack of diamonds. "Yeah, like, if he's not on his phone, he's like totally on his computer all the time."

"Has he bought you a bed yet?"

"Not yet, but it's no big deal. The couch in the living room pulls out into a bed. Every morning before we leave he makes me fold it all back up. He also likes my clothes folded or hung up in the closet. He's kind of a neat freak," she added, rolling her eyes. "You know, no eating in the living room, shoes have to be put away. But it's okay," she conceded with a shrug of her shoulders. "It's kind of nice that he takes care of his place. My dad never lifted a finger around our house."

Having lived with a man who'd had the same Stone Age mentality, Heather nodded. "Does Seth have a cleaning lady?"

"Nope. Can you believe he cleans the kitchen and the bathrooms and even vacuums?" She gave a disbelieving laugh. "I don't think my dad even knew how to turn on a vacuum. My mom had to work a lot, so I had to do most of the cleaning. I wasn't very good, though. Our house was always cluttered with my dad's beer cans and dirty ashtrays."

Heather cringed, wondering just what else she'd had to live with when her parents were alive. "Does your uncle ask you to help out around his place?"

She lifted her shoulders and shrugged. "Not really, but I help out with the vacuuming and cleaning the kitchen. He also likes for me to have the bed made since it's right in the living room. It's kind of cool sleeping there. I get to watch TV before I go to sleep and stay up as late as I want."

"So, that's why you fall asleep after lunch," she teased and elbowed Nicole in the arm. "Maybe you ought to turn off the TV and go to sleep earlier."

"Now you sound like my mom."

"I can't help it. I am a mom." She laughed and ruffled Nicole's hair, still trying to picture Seth pushing a vacuum and standing over a toilet bowl with a brush. She could personally attest that J.D. and Jared had never cleaned a bathroom in their lives.

After several more minutes of Go Fish, Kyle won with the most matches. Heather gathered the cards and handed them to Katie. "You and Kyle go up to the house and get your backpacks together. As soon as Seth gets here, I'll take you over to Auntie Debra's. I've got a meeting at the hospital tonight."

Katie tugged at Heather's arm. "Did you remember to call Kimberly's mom about her birthday party next week?"

"Yes, sweetie. We'll have to go shopping and get her a present. Do you know what she wants?"

"Yeah. She just got her ears pierced, so she wants new earrings. Can I get mine done, too?"

"Tell you what. Your birthday is next month. I got mine pierced when I was eight. We'll pick you out a pretty pair of earrings. How's that sound?"

"Awesome!" She sounded more like Nicole every day.

"Go on up to the house with Kyle. I'll take you over to Auntie Debra's after Seth gets here."

A wide smile crossed her face as she followed Kyle down the ladder. The familiar rumble of Seth's sports car sounded in the driveway.

Heather's stomach made a small flutter of its own as she glanced at her watch. "Looks like your uncle's a little early tonight. Let's go tell him how good a rider you've become. Maybe we could talk him into coming out next week and spending some time here, maybe even go on a trail ride with you."

Nicole shrugged her shoulders and picked up Spike, stroking his back like a little puppy dog. "He'll probably just have to work. I'm not even sure what he does, but it must be important. He'd probably forget to eat if I didn't remind him when it was suppertime. And then he usually just orders in a pizza. Between that and cereal for breakfast, I'd rather eat Spike's food. Even spinach and fruit cocktail sounds better than pizza and cereal."

"Hmmmm." Heather thought a minute then tapped a finger on her chin. "I have an idea. Next week we've got new counselors coming out. Maybe you and I can sneak off into my mom's kitchen. I'm not the greatest cook in the world, but I can teach you a few easy recipes. Uncle Seth would probably appreciate a home-cooked meal."

"Mom taught me how to make spaghetti, but Uncle Seth probably won't let me use the stove. He's pretty touchy about me going anywhere near his stuff, especially his stereo and computer."

"Remember, Nicole, it's only been two weeks. He's been living alone most of his life. Maybe you two could spend some extra time together this weekend. We don't have camp on Monday because of the holiday, so you two could do a little sightseeing. There's lots of wonderful tourist spots right here in Colorado Springs."

"You mean just me and Uncle Seth? How boring. Unless you guys came with us." Her voice had risen in hopeful anticipation. She folded her hands, pleading with her lower lip curled into a cute little pout. "Please, Heather? I know he likes you."

Heather gave a high-pitched nervous laugh. The way he'd come on to her last week, she had no doubt that he liked her, but that was before he'd found out she had kids. His cool demeanor this week was a pretty good indication he'd changed his mind. And besides, spending the day with three kids probably wouldn't be his ideal day of rest and relaxation.

"I think you and your uncle need some one-on-one time. Get a chance to really know each other. Just do me a favor."

"What's that?"

"Hide his cell phone. The last thing you want is for a call to interrupt your plans."

"Now, that's not a bad idea." She laughed. "We might just figure him out yet."

"Figure who out?" Seth's deep baritone bellowed from the barn door. "Or do I even have to guess who you two are talking about?" He whipped off his sunglasses and stared up at them, giving them a wary smile, almost looking shy. But somehow, the words shy and Seth didn't belong in the same sentence.

As always, he was handsomely dressed in a light-blue dress shirt rolled up to his elbows. The top two buttons were undone, exposing a sparse mat of curly chest hair at the V. His dark-blue tailored slacks still had the creases down the front. Did this man even own a pair of jeans?

Grabbing hold of the ladder, he shook the loft as he climbed up and peered over the top.

"Watch out, Casanova, you're going to get those expensive slacks dirty climbing up here."

He chuckled and draped his wrists casually over the top rung of the ladder, his sunglasses dangling from his fingers. His square jaw was stubbled with a dark five-o'clock shadow, only making him that much more irresistible. "Are you ready to go, Nicole?"

"Yeah, but Heather and I were just wonderin', if, like, you could come watch me ride sometime? I can handle the Palomino all by myself in the arena. J.D. says I'm not ready to ride in the pasture yet."

Heather cleared her throat, giving Seth a subtle hint.

"We'll see," he said noncommittally. "I'll have to check my planner. Why don't you go get Spike ready to take home for the weekend? I'd like to talk to Heather for a few minutes." He backed down and helped Nicole off the ladder.

Heather warily followed, acutely aware of Seth's gaze taking in the view of her dust-covered rump. As Nicole skipped out of the barn, Heather hopped off the third rung and found herself face to chin with him. It was only then she realized that for the first time since the auction, they were completely alone in the barn, unless she counted a buckskin mare sleeping peacefully in one of the stalls.

Even over the hay and horse smells, intoxicating manly scents drifted into her senses. He smelled of the hot-cinnamon disks that she'd come to learn he had an addiction for, and his after-shave was the same musky scent he'd worn to the auction.

Like, totally sexy.

He leaned a hand on the loft behind her, his arm barely brushing her shoulder. She backed into the ladder and grabbed a rung to steady herself. "What can I do for you, Mr. Roberts?"

Chuckling, he reached up to her hair, pulling out a piece of straw. "Why do you get all professional around me?"

"Because it helps me remember our relationship is strictly business."

"Business, huh?" He stepped closer, his shiny Italian loafers sliding to the outside of her scruffy cowboy boots, boxing her in. When his gaze dropped to her lips, she was determined not to fall victim to his little games again.

Taking the upper hand, she ducked under his arm and opened the stall door where the buckskin stood. "You're here early," she said, patting the horse's rump, silently apologizing for waking the mare from her slumber. She took hold of the halter and led the mare outside the barn to the corral.

"My last meeting let out early." He hurried in front of her and opened the orange metal gate leading into the paddock. "How is Nicole getting along? Is she giving you any problems?"

The horse whinnied and trotted into the corral. "She's doing great. She loves talking about her mother. Your sister sounds like she was a great mom."

"Yeah, I know. Nicole was her whole life."

"It would mean so much to Nicole if you could just spend a

few extra minutes here. Maybe we could set up some kind of schedule that would work into your plans. I'd even go so far as to offer an evening so it wouldn't interfere with your work. It doesn't get dark till later, and it would really mean a lot . . . to Nicole."

The annoying drone of his cell phone cut into the quiet ranch yard. She narrowed her eyes on his waist where the phone was clipped, silently daring him to answer.

He glanced at the caller ID and unhooked the phone from his belt. "I'm sorry, but I gotta take this. I'll only be a sec." On the third ring, he turned his back and answered, "Hey, Sue. Did Marty call? I had my phone turned off for a meeting this afternoon."

Heather started counting from ten to one, trying not to let the call irritate her. The man couldn't even give her five minutes of uninterrupted conversation. Maybe it was an emergency.

"Is seven-thirty still good?" Seth asked. "Great. That should give me time to get Nicole settled in for the night. I'll call and let you know when I'm on my way."

Didn't sound like an emergency. In fact, it sounded suspiciously like he was setting up a date. Not wanting to hear all the details, she headed back inside the barn and picked up the rest of the grooming supplies, dumping the utensils in a gear bucket.

An old, all-too-familiar ache started to creep inside her chest. She hadn't felt this way in a long time: the feeling that she wasn't important enough to keep a man's attention. A feeling she'd actually gotten used to when she'd lived with Eric. At times, he'd even taken a call in the middle of sex, leaving her without so much as a "Sorry, babe."

She strode toward the tack room where all the saddles and bridles were stored, then started separating the combs and brushes into their proper compartments. Gripping the prickly brushes in her hands, she felt a sting of moisture building in her eyes. She'd forgotten how much it hurt to be neglected, to be abandoned. To never quite be good enough.

When she turned to leave the tack room, Seth stepped in front of her, blocking the doorway—still talking on the phone.

"If he calls again, tell him I'll stop by before he goes to bed tonight. You're a peach, Sue. See you in a bit." He flipped his phone shut and hooked it onto his belt. "Sorry about that. I had to get things set for a meeting tonight at seven-thirty. As for next week, I'll check my schedule and try to set up some time with Nicole."

She couldn't help but comment. "I'll just bet you and Sue get a whole lot of business done."

"You mean my secretary?" he asked, playing innocent.

She rolled her eyes, completely understanding why Nicole made this gesture so often. "Look, I'm tired and I don't have the energy for your games tonight. If you'll excuse me?"

"Games?" He didn't budge from the tack-room door. "Do you think I've got something going on with my secretary or something?" His lips twitched, as if suppressing a grin.

"Hey, what you do on your personal time is none of my business, unless of course it affects Nicole. She is at a very impressionable young age, you know. I hope you keep your dates discreet when you bring them home."

He took in a deep breath and puffed out his chest, cracking his knuckles. "I don't bring dates to my place. It sends them the wrong signal. You know, they start getting serious, possessive, wanting a commitment and all." He smoothed his hair behind his ears. "Nope. I like to play the field. Keep my options open."

"Ugh! I've heard enough." She tried to brush by him in the doorway, but he propped his loafered foot on the wooden frame blocking her way.

"Hold on there, Ace. I'm only teasing. Sue is my secretary, but with false teeth, silver hair and three grandchildren, she isn't exactly my type."

He was still laughing, but she wasn't amused, especially when she had a pretty good idea of what type he did prefer, and nowhere did she fit into that category.

He touched her chin, his voice turning serious and sincere. "I really do have a meeting tonight, Heather, and if everything goes the way I think it will, I might just make vice president of my firm. It's what I've worked so hard for all these years."

She backed away from his touch, the warmth of his fingers still hot to her skin. "I know you're some kind of a financial genius, but what exactly do you do for your company? Nicole doesn't even know."

He dropped his foot from the wall and leaned against his shoulder. "Promise not to hold it against me?"

"Right now, I'm not promising anything."

"Well, for one, I'm a stock broker. I also help folks with financial planning, setting up individualized portfolios, like Jared. He's been coming to me for the past five years or so. But, in the last two years I've specialized in real-estate development."

"You're a realtor?" Now she understood why he was hesitant to tell her what he did.

"No, I'm not a realtor. I put together proposals and act as an investment specialist between the realtor and an investor who usually needs some kind of tax shelter. I'm meeting with a realtor and his investors tonight."

She circled that for a moment, maybe a little impressed by what he did, but she couldn't help but wonder if all these late-night meetings would interfere with raising Nicole. "Look, I know parenting is all new to you, Seth, but you're not a carefree bachelor anymore. You can't just leave your niece alone night after night to go off to all these meetings."

"What meetings? Other than last Friday at the charity auction, this is the first time I've left Nicole since I brought her here. If I didn't meet with the investors tonight, I'd have to fly off to Japan next week."

"Japan?" she repeated, wondering if he was serious. She remembered Jared's comment at the airport about which country he'd just flown in from, and Nicole's description of him being a jet-set playboy, dating women from all over the world. "Sounds like you're quite the world traveler, but you're not the only one you have to think about now." She knew she sounded preachy, yet she couldn't help but add, "You can't just go gallivanting all over the world with your girlfriends anymore and leave her at home with the neighbor."

His lips did that annoying twitch, as he tried not to grin. "Who said I go gallivanting anywhere with girlfriends?"

She looked down at the ground. "Nicole may have led me to believe that you've had your share of affairs on your travels. She said her mother talked about it a lot."

He laughed, this time not hiding his amusement. "Shelli always did like thinking of me as the billionaire playboy type. But I have to admit, I may have fed her a few exaggerated stories over the years just to see a smile on her face. I don't think she had a very happy marriage. You might say I let her live vicariously through me."

Giving a casual shrug, he slid his hand into the pocket of his trousers. "But seriously, whenever possible, I try to meet my clients here in Colorado or in Texas. Our headquarters is in Dallas, but I work out of the division here in the Springs. As far as ditching my niece, I've already arranged for her to stay with a girl she met one floor below my penthouse. Personally, I think Nicole is bored to tears with me and will love it if I leave."

Heather wasn't sure what to say now. It seemed she'd misjudged him. Would there ever be a day when she could let her guard down and trust men again?

"Anything else you want to know about me, Ms. Thomas?"

His voice sounded lower, huskier, maybe. "My driving record? My credit history?"

She blew a strand of hair out of her eyes, somewhat embarrassed at giving him the third degree, but she was only thinking about Nicole. At least that's what she'd been trying to convince herself. "Not at the moment, so if you don't mind, I need to be getting home. I have a meeting myself at seven."

"O-o-o-h-h-h-h," he drawled, stretching his arm out and bracing his hand on the door jam, blocking the exit. "So, it's okay for you to ditch your kids for a meeting, but it's not okay for me?"

"It's not like that, Seth."

"It's not? What's the difference?"

"Well, uh," she stammered, trying to come up with a good excuse. "My meeting is for the benefit of my kids, so if you'll kindly move out of my way, I need to get them settled in with Debra at her house before I leave."

"Just hang on there, Ace." His arm still blocked the doorway, preventing her escape. "What's got you so all fired up tonight, anyway? You've been about as friendly as Spike since I've arrived."

What could she say? It was true. She'd found any reason she could to jump down his throat. Maybe it was this meeting tonight and trying to figure out where they would all go after Saint Anthony's shut their doors this Christmas. But the fact that Saint Anthony's was closing their doors wasn't Seth's fault, and he had been nothing but prompt and cordial all week.

That was it, of course. He'd been a little too polite. If he didn't want to take her out on a date, why didn't he just come out and say so? She was a big girl. She could handle rejection. If she'd survived ten years of rejection from Eric, she could certainly handle being stood up by Seth.

She whipped off her cowboy hat, banging it against her leg.

"I guess I'm a little anxious about this meeting tonight at Saint Anthony's."

"The hospital? You know they're shutting their doors don't you?"

"Oh, yes. I'm very well aware of that fact. I've heard rumors that the new owner is going to knock down the whole thing and turn it into another golf course."

"I heard it was about to be condemned anyway. They had a fire in the boiler room and a roof collapsed last winter from the heavy snows."

"It may have had a few problems," she admitted, knowing full well the extent of the damage. She blew out a frustrated gust of air. "I lead a support group there and we're worried about our kids right now. I'm sorry for taking my anger out on you. It's not like you have anything to do with the hospital being torn down."

He cleared his throat and slid his hand into the pocket of his trousers. "I didn't realize you were so passionate about Saint Anthony's. Can't you meet anywhere? What about another hospital?"

"Yes, of course, we can meet in other locations, but it's not just about where we meet." How could she explain her attachment to Saint Anthony's? She and all the other Garrisons had been born there; her own kids had both been delivered in the birthing suites. Then there was their little cousin, Dillan, who'd made it through several lifesaving heart-transplant operations. And, sadly, her father had died in the emergency room after he'd crashed his plane into the side of the mountain.

Since Kyle's diagnosis, she'd spent at least three days a week in the family development center, volunteering, tutoring and leading support groups. Now she and hundreds of families who'd relied on Saint Anthony's for so many years were being forced to pull up stakes and start all over.

Losing friendships, breaking close bonds, and learning to trust again upset her the most. The hospital had become a sort of haven away from the loneliness and frustration she'd often felt at home. She could go to Saint Anthony's for support, for strength, for guidance. How could she explain this to a man who only saw a crumbling-down old building with a collapsed roof?

"Look, I really don't have time to discuss this with you right now. I still need to get supper for Kyle and Katie before I leave. So, would you please just move away from the door?"

"There you go, gettin' in a hurry again. I've still got a little business to discuss with you." He tipped her hat back, staring down at her with those delicious, dreamy blue eyes. His voice lowered to a slow, seductive drawl. "I'd like to see about cashing in on my purchase."

"Your purchase?" she repeated, knowing darned well he was referring to the charity auction.

He took a step toward her, closing the gap between them. The eight-foot-by-eight-foot tack room suddenly shrank to the size of Spike's cage, and if she had her druthers, that's where she'd rather be right about now.

"How about you get that babysitter lined up for tomorrow morning?"

"Tomorrow?" she repeated.

"Not too early, say around nine or so."

"Nine?" She couldn't seem to get out more than a one-word response. She swallowed then licked her lips, thoroughly aware of his broad expanse of chest muscles stretching his pressed tailored shirt. His breathing was deep and even, a steep contrast to hers. Shallow, short breaths were all she could manage at the moment.

"You seem to have a problem understanding me this evening, Ms. Thomas. Let me see if I can make it clearer." He set his hands on her shoulders and pressed her gently back against the tack room wall. "I want to cash in on my charity auction purchase, and for ten thousand bucks, I'd like to get a full day's worth. How about it? I'll pick you up and take you away for the day."

She blinked, trying to find some simulation of coherency in her speech. "What about Nicole?"

"I've already planned for her to stay overnight at her friend Maggie's. She lives on the floor below ours. I'll just arrange for her to stay for the day tomorrow. What do you think?"

"Um, I don't know. It's kind of last minute."

"I was going to say something earlier this week, but I get this feeling you would have found any reason to back out on me if given the chance to think about it. What do you say? I thought I'd take you up flying."

Her eyes widened. "Flying?"

"Yep. I own a Cessna 210. I thought I'd help you overcome this little fear you seem to have."

"Cessna?" At a loss for words, she shook her head and tried to form a complete sentence. "My father was killed in a Cessna."

He brushed a few wisps of hair off the side of her face, the tender movement weakening her state of mind, not to mention her knees. "I know all about your father, honey. I talked to Jared. Ice built up on the carburetor causing the engine to die, and he had nowhere to set down. Jared also told me how much you used to love flying, and that out of all the Garrisons, you were the one who'd always wanted to be a pilot."

"But that was before—"

"What's that old saying about being bucked off a horse? Maybe you need to get back in the saddle, or in your case, back in the cockpit." He lifted her braid and let it slip through his fingers as it draped down her front. "I thought we'd fly down around Pueblo, maybe even go over to Canyon City. You said your father used to fly you over the Royal Gorge. What do you say? I'll make it a nice short trip your first time up."

She shook her head. "I-I'm sorry, Seth, but there's absolutely no way you'll ever get me on one of those things again." Her voice sounded trembly. Her knees started to shake.

"Hey, hey, hey. Take it easy. I'm not going to force you to do anything you're not ready for." He massaged her arms and inched closer. "Tell you what. How about we just sit in the cockpit the first time? We won't even fire up the engine. How's that sound?"

The thought of even sitting in a Cessna made her stomach churn. Blinking back a threatening sting of tears, she could only shake her head.

"Okay, okay. I won't pressure you." He reached down and took her fingers and rubbed the pad of his thumb over her nails, chipped and uneven from ranch work, but he didn't seem to care as he gazed deeply into her eyes and spoke close to her face. "Just promise me you'll at least think about it? I may be a lousy uncle, but I'm a good pilot." He gently squeezed her hands. "You can trust me."

"My father was a good pilot, Seth. It has nothing to do with trust. I've got my kids to think about now. I can't take that kind of a risk."

"You take more risk every time you climb behind the wheel of your van. I could get into the statistics if you want."

She pulled her hands from his grip. "No. I've heard them all before."

He rested his hands on his waist and stared down at her. His lips were pressed together, his expression looking as if he were contemplating his next move.

"So, what happens when plan A doesn't work? Go to plan B? Maybe bungee jumping off the Royal Gorge? Or, hey, why don't we go white-water rafting down Bridal Veils Falls?"

He chuckled. "What about hiking? Is that too risky?"

"Hiking?" She cleared her throat and leaned against the wall, clenching her fingers around a leather bridle hanging on a hook behind her. "This is kind of short notice. I doubt I could even get a babysitter." She hated that her voice sounded shaky and breathless.

He moved closer and gave a low, husky laugh that made her insides quiver. It was amazing how this man could make her blood boil in anger one minute, then turn around and convert it into heated desire the next. She locked her knees, trying to remain unfazed by his nearness. Her gaze lowered to the V of his shirt, his Adam's apple bobbing heavily as he gave several heavy swallows.

Crouching down slightly to get at eye level with her, he arched his eyebrows. "What can I do to talk you into spending some time alone with me, Heather?"

"You're alone with me now."

He cocked one dark brow as he casually observed the deserted barn. Other than a cat curled up sleeping in a sunny spot, they were definitely alone. Boy, she walked right into that one.

"As a matter of fact, we are, aren't we?" He flicked a glance to her lips then back to her eyes.

Oh, no, not again.

He lowered his face close to hers, but she forced her eyes to remain open. She wasn't about to be lured into this game again. His warm, cinnamon breath and sexy musky scents had no bearing on her whatsoever. She was in complete control.

When he closed his eyes, she started to panic. Maybe he was actually going to kiss her this time.

Should she duck and escape? Or play chicken and see who backed down first?

CHAPTER SIX

Every part of her brain screamed at her to just scoot right out the tack-room door, but some magnetic force kept her grounded to the splintered, plywood plank. She actually held her breath, fully expecting him to pull away at the last minute.

But then it happened.

He gently pressed his mouth over hers. She looked up to the ceiling to divert her attention away from what was happening, trying to appear unfazed by his kiss. His lips were full and hot and wet and . . . Oh God. The soft whiskers of his jaw only heightened the pleasure as his lips lingered on hers, caressing more than kissing. She still hadn't closed her eyes, nor had she breathed, afraid of what might happen if she did.

He brought both hands up and slid them around the sides of her neck, his thumbs brushing the sensitive skin beneath her jaw. Keeping his eyes closed, he drew apart slightly and spoke barely over a husky murmur next to her mouth. "You can trust me, honey. I won't hurt you." Then he kissed her again, but this time it was with more mastery, more urgency.

Finding his lips too tempting, she slowly exhaled into his mouth, responding to his masterful persuasion. Her lips softened, melding into his. A force greater than gravity pulled her eyelids completely shut, and she found herself shamelessly leaning into his kiss. A soft moan escaped the back of her throat as she breathed his name. "Oh, Seth."

Seth. His name was like a soothing balm to her lips. She

couldn't remember, ever in her life, being kissed so tenderly and with such compassion.

As if sampling a fine delicacy, he kissed her top lip, sweeping over to the corner of her mouth and then along the bottom to the other side. His breathing was heavy against her face, his hands tightening their hold on the side of her face as he took her mouth again. Just when she thought she couldn't stand another moment, he lowered his hands to her shoulders and drew slowly away, pressing his forehead against hers. "So, have we got a date?" His voice was husky, his breathing heavy.

What was he asking? She couldn't seem to clear the fog from her mind. She couldn't even open her eyes, and at the moment, she really wasn't sure where she was. How could the sensations of one simple kiss turn all her wits into oatmeal?

The barn. Something about a date. Hiking. It was all starting to come back. Somehow, she had to get away and regain control. He couldn't know the effect he'd had on her.

She turned her head to the side and forced her eyes open, but diverted her gaze to her boots. "I just remembered, I told J.D. I'd come out and tour a new family around the ranch tomorrow morning." She ducked under Seth's arm and escaped the tack room.

Undaunted by her attempt to flee, he followed close on her heels. "What time will that be?"

"I don't know."

"You don't know?" He strode up beside her, his steps matching hers perfectly.

"Yes. Nine, I think."

"How long does that usually take?"

"It just depends. An hour maybe."

"Great. I'll pick you up here at ten."

"No." His persistence was starting to annoy her. "I mean . . . I don't think it would be a good idea."

"You're not going to renege on our date, are you?"

She didn't answer as she hurried up the ranch yard toward the house.

He easily kept up with her and expelled a heavy breath. "Look, if it's because of what just happened, I'm sorry. I shouldn't have kissed you."

When she didn't answer, he angled in front of her, making her come to an abrupt halt in the middle of the ranch yard. "I said I'm sorry. Please, stop and talk to me a minute."

Avoiding his gaze, Heather looked around, breathing heavily, not sure if it was because of her jaunt up the hill or from the untapped desires running rampant through her body. She'd never in her life had these overwhelming feelings for a man. She didn't know whether to throw her arms around Seth and tackle him to the ground, or go running for the hills.

He angled his head, catching her eye. "Did I blow it?"

She knew she couldn't resist this man, even if her life depended on it. "No, you didn't blow it." Staring at him from the corner of her eye, she returned his guilty smile. "And you don't have to be sorry."

He held her amused expression as if contemplating what she'd meant. Then as if he'd just won first place in a pie-eating contest, his smile broadened and he moved closer, his hands reaching out and touching her waist. "So, I wasn't the only one affected back there, huh?" A dangerous flicker of desire sparked in the depths of his iridescent blue eyes.

Laying a palm on his chest, she shoved him away, trying to keep her distance. "But I can't take off for the entire day, either. I don't like to leave my kids for very long."

He cleared his throat and scratched his chin. "Well, we'll just have to take them all with us."

"All?" she asked with an incredulous laugh.

"You seem to have trouble understanding me today. Yes, all.

Let's load up and go hiking in the mountains. What do you say? I haven't had a chance to do much with Nicole, and I know she loves you and your kids. I'll pack us a lunch, and we'll have a picnic overlooking the Continental Divide."

She arched her brows. "Have you ever hiked with a seven-year-old little girl terrified of spiders, a nine-year-old boy who gets into everything, or an adolescent young woman whose biggest hiking excursion has been up and down the aisles of a mall—much less, all of them at the same time?"

He tipped his head back and let out a loud, bellowing laugh, as if she were joking. "I think I can handle three kids. I'll pick you all up at ten. No excuses."

Heather flung her hands in the air and laughed. She wanted to go, if only to see his face at the end of the day after traipsing through the mountains with three exhausted, whiny kids. She lovingly pushed him away and walked backwards toward the house. "Looks like you've got yourself a date. But I'll pack the picnic lunch. From what Nicole tells me, you're not exactly Mr. Lean Cuisine when it comes to food."

"Sounds like I need to have a little chat with Nicole. She's giving me a bad reputation. Speaking of which," he paused, glancing at his watch. Then he slipped her a wink. "I'd better be going. Sue hates it when I'm late."

"We've got a good turnout tonight." Tracey Watson, Kyle's favorite therapist who had been laid off, dumped her purse on the counter of a small classroom where their meeting would begin in a few minutes. She grabbed a coffee mug from the cupboard. "I don't see Jared." She eagerly looked around at all the attendees for tonight's meeting. "I thought you said he'd be here."

"He called and said he had an emergency come up at the clinic. He'll try to stop by later."

Tracey's smile faded into a disappointed sigh. "Oh, I was hoping to see him tonight." Heather smiled, wondering if Jared knew just how popular he was in this town.

Some twenty-five or so employees of the hospital had shown up, along with at least twenty parents, mostly from her support group. She set a stack of notebooks on the front table. "I need to run back out to my van and get the rest of the information about the different sites I've come up with for a potential new learning center."

Heather hurried outside just as a sleek black sports car zipped into the front parking spot. Recognizing the expensive foreign convertible, Heather's feet stopped dead in their tracks.

Eric?

When the door swung open, her ex-husband's large hand grabbed the top of the door as his shiny black shoes lowered to the ground. A gold wedding band circled one of his fingers. An emerald bauble the size of a dime adorned another finger.

When he pulled the rest of his husky body out of the car, her mouth gaped open without a single sound escaping. Then it all registered. Eric had remarried.

Dressed in a tailored dark-brown suit, he straightened and shut the door behind him. His hair was thinner in the crown, and he looked thicker through the middle. She hadn't seen him in nearly three months, since his last impromptu visit when he'd shown up on her doorstep. He'd bought Katie another Barbie doll, not even bothering to bring anything for Kyle. Heather had covered for Eric, digging out a new Artemis Fowl book she'd bought for him to read for his free reading time. His reading comprehension was at an eighth-grade level, way beyond most of his fourth-grade peers. Not that Eric cared.

As soon as he spotted her, his narrow-set gray eyes captured her gaze. His thin lips pressed together in what she'd learned over the years was a smile—a smug smile of satisfaction when

119

he knew he had the upper hand.

"Hello, darlin'," Eric drawled, stepping onto the curb. "I see you still live at this dump."

She squared her shoulders, unwilling to let him know how intimidating he could be. "Are you here to attend our meeting? Since Saint Anthony's is closing their doors, we're trying to come up with some ideas on where to relocate. Maybe you could even help us come up with some funding for the new learning center. It is in the best interest of our child."

"No one's going to want to throw their money away on a bunch of misfits. You're all wasting your time." He glanced at his Rolex. "In fact, I don't have time to stand here and talk. I'm here to get rid of a burr that's been under my skin since I was born."

"What does that mean?"

"All those years I took the backseat while my mother went off to deal with one hospital crisis after another, and then when Kyle got sick, you practically lived at this place."

She had to speak through gritted teeth. "I don't know how many times I have to tell you this, but Kyle is not sick."

"Doesn't matter now, anyway. Do you know I could have bought two Mercedes for the money I've dumped into this crumbling-down piece of crap? Now I'm getting what's due me," he added contentiously. "It's time I got some return on my investments."

Comprehension dawned. "You're the realtor working with the new owners of Saint Anthony's?"

"I never said you weren't quick," he chided, chucking her under the chin.

She jerked away. "You're pathetic, do you know that? Is money all you can think about? What about your son? Do you have any idea how the closing of Saint Anthony's will affect him?"

"Our son should be at the Pine Tree facility where he can get the proper education and training he needs."

She crossed her arms over her chest. "You don't have the slightest idea what Kyle needs. He's made some amazing accomplishments. Maybe if you'd spend more than five minutes with him, you'd see that he's an intelligent, bright little boy." Glaring down at his hand, she added, "But I guess you've been too busy getting married to visit your own kids. We've only officially been divorced for what, two weeks? Who is she, anyway? Some young ski bunny you found on the slopes?"

"Actually, she's from Denver. Her father's a congressman," he added, as if to impress her.

"You'll forgive me if I don't send you a wedding gift. When were you planning to tell the kids?"

"Soon enough. Maybe I'll stop by one of these days when I can work it into my schedule." He brushed by her, heading toward the front doors. "Right now, I'm late."

She reached out and grabbed his arm. "Do you actually think walking away and marrying another woman will just wipe out your past? Whether you want to admit to it or not, you have two kids who need you. Not a birthday card once a year with five bucks stuck inside."

"You're absolutely right," he said, stopping and getting into her face. "My new wife and I have had the same conversation. She has a little girl from her first marriage who would simply adore having a little sister."

Heather jerked her head back. "What's that supposed to mean?"

"It means, little darlin', that I want Kyle reevaluated and I'm appealing for sole custody of Katie."

Heather's heart slammed against her chest. When she spoke, her voice sounded weak and pathetic. "Why, Eric? You've never wanted anything to do with your kids. Why now, all of a sudden?"

He only shrugged. "You know how much I adore Katie, and, like I said, my wife wants her. Apparently, she's unable to bear any more children, and her daughter needs a playmate. We can certainly give her the kind of stable home life with two parents that a six-year-old deserves."

Heather narrowed her eyes. "She'll be eight next month."

"All the better. Kyle's a danger to be around. He's clumsy and I don't want her endangered by his stupidity."

She balled her fists at her sides. "He is not stupid. He just has to learn things differently. How many times do we have to argue about this?"

"Not much longer if I have anything to say about it." He stared up at Saint Anthony's and gave a huge tooth-filled grin, tugging his trousers up over his bulging waistline. "You'll be hearing from my attorney soon enough."

Seth turned into the Saint Anthony's parking lot and parked at the west entrance where the administrative offices were located. Seth's boss, Joe Ferguson, had arranged a meeting between Chang Liu and his associates at Five Seasons Athletics, along with a realtor from Telluride who'd brought some very interested investors.

When Seth had learned how involved Heather was with Saint Anthony's and her aversion to the new resort, he was somewhat reluctant to go through with this meeting. But canceling at the last minute had been out of the question. Joe was meeting with the investors first at seven, touring them around the grounds, and then Seth would pitch his proposal at seven-thirty.

The administrative offices were located in the west wing, the oldest section of the hospital where the roof had collapsed last winter. They'd managed to repair the roof temporarily, but other than the cafeteria and a few classrooms on the first floor, the rest of the five-story building sat unused.

The newer addition, a seven-story brick building erected in the late fifties, was where the emergency entrance was located along with the admitting office. Ten years ago, the third floor of the new addition had been remodeled into several modern birthing suites, giving the hospital a much-needed booster shot for falling revenues. Unfortunately, with the Penrose Birthing Center and Neonatal ICU only five miles away, the competition was too steep for Saint Anthony's.

Staring up at the decaying walls and the overgrown landscape, Seth tried to convince himself that this was the right thing to do. The repairs alone would cost more than tearing the whole thing down and starting over. Shutting their doors was the only real, logical solution.

But ever since he'd found out about Heather's deep involvement with Saint Anthony's, he'd gone around and around in his head with how he was going to tell her that he'd been working for months on a prospectus for timeshare condominiums complete with a health spa, an eighteen-hole golf course, and a tennis and racquetball facility. He couldn't back down now. Dallas was on the line.

Funny, Dallas didn't seem near as exciting when he thought about it tonight. Probably still getting over his reaction to Heather's kiss.

He closed his eyes briefly, his heart still feeling the aftershocks. He'd been wanting to kiss those perfect pouty lips since he'd first seen her on the plane. He hadn't been prepared for the jolt to his heart the moment he'd lowered to her mouth.

At first she was wary, understandably cautious, but when she finally succumbed to the temptation and breathed deeply into his mouth, she'd practically clung to his shirt as if she'd found it hard to stand.

For God sakes, his knees had even gone weak.

He gave himself a mental shake, trying to focus on why he was here at the hospital in the first place.

This was it. The moment of truth.

He grabbed his briefcase and laptop computer then headed for the side entrance, shoving through the metal exterior door. He made his way down a long dark corridor toward the atrium that separated the east and west wings. He pressed the elevator button that would take him up to the second floor where the administrative offices were located.

As he waited for the elevator, a strong aroma of disinfectant soon drowned out what he thought smelled like meatloaf coming from the cafeteria. His stomach growled, reminding him he hadn't eaten since lunch. Shelli used to cook a mean meatloaf. Besides spaghetti, it was about the only thing she'd cooked that was edible.

He punched the up button again, then heard a woman's familiar laugh filter down the hallway from one of the classrooms. The moment he heard the sweet lift of her voice, his gut did the same flip-flop it had done on the plane.

All the doors were wide open. He took a step to the side, craning his head around to peer into the first classroom. His palms began to sweat. Heather said her meeting was at Saint Anthony's, he just hadn't counted on running into her.

Several small school desks were positioned on one end of the classroom, along with a bookshelf and three colorful bean bags in the corner. A large toy box overflowed with blocks and an array of building tools for kids. A play kitchen filled another corner, complete with refrigerator, a fake stove and an old cash register. At least a dozen people sat on folding chairs in a circle at one end of the room.

He heard Heather again and spotted her off in the corner near the coffee bar, standing with a tall blonde. Heather had her back to him, but with her mane of wavy brunette hair hanging below her shoulders, he knew without a doubt, it was the same woman who'd practically brought him to his knees with her kiss.

She wasn't wearing tight-fitting jeans that he'd come to look forward to seeing her in every day. Instead, she wore a pair of crème knit pants and a short-sleeved blouse of the same color. She had on open-toed leather sandals, and even from across the room, he could see her toenails were painted a pretty shade of pink.

Sleek and professional . . . and sexy as hell. Any man would be proud to have her as his wife. Eric Thomas was a fool.

Without being seen, Seth regrettably stepped onto the elevator and rode up to the second floor where he grabbed a cup of coffee from the executive lounge. As he entered the conference room, several men wearing expensive tailored suits and silk ties turned their attention toward him.

He set his coffee and briefcase on the end of a large cherry conference table and smiled. "Gentlemen? Glad you could all come. I trust you've already seen the grounds. So, please, let's get right to business."

William Tate, the other partner of the firm and head of the Dallas division, strode toward Seth. He was an older man with glasses, a paunchy stomach and skinny legs. "Seth, I'd like you to meet the realtor representing the Telluride investors. This is Eric Thomas. His mother was the administrator of Saint Anthony's up until about ten years ago. Eric, this is Seth Roberts. He's heading up this deal."

Son of a bitch. Eric Thomas was the realtor Joe had told him about? Then he remembered Heather telling him her ex-husband lived in Telluride. Seth should have made the connection. He reluctantly reached for Eric's outstretched hand. "Is your mother retired, Mr. Thomas?"

Eric slid his meaty hand into Seth's. "No. She and my father were killed in a car accident a few years back. Never made it past the emergency room downstairs."

"I'm sorry to hear that."

Eric gave an unemotional shrug. "A bunch of idiots, if you ask me. It's about time this place got shut down." He clapped Seth on the shoulder. "I've heard nothing but good things about you. I'm looking forward to your presentation."

Too bad Seth couldn't say the same for Eric. He obviously had no love lost over Saint Anthony's, which was surprising given the attachment Heather had with the facility.

Eric was a big man, maybe an inch shorter than Seth, but he had broad shoulders and a widening midsection. His thinning brown hair and close-set, dark-gray eyes made him appear years older than Heather. Yet Jared had said he'd graduated just one year ahead of her in high school.

Not in the mood for small talk with this man, Seth gestured his hand toward the conference table. He had to keep his mind focused on business. "Why don't we all have a seat so we can get started?"

After several introductions, Seth gave an in-depth PowerPoint presentation from his laptop, projecting each slide up on a large screen. He pitched his ideas, giving statistical marketing reports of the area, as well as breaking down the predicted rate of return on their investments.

He clicked through several slides of the proposed Golden Springs Golf Club Spa and Resort. "The ideal location reflects the expansive grandeur of lush green meadows racing to meet snowcapped mountains. The exquisite views of Cheyenne Mountain combined with impressive accommodations and high-quality services are only a few of the benefits you'll receive at this exclusive resort."

Stopping on the next slide, he added, "The Ferguson and

Tate name has represented more than twenty years of expertise and integrity in real estate, investments, and finance. It is our day-to-day commitment to working closely with each other and with our clients that represents our vision of being a leader in the commercial real-estate investment and finance industries. Our proven track record shows that we are committed to providing the best in quality and value to our clients and investors."

Making eye contact with each of the investors, Seth made the final pitch. "At Golden Springs Golf Club Spa and Resort, and at all Ferguson and Tate properties, the legacy of success is anchored in our philosophy of balancing living, learning and leisure. It is this formula that creates the signature of unparalleled excellence in quality and service throughout our network of resorts, hotels and conference centers." He left the final slide up on the screen. "Thank you, gentlemen. I look forward to a most-profitable business venture."

Applause confirmed the success of his presentation. As everyone converged into conversation, Seth clicked his briefcase shut, knowing the reactions from everyone in the room were right on. He glanced at his watch, realizing how late his meeting had run. He'd hoped to give Nicole a call before she went to bed.

Seth cleared his throat and extended his apologies for leaving the meeting early. When Eric approached him, Seth had to grip his briefcase as he questioned his own code of ethics. How could he even think about doing business with a guy who'd deserted his wife, forcing her to raise their two kids alone?

Eric clapped a meaty hand on his back, ushering him toward the door. "I look forward to doing business with you. Maybe we could go get a drink and discuss some of your ideas."

"No wife or kids waiting up for you tonight?"

He gave an arrogant chuckle. "My wife understands how these things work. Her daddy is Lawrence Sullivan."

"The congressman?" Seth repeated, maybe a little impressed.

Eric nodded and pulled out his billfold, flipping to a wedding photo with his new wife. Tall, blonde, rounded in just the right places. Gorgeous.

"Got yourself quite a trophy wife, Mr. Thomas."

Eric grinned, puffing out his chest. "Laura Lee has certainly helped me on my career path, if you know what I mean."

"Any kids?" Seth asked, trying to keep his voice level.

"As a matter of fact, she's got a nine-year-old little girl that kind of came with the package. She sleeps upstairs with the nanny, so Laura Lee and I have plenty of privacy." He flipped to another photo. "This is Katie. She's from my first marriage. Ain't she just a little sliver of sunshine?" The wrinkled, worn picture showed Katie with all her teeth, and she looked only about four or five years old. When Eric slipped his billfold into his back pocket, Seth thought it strange that he didn't even mention Kyle. Most men bragged about their firstborn sons.

"Keep up the good work, Mr. Roberts. I have this feeling we'll be doing a lot of business together in the future. How about we go get that drink? We can talk more in private."

Spending another moment with Eric Thomas was more than Seth could stomach right now. He shook his head. "Not tonight. Let Ferguson know when you want to sit down and talk numbers."

"I'll set something up for next week."

Frustrated with the turn of events, Seth punched the down button on the elevator. Now the big question. Should he tell Heather about this little business venture and that he would be working with none other than her ex-husband? Or did it even matter? After all, business was business. This wasn't personal.

So, why did he feel like he was betraying her? A woman he hadn't even met when he'd started this project.

Dammit. How did things get so turned around? Up until a

few months ago, his career had been the most important thing in his life. The vice presidency was his dream. Now it was practically sitting in his lap, and all his focus had turned toward his niece and her pretty brunette counselor.

Mulling everything over in his head, Seth drove across town and pulled into the parking garage of The Royale. The loud thumping bass of a car stereo drew his attention to a hardtop jeep that had just parked near the garage entrance. When the driver stepped out of the vehicle, Seth didn't recognize him as one of the tenants. His height and broad shoulders made him look college age.

As soon as the passenger door opened, two young girls spilled out, giggling and chomping on gum. Their faces were covered with pink rouge and their lips were a vibrant purple. He immediately recognized the strawberry blonde. Seth's heart jumped to his throat. Who the hell was this guy, and why were Nicole and Maggie driving around in his jeep?

Images of his sister and how she'd turned to boys at such a young age made his stomach churn. Acid burned in his throat. He switched off the engine and shoved open the door of his Vette. "Nicole!"

She and Maggie both whirled around, their eyes practically bugging out of their heads. "Uncle Seth? Why are you home so early?"

Narrowing his gaze on the young man, he forced himself to keep his voice level. "Looks like it's a good thing." He slammed the car door, the keys firmly clenched in his hands. He switched his gaze to Nicole. "Where exactly have you been?"

"Like, we just went out for a second. No big deal."

"I asked you a question, Nicole. You've got thirty seconds to explain where you've been, then I want you upstairs and washing that crap off your face."

Nicole shoved her hand on her hips and grunted. "Like, who

tied your tightie-whities in a knot?"

"Listen, young lady, I don't know if your mother allowed this kind of behavior, but I'll not have it while you're living with me."

"Whoa, take it easy, pops." The young man in faded baggy jeans and a T-shirt hanging untucked, stepped up next to the girls. "Everything's cool."

Pops? With his eyes narrowed on the boy, Seth pointed his finger to the security-coded parking-lot doors. "Nicole. Maggie. Upstairs. Now."

Maggie looked over at the boy. "Are you going to let him talk to us like that, Mitch?"

Mitch nodded his head toward the door. "Maggie, you and Nicole head on up. I'll explain everything."

Nicole shot Seth a spite-filled glare. "Oooooh! I hate you! You're just like my father. He never let me do anything!" She stomped her feet all the way to the lobby doors.

As soon as the doors swung shut, Mitch held up both hands. "Hey, it's not what you think. Mom needed some more formula for the baby, and she thought the girls would like to pick out a movie to watch." He reached inside the jeep and grabbed a brown paper sack. He opened it and pulled out a can of Similac. "See? No harm done."

"Milk?" Seth repeated, suddenly feeling about as tall as a worm. "You went to get milk?"

"Yeah." He stepped forward and held his hand out in greeting. "I'm Mitch Swanson, Maggie's brother. I just got home from college tonight. I'll be spending the summer here."

Seth looked down at his outstretched hand and swallowed his pride. "Nice to meet you, Mitch. I'm Seth Roberts."

"Nicole's uncle," he finished. "She told me about you."

Seth pinched the bridge of his nose and blew out a huge gust of frustration, but also relief. What just happened to him? He'd never felt this overwhelming need to protect anyone in his life. He gave a slight shake of his head. "Guess I owe you an apology. I kind of jumped to conclusions."

"Think nothin' of it. It was a perfectly understandable mistake. Mom let the girls do makeovers this afternoon. I guess I should have had them wash up before we left."

Feeling like an idiot, he asked, "So, what's your major?"

"Premed."

Impressed, Seth nodded. "Wow. Tough schedule."

"Tell me about it."

"Listen," Seth said, locking his Vette. "Nicole's been through a lot in the last few months—years if I had my guess. I just don't want to see her get into any trouble."

Mitch shifted the sack of baby supplies to his other arm and locked his jeep. "From the little I've been around Nicole, she's a great kid. She's seems pretty mature for her age."

Seth didn't know a lot about girls her age, so he just nodded. "Maybe we ought to head on up. I've got some major sucking up to do."

Mitch laughed and clapped him on the shoulder as they strode toward the elevator. "If she's anything like Maggie, she'll already be worrying about her hair and talking about boys."

Seth gave a nervous laugh. "That's what I'm afraid of."

CHAPTER SEVEN

Saturday morning, Seth pulled out his four-door SUV from the covered garage. He normally only drove it during the winter months, but with Nicole and Heather's crew, he had a feeling he was going to need the extra space of his SUV.

After he'd grudgingly fed Spike his vegetables and a dried apple, he'd picked up Nicole from Mrs. Swanson's. Letting Nicole stay overnight had been his only saving grace with her. He'd screwed up royally, and now he had to figure out how to earn back her trust. Maybe this hiking excursion into the mountains was just what they needed. A chance to get back to nature and back to the basics. With any luck, maybe by the end of the summer, he and Nicole might actually be a family.

The end of the summer. After the success of his meeting with Mr. Liu last night at the hospital, Dallas was in the bag.

Funny. The prospect of moving to Dallas suddenly didn't seem as appealing as it had before. Before he'd taken Nicole under his wing and had her future to consider. Before he'd met Heather . . . and couldn't imagine a future without her.

With just one kiss, she'd ignited a flame somewhere in the depths of his belly that had never been lit before. Just thinking about Heather's kiss made his chest swell, not to mention other areas of his anatomy. He adjusted the rearview mirror and finger-combed his hair, still wet from his shower. The breeze from the opened window dried his hair as he headed toward the J Bar D Ranch.

132

He had a few qualms about taking three kids hiking today, but then he remembered his own youth and how much fun he'd had scaling the rocks and boulders with Shelli. They didn't have much else to do in the way of entertainment. Pop couldn't afford cable, and they'd only been able to get one TV station tuned in halfway decent.

He glanced over at his niece who was writing something in a spiral notebook, something he'd seen her doing quite a bit since she'd started at Heather's camp. He still couldn't believe Nicole was almost thirteen. Seeing her last night with Mitch made him realize that these next few years would be the most important of her life.

Should he take his boss's suggestion and send her to a prep school in the fall? She'd be with girls her own age and, more importantly, away from boys. He could certainly afford it. She'd get the opportunities that most girls her age only dreamed about. College was just around the corner, and with the proper schooling, her acceptance into any Ivy League college in the country would almost be guaranteed. And after last night's misunderstanding with Mitch, Seth had this feeling she'd probably jump at the opportunity to get away from him.

He still wondered what she'd meant when she'd said he was just like her father. It didn't sound like a compliment.

When she caught him watching her, she slammed her notebook shut and stared out the window. "So, where are these exciting trails, anyway?" Her voice was less than enthusiastic, but at least she was speaking to him.

"I thought I'd take you where your mom and I grew up, near the mines of Leadville."

"Mom never said much about where she grew up." She started doodling the word Mom on the cover of her notebook, retracing it several times. "She said she always wanted to take me there, someday."

Seth draped his wrist over the steering wheel. "You miss her, don't you?"

Circling the word several times, she finally gave a small lift of her shoulders. "Yeah, I guess."

"You look like her when she was your age. I've got some old photo albums at home if you ever want to go through them. I'll set them out."

She rolled her eyes and looked out the window. "Whatever."

He kept talking, even though she clearly didn't want to have a conversation. "Every time I called her over the years, you were all she'd talked about, bragging about what a great dancer you are. I bet they've got a lot of good studios in the area. Maybe we could call around and get you started with one."

She didn't answer.

"She also said you used to do a lot of painting. Maybe we could go to the hobby store, set you up a little studio in the den?"

She gave a disgruntled huff and glared over at him. "I know what you're doing."

He gave a confused shake of his head. "What am I doing?"

"Just forget it. I don't want to talk about it."

"About what? I thought you'd like to start doing some of the things you used to do in California."

"You're wrong, okay? I don't want to dance, and I don't want to paint. I just want to be left alone." She gave a heavy sigh of exasperation then stared out the window and didn't say another word.

What was he doing?

With a thick cloud of tension looming between them, Seth pulled into the J Bar D Ranch lane next to Heather's minivan. As soon as he slipped his SUV into park, Nicole bolted out the door and headed down toward her cabin. Disillusioned, he switched off the ignition and heaved out an exhausted sigh. So much for his great attempt at bonding.

His heart actually skipped a beat when his eyes found Heather as she crossed the asphalted parking lot, heading toward him. After living with Miss Attitude for two weeks, he could certainly use a friendly face today.

A forest-green T-shirt fit snuggly over Heather's breasts, covered slightly with a hiking vest with pockets. Shiny tanned legs slid out from under a pair of khaki shorts with more large pockets on the thighs. Her legs were long and proportionately muscular, not surprising with all the work she did around the ranch.

She wore a pair of brown leather boots with thick socks crumpled around her ankles. A baseball cap with the J Bar D Outreach Camp for Kids logo shaded her face. A thick brunette braid hung down the middle of her back. She was by far the sexiest creature he'd ever laid eyes on.

Eric Thomas was a fool. And now that he knew Heather's animosity toward the man, as well as her involvement with Saint Anthony's, Seth found himself in quite a pickle, as his mother used to say.

He clenched his hands around the steering wheel, questioning his sanity for the hundredth time. He was in the prime of his life, and he'd just taken on the role of father to a preteen— and failing miserably at that. Pursuing a mother of two children was nowhere in his grand plan. Maybe after today he should heed Heather's advice and keep his relationship with her strictly business.

After today he'd go back to a client-and-counselor relationship. No flirting. No kissing. No problem. He'd never had any trouble backing away from a woman before. Why should Heather be any different?

A loud thud at the base of his heart warned him that Heather wasn't like any other woman he'd ever met.

He returned her smile as she approached the driver's-side window. She leaned forward, tucking her fingers into her hip pockets. The low-scooped neckline of her T-shirt made it almost impossible for him not to drop his gaze to the generous curves of her breasts.

Yep, after today, he'd back off. No more touching, no more fantasies about the future . . . after today.

"You sure you're ready for this?" she asked, sounding less than enthusiastic herself.

"Absolutely," he reassured, shoving out his door. The moment he stood, he noticed the way she was fidgeting, looking down at the ground, switching her weight from foot to foot, pushing her sunglasses up on the rim of her nose, then tugging her baseball cap low over her forehead. He bent his knees slightly, trying to catch her gaze. "Heather? You're not having second thoughts about going today, are you? I promise. We'll all have a great time."

"No, it's not that. It's just. . . ." She drew her bottom lip into her mouth, staring down at Kyle and Katie who were standing on the fence, petting the horses.

"Just what?" he asked, tipping the brim of her hat back. Looking closer over the rim of her sunglasses, he thought her eyes appeared bloodshot, almost like she'd been crying. "Hey, is something wrong, honey?" He gave her shoulder a gentle squeeze. "Don't take this the wrong way or anything, but you look like you've had a rough night. Is it Kyle? Are his hands bothering him?"

"No, I just don't think I'm going to be very good company today." Her voice cracked and she looked away, avoiding his gaze.

"Heather, has something happened?"

She crossed her arms over her chest, rubbing her skin like

she was cold. "I kind of had a run-in with my ex-husband last night."

At the thought of Eric anywhere near this woman, Seth stiffened. "Did he hurt you?"

"No, at least not the way you think."

He stepped closer, bending slightly to catch her gaze. "What is it then? Can you tell me?"

"He wants the kids, Seth. He's going to file for full custody."

He mumbled a low curse, unable to hold his anger. "Can he do that?"

She gave a cynical laugh. "You obviously don't know my ex-husband."

He gulped, not sure what to say. Unfortunately, he knew him far more than he wanted to admit.

Pacing in front of him, she spoke with a tremble to her voice. "I found out last night that he's already remarried. He works fast, huh? Some congressman's daughter."

He whipped off his baseball cap and dragged his fingers through his hair. "What are you going to do?"

She stopped pacing and shoved her hands on her waist. "Fight him, of course. What choice do I have?"

"Yes, of course. I'm sorry. Look, if you need a good lawyer, I can—"

"Thanks, but I've already contacted the lawyer who handled my divorce."

"So, what does he say?"

"*She* said all we can do right now is wait for him to contact me. With any luck, he's bluffing. Only doing it to pacify his new wife."

"What does that mean?"

"Apparently, she can't have any more kids and she wants a playmate for her daughter."

Seth rubbed his eyebrows. The more he learned about Eric

Thomas, the more he wished he'd never taken on the hospital account. Maybe it wasn't too late to give it over to Davison. Or better yet, drop him altogether and find new investors. Joe would have his ass fired for sure.

Angered, Seth slid his cap back on. "Eric's not going to take your kids, Heather. Any self-respecting judge will see how they've thrived under your care."

She tilted her head to the side, almost looking puzzled. "How did you know his name was Eric?"

Thinking fast, he said, "Oh, Jared mentioned it at the airport. Said he's been a real jerk."

She rolled her eyes, reminding him so much of Nicole. "That's putting it mildly."

"He's probably just blowing smoke, trying to get you all rattled."

"I'm rattled all right." Her voice choked and she looked away, stabbing the toe of her hiking boot into the ground.

Seeing her so distressed, he gently took hold of her shoulders. "Hey, now. Like your lawyer said, Eric might not even go through with it."

"I know, but—"

"But nothing. Don't let him get you down like this. You're a good mother. You deserve some of your own happiness. Until he actually gets the lawyers involved, let's forget all about Eric and his idle threats and have a good time in the mountains, okay?"

She looked back at her kids and dabbed at the tip of her nose. "You're probably right. If I've learned anything over the years, it's that he never keeps his word."

"We're agreed, then? A day in the mountains taking in all that the good Lord has to offer?"

Her lips slowly curled into that sweet smile he'd come to adore. "You've definitely got the power of persuasion on your side." She motioned her head toward her van. "Do you want me to drive? My van's old, but it's functional. Hopefully, it will make it over the pass."

"Hopefully?" he said with a laugh, glad for the change of subject. "If you don't mind, I'd like to drive my SUV. There's a few places we might need four-wheel drive."

"Fine with me. Everything's in the back of my van."

He arched his brows. "Everything?"

"Yep. The coolers and a few other things we might need."

"Cool-ers? As in more than one?" Seth walked around to the back of his SUV and popped the hatch. He met Heather carrying a large Coleman cooler and shook his head. "All that for one picnic?"

Her pretty laughter floated across the ranch yard. He was glad to see her mood lighten, although he wondered how long that would last when she found out he was dealing with none other than the same man who was making her life hell.

She hoisted the cooler inside with a thud. "This is just the drinks. There's another one holding all the food."

"All the food?"

She headed back to her van, still laughing. "You seemed to have caught my disease of repeating everything."

He strode over beside her and swept off his cap, chuckling. Another cooler plus a Rubbermaid tote bucket filled with bread, chips, and cookies waited to be loaded into his SUV. "We're just going for the day, right?" He scratched the back of his head.

"Believe me, by the end of the day, you'll be glad I brought what I did. You're in for a real adventure, Uncle Seth." She gave him a swift pat on the rump as he lugged the cooler and tote from the van. He suddenly had a wary feeling about this outdoor excursion. Was it too late to back out?

As he slung the cooler in the back of his SUV, she set the tote off to the side and nudged against his shoulder. "By the way," she said, peeking over the rim of her sunglasses, openly scanning him from his baseball cap down to his leather hiking boots. "Nice legs."

With the heat of her bare skin against his arm, he could actually feel his face blush under her visual scrutiny. When she dragged her gaze back up till their eyes met, he knew right then there was no way he could back out now, even if his life depended on it.

He tried to remember his deal with himself about not pursuing her after today. Watching her trot back to her van, he was thankful it was only morning. A lot could happen in a day.

"Come on, Kyle!" Heather yelled to her son down at the corral.

Kyle jumped off the fence and shuffled up the hill, kicking rocks and twigs along the way. For only nine, he sure was a big kid. Not overweight, but big-boned. Maybe he was at that awkward age where his coordination didn't seem to keep up with his body. In the two weeks Seth had been around the boy, he noticed Kyle rarely smiled and never made eye contact with anyone, not even Heather. Other than the first day when he'd acted out with J.D., he'd been quiet for the most part. The boy almost seemed slow, mentally, for lack of a better word. Not retarded like Marty, but Kyle's speech was often slurred, and he spoke in incomplete sentences, making him difficult to understand at times.

But there was a definite clarity in his big brown eyes that made Seth believe Kyle was actually a pretty smart kid behind his somewhat detached demeanor. Watching him with Spike and the animals on the ranch, he could tell Kyle had a curious nature about him. He usually had a different colored rock in his hand that he'd found somewhere on the ranch. He had an obvious love for horses, spending most of his time in the corral with his uncle J.D. Kyle's love of animals and the great outdoors were traits he'd definitely inherited from his mother.

Since Nicole barely said two words to Seth when he'd picked her up every night, she'd never mentioned anything unusual about Kyle, or his sister Katie, for that matter. Like today, every attempt he'd made at talking to Nicole had ended up in disaster. Whether it was talking about the weather, or what was on television, their conversations usually ended with Nicole rolling her eyes and giving him the silent treatment.

What was he doing wrong?

A high-pitched giggle drew his attention to the playground where Katie jumped out of the swing, landing in the sand. Her long brunette pigtails flopped over her shoulders as she galloped toward them, neighing and pretending to be a horse.

"Uncle Seth! Uncle Seth!" she squealed with her arms held wide.

It was the greeting he'd received almost every morning and every night . . . and his heart swelled every single time. Since he couldn't sweep her mom into a huge embrace, he settled for her daughter instead. He hunkered down on one knee as she wrapped her arms clear around his shoulders. "How's my little Katie-did this morning? Are you ready to go feed some hungry bears?"

She giggled when he tickled her tummy. "There's no bears, but Mommy brought some peanuts to feed the ground squirrels."

He glanced up at Heather over the rim of his sunglasses and quirked a wry grin. "You sound prepared for everything."

"I'm Katie's den mother for Girl Scouts. I have to be prepared."

Seth stood and took the last backpack from Heather then threw it in with the other gear. "Is this everything? Did you forget the kitchen sink?"

"You may want a sink if somebody falls in a mud puddle or

steps in animal droppings."

Katie crawled into the backseat between Kyle and Nicole. Seth walked around to the passenger door and held it open for Heather. As she approached, he nudged the door shut, forcing her to come right up next to him.

She tipped the bill of her hat back and whispered, "Are you sure you're up for this? It's not too late to back out."

Seth leaned closer to her face and spoke in a low murmur. "If I have to tow three kids along to be near you, then it'll be worth every minute."

"I have a feeling you're in for a rude awakening, Mr. Roberts. Don't say I didn't warn you."

Just as he lowered close to her pink heart-shaped lips, she sneaked two fingers between them, pressing gently against his mouth. "Not in front of the kids," she whispered, her suntanned skin turning rosy pink.

"Hmmm," he said, tapping the bill of her cap down. "Sounds promising, then."

Heading north out of Woodland Park, Seth stared out the window at the mountain terrain stretching for miles. Rocky cathedrals jutted out of steep crevices and watery ravines. The snowcapped peaks were a reminder that winter could still spring another storm at the higher elevations. Tall pine trees shot straight out from stony ledges, defying Mother Nature. Several small waterfalls cascaded into a rapidly flowing creek as the sun beat down, melting the winter snows.

As they headed toward the Continental Divide, Kyle started banging his forehead against the window. Seth glanced into the rearview mirror. "Is he okay?"

Heather reached down into her tote bag at her feet and pulled out what looked like a set of headphones. She handed them back to Kyle who immediately slipped them on over his ears.

"He's very sensitive to the altitude change. It'll take him a few minutes to adjust." She handed Kyle a stick of gum, offered some to Nicole and Katie, then took out a stick for herself. When she offered Seth a piece, her lips slanted into a sexy, crooked grin, and that's when he saw that the gum was cinnamon flavored.

"Thanks," he said, folding a piece into his mouth. "My favorite."

"Yeah, I kind of guessed that."

As soon as they planed out, Kyle sat back against the seat and began humming what sounded like "Yankee Doodle Went to Town." Katie and Nicole chanted a fast-paced rhyme while they expertly executed a hand-clapping game. If he remembered right, it sounded like one of the games Shelli had taught him when they were kids. Although chaotic, it was a nice change from total silence or the radio playing the same songs over the airwaves.

Heather leaned across the center console and elbowed him gently in the arm. "You're handling this better than I thought."

"I'll admit, it's a little noisier than I'm used to, but I'm having a great time." He perched his elbow next to hers on the console, their arms barely brushing. If he didn't know any better, he'd swear she'd scooted closer. It took all his strength not to reach down and hold her hand as he'd done on the plane, feel the softness of her skin.

"Did you and your sister do a lot of hiking?" she asked, smiling.

He nodded. "We didn't have a whole lot of options for entertainment. Shelli and I spent hours scaling the foothills, searching for caves."

"Sounds like you two were pretty close. How old was she when she died?"

"She'd just turned twenty-eight. I'm only a year and a half older. Our mom died of a brain tumor when I was five, and since Pop pulled double shifts at the factory, we pretty much raised each other." Heather's eyes widened as she counted silently on her fingers.

Seth flicked a quick glance back at Nicole. She'd pulled out her MP3 player and two headsets, giving one to Katie. When they started singing what he recognized as a Taylor Swift song, he lowered his voice and filled in the story about his sister. "Shelli was sixteen when Nicole was born." He rubbed the back of his neck, admitting out loud what he'd always felt about his sister's situation. "I feel kind of responsible."

"What do you mean?"

His knuckles whitened on the steering wheel. "I was so hell-bent on getting out of that town, that I worked every night of the week at the local grocer. I graduated early and headed off to college, which left Shelli alone with Pop. She wanted out, too. She just took a different route. Boys. She got pregnant, dropped out of school and moved out to LA with Nicole's father. Pop died a year later. I was a sophomore in college."

Her elbow still on the console, Heather reached over and gently caressed his forearm. "Sounds rough. Did you and Shelli keep in touch?"

Seth shook his head, still feeling the guilt at having deserted his sister. "We talked on the phone a few times a year—Christmas, birthdays, that sort of thing—but I'm not a big letter writer. I'm afraid we kind of lost touch. When I went to work for Ferguson and Tate, I visited whenever I could schedule a meeting at the same time." Knowing how close Heather was to her family, he felt ashamed at admitting what a lousy brother he'd turned out to be. Hoping to steer clear of the unhappy subject, he nudged her arm with his own. "You and your family sure are close."

Her face immediately brightened with a smile. "Yeah, they've always been around for me. I don't know where I'd be without their support. My brothers are great father figures, and even though my sister has been away at college, she's always calling or sending them letters in the mail. My mom and my stepfather, Brad, help me with the babysitting when I have a speech to give or I'm volunteering at Saint Anthony's."

At the mention of Saint Anthony's, he straightened and cleared his throat. "How'd your meeting go last night?"

"We've come up with a few new locations, but either there's not enough space, or there's not enough money for the amount of space we want. It's all so frustrating. Maybe if I throw myself in front of the wrecking ball, they'll stop the demolition."

She said it as a joke, but he knew how serious this was for her. "Sounds like you're pretty attached to Saint Anthony's."

"It's almost like a divorce of sorts. It's tearing us all in different directions. Even if we find a new location, it'll never be the same. Some folks are going to try the new hospital in Denver, but that's too far for most of us to drive several times a month. There are a few small facilities locally, but they'll never be Saint Anthony's."

Seth glanced out the driver's-side window, suddenly feeling warm. He pressed the automatic-window button, hoping to circulate some fresh air. "So, what's made you become so involved with Saint Anthony's?"

She swiveled around and smiled back at the kids. Nicole and Katie still had their earphones on, singing songs while flipping through a teen magazine that Nicole had brought. Heather switched her gaze to Kyle who continued to sing only the first line of "Yankee Doodle" as he rocked back and forth. She turned back to Seth. "Nicole hasn't told you about Kyle?" Her voice had lowered to almost a whisper, as if not wanting him to overhear the conversation.

He arched his brows, keeping his voice low as well. "Told me what?"

"Kyle's autistic."

The moment she said the word, he looked back at Kyle, and immediately saw all the characteristics. Having been around a lot of autistic kids at Pine Tree over the years while visiting Marty, Seth understood now why Kyle acted they way he did. "I'm sorry. I didn't know."

"No need to be sorry," she almost snapped, sounding defensive. "He's still a bright, outgoing little boy."

"I know, I know. That's not what I meant," he said, reaching over and taking her hand, trying to reassure her he wasn't judging. This was obviously a sensitive subject for Heather. "Believe me. I just meant that I know it can be very challenging on the adult caretakers. When did you find out?" he asked, rubbing the back of her hand, hoping to ease her tension.

She squeezed his hand and gazed up at him, looking apologetic. "I'm sorry I snapped. You're absolutely right. It's been a very long road." She blew out a heavy sigh and lowered her shoulders. "We found out officially when he was three. But we noticed things before that we thought were not normal development for a baby. He hadn't talked. He rarely smiled or laughed. Loud noises sent him into crying fits. When he was two and a half, we had him tested and evaluated at Saint Anthony's."

Still holding his hand, she looked away and stared out the window. "That's probably the biggest reason my marriage failed. We couldn't agree on the method of therapy. I wanted to homeschool and raise him with the help of outside therapists and tutors, but Eric thought sending him away to Pine Tree Family Services Center would benefit him the most."

She let go of his hand and shook her head, clasping her hands in her lap. "There's no way I would've shipped him off to some cold and sterile building. No one to love him. No one to give him a hug every day. I just don't know how parents do it."

Seth gripped the steering wheel, thinking about Marty and how their father had been given no choice but to send him to the institute after their mom had died. Until now, Seth had never really thought about any other options for Marty.

Pine Tree Family Services Center had been instrumental in raising him into a productive young man, educating him with the latest techniques and therapies. Turning twenty-six in June, Marty was even responsible for a lot of the lawn maintenance around the facility. His favorite hobby was gardening and planting flowers. The way she talked, she made these places out to sound like Alcatraz.

Swerving around a slow-moving vehicle, he gunned the accelerator and headed over Woodland Pass. Truth be told, he and Shelli probably would have been better off living there themselves rather than sharing their beds with rodents, or sleeping by the woodstove because there was no other heat in the house. Marty received proper medical attention and had three square meals a day. He and Shelli survived on peanut-butter sandwiches, and on rare occasions, even got milk to wash them down.

Whenever they'd visited Marty as kids, he'd always seemed happy. He had a huge playground and a yard with lots of balls—every kind of ball a kid could ever want, basketballs, footballs, soccer balls. Seth only had a football as a young boy, and it had come from the neighbor's trash can and was half-flat. Marty shared a room with two other boys his age, and they even had their own bathroom with plumbing that actually worked. So, before this lady went judging anyone for their decision to seek an institution for help, she'd better damned well have done her homework.

He cleared his throat and struggled to keep his voice level. "I don't think you're giving these facilities a fair chance, Heather. I know several places in the area, and they're all warm and loving environments. You can't be swayed by what you see on TV."

"Oh, I know. You're right. I don't mean to sound so judgmental. There are wonderful places all across the country, and a few good ones right here in Colorado." She gave a heavy sigh and turned to look at her son. "I guess when it comes to either of my kids, I get very defensive and overprotective. The place could be a five-star spa and resort with specialized private tutors, and it still wouldn't be good enough for Kyle. It wouldn't be home." Her voice choked and she turned around, fiddling with her vest. "He wouldn't be with me."

His irritation suddenly dissipated, and for the first time, he was getting a small idea of the kind of challenges and decisions she'd had to face day after day. He craned his neck around, truly seeing the love and devotion she'd poured into both her kids, and how she only wanted to give them the best possible life. No matter how good of an environment it might be, nothing could outweigh a mother's love. Having grown up without a mother, he could personally vouch for the emptiness in his heart that would never be filled.

Heather propped her knees on the dash, slouching back against the seat. "Eric never came right out and said it, but I think he was just embarrassed." She'd lowered her voice so only he could hear over the noisy kids in the backseat. Nicole and Katie still had earphones in, singing another Taylor Swift song. Kyle continued to sing "Yankee Doodle."

He leaned closer, rubbing the backs of his fingers over the skin of her forearm. "What do you mean, honey? Why do you think Eric was embarrassed?"

She blew out a heavy sigh, shaking her head. "Kyle didn't fit into Eric's idea of what the perfect son should be. Sending him away would rid him of the constant reminder that I'd failed him, that I'd given him a less-than-perfect son."

Seth had to grit his teeth. Bastard. The more he learned about her ex-husband, the more he was thankful they'd divorced. "I think your ex-husband is the real failure. You had nothing to do with Kyle's autism. From the little I've observed, you're doing a great job with him."

"Thanks, but I'm afraid my confidence level is at an all-time low right now. Up until the last few months, I thought he was showing a lot of progress."

"What's happened in the last few months?"

"I don't know. He's just been reverting into some of his old behaviors. Like his shirt, for instance. He'll only wear his purple Colorado Rockies T-shirt."

"Can you buy him duplicates?"

She laughed. "I've tried. The one he likes has a black mark on the sleeve from a marker that stained it a while back."

"That's not a big deal. I remember growing up and never wanting to take off my Denver Broncos jersey. Pop finally had to yank it off one night so he could wash it."

"I know, I know. I keep telling myself he's just like any other normal kid. But it's more than just his shirt. The day you saw him throwing a tantrum? He rarely has fits like that. It only happens if he's bothered about something or eats something that might upset his system and trigger an outburst. But we're all very careful with what he eats, so I don't really think his diet was the problem. He'd burned himself with some matches while I was in California, and I assumed his behavior was from that, but now I'm not so sure. He was acting out even before I left for the trip. Of course, Eric would probably blame it all on me. I'm just hoping it's another phase Kyle's going through." She tried to sound upbeat, but he could see the doubt flickering in her eyes.

"Don't let Eric get you down, honey. I haven't been around Kyle that much, but what little I've seen, he's a great kid." He reached down and took hold of her hand again. "I'm not an expert, and I've never been a parent, but I'm pretty sure all kids have their moments. Just keep doing what you've been doing, loving them unconditionally, and they'll turn out great."

Without looking up at him, she covered his hands with hers and squeezed. "Thanks. I needed to hear that."

His heart swelled in compassion for Heather, and yet he knew the feelings she stirred ran deeper than he'd ever experienced with anyone else. Whatever was happening between them, it felt good. It felt right. He was going to savor this newfound closeness.

He pulled into a scenic mountain overlook and parked, then reached up and tweaked her chin, getting her to smile. "We're here. Are you sure you can handle this? I mean, you could wait at the bottom if you think you're not up to such a vigorous—"

She broke into a fit of hearty laughter. "Just lead the way. We'll see who gets tired first." Her sadness was replaced by a glow of happiness. He hoped he had something to do with it.

He turned and faced the kids in the back. "Everyone ready to hike to the top?"

"I am! I am!" Katie squealed, unbuckling her seat belt. She bounded out the door after Nicole and they both traipsed toward the overlook.

Seth glanced over at Kyle. "Ready to go, pardner?"

He'd taken off the headset, but he was chewing on the rim of his T-shirt, with his hands clamped over his ears. "Only Uncle J.D. calls me pardner," he mumbled.

"Oops, I'll just call you Kyle, then. Come on. Let's go feed some squirrels."

Kyle only stared out the window with his hands over his ears, still rocking back and forth.

Heather reached over and touched Seth's forearm. "It's okay. It takes him a few moments to get acclimated to his surroundings. I'm sure once he gets on the trail he'll loosen up a bit."

Still unsure, Seth climbed out and met Heather as she shut the passenger-side door. He slid a sideways glance toward Kyle through the rear-seat window. "Maybe this is too much for him."

"Oh, no. He loves to run and hike. I think he's still getting used to having you around. He's really only seen you a few times when you drop off Nicole at the ranch and pick her up. This will give him more of a chance to get to know you."

"Does that go double for his mother?" He cautiously touched her waist with both hands.

She opened her mouth to answer when Kyle shoved the door open, ramming Seth in the backside. Seth grunted and fell against Heather, shoving her against his SUV, her body molding perfectly to his.

As Kyle ran off with the girls, Seth braced his hands on the SUV behind her head and shoved away from her, but only enough to look down into her face. "Gee, I'm sorry. Are you all right?"

"Yeah, except that I can't breathe." She laughed and rested her head on the roof of his SUV behind her. "If I didn't know any better, I'd say you and Kyle were in cahoots with one another."

He slid a glance over the rim of his sunglasses toward the kids, making sure they were a safe distance away, then leaned into her, this time on purpose. Her face turned a delectable shade of pink that he just had to nibble. He snuck a quick kiss on her lips, noticing she didn't put up any form of resistance. When he went to pull away, she followed him, keeping him from breaking the union.

Sweet heaven. Did she have any idea what she was doing to him? He deepened the kiss, pressing her against the door, the growing desire in his shorts telling her exactly how she affected him.

Her lips parted in invitation, and he had to fight to keep his tongue from dipping inside her mouth and tasting all of her. Who needed a picnic when he could munch on her all afternoon?

"Mommy! Mommy!" Katie hollered from the overlook.

"Okay, okay," she said breathlessly through his kisses, pushing against his chest.

He moved away, but kept her boxed between his hands and hiking boots.

"You're very good at that," she said, dabbing her hand at the moisture on her lips. "And as much as I'd love to continue our little, er, chat, I think we'd better go catch up with the kids. I've suddenly found myself between a rock"—she glanced down and gave him a sheepish grin—"and a hard spot."

He laughed and allowed her to duck under his arms. "Is that why you wanted them to come along today?"

She gave an innocent giggle and tugged down the bill of her cap. "A girl can't have too many chaperones." She reached in the SUV and pulled out a bright yellow backpack with water bottles on the side. She shut the door and looked toward the kids. "Katie? You're getting too close to the edge. Wait for Mommy!"

"Hurry up!" Katie hollered.

Heather looked over her shoulder at Seth. "Are you coming?"

Still gripping the top of his SUV, Seth lazily rolled his head to the side and met her amused grin. "Not yet."

She covered her mouth, trying to stifle her laughter. "Well, then, I'll just be over with the kids while you get everything settled and"—she lowered her gaze and edged backwards— "locked down . . . tight."

As she twirled around and trotted off toward the kids, Seth bowed his head between his shoulders, trying to get a grip on his hormones. He grabbed a bottle of Evian from his backpack and gulped a huge drink then glanced at his watch. Only eleven-thirty. This was going to be one helluva long day.

He jogged over to where they had all climbed up on several boulders overlooking miles of rugged mountain terrain. Heather was busy slathering sun lotion on Katie's face and arms. Kyle had found a big stick and was tapping it against a tree, looking up through the branches. Seth stepped up beside Nicole, perched his big brown hiking boot on a boulder and leaned on his thigh. "Awesome, isn't it? You gotta admit, even this rates over the beach."

Nicole looked Seth square in the face then popped her gum. "Yeah, but it's no ocean. Let's just get this over with. Where're these exciting trails you keep talking about?"

"Over here!" Katie yelled. "Let's go this way!"

"Don't go off the path," Heather warned. "There might be poison ivy. And don't go too far ahead."

"Yeah, those bears will eat you up before we catch you."

"Like, I'm totally sure, Uncle Seth." Nicole rolled her eyes and trotted off toward the trail.

He caught Heather's gaze, raised his hands in frustration and mouthed, "What am I doing wrong?"

"Patience, Seth. She's just trying to act like she doesn't need anyone. After I lost my dad, I shut everyone out. I was mouthy and defiant. I don't know how anyone put up with me."

"So, what made you come around?"

"J.D.," she said matter-of-factly, hooking her backpack over her shoulder. "He never gave up on me. We had some pretty heated fights, but he made me realize that I could allow myself to love someone without worrying they'll leave me."

He touched her chin, forcing her to return his gaze. "So, what happened when Eric left?"

She leaned her face into his palm and gave him one of the prettiest smiles he'd ever seen. "I'm still working on that one.

Or hadn't you noticed?"

"Now that you mention it, you do seem to keep ducking away from me," he teased, stroking his thumb over her cheek. Eric Thomas was a real piece of work. How could anyone intentionally hurt this woman?

Inwardly, Seth fumed. If he had any balls at all, he'd tell that jerk what he could do with his money, and he'd find another realtor. Unfortunately, Ferguson and Tate had Seth by the short hairs. If he lost the hospital account, he could kiss Dallas and the vice presidency good-bye. As much as he was falling for Heather, he wasn't sure if he could give it all up right now. This was what he'd worked so hard for all his life.

She stepped backwards toward the trails. "I promised myself I wasn't going to talk about Eric today. It's a gorgeous day and I don't want to ruin it."

"You won't have any arguments from me," he said with a huge gust of relief. He wanted to forget about the hospital, forget about Ferguson and Tate. Today, he wanted to enjoy one of the few days off he'd had since joining their firm over five years ago.

Heather trotted up next to Katie and took hold of her petite hand. Kyle was several steps in front with his stick, hopping on one foot. As Seth fell in behind them, he had no doubt of the deep abiding love and devotion she had for her children.

Seth was surprised to find Nicole hiking beside him, her face alight with a glowing smile. She'd worn a cute summer hat, her strawberry blonde hair flipping up at the ends. When she looked up, he only nodded, giving her a little wink. She giggled and hurried up beside Heather. He caught her sneaking a quick peek back at him, then she started jabbering about all the mountains in California.

He stuffed his hands in his shorts pockets and grinned. Even though she could be the most irritating child, he found himself losing his heart to her a little at a time. With every smile that she'd let slip, he felt that much closer to her and Shelli. Maybe Heather was right. He just needed patience.

Was there somewhere a person could buy that stuff?

For the first thirty minutes of their hiking excursion, everyone sang and collected pocketfuls of nature souvenirs. They found acorns, pinecones and several smooth shiny rocks that turned different colors when they got wet in the cold mountain stream. Seth stuffed an array of collectibles in his oversized pockets of his shorts.

Several ground squirrels shimmied across the trail in front of them. The spring thaw had filled the streams, the gushing waters making their hike even more tranquil. Small waterfalls cascaded over huge boulders creating millions of tiny rainbows in the afternoon sunlight. The smell of pine trees and new spring grass filled his senses.

Using a broken limb as a hiking stick, Seth couldn't help but smile, silently patting himself on the back. Things were running pretty smoothly so far. What was Heather so worried about?

Kyle stood near the stream, pointing out several beaver dams to Katie. His curiosity about nature gleamed in his eyes. His enthusiasm for every type of tree, every kind of bird or animal proved he was an intelligent, inquisitive kid. At times like this, it was hard to believe he suffered from autism.

Nicole approached Kyle and Katie with her shirt filled with more colorful rocks, jabbering about which one was the prettiest. And then there was Heather, a beautiful brunette in snug-fitting hiking clothes matching his steps, stride for stride, smiling up at him from under the brim of her baseball cap. Wisps of hair framed her pretty oval face alight with a healthy pink glow. Her big brown eyes were filled with something he hadn't seen before. She looked totally happy and content to be surrounded by her kids, enjoying nature at its most spectacular.

Their hands brushed and she easily slid her fingers into his palm, giving his hand a squeeze. He smiled down at her with genuine affection and intertwined their fingers. Yep, life didn't get much better than this.

A loud splash jolted him into another reality—Heather's reality. His heart about jumped out of his chest when he saw Kyle struggling to stand upright in the rushing mountain stream.

Holy shit! "Kyle! Watch out!"

Chapter Eight

Seth plunged into the stream and gasped as the freezing water filled his boots and splashed on his bare legs. He grabbed Kyle by the shirtsleeve, struggling to get him to shore without letting him fall. He had to be at least a hundred and some pounds.

When he made it to the edge, Heather reached out and took Kyle's other arm. Several feet from the stream, Seth set him on a large boulder in the sun. Kyle's lips quivered from the cold. His whole body quaked.

Seth reached up and rubbed the boy's shoulders, hoping to give him a little heat. "Kyle? What happened?"

His lips quivered as he pointed to a shiny red boulder in the middle of the stream. "K-K-Katie . . . w-w-wanted . . . r-r-rock."

Heather draped a small towel over Kyle's head and patted his hair dry. "You can't just go wading into these streams. Besides the fact that they're freezing, the current is very fast and could carry you right down the side of the mountain."

He shook uncontrollably. His clothes were soaked, so Seth tried to pull off Kyle's T-shirt.

"No!" he screamed, flailing his arms.

Heather came around in front of him. "Kyle, honey. It's okay. Seth just wants you to get dry, and then you can put your shirt back on. Okay?"

"No! Leave on!"

Heather set her backpack on the ground. "I'll run to the

157

vehicle and get some dry clothes."

Unsure of how to handle Kyle, Seth touched her arm. "You'd better stay here. I'll go get his things. What does he need?"

"Just bring the brown backpack. There should be some big towels in the blue tote box."

"Okay, I'll be right back."

After an uncomfortable jog in his cold, wet boots down to his SUV, Seth grabbed the other backpack and pulled out a towel. As he ran back on the trails, his boots crunched through pine needles and rocks. He found everyone sitting next to the stream, soaking in the warm afternoon sunshine.

He slowed his pace and approached Heather from behind. Staring down at her, he took in her long, tanned legs that were crossed at the ankles in front of her as she sat comfortably on the grass-covered ground. She tipped her head back, accentuating her slender, graceful neck. His gaze wandered down to the generous swells of her full, rounded breasts, and he understood why she wanted so many chaperones.

She squinted up at him. "Did you have any problems finding everything?"

He chuckled at her upside-down smile. "It was all right where you said it'd be. Do you want me to take Kyle somewhere and change?"

"Oh, no. I'd better help him." She started to rise.

Touching her shoulders, he gently pressed her back down. "Really. I'd be glad to try. He is almost ten. Kind of old for his mommy to be helping him dress, don't you think?"

She shrugged away from his hands, her brows dipping into a frown. "I suppose you don't think I can handle Kyle, either?"

"I didn't say that. Please. Just let me at least try. You might be surprised."

Heather crossed her arms over her chest and watched Kyle jump up and down, trying to catch a bug. She lowered her shoulders and flicked the grass between her legs. "I suppose you're right. He is getting older. Go ahead and try, but use a low voice and be firm. Let him give you the cues. You'll know if you're doing something that bothers him. Oh, and be careful with his ears. He doesn't like them touched."

"Anything else?" he asked, half-kidding, but mostly serious. He wanted to do this right. How hard could it be to get a little boy dressed?

"Mommy! There's a spider on me!" Katie squealed.

"Never a dull moment." Seth extended his hand. "Think you can handle the spider emergency?"

"I got it covered, thanks." She grabbed hold of his hand and stood to his length, sidling up close so their legs barely brushed together. "I warned you, didn't I?"

"Hey, it wouldn't be an adventure without spiders and a dip in the stream." He slid his hand around her waist. "By the way, anyone ever tell you how sexy you are in hiking boots?"

She fluttered her lashes down, her lips curling into that delectable, kissable smile. "No." Stepping on the toe of his boot, she whispered close to his mouth. "You're not so bad yourself. You gotta admit, these shorts are a lot more comfortable than those fancy tailored slacks you wear all the time."

"Mommy! Quick! It's going to bite me!"

Heather glanced over her shoulder. "Duty calls. Holler if you have problems with Kyle."

As Heather trotted toward Katie, Seth warily approached Kyle, suddenly remembering how he'd never clicked with Brenda's kids last summer. He certainly wasn't doing a bang-up job with Nicole. Was this another test? Would he blow it with Heather's kids, as well?

He picked up a flat rock, tossing it into the water with a clunk. Kyle watched from the corner of his eye. Seth picked up another one and handed it to him. Kyle took the rock and imitated Seth perfectly, lobbing the rock into the water.

He touched Kyle's shoulder and turned him around. Even though Kyle wouldn't look at him, Seth stared into his narrow gray eyes. "I brought you some dry clothes, Kyle. How 'bout us men go over behind the trees and get you changed? We don't want any girls watchin' us, do we?"

Kyle peeked at his mother out of the corner of his eye. Seth found himself holding his breath, waiting for Kyle's reaction, but then he ran off behind the trees and began stripping off all his clothes.

Seth blew out a huge breath he hadn't even been aware he'd been holding, then handed Kyle a dry towel and his new clothes. The shirt was another purple Colorado Rockies T-shirt. It must have been okay because Kyle donned it over his head without a fuss. As soon as he'd pulled on his new shorts, he ran off barefoot toward his mother, leaving his wet clothes piled in a heap.

Seth gave a relieved chuckle and scooped up all the wet clothes, stuffing them in the backpack. That wasn't so bad. At least Kyle hadn't pushed him away. Maybe he could get used to this fathering stuff after all.

He caught a glimpse of Heather standing near the stream. She turned and smiled, and for a moment, they just stood there, fully taking each other in. Even though his serene hiking adventure had suffered one minor setback, he still couldn't deny these overwhelming desires he felt for Heather. He could definitely put up with a few spiders and squishy boots to have her by his side day after day.

Kyle ran up to her with his hiking boots, wanting her to put them on for him. Then Katie tugged at Heather's shirt, complaining about something that got on her shorts. She immediately turned her attention to Katie. Seth glanced around and found Nicole sorting through various rocks next to the stream.

A sudden twinge of pain shot down between his shoulder blades. He had to force himself to get a grip. Getting involved with a newly divorced woman with two kids, while just having undertaken the role as father to his niece, took their relationship clear into the next realm.

What had he been thinking? Things were happening all backwards. He needed to refocus, get back to his original plans. Vice president, Dallas, then find a woman to settle down with. After a few years of honeymooning, then maybe they'd be ready to have a couple of kids—when the time was right, and he had his future secure.

As he watched Heather pick up Katie and twirl her in the sunlight, their melodic laughter sent another ripple of warmth through his heart. She set Katie on the ground just as Nicole ran up to Heather and showed her something she'd found. Heather bent over at the waist, giving Nicole her undivided attention. They both laughed about something before Heather wrapped her arms clear around his niece, giving her a heartfelt hug.

When Heather glanced up and gave him an adorable wink, all his well-laid plans washed right down the side of the mountain. He knew then and there it would be like swimming up a waterfall to get Heather out of his system.

Overwhelmed with where his thoughts had led, Seth took in several deep breaths of every scent nature had to offer. Pine, spruce, melting snow, even a trace of animal droppings added to the natural surroundings. Sparkles glistened off the water, looking like millions of tiny diamonds in the sunlight. The sound of the rushing water made for a peaceful afternoon, and he didn't want to ruin it with thoughts beyond right now.

"Uncle Seth! There's a beaver!" yelled Katie.

He jogged over to the stream. "Where is it?"

"Over there! He's building a gigantic beaver dam!"

"Wow. He sure is. See his furry flat tail?"

"Do beavers eat people?" she asked, suddenly looking a little afraid.

He chuckled and hunkered down on one knee, wrapping his arm around her tiny shoulders. "No, sweetheart. Beavers are vegetarians. Do you know what that means?"

"They only eat plants?"

"That's right. People think beavers like to eat bark, leaves and twigs, but they'd much rather eat clover, grasses, and raspberry canes."

In the next breath, Katie whirled around. "I'm starving. Can we eat?"

Amongst all the confusion, he realized it was past two o'clock. He smiled and tweaked Katie's cheek where a little dimple only added to her sweetness. "Let's go find your mom and see what she thinks, okay?"

Heather set Kyle's boots on the ground, looked him square in the eyes and firmly held his face between the palms of her hands. "Stay away from the stream, Kyle. Do you understand?"

He flinched away from her hands and rocked back and forth, tugging the rim of his shirt into his mouth. She squatted down and began retying his hiking boots, relieved he hadn't been hurt, yet frustrated that he'd taken such a dangerous risk.

She couldn't help but wonder, *was it just Kyle?* Or did all little boys think they were invincible? Every time she turned her back, it seemed he found some new way to get into mischief.

Laughing and singing drew her attention to that big hunk of a man who'd dragged her out here today. Even with Kyle's little dip in the stream, she had to admit, it had been a long time since she'd had this much fun. She smiled and listened as they

162

sang "The Ants Go Marching," throwing rocks into the nearby stream.

When she'd told Seth about Kyle's autism this morning and he'd defended institutions, she couldn't help but notice a flicker of apprehension in his eyes. Was he just like Eric and thought Kyle would be better off in a structured facility?

Or was it disappointment she'd seen in his eyes? Like Eric, was he disappointed that her kids were anything less than perfect?

She looked up and smiled at Kyle as he studied some kind of rock he'd found near the stream. In her eyes, Kyle was the most beautiful little boy she'd ever seen. She'd lay her life down to protect him and guide him through this crazy world.

Seeing how grown up he was getting, she realized it wasn't the closing of Saint Anthony's that worried her the most. It was the hassles and worries of finding new therapists for Kyle, changing routines, adjusting to new environments. He needed stability, a place he could feel at home. He needed a place that would be around clear into his adult years, long after she was gone.

Was there such a place?

She'd looked into area programs where adults with challenging disorders could live under the supervision of a house parent. Unfortunately, they were usually located in the lower-rent districts because of their limited potential for income. She'd never considered herself a snob before, but she wanted more for her son. A life where he could be safe and secure in his surroundings, attend college and have a successful career.

Enjoy as normal a life as possible.

She finished tying Kyle's boots and watched him jump off the log and run toward Nicole. Bottom line? She wanted him to remain a little boy and live with her forever.

Giving an exhausted sigh, she sat down on the log that Kyle

had just vacated and watched Seth and Katie. They were up to "nine by nine" in their little ant ditty. He was swinging Katie's arm, her head barely reaching his waist, she was so tiny.

He'd worn khaki hiking shorts with a short-sleeved, button-down shirt of the same color. His legs were a deep bronze with dark hair, his calves bulging as he squatted next to her daughter. Poor guy. His feet had to be soaked inside those thick leather hiking boots, but he didn't seem to mind. His vibrant blue eyes reflected the majestic blue of the clear Colorado skies, and his smile radiated happiness in the warm afternoon sunshine.

Remembering how he'd plunged into the stream to rescue Kyle made her heart swell with admiration. Maybe she'd misread Seth's reaction earlier to her revelation about Kyle's autism. The way Seth went out of his way to include her son in his conversations, pointing out all the names of trees and birds, collecting nature souvenirs and stashing them into his pockets, he'd shown more interest in Kyle in one day than Eric had done Kyle's entire life. After he'd warmed up to Seth, it was like Kyle turned into a different kid, even letting Seth help him get dressed. Other than her brothers, Kyle had never let another man get that close before.

She recalled her tête-à-tête with Seth earlier as he'd pinned her against his SUV. A sudden heat tingled her skin. Other than Eric, she'd never let another man get that close to her either. What was it about Seth that made him so irresistible?

Although she was physically attracted to him, seeing him with her kids, watching his transformation from bachelorhood into fatherhood: that's what clinched it for her more than anything. Whether he'd admit to it or not, nurturing children was second nature for him. Even though Nicole had put up a defiant act in front of everyone, she'd admitted earlier that this was the best day she'd had in a long time. Seth was definitely breaking through Nicole's hardened shell.

As he hunkered down next to Katie, examining another rock, he turned and slid Heather a discreet wink but kept right on talking. She gave a wistful sigh, knowing he'd definitely weakened the shell she'd had around her heart for so long.

But something just didn't add up. A divorced mother of two didn't fit into the plans of a man like Seth. He was gorgeous, loaded, and would make a great father. He could have any young woman he wanted . . . without the burdens. Why was he showing interest in her?

"Katie's starvin'." Seth stepped in front of her. "What do you think? Should we head back and grab a bite to eat?"

She looked up, trying to jog her senses back into place. She hadn't even seen him approach. "Food? Yes. Food would be good."

He gave a deep baritone chuckle and hunkered down to her eye level. Resting his elbows on his thighs, he interlaced his fingers in front of him. "Where did your mind drift off to? And more to the point, was I there, too?"

Tilting her head to the side, Heather smiled. "Actually, yes. I was just wondering why a gorgeous millionaire bachelor like you has never married and had a whole slew of your own kids by now? You're a natural."

He swept off his cap, rubbed the top of his head and stared down at his boots. Was he actually blushing? "As a matter of fact," he said, sounding somewhat hesitant. "I came close to marrying a woman last summer."

"You did?" She straightened and couldn't help but feel a little deflated. "What happened? I mean, if it's not too personal."

Straddling the log, he slid his cap back on and nudged in close beside her. The soft texture of hair from his bare legs rubbed against the smooth surface of hers, stimulating a warm flutter in her female anatomy. A reaction she hadn't felt in years. She pressed her knees together, trying to ignore the sensations.

He gave a nonchalant shrug of his shoulders. "It's kind of complicated."

"Complicated? How?"

Without looking at her, he reached down and grabbed a stick lying at his feet. "She was divorced and had three young boys. She and I got along pretty well, but their father played quite a bit of interference."

"What do you mean? What kind of interference?"

He chucked the stick through the trees and wouldn't look at her. "He had a say in just about everything I did when it came to their kids. What movie we saw, what restaurant we took them to. It was like I had to get permission to even date their mother. In the end, everything just kind of came to a head, and I bailed. But it never would have worked anyway. Her kids never really accepted me and they resented me for taking their father's place. That's probably why I'm a little hesitant around Nicole. I don't want to blow it . . . if I haven't already." He peered over his shoulder at his niece.

Heather reached out and touched his arm. "Take it from me, Seth. You haven't blown it. She's just as unsure about how to act around you as you are around her. It all takes time."

Then she realized she was newly divorced with kids, the exact situation he'd just left. "Gee, after what I told you about Eric threatening to take the kids, I can't believe you didn't jump back in your SUV and run." She picked up a pinecone, flicking it with her fingernails. "Spending time with me has to scare you to death."

"It's scary, but not how you think. I'd love to be a father someday, but becoming a stepfather takes fathering into a whole new dimension." He touched her chin, turning her face so she was looking at him. "Not only do I have to convince the mom to like me, but I also have to get the kids to accept me, too. And that's not even taking the ex-husband into consideration, and how he'll be in the picture."

She nodded in complete agreement. "I guess grown-ups can be pretty complicated, huh?"

"Ahh, but sometimes that's a good thing." He arched his brows and smiled. "It definitely keeps things interesting."

"That's one way to put it," she said through a short laugh, but inside her heart was breaking. She had to let him know there were no hard feelings, and that he was not committed to her in any way. She rubbed her palms on her shorts. "Rest assured, Seth. After today you're off the hook. Your debt will be paid in full, and then you can go back to your carefree bachelor life with no one complicating things. All you have to do is concentrate on Nicole's welfare."

He nodded, staring off toward his niece. "She'll definitely keep my life interesting, that's for sure."

Noticing he didn't argue the point, she quickly changed the subject. "How'd your meeting go last night? You and ol' Sue have a good night?"

He laughed. "More than good. It's just a matter of getting all the paperwork filled out and acquiring all the investors' signatures."

"And their money," she added dryly, rolling her eyes. She stood and brushed grass and dirt off her rump.

Still straddling the log, he gazed up at her from under the brim of his cap. "I've seen that look enough times from Nicole to know there's something wrong. What's the matter?"

She dusted off flakes of dirt. "Nothing's wrong. It's just . . . I don't know. Is that really what life's all about? Money? Accumulating wealth? Eric was the same way. His whole life revolved around the bank account. Do all men think money is everything you need to be happy?"

"No, of course not," he answered, squaring his broad shoulders. "But I also know how difficult life can be with the lack of it, and I resent you even saying my name in the same sentence with your ex-husband." He stood and narrowed his eyes. "What's this all about, anyway? Why all the questions?"

She turned her back and rubbed her arms, embarrassed that she'd gotten so serious. She barely knew this man, and yet she'd allowed herself to get caught up with romantic notions. Thinking there could be a future with Seth was ridiculous. "I'm sorry. I don't know what came over me. I've had a lot on my mind lately, and I thought. . . ."

Stepping up behind her, he touched her arms, his fingertips trailing down her skin over her forearms until he interlaced their fingers. Sliding his booted feet beside hers, he wrapped his arms around her middle. "You thought what, honey?"

She closed her eyes and tipped her head against his chest. "Oh, Seth. I don't know what I'm thinking anymore. This is all so confusing."

"For what it's worth, I'm just as confused as you are." Brushing his cheek against hers, his voice was a velvet murmur next to her ear. "Everything you've said I've been telling myself the exact same thing all day." She stiffened at his admission. Before she could pull away, he slowly turned her in his arms, gazing deeply into her eyes. "But I also know that I've never wanted to be with anyone more than I've wanted to be with you." His lids lowered in sweet seduction as he gazed openly at her lips.

"I know. I feel the same way." Her voice turned breathless and heavy. "So, what should we do?"

He glanced over his shoulder. She followed his gaze to where the kids were a good distance away from the stream, tucked safely in the thicket, swinging from a tree. She slipped the tip of her tongue over her lips, wishing she didn't have so many chaperones right now.

He gave her a lazy smile, only making her desires burn that much hotter. Lowering to her mouth, he awakened wonderful new sensations that brought her back to the basics of human nature, the need for human contact, for physical intimacy. Just the simple act of his lips moving slowly over hers made her knees tremble. She curled her fingers into his hiking shirt and breathed out a small moan of complete contentment. "Oh, Seth."

He rolled his head to the side and sneaked another glance at the kids then backed her clear up around the trunk of a large tree, obscuring the kids' view. His vibrant blue eyes turned to a deep smoky haze that seared right to her heart.

She parted her lips, inviting him to take more as the rush of wonderful new feelings surged through her body. He tasted of cinnamon from the candy he chewed, mixed with the salt from his skin, making him that much more delicious. His masculine scent swirled together in a heady concoction with the earthy pine scent of the trees. This was definitely nature at its finest.

His bare legs brushed against hers as he backed her up to the tree, deepening his kiss. Standing full length against his body, she fed her fingers through his hair at the nape of his neck. Her thoughts of passion jumbled with thoughts of her kids, her future.

Where was this all going? Did he have any idea the kinds of responsibilities she had? Or was she just another one of his flings for the summer?

She rolled her face away from his, but kept her eyes closed. "We can't do this," she whispered with heavy breaths.

He bent and kissed her neck, speaking in a low sultry voice near her ear. "It's okay. I'll back off. Maybe we could find a babysitter tonight and go to my place."

"No. You don't understand." She swallowed and met his sensual gaze. "I'm not like your other girlfriends, Seth. I can't just mess around and have a casual affair. It's too dangerous."

He pressed his warm, wet lips against her forehead, making it that much harder for her to remain firm. "For the record, other than the woman I was with last summer, I haven't had that many girlfriends. I'm not into casual sex. You're safe with me."

Fiddling with a pocket of his shirt, she was suddenly feeling shy. "I don't mean that kind of dangerous. I just managed to get my heart put back together." She looked up and curled her fingers into his shirt. "I'm not sure if I'm ready for this." She paused and mouthed, "For you."

"I told you before, honey. I'm not going to hurt you. Please trust me."

"It's not a matter of trust anymore. I'm not a carefree, single woman, and I'm sorry I ever led you to believe otherwise. But the fact remains, I'm a divorced mother of two challenging kids, and you've got your own plate full with work and taking care of Nicole."

She swallowed and breathed in a deep breath of cool mountain air. "I think that after today we should go back to a business relationship, before it's too late and someone gets hurt." Even though the ache in her heart told her it was already too late for her. Funny, she'd never had this sickening feeling in the pit of her stomach when she and Eric had split.

"Mommy!" Katie yelled from behind the tree. "Kyle pushed Nicole! She's bleeding!"

Seth groaned. "We're not through with this conversation." Placing another quick kiss over her mouth, he shoved away from the tree and followed Katie.

Heather picked up her backpack that had fallen to the ground and ran up behind Seth as he approached Nicole. Tears dripped from Nicole's eyes as she held her leg. Blood dribbled from a small gash on her knee.

Looking around for Kyle, Heather found him several yards away tapping a stick on a tree. Did he even realize he'd hurt someone?

Seth squatted down in front of Nicole and assessed the situation. Tiny pebbles and chunks of dirt were embedded in the skin. "It's okay, Nicole." He carefully slipped his hand under her calf. "Looks like it's just a little scrape."

"Easy for you to say." She shoved his hand away. "Look at all this blood!"

"What happened?" he asked. "Katie said Kyle pushed you."

"No, he was helping me balance on a log, and I tripped." She shook her head in disgust. "Stupid log rolled over."

Standing behind them, Heather unzipped her backpack, relieved her son wasn't to blame after all. "I've got some antibacterial wipes and some bandages."

"You do it, Heather, please?" Nicole pleaded with those big green eyes sparkling with tears.

Remembering how Eric had practically fainted at the sight of blood, Heather nodded and pulled out the wipes.

"It's okay," Seth assured them both, staying in front of his niece. "I know what I'm doing. I used to do this all the time for your mom when she was a kid." Seth took a wipe and expertly swabbed the area around the scrape. Nicole flinched and gave Heather an obvious glare of distress, but Heather only smiled and peered over Seth's shoulder.

"I used to kid Shelli that she could be in bed and still find a way to get hurt. She always had a bandage taped somewhere on her body." He looked up and slid Nicole a wink then grabbed another wipe.

Nicole's shoulders relaxed as she watched her uncle closely, but she didn't pull away. "Did you and Mom used to go hiking a lot?"

"Almost every day. One time we saw a mountain lion and pretended to be on a safari."

Her eyes widened. "What happened?"

"I heaved a rock at it with my slingshot. Got him right

171

between the eyes. He growled and scampered off like a scared little pussycat."

"Awesome. Did you ever see any bears?"

Heather smiled, listening to Seth reminisce with Nicole. She needed to hear good things about her mother, and Seth needed to talk about his sister. Heather had never seen these two actually have a full-fledged conversation without any sarcastic retorts or Nicole stomping off mad.

As he tenderly ministered to her wound, carefully dislodging pea-sized pebbles, totally unfazed by the blood, she chalked a mental mark in the win column as he and Nicole took another step toward a positive father-daughter relationship. Heather unwrapped a bandage and handed it to him, thankful that she'd been able to help smooth the edges between them. Once school started up this fall, they wouldn't need her at all.

The way her chest tightened, she knew she'd allowed herself to become too emotionally involved with Nicole . . . along with her adorably sexy uncle. Nicole had lost her mother only three months ago. She needed time to heal, time to bond with her uncle. This was not the time for him to become attached to Heather. And the way Kyle and Katie had taken to Seth, she couldn't bear for them to lose another man in their lives. Somehow she had to distance herself from both Seth and Nicole.

After today, they had to go back to a business relationship before anyone got hurt. New counselors started on Tuesday along with a whole slew of campers Nicole's age. That should help alleviate Nicole's dependence on Heather and her kids. Rubbing her fingers over her lips, still tasting Seth's kiss, she let out a breath of disenchantment and glanced at her watch. Almost two-thirty.

After today, she thought, still giving herself plenty of time to soak in as much of Seth as she could. It would probably be a long time before she ever felt this way again.

She stood and zipped the backpack shut. "Looks like you two have everything under control. I'll take Kyle and Katie on ahead and get our picnic set up."

"Hold on. We're ready to go." He stuffed the wipes and bandage wrappers in a plastic bag that she'd given him. After checking her knee one last time, he looked up at Nicole. "How about a piggyback ride down? I used to give your mom rides all the time."

Nicole looked up at Heather, as if checking to see if she should. Heather gave a slight nod of her head and smiled. "Just remember, if you go over the mountain, he goes."

She giggled as Seth turned around, allowing her to slide her petite arms around his brawny neck.

Seth gave an exaggerated grunt and shoved to standing. "Gee whiz, girl. How much do you weigh?"

"Uncle Seth!" she gushed, trying to get down.

He laughed and scooped his elbows under her knees. "Hold on. This terrain gets pretty steep. Grab a tree if we go over the side. I'll hang onto your ankles!"

CHAPTER NINE

As Heather strode ahead of them, Seth realized they'd actually only hiked a total of one mile before they'd headed back down to eat. He'd been used to ten-mile hikes and eating a granola bar on the trails. Yet, he had to admit, he didn't think he'd ever had this much fun before today. Kyle's frolic in the stream and Nicole's skinned knee only added excitement to their adventure.

He sat down at a picnic table across from Heather as she handed everyone a sandwich. He passed out grape-juice boxes and opened a couple of bags of chips. When he glanced down at his sandwich, he gulped. He hadn't eaten a peanut-butter sandwich since the day he'd moved away from home after high-school graduation.

Except for the occasional splurges when his father brought home hot dogs or a frozen pizza, they'd eaten peanut-butter sandwiches morning, noon, and night. He'd sworn he'd never eat peanut butter again.

"Mommy, you left the crust on," Katie complained, shoving it in front of Heather.

She pulled the edges away and handed it back. "There, perfect. Just the way you like it."

"I can't get the straw in the juice box," she whined, trying to jam the straw into the hole.

Heather quickly remedied the situation. "There, now eat, and try not to get any grape juice on your shirt."

Seth couldn't help notice how Heather hovered over her

daughter, but then again, he'd been raised without a mom, and didn't have the slightest clue as to how a mother should act. He opened his juice box, remembering the basket he'd packed with French bread, a block of cheese, and a bottle of wine. Now, of course, he realized how impractical it was, not to mention out of place. He stared down at his sandwich that was made with Heather's loving hands and decided not to even mention his picnic.

He picked up his sandwich and took a huge bite out of the corner. "Mmmmmm," he said, grinning toward Heather. "These are the best sandwiches I've ever had. You didn't tell me you were such a great cook."

"This is nothing. You should taste my grilled cheese sandwiches." She laughed and crossed her legs, her foot brushing against his calf. With her eyes bearing into his, she rubbed his leg while sipping her grape juice. The peanut butter suddenly caked to the roof of his mouth, making it impossible for him to say another word.

After they ate and cleaned up their wrappers and cans, they repacked the coolers into the back of the SUV. Katie whined that she wanted to go home. Nicole, overexaggerating her limp, absolutely refused to go back on the trails. Everyone loaded up and they headed over the mountain pass toward Colorado Springs.

Seth glanced at the threesome in the rearview mirror, all sleeping soundly. Katie's head rested on Nicole's shoulder, her head draped over Katie's. Kyle rested his head against the door, his eyes slowly drifting shut as he watched the mountains through the window. An overwhelming contentment swept through Seth's body, a feeling that he'd never experienced before.

Heather's eyes were closed, her head tipped to the side, but her lips seemed to be curled into a small smile. He remembered what she'd said about it not being possible for them to be together. Could they go back to the way they were? Client and counselor?

She definitely had her hands full, but that didn't make her any less desirable. If anything, his attraction had grown deeper after witnessing how good a mother she was. He barely remembered his own mom, but he'd always imagined her just like Heather.

It was after six when he rounded the corner and pulled into the asphalted parking lot of the J Bar D Ranch. Several vehicles were parked haphazardly along the drive.

Heather sat up and stretched. "Looks like Mom and my stepfather, Brad, are back from vacation. My sister, Megan, was supposed to arrive home from California this afternoon, too." She pointed to a white crew-cab pickup. "That's Jared's truck. I bet he picked her up. Megan's only home for a few days before she starts her residency up in Denver."

"What's she specializing in?"

"Geriatrics. It'll be great to have her back in the area."

Just as he shifted into park, a short, blonde-haired woman trotted out the side door of the yellow ranch house. Heather's face broke into a huge smile. "Look, kids. Megan's home!"

"Auntie Megan's back?" Katie groggily opened her eyes. When she spotted her aunt, she squealed. "Auntie Megan! Hurry! Let me out!" She shoved against Nicole, trying to get her to wake up.

"Okay, okay. I'm awake." Nicole pushed out her door, followed by an excited little seven-year-old Katie. She ran up to Megan and jumped into her arms. Seth had to chuckle. Megan squealed just about as loud as Katie as she twirled her around in circles.

Kyle had awakened, but he only sat there, staring down toward the corrals. J.D. stood grooming a big black quarter horse with a white star on its forehead. He glanced up when he heard the commotion, tossed the brush in a bucket and led the horse into a nearby paddock. The few times he'd spoken with J.D., Seth had really enjoyed their talks. His wife Debra was one of the nicest and—with the exception of Heather—one of the prettiest ladies he'd ever met, even seven months pregnant.

J.D. owned most of the ranch, raising and training horses in addition to running the outreach camp. With their first baby due the end of July, J.D. had it all. He was surrounded by all of his family, cherished and respected by everyone. All the money and prestige in the world couldn't buy that kind of love.

Seth almost groaned. How could he live up to someone like J.D. or even Jared? Heather boasted on them and how much they'd done for her over the years, how close they'd all stayed. How could he possibly compete with such perfection?

Kyle shoved out his door and pulled several rocks and arrowheads from his pockets. "Gonna show Uncle J.D." He slammed the door then shuffled down the asphalted drive as he juggled everything in his hands, trying to keep from losing his collection from this afternoon's hike.

J.D. strode toward the fence, climbed over the rails then trotted up the yard toward Kyle.

Heather unbuckled her seat belt. "Are you sorry you asked us all to go with you today?"

Seth reached across the console and grabbed her hand. "I'd do it all again in a heartbeat, soggy boots and all."

She gave a gentle squeeze in return. "Is my debt paid in full? Or are you going to hold me to another date?"

He reached up and stroked the side of her cheek with the backs of his fingers. "I think you know what I want, but I'll do whatever you say."

She gave an exhausted sigh. "I think we'd better keep this to a business relationship, Seth. Any more, and I'm afraid someone's going to get hurt. I can't risk putting myself or my children through that again, and now we've got Nicole's well-being to consider. I think she's becoming very attached to my kids and me."

He leaned close and placed a kiss over her cheek. Her long lashes brushed his cheekbones as her eyes fluttered shut. "She's not the only one," he whispered. "And I have no intentions of hurting you or the kids."

She drew apart and gave him a sad smile. "They never do."

A light tap at their window jolted their heads back. "Do you two need to take this behind the barn?" Megan teased.

With regret, Seth let go of Heather's hand, wondering if she'd ever allow him to get this close again. "Go on." He motioned his head toward Megan. "I'll load everything into the back of your van."

She laid her palm on his cheek and smiled, but it was an apologetic smile, as if saying she'd had a good time, but this was it. Don't pursue her after today.

He only nodded, not knowing if he could honor her request. She slid out and gave Megan a heartfelt hug, her tall physique dwarfing her younger sister's.

He stepped out of his vehicle and did an upper-body stretch, twisted at the waist and breathed deeply. The aroma of barbecued hamburgers and steaks drifted into his senses. He glanced over the roof of his SUV toward the backside of the ranch house. A tall, dark-haired man stood near a large outdoor brick fireplace, holding a long-handled spatula in his hand. A shorter woman with shoulder-length brunette hair stood next to him holding a plate of hamburgers, hot dogs and steaks. Although shorter, the brunette was a dead ringer for Heather. He assumed that was her mom and her stepfather, Brad Dalton.

Heather said they'd just returned from an architect convention in Seattle. Although Ferguson and Tate had never used

Dalton & Jones Architects, Seth had heard nothing but good things about them. Apparently, they were behind the Blue Ridge Condo Development, as well as several outstanding developments in the area. Seth would definitely give them a shot when it came down to roughing out this new resort.

He strode around his SUV and met Heather and Megan, still wrapped in an embrace. Heather stepped back, a good head taller than her younger sister. Megan's emerald-green eyes sparkled with excitement. Wild strands of kinky blonde hair blew in disarray, framing her small oval face. She didn't look much older than eighteen.

"I'm so glad you're back," Heather gushed. "I wish you could stay longer than a few days."

"I know, but I had to jump on this opening up in Denver."

"Did you hear about Saint Anthony's?" Heather asked.

"Yeah. I heard it was going to be converted into another resort. Like Colorado needs another golf course," she added dryly.

Seth cringed and shoved his hands into his shorts pockets, avoiding either of their gazes. It didn't sound like any of the Garrisons would be too thrilled if they found out he was behind the whole conversion.

Heather looked up at him, her smile not as confident as those he'd seen this morning. "Megan, I'd like you to meet Seth Roberts. His niece is attending our camp this summer."

He extended his hand in greeting. "Nice to meet you, Megan, or should I call you Doctor Garrison? I hear congratulations are in order for graduating medical school."

She slid her petite hand into his and squeezed. For a little thing no bigger than five-three, she had quite a grip. "Thank you. I'm just glad to be home for a while."

"Heather said you were leaning toward geriatrics?"

"Yes. I'm starting my first year of residency up in Denver

next week."

"You're going to drive your patients crazy," he said with a chuckle.

She cocked her head to the side. "Why's that?"

"Well, don't take this the wrong way, but they'll probably want to know your secret."

"My secret?"

"For staying so young."

A bright pink blush covered her cheeks as she looked down at her fingernails. "I know. Some people think it's a gift, but sometimes I feel like it's a curse. I think that's why I put in so much effort. I want to be the best, even if I don't look the part."

"How'd you do in school?"

She gave him a timid smile and rolled her gaze up to meet his. "I got top honors, beating out all the males."

He tipped his head back and laughed. After only just meeting her, he could tell that the Garrison spunk definitely ran in the genes, no matter what size they wore. "You two go on and catch up while I unload everything, then Nicole and I had better be going. Looks like you have quite a crowd tonight."

"There's plenty of food," Megan said. "Why don't you two stay?"

He couldn't help but notice a look of apprehension cross Heather's face when she met his gaze. He took it as a cue to bow out gracefully. "I'd better not. I promised Nicole I'd take her shopping for a new bed. She's been inhabiting my pull-out sofa in the living room for two weeks."

"Auntie Megan!" Katie squealed from across the yard. She was sitting on a swing, her feet dangling below her. "Push me high! Watch me do a parachute!"

"Okay!" Megan trotted away giggling, obviously happy to be back home.

Seth opened the hatch of his SUV, speaking over his shoulder to Heather. "Let me get this stuff transferred to your van, then you can get back to your family. I don't want to intrude."

She stepped beside him, her smooth legs brushing against his as she reached in and grabbed a backpack. "You're not intruding. If you'd like to stay, I'm sure there's plenty of food." She avoided looking at him, revealing that she'd only asked him out of courtesy.

He grabbed a cooler and shook his head. "Better not. Why don't you find Nicole and tell her I'm ready to go?"

They both walked over to her van. She opened the rear door and waited for him to set the cooler inside before tossing the backpack on top. "I'm assigning Nicole to a new counselor on Tuesday. I'll be busy with the new campers, and I probably won't have as much time to spend one-on-one with her. She's also getting three new cabin buddies. She probably won't even notice."

"Whatever you think is best," he said, stowing the last cooler and tote box in her van. He slammed the door, maybe harder than necessary, before he turned to face Heather. Rolling his head around on his shoulders, he gave a loud sigh of frustration. It was better this way. End it now before anyone got too involved. A twinge at the base of his heart made him grimace, knowing he'd already allowed himself to get too involved.

Her fingers fiddled nervously with the pockets of her hiking vest. "Thanks for taking us with you today. You were right. I needed to get out and have some fun. I think Nicole even had a good time, scraped knee and all. You were a great hiking guide."

He took her trembling hands and closed the gap between them, feeling a gentle squeeze as her lips curled into that pretty smile he'd come to adore. "It was my pleasure, believe me." He lowered to her mouth, knowing he couldn't leave without one last kiss, one last taste of the sweetest woman he'd ever known.

"No," she whispered, placing two fingers over his lips, her warm breath fanning his face. "Don't make this harder than it already is."

Clamping his back teeth together, he dropped her hands and fished his keys from his pocket. "If that's the way you want it. Tell Nicole I'm waiting."

She touched his arm. "Please, Seth. Don't leave mad."

He knew she was right. He'd been telling himself the same thing all day. "I'm not mad," he said, even though he knew he sounded more than a little irritated. "It's just been a long day. I've got a lot of things on my mind right now."

"I understand. I'll go get Nicole." Without another word, Heather turned and trotted down to Nicole's cabin.

He strode around his vehicle and slumped back against the driver's-side door, crossing his arms over his chest. So, this was it, the big brush-off. Although he'd never really dated till after college, he'd always been the one to end relationships. Getting dumped after a first date was a definite first.

He didn't like it.

"Joshua?" Debra called, drawing Seth's attention to the back patio. "Hamburgers are ready." She waddled down the yard with her hand on her lower back. Once she joined J.D. and Kyle, she slid her arms around her husband. J.D. straightened and planted a big kiss square on her mouth, his hand splaying over her pregnant belly in loving affection.

"See this one?" Kyle asked, trying to get their attention.

J.D. ruffled Kyle's hair. "Come on, pardner. Let's get something to eat. You can show me the rest later. Auntie Debra says her baby's starvin'."

"No! Now!" Kyle yelled and shoved the arrowhead into J.D.'s stomach.

"Kyle? I said it's time to eat." J.D.'s voice turned firm. "Now go put these rocks away and get washed up."

Kyle threw all his treasures on the ground and stomped away toward the house. J.D. swept off his hat and shook his head, his mouth formed in a grim smile. Together, he and Debra bent over and gathered everything into his hat. They appeared unfazed by Kyle's tantrum as they exchanged another kiss before strolling off to the backyard, hand in hand.

"I'm ready, Uncle Seth." Nicole slid into the front passenger seat.

He opened his door and took one final glimpse at the tall brunette standing near Jared and her sister, laughing, completely content with her life. She was right. She didn't have any room for anyone else. This was her family. They were all she needed.

Now that he and Nicole were on the right track, he had to get back to his original plans. Get this new resort funded, get that promotion to senior vice president of the southern region, then move to Dallas. All, hopefully, before school started in the fall. He didn't need a woman and her two kids messing up his plans.

With firm resolve, Seth slid into the passenger seat and switched on the ignition. "What do you say, Nicole? Should we get you a bed?"

"That'd be awesome. Can I get a dresser to match?"

"I don't see why not."

"What about a computer? I'll need one for school this fall, and maybe we could even get a DVD—"

"Hold on," he said with a chuckle. "One thing at a time." He reached inside the console and switched on his cell phone. Several messages waited in voice mail. He knew how his phone irritated Heather whenever it rang, so he'd opted to keep the phone in his glove box.

He scanned through the missed calls, relieved there were no calls from Marty. "I thought maybe tomorrow we could take a drive down to Pueblo. My dad's brother owns a small ranch. I haven't seen him since I was in high school. Maybe you'd like to meet one of your long-lost relatives."

"Sure. I guess."

He'd no sooner had his phone turned on before it rang again. He dropped the gearshift into drive, flipped open the phone, and answered, "Roberts here."

"Seth?"

"Hey, Joe. What's up?"

"I've been trying to get a hold of you all day. I left a few messages on your home answering machine and your cell phone."

"Sorry about that, I forgot my phone today." He turned and slid Nicole a conspiratorial wink.

"We got a call from Eric Thomas. He's got several clients itching to spend their money and wants to meet you for a drink. I'd go myself, but my wife has theater tickets. I think you'd better jump on it."

"Tonight?" Seth rubbed his brow. "Can't this wait till next week? I've already made plans with my niece."

"Look, if this account is too much for you to handle, maybe we should give it over to Davison. He just closed on the new Prairie Vista Aeropark project up north. He knows what it takes to make things happen."

Seth gritted his teeth, rubbing his hand over the back of his neck. The Prairie Vista Aeropark subdivision was the account Seth had worked on night and day before his sister had been killed. He'd had no choice but to hand the account over to Davison so he could handle his sister's estate.

The highly sought-after development of the new aeropark had a private runway for all the homeowners to use, along with a clubhouse and an indoor swimming pool. If it weren't for the promotion and move to Dallas, he himself would invest in the development. It was costing him hundreds of dollars a year to hangar his plane out at the airport.

Knowing he couldn't let Davison have this one, he grudgingly agreed. "All right, I'll be there. What time?"

"Eight at the Royal Rock Lounge."

"The Royal Rock is clear across town." He glanced at his watch. "Nine is the earliest I can make it."

"Maybe I should call Davison."

"I said I'd be there. Just give me an hour to get Nicole settled in with the neighbor."

"That reminds me. My wife got all the information on the Nantucket Girls School in Maine. Looks like they've got room if you act fast. Didi left a phone number and a person for you to contact on your home machine. Good luck tonight. This is what you've been working so hard for all these years. Make us proud."

Seth flipped the phone shut and heard Nicole give a grunt of frustration. She crossed her arms over her chest and stared out the window, shaking her head.

He gave a heavy sigh and pulled into a front parking stall near the entrance of his building. Before he even shifted into park, Nicole flew out the door and fled through the revolving glass doors. The doorman jumped back when she almost knocked him down.

Seth swore under his breath as he jogged up to the front. "Sorry about that, Freddy."

"Don't worry about it, Mr. Roberts. I got me a granddaughter just about her age. She's always running here and there, her mouth always going a mile a minute. I swear that girl never runs out of things to talk about. Just last week, she was over and I couldn't get a word in edgewise. Seems she's got this project she's working on at school, some kind of an invention of sorts. Well, anyway, her partner just up and—"

"I'm kind of in a hurry tonight," Seth interrupted. "Maybe you can tell me about your granddaughter some other time.

Bring her by and have her meet Nicole."

"Sure thing. You got it. Have a good evening, sir."

Seth jogged over to the elevators and punched the buttons several times. Just when things were smoothing out between Nicole and him, he blew it. How could he get her to understand that he was doing this all for her? Well, at least a lot of it had to do with her. He could give her anything she ever wanted if he got this promotion.

He stepped off the elevator onto the fifth floor and heard a loud thud as his penthouse door slammed shut. The dead bolt slid into the latch. Jiggling the knob, he pounded his fist on the door. "Don't do this, Nicole. Let me in . . . now."

"Why? You're leaving anyway!" she yelled back. "Just go to your stupid meeting!"

"I'm not leaving till we talk about this." His voice bellowed down the corridor.

He searched through his key ring and fed the house key into the lock. The deadbolt clicked and he reached down and grabbed the doorknob, flinging the door wide. The knob slammed against the wall with a loud thud. He stepped over the threshold, narrowing his eyes on his niece. "We need to talk."

She covered her hands over her head, cowering in front of him. "I didn't mean to lock the door. I'm sorry!" she whimpered, the sound tearing his heart out. "Please don't hit me. I won't do it again!"

Seth stopped dead in his tracks. He'd never seen this look of pure terror before. It wrenched a hole clear through his gut. He held up both hands in surrender and lowered his voice. "Take it easy, sweetheart. I'm not going to hurt you."

"Just leave me alone!" she cried through her tears. "I don't need you. I don't need anybody!" She ran to the bathroom and slammed the door. Another click sounded as she locked it.

He hurried across the living room, around the sofa, still

pulled out and unmade from this morning, then approached the bathroom. He could hear quiet sobbing coming from behind the door, sounding like she was slumped on the floor.

"Nicole? Please. Let's talk about this." He splayed his palm on the oak panel. "I'm sorry I yelled at you. I'm just as frustrated about having to leave as you are."

He rested his forehead against the door. "Look, I'll call my boss and get Davison to cover the meeting. I don't want to leave you like this, okay? But you have to promise to come out and at least talk to me. I swear, I'm not mad. I would never do anything to hurt you."

When she didn't answer, he headed for his phone in the den. To hell with Eric Thomas. If he had a shred of common courtesy, he'd have given more than a day's notice and would be willing to meet next week.

The answering machine beeped, indicating two missed calls. The first was Joe's wife Didi calling about the Nantucket Girls School. He jotted down the contact name and phone number, not sure if he should send Nicole away right now. He was actually getting used to her being around.

"I knew it! You do hate me!"

He jerked his head up and found Nicole standing near the door of the den, shaking her head back and forth.

"You don't want me either! You're just like my dad! You're all the same!"

She turned and ran down the hall in tears. He barreled after her, hoping to keep her from locking herself in the bathroom again. He shoved his arm inside the room and cringed the moment the door pinned him against the doorframe. He let out a low curse and shoved the door open, rubbing his forearm, trying to catch his breath.

Nicole climbed into the bathtub and crouched into a ball in the corner. Her little body trembled. Tears coursed down her cheeks. Any pain he may have felt on his arm was replaced with a sickening sensation in the pit of his gut. He took a hesitant step toward her, stopping when she covered her head with her hands.

"Please," she cried. "P-please d-don't hit me."

What's going on here? What did she mean, he was just like her dad? He slumped to his knees and sat back on his haunches, his chest swelling in compassion for Nicole, and at the same time he seethed in anger at her father.

Dear God, what kind of hell had her father put her through?

Her little hiccups ripped a piece out of his heart. He swallowed, hoping he wouldn't say or do anything else to upset her. "Nicole? I don't know what's going on here, but you have to know I would never hurt you."

She tucked her knees to her chest and continued to cry. Sometimes, he forgot how old she was. At times she looked on the verge of womanhood, and at other times, like now, she looked about as fragile as a newborn chick.

Hesitantly, he scooted closer to the side of the tub. "Please, will you talk to me?"

She swiped at her nose with the back of her hand. "I thought you had a meeting."

"The meeting can wait. I don't want to leave you like this. Please, tell me what's wrong."

She snuffed and turned her head to face him. Her big green eyes were red and puffy. Tears streaked down her face, leaving tracks through the dirt and dust of hiking all day.

Her voice was a trembly whisper when she finally spoke. "Are you sending me away?"

He shook his head, confused. "Sending you away?"

She reared her head back and glared. "I'm not stupid, Uncle Seth. I heard that lady tell you about the Nantucket Girls School."

The message on the machine. Was that what this was all about? "My boss only thought the school would be something you'd be interested in, but I assure you, I won't do anything unless it's what you want."

"What I want? That's a laugh. Since when does anyone care what I want?"

"What do you mean?" he asked, softening his voice. "I care very much what you want."

"Yeah, right," she mumbled, rolling her head to the side. She wiped her face with the sleeve of her shirt.

He reached up and grabbed a towel and handed it to her. Without looking at him, she took it and pressed it against her face, leaving the towel there for several moments, as if garnering strength to face him again. Somehow, he had to get her to know he really was concerned about her. "Nicole, whether you realize it or not, I do care about you. I've tried to get you to open up and tell me what you need, but all I've gotten is a cold shoulder and this constant sparring."

When she stopped crying, he sat back and braced his elbow on his bent knee. "I know this has all been tough on you, losing your parents, leaving your school, your friends. But if we're going to live together, we have to learn how to talk to one another."

He wanted to clear the air about the boarding school and hoped she believed him. "As far as what you heard on the machine about the boarding school, when I brought you home from LA, I'll admit, I was panicking. I thought, what did I know about raising a little girl?"

She gave a huff and tossed her towel down in the bathtub.

"I mean young lady, Nicole. Believe me, I know you're not a little girl. You're almost a teenager. I think that scares me more than if you'd been six weeks old, still in diapers."

She gave a muffled laugh and turned her face toward the tiled bathroom wall. Sensing an ease in tension, he relaxed his shoulders and picked up a bottle of shampoo, flicking the lid with his thumb. "My boss has a daughter your age, and she attends this Nantucket Girls School on the east coast. They say she loves it there. At first, I honestly thought you'd be thrilled with the opportunity. You'd get to be with girls your own age, get the best schooling, and you wouldn't have to put up with an inconsiderate uncle you don't even like."

She tipped her head back and stared toward the ceiling, her eyes filling with tears again. "I think it's the other way around. You're the one who doesn't like me."

A swift pain hit his heart. "Why would you think I don't like you?"

"I don't know." She swiped her eyes, trying to keep from crying. "You're just, like, always so busy with your work. You never say much except, turn the TV down or it's time to go to bed. I feel like I have to stay away from you or you'll get mad at me."

"Awe, Nicole," he said, rubbing his brows. "If I don't say much, it's because I don't know what to say. It seems like every time I open my mouth I say something stupid or I offend you. After everything you've been through, I figured you just needed your space, so I backed off. But it's not because I don't like you. My God, I'm sorry if you ever got that impression."

He pushed back and slouched against the wall, staring up at the ceiling. "I really suck at this parenting stuff, don't I?"

She gave a muffled laugh. "You don't suck," she said through her tears. She picked up the towel and started picking at the fringe. "I'm not exactly the most likable person in the world either. My dad let me know that every day."

He had a sickening feeling that her dad wasn't the nicest person in the world. Seth had known Richard from high school. A year older than Shelli, he'd been involved in the drama club and had wanted to pursue a career in acting. Unfortunately, things had never panned out for him in California. He'd had several different jobs over the years. Seth wondered if there was something Nicole wasn't telling him.

"You keep saying something that kind of bugs me. What do you mean I'm just like your father? It doesn't sound too complimentary."

She crossed her legs beneath her, fiddling with the corner of the towel. "Let's just say my dad didn't do a whole lot of talking to me either. I know my mom was only sixteen when she had me, and I don't think Dad wanted me." She dabbed at her eyes.

Her earlier reaction to Seth still made his heart ache. He had to know if she'd ever been abused. "Nicole? Did your dad ever hit you?"

Leaning her elbows on her thighs, she lowered her face into the towel. Her silence was answer enough. He felt the sting of moisture behind his own eyes. When she looked up, he asked, "Wanna talk about it?"

"Doesn't matter anyway. It's not like he can do anything to me now."

Seth had to grit his teeth, not at all liking where this was headed. Shelli had never given any indications that this was going on in their home. Had Richard hit her, too? Angered, he tipped his head back against the wall. "I know this must be difficult to talk about, but you can tell me anything. I really do care."

Turning to face him, she let out a big breath and leaned against the backside of the tub. "It all started when I was around ten."

Ten? Almost three years ago? Bile rose in the back of his throat, and he had to force himself to keep from saying anything.

"Dad got a job at some advertising agency, made a whole lot more money than anything he'd ever made before. They sent him on a lot of trips though, so he wasn't home much. And when he did come home, it seemed like him and Mom always ended up arguing." She wiped her eyes again and swallowed. "Anyway, Mom had enrolled me in dance lessons."

"What kind of dance?"

"Ballet and tap. Then I started jazz. That was my favorite." Her voice sounded brighter just talking about it.

"Mom also signed me up for art lessons. I did pretty good in school, and the teacher thought I should take some courses from the local community college."

"Wow. I didn't know. Do you still have some of your work? I'd like to see it."

She shook her head and picked at the towel. "Dad . . . well, he wasn't too thrilled to see all his hard-earned money being poured down the drain on dance tutus and a palette of paint. Or as he'd put it, a bunch of sissy crap for a spoiled little brat that shouldn't have been born in the first place."

Seth sucked air through his teeth. "That must have hurt."

She only shrugged. "I guess, but he was gone so much, I tried not to think about it. I knew Mom loved me, and that was all that mattered."

Hoping to keep her talking, he asked, "Did your dad make you quit your lessons?"

"Not right away. He had to work late most every night, and then when he did get home, he smelled like alcohol and a weird kind of perfume. Mom didn't wear much perfume, and I knew it wasn't hers."

So, the bastard had cheated on Shelli. If Nicole knew, Shelli had to have known, as well. Why hadn't she left him?

"One night, I couldn't sleep and I was up working on a painting that I wanted to enter into a contest at school. He stumbled in late and tripped over the easel. He kind of went berserk."

"What do you mean?"

"He threw everything right out the front door. Dumped the

paints all over the lawn. Even poured it all over my canvases."

Angry, he forced himself to keep his voice level. "What did you do?"

"I yelled at him. Then I told him I hated him." She gave a short laugh. "Daddy didn't put up with any back talk, but when I saw my paintings get ruined, I just started screaming at him."

He was almost afraid to ask. "What did he do?"

She rubbed the back of her hand over her lip. "Smacked me right across the face," she said matter-of-factly. "I probably deserved it, though."

"Did you go to a doctor?"

She shook her head. "It wasn't that bad, and he said he was sorry, and that he'd never hit me again."

"But he did, didn't he?"

"It was only when he drank." As if that made it all okay. "He got mad at the littlest things." She closed her eyes, her lips quivering as if she were trying to keep from letting it all loose.

"Where was your mother when he started doing this to you?"

She swiped at her eyes with the towel. "He only hit me when Mom was at work. If she saw a bruise or anything, Dad said I fell in gym class or some other lie like that."

Seth's gut tightened. Blood surged through his veins on fire. If that bastard hadn't already been dead, Seth would have gone out and strangled him with his bare hands.

He sat forward and cupped his hands around the back of his head, trying to stifle his anger. Right now, Nicole needed comfort, not anger. He wasn't sure he knew how to do that right now. He wasn't a counselor. Maybe he should leave this up to Heather to deal with. What if he said the wrong thing?

He gazed up at this broken girl who was stuck somewhere between a woman and a child. She'd suffered through more traumas in her short lifetime than most people had in their entire lives. Another sickening sensation made his gut churn.

She was developing into a mature young woman. What if her father had done more than beat Nicole?

Although he was afraid to ask, he knew he had to anyway. "Nicole? Did he ever. . . ." He swallowed, not quite sure how to word his question. "Did he ever force himself on you? I mean sexually?"

CHAPTER TEN

Nicole's eyes widened as she backed toward the end of the tub. "Oh, no. It was never like that." Her face reddened as she looked down at the swells of her breasts then crossed her arms over her chest.

"I'm sorry, honey." Seth found himself letting out a sigh of relief. "I didn't mean to make you feel uncomfortable. I just need to know what you've been going through. Did you ever tell anyone? A friend or a teacher?"

She shook her head. "I couldn't. He swore that if I ever told anyone, especially Mom, he'd kill Spike and use him as a hood ornament on his truck." She stared at him with tears in her eyes. "I know you hate him, Uncle Seth, but I couldn't let anything happen to Spike. He's the only real friend I've ever had."

Seth could only sit there with his eyes wide, amazed at the fortitude of this young girl. She'd endured beating after beating from her drunken father, only to save the life of an iguana?

"I never said I hated Spike," he croaked out in a choked voice. "I'm just not overly fond of anything that sticks its tongue out at me every time I come near it. I tend to back off, kind of like when a certain girl rolls her eyes at me every time I try to say something to her."

She rolled her eyes then covered her mouth when she realized what she'd done. "I guess I do that a lot, don't I?"

Not wanting to upset her further, he tried to give her a smile.

"How about you and I start all over from the beginning? We seemed to have gotten off on the wrong foot from the moment I showed up in LA with the Barbie suitcases."

She gave a small snort of laughter.

He took that as a good sign. "What do you say? Should we get out of the bathroom and find us something to eat? Heather gave me the rest of the cookies and sandwiches that were left from our picnic. For some reason she thinks I'm not a very good cook." He slanted his head and gave her a wry grin.

"Uh, I may have made one teeny weenie remark about being sick of pizza."

"You're kidding, right?"

"What do you mean?"

"The only reason I've had so much pizza was because I thought that's the only thing you liked. Believe me, if we keep eating like we have, I'm going to end up with a massive coronary before my thirtieth birthday."

She drew her head back. "Wow, you're that old?" She said it like he was a hundred.

"Hey, now, I've still got a few good years left in me." He was glad to at least see her smile. "Tell you what, let's plan our big shopping day for tomorrow. We'll stop by the grocery store and pick up some real food. Maybe Monday, we'll drive down and visit your great-uncle in Pueblo. Now that you're learning all about horses, maybe you can spend some time down there this summer, too."

Standing, he extended his hand to help her up. She slid her slender fingers into his palm and stepped out of the tub, directly in front of him. For a minute, they both just stared at each other as if meeting each other for the first time.

He squeezed her hand. "Nicole?"

She looked down and swayed nervously back and forth between her feet. "Yeah?"

Touching her chin, he bent his knees slightly to get more at her eye level. "I'm sorry."

She gave a heavy swallow. "Me, too." Her voice cracked as she broke into another sob.

In the next instant, he pulled her tight and wrapped his arms clear around her bony little frame. She was so petite. Her fragile body melted into his arms like a little angel. Then he realized it was the first time she'd permitted him to hug her since she'd come to stay with him. Even at the funeral, she'd only allowed him one quick hug at the cemetery.

He placed a soft kiss on the top of her head, his heart exploding with love and compassion for this child. He knew then and there, he could never let her go. She needed him, and for some reason, he needed her.

She pulled back and wiped her tears. "I got your shirt all wet."

Tugging the tails of his khaki shirt out of his shorts, he wiped her face. "That's okay. It blends in with the water from the stream this afternoon." He lifted up one of his soggy leather boots. "I think my feet are all shriveled up inside."

When she laughed, he stepped back and smiled. "Tell you what. Let's make a deal. I'll try to be here more for you, and you try to treat me more like a friend. Think we can do that?"

Her big green eyes shimmered through a puddle of tears. "Are you going to send me away to school? Or will I get to go to eighth grade here and live with you?"

Should he tell her about Dallas? The only reason he hadn't was because he didn't want to jinx himself and not get the promotion. Now he didn't want to keep anything else from Nicole. "Listen, I need to tell you something. I'm up for a big promotion in the fall. If I get it, it means we'll be moving to Dallas. What would you think about going to school down there?"

"Really? That's, like, in Texas!" she almost squealed.

He laughed, feeling relieved. "You're okay with that, then?"

"I guess. I've never been to Texas."

"Don't completely write off the prep school though. From what my boss says, it's every girl's dream. But it's your choice. I won't do anything without talking to you first, okay? Do you believe me?"

She nodded and wrapped her arms around his waist.

"Umph," he grunted and hugged her again. "You remind me so much of your mother. She was short and petite just like you, and she could hug tighter than a grizzly bear."

She looked up at him and smiled. "You know? You might just make a great dad, Uncle Seth."

"Thanks. That means more to me than you'll ever know." He tapped her nose. "Come on, let's get our stuff from the truck and have some cookies and milk."

"What about your meeting?" she asked, walking side by side with him to the living room.

"I'll reschedule it for next week. I'd rather spend some quality time with my niece tonight."

Her big green eyes widened. "It's really okay if you want to go. I mean, it's only eight-thirty. You could still make it if you hurried. I wouldn't want you blowing it with your boss."

"You sure you wouldn't mind?"

She tilted her head and glanced sideways toward his entertainment center. "As long as I can play your stereo."

He rubbed his chin and groaned. "You're quite the little negotiator, aren't you? I see these two weeks with Heather has rubbed off on you."

"Does that mean you'll let me? I promise, I won't break it. Please, please, please?" she begged, clasping her hands together.

"Okay, just don't crank it up too loud. Old man Doogan next

door can be pretty grumpy. Are you sure you'll be okay here by yourself?"

"Positive. I'll lock the doors as soon as you leave. I'll call Maggie's mom if I need anything."

He glanced at his watch. "Okay, but I won't be long. Call me even if you get scared. I can be home in twenty minutes."

"Okay. But I'll be fine. Remember, I'm almost thirteen."

He scratched his head and squinted his eyes, trying to remember when her birthday was, then snapped his fingers. "June eleventh, right? That's only two weeks away."

"Yep, only two days before Uncle Marty's."

"That's right. Maybe we'll have to pick him up and all go to the Pizza Palace. He loves the big bear band."

"Maybe Heather and her kids could come along."

Knowing that Heather didn't want to see him anymore, at least on a personal level, he simply said, "She's got her own family to take care of, and besides, she's not interested in anything beyond business right now."

"You're kidding, right?" She looked at him as if he'd just grown a third arm. "She's like totally crushing on you."

"Crushing?" he repeated, giving an incredulous laugh. His cheeks actually started to feel warm. "I don't know about that, but for right now, it's just you and me, kid. Think we can be a family?"

She looked down and nodded less than enthusiastically. "Yeah. I guess."

He touched her chin. "Hey, don't sound so happy."

"I'm sorry, it's just that I really like Heather. She's pretty cool, for an old chick," she clarified.

Knowing Heather was probably younger than he, Seth tipped his head back and laughed. "Don't let her hear you say that." He glanced at his watch. "Listen, I need to change. Then, you'll be on your own. Do you want me to show you how to work the

CD and DVD player?" He couldn't help but notice the little grin that swept across Nicole's face when she eyed his stereo again.

"Mitch has one just like it. He showed me how to use it last week. If I have problems, I'll just call him."

Seth smiled. If playing with his stereo was all it took to make an almost-teenager happy, then by all means, let her have at it.

If only it was that easy with a certain camp counselor. But for some reason, bribing Heather with any kind of electronic equipment probably wasn't going to win her heart. And judging from the kind of jewelry she'd worn at the auction, he guessed Eric himself had done more than his share of bribery over the years.

Frustrated with where things had ended up between him and Heather, he headed into his bedroom and shut his door. Distance. That's what he needed between them right now. Nowhere did a divorced mother of two kids fit into his plans. Now, if he could just convince his heart she didn't belong there, either.

Sitting at her office desk at the ranch, Heather flipped through the mail she'd brought from home. She practically held her breath, looking for an envelope from McLaughlin and Smith, the law firm of Eric's attorney. Two weeks had passed since she'd run into Eric at the hospital where he'd told her he wanted Kyle reevaluated, and that he wanted to petition for custody of Katie. But so far, no one had tried to contact her.

Thank you, God, she breathed in relief, dumping the pile of mail off to the side. Maybe her lawyer and Seth had been right, and Eric was just bluffing. She should know better than anyone, Eric's word was about as dependable as wet toilet paper.

Staring down at a large calendar desk mat, Heather noticed it had also been two weeks since the hiking excursion into the mountains with Seth. She wrote his name on that Saturday's date, tracing and retracing his name, realizing how much she'd actually missed talking with him every day.

True to his word, he'd backed off and hadn't made any further personal advances since their hiking trip. Other than a nod or an occasional smile when he'd picked up Nicole and dropped her off, Seth had been dealing with Nicole's new counselors and hadn't even made an attempt to talk to Heather.

She doodled a heart around his name, knowing that deep down, she'd kind of hoped he would have pursued her a little more, the way he'd done before their hiking trip . . . before he'd discovered she was a divorced mother with two young children.

Despite how things had turned out between them, remembering their hike into the mountains always made her smile. Even though he'd never said anything, she'd peeked in his picnic basket when they were unloading everything into her van and found Italian bread, cheese, health-store granola bars and several bottles of water. He'd even thrown in a beautiful red-and-black afghan and a bottle of white wine. She'd lay odds the wine hadn't come from the local grocery store.

Now she realized he'd never even brought it out of his SUV. He'd eaten peanut-butter sandwiches along with the rest of them, drinking grape juice and pretending they were the best things since the invention of chocolate.

Heather leaned an elbow on her desk and slumped into her hand. If truth be told, he was probably relieved to be let off the hook. This way he didn't have to live with the guilt of breaking it off with her.

Ice clinking drew her attention to her sister-in-law sitting at the desk behind Heather. She craned her neck around and smiled. Dressed in maternity shorts and a cotton maternity top, Debra sat slouched in a cushioned office chair with her bare feet up on the desk fanning her face.

"Gee, Debra, are you hot?" Heather asked with an amused smile.

"Honey, I'd be hot in the middle of Antarctica. I don't know if I can hang on another month."

"Don't rush it. That baby will be here before you know it. Then your days of putting up your feet are over. Treasure these last few weeks of quiet."

"Did Joshua tell you he's driving me to my doctor's appointment this afternoon? We should be home by five-thirty. We're down to our two-week checkups."

Heather shook her head. "I don't remember him saying anything, but it shouldn't be a problem. Is he still taking Kyle to the Colorado Rockies baseball game tomorrow afternoon?"

Frowning, Debra glanced down at her calendar. "I don't think he remembered. He and I planned on going to Boulder for a sale."

The front door swung open and J.D. sauntered in. "How's my two favorite girls doing this afternoon?" He threw his straw Stetson cowboy hat on a rack of antlers hanging on the wall and took three determined strides toward his very pregnant wife.

He planted a noisy kiss on her lips then affectionately rubbed her bulging belly. "How's it goin' in there, lil' fella?"

Debra rested her hand over J.D.'s and smiled. "I think I may have a steer wrestler in the makings. He's determined to jab me in every quadrant of my stomach."

J.D. chuckled, his eyes sparkling with his new title of expectant father. "Let me wash up and I'll be ready to take you to your appointment."

"By the way," Debra said with a grunt as she brought her legs down to the floor and sat forward. "Did you promise to take Kyle to the baseball game tomorrow afternoon?"

J.D. stood back and shoved his hand on his waist. "Oh, man. I forgot all about that. I already told Mr. Wilkes we'd be up around three to look at his mare."

Heather raised her hand. "Don't worry about it. I'll see if I can take him. Maybe another time?"

"Count on it. I'll try to bring something back for him from the sale," J.D. added, helping Debra to her feet.

Debra motioned her head toward the kitchen while holding her lower back. "I set the cupcakes you wanted for Nicole's birthday on the counter. Tell her we're sorry we'll miss her party."

"I will, and thanks for making them. I'll lock up after everyone leaves. Brad and Mom went up to Denver for the weekend. They're helping at a church social at her sister's parish, then they're going to a play and staying overnight. I swear, those two are like a couple of honeymooners, even after twelve years of marriage."

"Keep the faith, sis." J.D. gazed into his wife's eyes. "Love will find you again, too." Glancing down at Heather's doodles on her calendar, he grinned. "If it hasn't found you already." He gave a knowing wink then helped Debra out the front door.

Feeling a hot rush of blood to her cheeks, Heather grabbed a pen and quickly scribbled through Seth's name. She never could hide anything from J.D.

The front door swung wide, and Jillian Stone—or Jillie, as she liked to be called—peeked her head in the door. She was a perky, twenty-two-year-old psychology major. She had cropped blonde hair and at least six earrings pierced through both ears. Always dressed in wild colors, it was easy to see why all the girls loved her. Their other two counselors, Hannah and Stephanie, were more of the rugged horsewomen type whose wardrobes mainly consisted of frayed jeans and a tank top. All the girls were equally attractive in their own light, which had Jared stopping by the ranch a few extra times—to check on the horses, of course.

"Heather?" Jillie stepped in the door. "Do you want us to start on the nature poster?"

Glancing at her watch, Heather nodded. "Yeah, it's only three o'clock. That should give us time to clean up before the campers have to leave for the weekend. I'm getting ready to bring the cupcakes out to surprise Nicole. Make sure everyone's around."

"Okay, but we need more glue. We're down to half a bottle."

"I'll bring some out when I bring the cupcakes. Have you seen Kyle?"

"I saw him down at the corral sitting on the fence. He said he was waiting for J.D. to take him riding."

Heather cringed. J.D. must have forgotten to tell Kyle he had to leave early today because of Debra's appointment. "See if you can get him to come up for the birthday party. I'll be out in a minute."

After rummaging through the craft closet, Heather found a large bottle of glue, then went to the kitchen where she grabbed a tray full of cupcakes. It was a good thing Debra had made them because the last batch of cupcakes Heather had made had been burnt to a crisp and thrown to the potbellied pig in the petting zoo.

She put a candle in the middle of one and strode outside to join Jillie and the other campers at the picnic table near the playground. She glanced down at the barn and found Kyle, still perched on the fence. "Didn't Kyle want to come up?"

Jillie shook her head. "He didn't answer. He just sat there, staring at all the horses."

High-pitched giggling drew her attention back to Nicole and a little girl her own age. Chloe was thirteen and of African-American descent, and had been diagnosed with leukemia when she was ten. She'd been in remission for the last year. To watch her smile and fill the camp with her laughter, no one would ever guess the kind of pain she'd had to endure.

Stepping up behind the twosome, Heather set the bottle of glue between them, and then presented the tray of cupcakes to Nicole. "Happy lucky thirteen, Nicole, one day early." She started a chorus of "Happy Birthday," and everyone joined in with them. When the song ended, Heather gripped Nicole's shoulder from behind and leaned close to the side of her face. "Okay, honey, make a wish."

Nicole closed her eyes and held her breath for what seemed like several moments. As much as she'd suffered over the last several months, Heather couldn't help but wonder what she was wishing for today.

Chloe nudged Nicole's shoulder. "Hurry up. Wax is dripping all over." Both girls giggled as Nicole blew out her candle. Everyone clapped and chowed down on their confections.

Heather reached between the girls and picked up a poster filled with drawings of the ranch and some of the animals. "Wow, you two have made a wonderful poster together. We'll have to display it up in the camp office for all the parents to see."

Nicole turned quiet, then looked up at Jillie. "May I use the restroom?"

"Sure, but hurry. We've only got about forty-five minutes before it's time to go."

As soon as she ran off, Heather realized what she'd said about displaying their posters for their parents. She walked around to Jillie and pulled her aside. "I could kick myself for being so insensitive."

Jillie watched as Nicole slammed the bathroom door. "I don't know. I think there's something bothering her. At times she's laughing and having a great time, but then out of the blue, she clams up and doesn't want to be around anybody."

"Maybe I can have a talk with her before she leaves tonight."

"Might be a good idea," Jillie agreed, cleaning up the craft table. "Has she ever talked to you about her parents?"

Heather shook her head. "Other than the first day, she's never really shown any emotion. She and Seth might be having troubles, too. Maybe I can find a way to reach her."

Jillie's expression turned ornery as she elbowed Heather in the arm. "I'd love to find a way to reach her uncle. He makes all my college friends look like high school kids."

Inwardly agreeing, Heather gave a nervous laugh and picked up a cupcake. "I guess he's kind of cute if you go for the rich, powerful, executive type." She took a bite, knowing that was exactly the type she should be avoiding right now.

"Nicole says he's up for a big promotion at work. If he gets it, they're moving to Dallas."

"Dallas?" Heather about choked on the cake. "I hadn't heard. I mean, I knew he wanted a promotion, but I had no idea it was in Dallas."

Was Seth really moving to Texas? She glanced down just as Nicole entered her cabin. Heather swallowed the lump of cake and licked her fingers. "Keep an eye on Kyle, will you? I'll be right back."

She strode down and tapped at the cabin door. When no one answered, she peeked her head in the crack. "Nicole? Can I come in?"

"It's your camp," she retorted.

That didn't sound good. Heather warily stepped inside and strode over to Spike's tank, lifted the lid and reached her hand in and stroked his back. He really was a cute little guy in a weird sort of way.

She replaced the lid and warily turned to face Nicole who was lying on the bottom bunk on her side, facing the wall. Heather approached and braced a hand on the top bunk, staring down at her. "I'm sorry if I upset you earlier when I talked about showing your posters to the parents. I don't know what I was thinking."

Nicole lifted her shoulders. "Doesn't matter."

Heather pulled a wooden rocking chair next to the bed and sat down. "Sure it does. It's difficult not having your mom and dad to share things with. I think that's one of the things I missed most when my dad was killed. He never got to see all the things I could do, all the accomplishments I'd made."

Rolling on her back, Nicole stared at the underneath side of the top bunk. "My dad didn't either. He was always on the road. Too busy."

"What about your dance recitals? Did he ever see you perform?"

She dabbed at her nose and sniffed. "Only once." A tear rolled down her cheek. She swallowed and closed her eyes.

Heather braced her elbows on her knees and leaned closer. "What is it, Nicole? Will you talk to me?"

"I don't know. It's just so hard."

"Ahh, sweetie. I know it's hard." Heather whisked a strawberry blonde curl off Nicole's forehead. "Sometimes thinking about it and keeping things stored up is the hard part. It might make you feel better if you get it out in the open."

Nicole's voice was barely over a murmur when she finally spoke. "It was all my fault."

"What was all your fault?"

She closed her eyes and whispered, "Their accident."

Heather frowned. "Why do you think it was all your fault? You weren't even in the car."

"Yeah, but if it weren't for me, they'd have been home and wouldn't have been in an accident at all."

"Can you tell me what happened that night? Where were they going?"

Nicole gave a heavy swallow. "I had a big dance recital at seven. I was the lead dancer in one of the performances, so I

207

asked Daddy to come watch me. He didn't want to, of course, but Mom and I begged him. He'd never seen me dance before."

An emotional stab of pain wrenched Heather's stomach, as she feared what must have happened next. "Did he get to see you dance, honey?"

"Yeah. I even got my teacher to reserve the front two middle seats so he'd have the best view in the theater."

Heather gave a small smile of relief knowing Nicole's father had at least been there, but still couldn't understand why Nicole thought their accident was her fault. "What happened after the recital?"

"Mom came backstage and brought me flowers. Said they were from my dad." She swiped the tears from her face. "I know Mom got them. She just said that to make me think he actually cared."

"Oh, honey, of course he cared about you."

She rolled her eyes, forcing more tears down her cheeks. "Then why did he always leave Mom and me alone so much? Why was he always going out to those stupid bars? Why did he . . . ?" She choked on her words and rolled away from Heather, facing the wall.

Why did he what?

Sensing a breakthrough, Heather had to keep her talking. "So, your mom brought you roses, then what?"

Her voice came out muffled as she spoke into her pillow. "A bunch of my friends were having a sleepover, but Dad said I couldn't go. He didn't like any of my friends."

"Did you go?"

She wiped her eyes with the sheet. "Yes."

"Did you tell your mother?"

She paused and lowered her voice. "Not exactly."

"What do you mean, not exactly?"

Sitting up, she hugged the pillow to her chest. "There was

also this post party for all the dancers and their families, but Mom said we couldn't go because Daddy was waiting out in the car." Her voice always took on a cynical air when she talked about her father. "Anyway, I told her I would get a ride home with one of the teachers, only I didn't go home."

"Where did you go?"

"I told my friend I could come to the sleepover."

"I bet your mom and dad must have been worried when you didn't come home."

Tears coursed down her freckle-covered cheeks. "Don't you see? That's why they were killed. They were out looking for me. If I'd have gone home with them, they wouldn't have gotten into that stupid accident. My mom would still be alive."

"Oh, honey." Heather leaned over her and gave her a heartfelt hug. She wasn't sure what to say to this girl. How could she assure her that it was not her fault?

She reminded Heather so much of herself as a young girl. After her father's plane crash, she'd held herself responsible for his death, reasoning that if she'd been with him, helping him navigate, he would have been able to set down safely. Of course, now she knew she couldn't have prevented it, and she probably would have been killed herself had she been with him.

But she also remembered how everyone had tried to convince her it hadn't been her fault. Until she'd come to that realization on her own, it hadn't done any good to tell her otherwise.

She drew apart and stroked her fingers over Nicole's arm. "Sweetie, you can't blame yourself for something you had no control over. It was an accident. I know it's hard to understand when things like this happen, but you have to let it go or it'll eat you up inside. No matter why they were in that car, it doesn't matter. You have to trust that God was in control that night when He took your parents."

Several car doors slammed, and Heather could hear the rest

of the campers being picked up for the day. She glanced at her watch. Almost five. Seth had picked up Nicole every night around five-thirty. Even though they'd made a huge break-through, Heather didn't want him finding his niece in tears. She still had a lot of healing to do before the summer was out.

Hoping to lighten her mood, Heather reached out and rubbed her arm. "Hey, I've got an idea."

Nicole rolled over and gazed up at her through reddened, puffy eyes. "What?"

Heather grabbed a box of tissues and handed them to her. Turning thirteen was a huge deal in the Garrison family. Becoming a teenager was always marked with a big outing with their mom. Although no one could ever replace Nicole's mother, Heather wanted to give this girl something to remember.

She sat back and smiled. "How about you and me do a little birthday shopping?"

"Really?" She sniffed and wiped her eyes with a tissue. "You mean, like in a mall and everything?"

Heather laughed. "You bet. We'll take Katie and go to lunch. Make it a girl's day out. How's that sound?"

"I'd love to go shopping with you and Katie. I might be need-ing some new clothes anyway if I'm going to a boarding school this fall."

Heather drew her head back in surprise. "Seth's sending you to a boarding school?"

"Well, he said it was up to me, but he's supposed to be get-ting this big promotion at work, and then we'll be moving to Dallas. I'm guessing he'll be busier than ever and would rather I went away to school anyway. That way he won't have to worry about me being alone all the time."

So, what Jillie said was true. A tight knot of tension coiled in her stomach at the thought of Seth and Nicole moving away. "What do you want to do?"

Nicole shrugged, looking down and shredding her tissues. "I don't know. The brochures looked pretty cool and everything. I guess Seth's boss has a daughter my age that loves it. I'd get to ride horses there, too, but I don't know. I just can't decide. Everything's so confusing right now."

"You've been through a lot, honey. Don't feel like you have to make a decision today."

"I know. Uncle Seth said the same thing." She flipped on her side, bracing her elbow on the bed. "I can see why he likes you. You're so easy to talk to."

Feeling an unwanted blush creep up her face, Heather stood and began straightening the covers on the top bunk bed. "Yes, your uncle has been very kind this summer, and I must say, very prompt. He hasn't been late in two weeks."

"No, I mean he totally likes you, Heather. Can't you tell? He's always watching you whenever he picks me up."

Heather fluffed the pillow, hoping to hide the giddiness spreading through her limbs. "I think you're imagining things, sweetie. He hasn't spoken but a few words to me since our hiking trip."

"Yeah, but isn't that because you told him you didn't want to see him?"

Heather smoothed her hand over the pink quilt. "I may have given him that impression," she conceded, flipping the quilt over the top of the pillow. "But it's because big things are happening with his career. He can't be bogged down with a woman who has so many responsibilities. I'm not like all his other girlfriends."

"What other girlfriends?"

"Oh, you know what I mean."

"Hmph, I think he took a woman to the Ice Capades at the Broadmoor last weekend, but other than that, Uncle Seth told me he hasn't been serious with anyone since last summer." She grabbed her backpack and slung it over her shoulder. "Actually, from the few weeks I've lived with him, he's been pretty cool. He even bought me a whole bedroom set and took me to Pueblo to visit his uncle Cyrus."

"That's wonderful. How'd that go?"

"Pretty good. I even got to ride one of the Arabians. It was awesome. He said I could come back and visit anytime I wanted."

A loud whinny from the stables jolted Heather's attention toward the barn. "What was that all about?" Her cowboy boots clomped noisily on the hardwood floor as she trotted across the cabin and stared out the door toward the stables.

Kyle had taken off his bandages and had caught Evening Star, J.D.'s black gelding quarter horse. Kyle held the leather headstall, trying to slide it over Evening Star's head. The horse snorted and pranced backwards, almost stepping on Kyle's foot.

"Kyle! Wait!" Heather hollered as she sprinted off toward the barn. "You can't force it!"

When she neared the fence, she hoisted herself over the top and hopped down on the other side. "You know you're not supposed to do this by yourself, young man. You could have been hurt!"

"Do it alone!" he said, yanking Evening Star's head.

She grabbed hold of the lead rope and Kyle's arm at the same time. "Let go of the bridle, Kyle. You can't force the headstall on." She took hold of the leather straps and rubbed the horse's muzzle. "Easy, boy. Calm down."

She took a deep breath, straightened the bridle and carefully slipped the metal bit into the horse's mouth. He chewed several times and snorted, adjusting to the tack. "Good boy. That's it." She buckled the leather strap loosely behind his ears.

"Do it alone," Kyle repeated.

She reached down and took hold of his hands, examining his

burns. The skin was still red, but the blisters were almost healed. "You need to be careful with your hands. You don't want to make them worse."

"Ride Evening Star."

Knowing it did no good to argue with her son, she headed over to the tack barn and grabbed Kyle's saddle along with a red-and-brown saddle blanket and his riding helmet. "I'll finish saddling him then you can walk him around the arena like you do with J.D. But you have to promise you won't come in here by yourself again."

"Not a baby," he retorted.

She hoisted the saddle over the horse's back, situating it over the blanket. "I know you're not a baby, Kyle, but riding a horse is a big responsibility. You know the rules. No riding alone, and there has to be an adult to supervise. Those are the rules for all the kids who attend this camp, not just for you. Now come over here, and I'll give you a leg up."

After adjusting his helmet, Kyle shoved his foot into the stirrup and tugged on the saddle horn, hoisting himself clear up on top of the big black. For a minute Kyle just sat there with his eyes closed, then he leaned over and wrapped his arms around Evening Star's neck. It was one of the few times he'd ever shown that kind of emotion.

Heather rubbed Kyle's leg. "I think Evening Star likes you. What's he saying?"

Without looking at her, Kyle pulled himself upright and grabbed the reins. He nudged the flanks of the horse with his boots and clicked his tongue. Holding onto the lead rope, Heather fell into step next to Evening Star as he plodded through the dusty arena at an easy walking gait. His head bobbed up and down as he snorted several times to clear his nostrils.

She reached out and patted the horse's neck. "How's it going with the new kids here at camp? Have you made any new friends?"

He only stared down at Evening Star's head with his normal blank expression. She hated when he turned into himself like this. It was hard to tell what he was thinking. She kept speaking anyway. "Nicole sure likes playing with you. She says you're the champ at Go Fish."

She continued to walk around the large fenced-in paddock, the sun bearing down hot this mid-June afternoon. She tugged her flannel shirt off and draped it over the fence then adjusted her tank top to catch a few sunrays.

"Guess what? I'm taking you and Katie to the baseball game tomorrow. J.D. and Debra have a sale, so I get to go have all the fun. How's that sound? I can't wait to get a hot dog."

"Faster."

"Okay, but keep it at an easy trot." She picked up her step and stayed beside Kyle, still holding onto the lead rope.

"No. By myself," he demanded, his face turning red with anger.

Not wanting to spur her son into a tantrum, she slowed Evening Star to a stop and patted his neck. She'd seen J.D. let Kyle walk his horse alone a few times. Maybe Kyle would be okay for a few minutes. She reached up and unhooked the lead rope and stared into her son's stony expression. "I've seen you ride before, so I know you can handle him. Just don't jerk him too fast. Okay? I'll be right here if you need help."

Reluctantly, Heather backed away. Kyle clicked his tongue and started at a nice easy trot. Evening Star's gait held an even rhythm as Kyle posted like a professional, even cueing lead changes in the corners. They circled several times around the arena, and Heather found herself relaxing her shoulders, seeing her son for the first time as a responsible little boy. Maybe she'd been too overprotective and needed to let out the reins herself where her son was concerned. When she was his age, she'd been out riding the trails all by herself.

She stepped out of the way as Kyle nudged Evening Star into a faster canter. Heather practically held her breath as he rounded the paddock like a pro, gentling Evening Star into long, even strides.

"Good job!" Heather yelled as he rode by in front of her. His eyes filled with expression, almost twinkling, unlike the blank stare he usually had. "Not any faster. You're doing great!"

Heather smiled at the accomplishment he'd achieved over the last several years. It showed in his posture as he sat tall in the saddle like a real cowboy.

Gently kicking the horse, he urged it into a quicker-paced gallop. Heather's heart about jumped out of her chest. He leaned over and rode gracefully, holding tight to the reins. As he whisked by, it was as if he'd been transported into a different realm of the universe, totally oblivious to her or anything around them.

"Kyle! Pull back on the reins!" She waved her arms as he galloped past her, spurring his horse faster. "No, Kyle! Slow down!"

But Kyle continued to barrel around the arena. She jumped back to the fence as he rode Evening Star faster and harder. Heather could only watch, mortified as he sat forward, allowing his horse to do all the work. Dirt clods spewed from behind as the horse churned the dry dusty soil.

"Kyle! Hold up! Bring him to a halt!"

As if something clicked, he pulled back gently on the reins, easing into a canter, then a fast trot, then finally slowing down to an even walking gait.

With her chest heaving, she charged across the corral and caught up with the horse and rider, both breathing heavily. Evening Star snorted, prancing anxiously from his exercise session.

Heather reached up and patted the panting beast. "Whoa, boy. Take it easy." She glared up at her son, who stared off into the ranch yard. "What was that all about? This arena is too small to go that fast. What if you'd been thrown? Or what if something had happened to Evening Star? What do you think J.D. would have done?"

Kyle stared down at his saddle.

"If he finds out what you've done tonight, he may not even let you ride him again. Is that what you want?"

Swinging his foot over the saddle horn, Kyle hopped down, standing almost face to chest with her. When had he gotten so big? She took hold of his hands and cringed. A trace of blood tinged his palms from holding onto the leather reins so tight.

With her adrenaline still surging through her veins, she handed him the lead rope. "You need to walk the horse around to cool him down. That's part of your responsibility. Then we need to put some salve on your hands. We don't want to get them infected."

He brushed by her, ignoring her. She grabbed hold of his arm and spoke through gritted teeth. "Kyle. Don't you dare walk away from me. You need to take care of the horse, then he'll need to be unsaddled and groomed before letting him out into the paddock."

Kyle shook his head. "You do it!"

Heather gripped his hand and curled his fingers around the lead rope. "If you want to show me how grown up you are, then you have to take care of your horse. Now, march!"

"No!" Then he bolted out of the coral, slinging the rope at her as he ran off.

The metal clip caught her in the eye. She gasped and clamped her hand over her face. Pain seared her eye. Blood trickled down the edge of her brow bone. She doubled over at the waist, but the pain in her eye was far outweighed by the torment at not being able to control her own son. She loved him with all of her heart, but this constant rejection and his inability to love tore at the most inner fibers of her being.

Evening Star snorted and nudged his head into Heather's side. She grabbed hold of his halter and tugged herself upright, holding the gentle beast in her arms. "Thank you for taking care of my son," she whispered with a trembly voice.

The familiar low rumble of Seth's Corvette sped up the lane toward the house. Squinting through what felt like a swollen eye, she quickly wiped her face and led the big black toward the stables. She didn't want Seth seeing her like this. Hopefully, he'd pick up Nicole and leave like he'd been doing for the past two weeks.

She led Evening Star inside the barn and put him into an empty stall. Storming over to the utility sink in the corner, she found a clean rag and wetted it under the cold running spray. Squeezing the excess water into the sink, she gingerly placed the cool compress over her eye, soothing the swollen socket as well as her exhaustion.

She braced a hand on the edge of the sink and bowed her head between her shoulders. *Dear God, help me with my son. I don't know what to do anymore, who to turn to. Please, tell me what to do.*

"You okay?" Seth's familiar baritone sounded from behind, near the entrance of the barn. "Nicole said you were having some trouble with Kyle. Can I help?"

CHAPTER ELEVEN

"I can handle Kyle," Heather assured Seth, keeping her back to him. "He just didn't want to quit for the day. I think he'd ride his horse from morning till night if I'd let him." She tried to sound lighthearted, but her voice sounded scratchy.

His steps through the straw became louder as he approached her from behind. "You sound winded. You sure you're okay?"

"Just a little hot. This cool compress hits the spot." She cleared her throat and tossed the rag into the sink. Turning opposite from him, she stepped quickly to the stall where Evening Star stood and began unsaddling him. "I told Nicole I'd take her shopping for her birthday. I hope that's okay."

"Sure. That'd be great. I'll have a credit card authorized for her to use anytime she needs something."

"I think she's out behind the cabins cleaning up some crafts. I'll see you Monday." She hoisted the heavy Western pleasure saddle down from the tall horse.

"I thought maybe we could talk. It's been a couple of weeks. How's Nicole doing?"

Keeping her head low, Heather carried the saddle to the tack room, feeling the weight of it banging against her thigh. She spoke over her shoulder as she arranged the saddle over a barrel. "Nicole finally opened up to me tonight. Maybe we could meet next week and talk about it when we have more time."

She adjusted the straps and folded the cinch, stalling mostly, hoping Seth would just leave her alone. The last thing she wanted was for this man to see how incompetent she was at parenting. It might make him question her skills as a counselor, though at this point, she had her own concerns. Maybe she just wasn't cut out for this.

"I'm in no hurry, if you want to talk now," he said, standing in the doorway behind her. "Is there anything wrong?"

"No, she's actually doing pretty good. Maybe we can get together on Monday." She yanked her baseball cap low over her forehead and brushed her hands on her thighs. With her head down, she shouldered past him, leaving him standing in the doorway.

He didn't answer as he followed her back to the stall with Evening Star. She slid the bridle off and brushed by Seth, avoiding any eye contact. Why wouldn't he just leave her alone like he'd done all week?

She stepped into the tack room and swung the bridle up on a hook. When she turned around to leave, she ran into a broad set of chest muscles. Her hat brim bumped his shirt. Keeping her head down, she grimaced and pressed her hands on his tailored dress shirt, his heart pounding heavily under her palms.

"Heather?" he said sternly, but gently. "Why won't you look at me?"

The lump in her throat made it hard to breathe. "Please, just go," she barely whispered. "I don't need this right now."

"Need what? What's wrong, honey?"

God, she loved it when he used such sweet endearments with her. But she couldn't keep dragging him into her problems. She shook her head. "Nothing. I need to go check on Kyle."

"He was on the swings with Katie and Nicole when I came down. Has something happened? You sound like you've been crying." He took her wrists and slouched down below the brim of her hat. She closed her eyes avoiding his intense gaze.

"My God, Heather. Your eye." He pulled her hat all the way

219

off and dumped it on a saddle behind her. "It's almost swollen shut. What happened?"

She twisted free from his grip and strode over toward the horse and grabbed the lead rope. "It was an accident. I'll be fine. I just need some ice."

He jogged in front of her and opened the corral gate. She unclipped the rope and sent Evening Star into the paddock toward the automatic watering system. The gate swung shut with a loud clank, then the rustling of chains as Seth latched the fence. Without waiting, she took long determined strides up the ranch yard toward the house.

Seth jogged up beside her. "Are you here alone?"

She shook her head. "Jillie's still here. You can probably find her in the girls' cabin. I'll call you next week. If you'll excuse me?" She pushed through the office doors and made her way into the kitchen.

Seth followed, undeterred.

She yanked open the freezer and pulled out an ice pack, grabbed a towel, then wrapped it up and placed it gingerly over her eye. She rounded the corner to the bathroom and removed the cold compress to take a peek in the mirror.

A black shadow already surrounded her socket. The lid had almost completely sealed shut. Seth's hand covered her lower back as she tried to assess the damage. She forced a short laugh. "You should see the other guy."

His hand tightened around her waist as he caught her gaze in the mirror. "Who was the other guy, Heather?"

"I told you. It was an accident. When Kyle finished riding, he tossed me the rope and I caught it with my eye."

"Let me take a look. Turn around and sit on the counter."

She lowered her shoulders and blew out a quivery breath. "You're not going to leave till you do, are you?"

"Nope. So be a good girl and let me help you."

He turned her around and helped her sit up on the counter. Gently gripping her chin between his thumb and forefinger, he tipped her head back. "Can you open your eyes?"

She tried to open both eyes, but she could only see through one. He stood so close his thighs brushed into her knees, his musk aroma wafting into her senses. He'd taken off his tie and unbuttoned the top two buttons of his dress shirt. The sleeves were rolled up to his elbows.

Her heart beat a little faster as his fingers, soft and smooth, touched the side of her face. "This might hurt," he warned, then proceeded to part the swollen tissue surrounding her eye.

She winced and grabbed his forearm, which felt strong and firm. "Yeah, it definitely hurts."

He examined her eye closer. "It doesn't look like there are any blood vessels damaged."

The warmth of his breath washed over her face. She breathed deeply, enjoying the smell of cinnamon. "You know, your teeth are going to rot, the way you eat so much candy," she teased as he continued to poke and prod.

He slid his palms over the side of her cheeks. "Do you see any lightning bolts or have any sharp shooting pains?"

"No, it just feels like a baseball got shoved into my socket. How'd you get to be such an expert on black eyes?"

He chuckled but didn't answer her question.

"Got any antiseptic? Looks like the skin is broken above your brow. Must be where the metal clip hit you. I don't think you'll need stitches."

She rummaged through the medicine cabinet and found a bottle of peroxide and a cotton ball. She let out a sigh of frustration and sat back on the counter allowing him to minister her wound. He soaked the cotton ball and dabbed it over the cut. She winced, sucking air through her teeth, but it was her pride that hurt more than anything.

"Ouch!" She grimaced, pulling back. "I think it'll be okay. I just need to ice it down."

He gripped the counter on each side of her thighs and gazed into her face. "Wanna tell me what happened? It looks like you've been crying. Is it more than just your black eye?"

"No. It was just an accident."

"Where's J.D.? Doesn't he usually give the riding lessons?"

"Yes, but he had to take Debra to her doctor's appointment."

"So, he left you here alone with twelve campers plus your two kids?"

"Most of them have already been picked up, and besides, I wasn't alone. I've got three college graduates helping me, as well as three parent volunteers. And I'm perfectly capable of teaching my own son how to ride a horse, thank you. I've ridden horses since I was old enough to hold up my head."

He pressed his hands on her thighs, moving closer. "So, are you through here for the day, then?"

She scooted back and bumped into the mirror on the wall. Once again, it seemed his blue eyes cast a spell over her and she found it hard to breathe. How did she always manage to find herself in these kinds of predicaments with Seth?

She squared her shoulders and pulled away from his penetrating gaze. "I can go just as soon as you and Nicole leave. She's out back with Jillie." Slipping him an ornery grin, she added, "Jillie thinks you're pretty hot, by the way. You'd be better off putting all this energy into a single, young, college graduate."

"I'm not interested, and you're in no shape to drive. I'm taking you and your kids home. We'll grab something to eat on the way, maybe even rent a movie. How's that sound?"

"It sounds like you've completely gone over the brink. Why would you want to spend a Friday night being cooped up in a small condo eating pizza and watching a Disney video with a bunch of kids?"

"Because I like your kids and I've been wanting to find out if the Little Mermaid gets her tail back in the sequel. I watched the first one when Nicole was two. I've been trying to come up with an excuse to rent it. What do you say? It's my treat."

He lowered to her mouth, but she pressed back against the mirror. "Don't you have a date or a meeting to go to?"

"I do have a meeting, but I'll just call and reschedule."

"You? Reschedule a meeting?" She shook her head and swung her legs to the side, trying to brush by him. "Thanks, but that's really not necessary. I'll be fine. If I have to, I'll have J.D. drive me home. He should be back any minute. Jared can bring me out tomorrow to get my van."

"Heather!" Nicole charged into the house. "Katie's hurt!"

"Oh, no. Now what?" Heather slid to the floor and followed Seth who was already halfway out the door. They rounded the backside of the house and found Katie hunched under the swings holding her arm and screaming.

"Did you see what happened?" Seth asked Nicole. His concern for Heather's daughter rang apparent in his voice.

"I'm not sure. I was in my cabin with Jillie. When I came out Katie was under the swing crying." As they all approached the playground, Jillie was there huddled next to Katie. Kyle's backside disappeared into the house. Heather cringed. Was Kyle somehow responsible for this, too?

Seth hunkered down next to Katie. "Hey, sweetheart, take it easy," he soothed. "Will you let Uncle Seth take a look?"

"No. Mommy!" she cried, keeping her arm huddled close to her stomach.

Heather dropped to her knees and touched Katie's shoulders. "Is it just your arm? Nothing else hurts?"

"No. I think it's broken!"

Heather's heart suddenly surged into overdrive. She'd never experienced a broken bone before. "Let me see. Maybe it's just bruised." Katie squealed the moment Heather tried to move it. The skin hadn't been pierced, but she couldn't move her fingers without screaming.

Remaining outwardly calm, she wrapped her arms around Katie and gave her a gentle hug. "It's going to be okay. Can you stand?"

She shook her head, crying and rocking with her arm in her lap. "Kyle pushed me, Mommy! He's such a bully. I hate him!"

Heather's heart lunged to her stomach, afraid her suspicions were right about Kyle. "Katie. You don't hate him. I'll talk with him later. Right now we need to get you to the hospital. They'll make your arm feel all better." She looked up at Seth. "Can I borrow your phone?"

He unclipped it from his belt and handed it to her. "Why don't you let me take you into the emergency room? Kyle can stay with Nicole and me until you're through."

She held up her hand and shook her head as she dialed J.D.'s number. "J.D.'s the only one who can calm Kyle down when he's like this." She just hoped J.D. was on his way home.

"Yeah, this is J.D."

"How soon before you and Debra get home?"

"Heather? What's wrong?"

"It's Katie. She may have broken her arm."

"We're coming down the road now."

She breathed a sigh of relief. "Can I leave Kyle with you? I don't know how long I'll be at the hospital."

"No problem. We'll be there in five minutes."

She hung up and handed the phone back to Seth. "J.D. will be here any minute. He said Kyle can stay with him and Debra."

"I'll stay, too, if you want," Jillie added.

"Thanks, but that's really not necessary. I need you to run into the kitchen and grab a large towel. We'll use it as a sling to keep her arm immobilized against her body."

"Got it. Anything else?"

"Yeah. Pull the van over near the playground. The keys are in it."

"I'll get it," Seth intervened, already on his feet.

Jillie turned. "I'll be right back with a towel."

Nicole touched Heather's shoulder. "I'll go stay with Kyle till J.D. gets here."

"Thanks, sweetie. That would be a great help."

Jillie was back with a towel in seconds, followed swiftly by Seth after he'd moved the van closer to the playground.

With Seth's help, they managed to wrap Katie's arm in a sling. She was still crying, but had calmed down to a low whimper. Heather's heart was thumping so hard her chest started to hurt. She swept a few wispy brown tendrils behind Katie's ears. "Let's see if I can carry you to the van. You're getting to be such a big girl."

"Please, let me carry her for you." Seth slanted Katie an ornery grin. "I promise I'll try not to drop you in any horse apples." He carefully scooped her tiny body into his big brawny arms and stood. Her crying softened as she curled against him, safe, secure. He placed a tender kiss on Katie's forehead. "I got you, my little Katie-did. Everything's going to be all right."

Heather gave her a kiss, too, Katie's skin still moist from Seth's kiss. She needed his strength now more than ever. But she had to do this on her own. She couldn't be weak now. She'd made it all alone through chicken pox, pneumonia, and several long nights with the croup. She could handle a broken arm.

As Seth hurried toward the van, he said, "Get in the back. I'll hand her to you so you can be with her. I'll drive."

"I said I can handle this, Seth. Please. You don't have to chauffeur me around." She was relieved to find J.D. pulling into the drive.

He parked and jogged over to the van, looking down at Katie, still in Seth's arms. "Hey, sweetie pie. Did you hurt your arm?" She nodded and began screaming again.

"I'm driving them to the ER." Seth said matter-of-factly. "Help your sister in the back so I can hand Katie over to her."

J.D. took Heather's arm and helped her into the backseat. "What happened to your eye?"

Heather had almost forgotten. It had practically swollen shut, and she could barely see through one eye. "Nothing. I'll explain later. Hand me Katie."

"Debra and I will take care of Kyle." Then he looked up at Seth. "Nicole's welcome to stay, too."

"That'd be great," Seth said, carefully depositing Katie next to Heather. Katie let out another ear-piercing scream from being moved. Seth quickly secured the seat belt, allowing Katie to lean against Heather who had already wrapped her arms around her tiny shoulders, careful not to bump her arm.

As Seth jogged around to the driver's side, J.D. reached in and gave Heather's leg a reassuring squeeze. "Don't worry about Kyle. We'll barbecue some hamburgers and have a great time. You just worry about Katie."

After he shut the door, Seth dropped the gearshift into drive and eased out of the driveway. Neither of them spoke. Just Katie's anguished cries sounded over the crunching gravel of the rock roads as they headed toward the highway.

Heather dreaded what was yet to come. X-rays. Setting the bone. More pain. She cringed and closed her eyes, wishing she could be the one going through all her daughter's pain. Heather dabbed the pads of her fingers around her brow bone, already feeling the makings of a nice bruise. She squinted out of her good eye and caught Seth watching her, not saying a word.

The drone of his cell phone startled both her and Katie.

"Roberts," he answered simply. "Thanks for getting back to me, Sue. Looks like I'm going to have to cancel tonight's meeting. There's been a family emergency."

Family? Heather met his gaze briefly in the rearview mirror. Did he know he'd just included himself in her family?

Seth gripped the steering wheel, trying to keep from losing his temper with this bullheaded woman. Why wouldn't she allow him to help her? It was like pulling teeth, trying to look at her eye earlier, and now she acted as if he was intruding on her life by taking her and Katie to the hospital. He'd even canceled a meeting to help her out. He threw his cell phone on the seat and focused on the road.

He was supposed to meet Eric Thomas at the hospital to discuss more ideas on the new resort. He just hoped Sue got a hold of him in time. The last thing Heather needed tonight was another confrontation with her ex-husband.

Seth's phone rang again. He caught Heather's annoyed expression as she rolled her one good eye, obviously irritated with his cell phone. He picked it up, saw it was the office, and had to make sure Sue had rescheduled the meeting. "Hey, Sue. What'd you find out?"

"I rescheduled for next week."

"Great. Thanks for your help. I won't be available the rest of the night. Forward everything to voice mail." He powered his phone off and threw it on the seat with his briefcase.

With adrenaline racing through his body, Seth pulled into the emergency lane of Saint Anthony's Children's Hospital and parked near the entrance. He carried Katie into the emergency room and held a limp little girl in his lap while Heather filled out all the paperwork.

A nurse approached with a wheelchair. Seth stood and carefully deposited Katie, giving her a kiss on the cheek. He straightened and touched Heather's arm. "Maybe you need to have someone take a look at your eye. I could stay with Katie."

"Nonsense. I'm fine. It's just a bruise. Katie needs her mother right now." She placed a hand on his arm. "Thank you so much for bringing us in. You've been wonderful with Katie, but I would really feel a lot better if you'd kept your meeting tonight. Take my van. I'll call Jared and have him come pick us up when we're all through here." Her voice choked. "I need to go now." She hurried away and left Seth standing near the emergency-room doors.

Frustrated, he pulled out the van keys and headed out to the parking lot.

After several hours of waiting, X-rays, and more waiting, it was determined that Katie's radial bone had suffered a clean break below the elbow. The bone was set and casted. Exhausted but glad the ordeal was over, Heather wheeled a sleepy little girl out to the lobby. She fumbled through her purse for her keys and realized Seth still had them and was probably still at his meeting. She rummaged through her purse for her cell phone to call Jared. Hopefully, he was through with his vet emergency.

"How's she doing?" Seth's deep baritone sounded from behind. A familiar gentle hand circled her wrist.

Surprised, she slowly turned and found a pair of expensive leather loafers sliding into view. Her gaze traveled up his wrinkled Dockers to his toned waistline. When she met his gaze, a small smile crept into the corners of his perfect full lips as he eyed Katie's new pink cast, molded clear past her elbow.

Seeing Seth sent a wave of comfort through her body. Just his presence gave her strength. She blinked, wondering if maybe she was so tired, she'd dreamt him up. "I saw you leave earlier. Did you make your meeting?"

His brows drew together, looking confused. "I told you, I rescheduled the meeting. I went out to move the van from the emergency parking, but I've been here all night. Is she okay?"

Still a little awestruck, Heather nodded. "She'll be fine. Just tired. The doctor gave her some pain meds to help her sleep." Katie closed her eyes as fatigue gripped her eyelids. "I think that says it all. The doctor says we can go. I'll have to bring her back in a few weeks for more X-rays."

"Do you need to call her father?"

"Eric?" Heather repeated, giving a nervous glance at her daughter's cast. She still hadn't told him about Kyle's burns. "Yes, I'll give him a call tomorrow. No need to worry him this late at night. Katie just needs to rest now."

Seth swept a piece of hair from Heather's face, tucking the strand behind her ear, his warm fingertips a much-welcome touch that she needed so much right now. "How are you holding up? Your eye looks better."

"The doctor took a look at it and said everything's okay. They gave me an ice pack, which seemed to help. Katie went through all the pain." She held up all the prescriptions the doctors had given her. "I need to stop and get these scripts filled before we go home." Glancing at her watch, she was shocked at how late it was. "Eleven-thirty? You shouldn't have stayed so late, Seth."

"Yes, I should have. Now, come on. Let's get Katie home."

When he mentioned home, Heather got the same warm, fuzzy feeling she'd gotten when he'd included himself in her family. She decided she could get used to that feeling.

Taking control of the wheelchair, Seth headed out to the van and unlocked the sliding door. She crawled onto the bench seat before he carefully deposited a sleepy Katie next to her. She strapped on their seat belts and laid Katie's head on her lap, propping her arm on a small pillow.

Seth rested his hand on her shoulder. "I called J.D. about an hour ago. Kyle's doing fine and Nicole's staying with them tonight. Why don't I drop you and Katie off at your condo, get you settled in, then take your van home? I can swing back by in the morning with clean clothes for Nicole and take you out to the ranch. How's that sound?"

"Sounds like the man with the plan." Heather smiled and tipped her head back on the seat. "I just want to crawl into bed and sleep for about twenty-four hours."

"Hmmm, I think I like your plan better." He arched his brows in lazy seduction and squeezed her thigh. She only smiled, thinking she kind of liked that plan, too.

Seth swung by an all-night pharmacy before heading back to her condo. She was grateful he was there to carry Katie in from the van, but was a little embarrassed when he followed her through her cluttered living room, stepping around a farm play set and a basket of laundry that still needed to be folded. Remembering how Nicole had described him as a neat freak, Heather almost cringed. Unfortunately, after working full-time at the ranch and tutoring Kyle and Katie, housework tended to fall to the bottom of her priority list.

She gave a resigned sigh and flipped on the hall light, then headed into the master bedroom where she turned back the covers of a thick downy comforter. At least she'd made the bed that morning. "Since it's just the two of us," she whispered, "I think I'll let her sleep with me tonight. If she has any problems, I can be here for her."

Seth laid Katie on the bed and helped take her shoes and socks off. Heather slipped one of her T-shirts over Katie's head, carefully feeding her cast through the sleeve. Tucking her under the covers, she placed a kiss on her forehead. Her little girl looked so fragile. Tears formed, brimming Heather's lower lids.

Seth's comforting arm surrounded her shoulder. "Come on," he said, pressing a kiss to her temple. "She'll be okay for a while."

Heather didn't resist his lead as he guided her down the

hallway, shut out the light, leaving her condo dark except for a pole light shining through the opened living-room curtains. She hoped it would disguise the mess she'd left that morning.

They stepped around a Barbie playhouse and found their way to the couch where Seth slumped down onto a thick cloth-covered cushion. He grunted and reached behind him, pulling out a naked Ken doll. He laughed and tossed it to the Barbie house. "Sorry, Ken, I don't like to share."

Heather started straightening a few pillows and blankets. "I'm not exactly the best housekeeper in the world. It's hard for me to keep up with all their toys sometimes."

"The place is fine. It's the way a home is supposed to look."

"Can I get you something to drink? Some tea or a soda?"

He shook his head and toed off one of his shoes. "You've had a long day." Slipping off the other shoe, he took hold of her hand. "Why don't you sit down here," he said, gesturing to the spot on the floor, directly between his legs, now casually spread wide and much too inviting.

She bit her bottom lip and stared down the hall. "I don't know. Katie's just in the next room."

He chuckled and tugged her down to the carpeted floor in front of him, situating her between his stockinged feet. "Don't worry. I'll try to keep all your clothes on, at least until we know she's asleep."

"Seth?" she warned, trying to escape his hold.

He pressed her shoulders down. "Relax, Heather. You can take off your mommy hat now."

"And what hat should I be wearing?"

"None. You're off duty for a few minutes."

When he started massaging her shoulders, she moaned and bowed her head. "Ohhh, my gosh, that's wonderful. I can't remember the last time I had a shoulder rub." After he massaged her upper back and shoulders, he proceeded to slide his fingers through her hair, massaging her scalp in small circles. He worked his way to the nape of her neck then began rubbing the muscles between her shoulder blades again. He swept her hair up into a ponytail, twisting the strands and making her scalp tingle.

"That feels so-o-o good. Where did you learn to do this?"

"I used to play with Shelli's hair all the time when we were kids. She didn't have a lot of friends and I always ended up being her hairdresser." He pulled her head back and smiled down at her. "I even cut her hair. Didn't do too bad a job either, if I do say so myself."

"Sounds like you two were pretty close. I bet you miss her."

"More than I thought possible. It's weird," he said, twisting her hair into what felt like a braid. "I didn't call her but a few times a year when she was alive. Now that she's gone, I think about her all the time. Mostly, how I let her down."

"I guess we all tend to get caught up in our own lives. It's easy to take the ones closest to us for granted."

"Yeah, but I completely blew her off. No wonder she ended up pregnant. Now I'm supposed to be responsible for her daughter? Every time I think about the enormous responsibility, it scares the hell out of me." He let out a loud sigh and dropped the strands of hair over her shoulder, slouching against the back of the couch.

Heather shoved to her knees and turned around to face him, pressing her hands on his thighs. "You're going to be fine, Seth. Just watching you with Nicole on our hiking trip tells me you're a natural when it comes to kids. And Katie absolutely adores you. Don't be so hard on yourself."

He gave an exhausted sigh and stared up at the ceiling. "I don't know if I'm cut out for this parenting stuff. I mean, I'm a twenty-nine-year-old bachelor. What do I know about raising a young girl? She becomes a teenager tomorrow, for crying out loud. Soon there'll be boys. And, oh, God," he mumbled, rubbing his eyebrows, "I don't even want to think about all that female crap you girls have to go through. That was one area I let Pop handle."

Heather climbed onto the couch next to Seth, letting him wrap his arm around her. The muscles through his shirt felt hard, sensually warm. "You're going to be fine, Seth. The most important part of being a good parent is listening. You need to learn how to talk to Nicole."

He looked down at her and quirked a wry grin. "What do girls like to talk about anyway?"

"It really doesn't matter as long as you're making an effort. Talk about your work. Tell her how your day went. Believe me, once you get a young girl talking, it's like trying to stop Niagara Falls to get them to shut up."

She pulled her knee up to her chest. "Have you ever talked to her about her relationship with her parents?"

He massaged her calf up and down through her jeans as he talked. "As a matter of fact, we kind of had a breakthrough after our hiking trip."

"What kind of a breakthrough?"

"For one thing, I found out that her dad used to hit her."

"Oh, no," she gasped, pressing her fingers to her mouth.

"He drank pretty heavily, too. I still haven't told her that her dad was drunk when they had their accident."

"That's horrible. Tonight, she told me that she thinks the accident was all her fault."

He angled his head toward her, drawing his dark brows together. "Her fault? Why would she think it was her fault? She wasn't even in the car."

"I know. That's what I tried telling her, but apparently they had attended her dance recital that night. She'd told them she was getting a ride home with one of her teachers, but she went to a sleepover instead. She never called her parents to let them know. Now she thinks they were out looking for her when the accident happened."

"I don't think they even went home after the recital. The police report said witnesses saw them at a bar around eight-thirty and they didn't leave till around eleven-thirty. They crashed into a telephone pole shortly after that."

"Maybe you should tell her about her father's drunkenness. That might take some of the guilt off her shoulders. Has she ever said anything about her mom? Did he ever hit Shelli?"

"She said she'd never seen him hit her. But get this: he'd threatened to kill Spike if Nicole told anyone. My God, Heather, she protected Spike over her own welfare. What kind of a kid would do that?"

"One with a big heart. That explains why she's so attached to Spike. Did she say anything else? What about some of the things she used to do when she lived at home?"

"She used to take art lessons. I guess she's pretty talented."

"She's made some wonderful drawings at camp. Have you looked into some area art or dance studios? Maybe if she started doing what she used to love, it would help her get back part of her old life."

He nodded. "I've asked her several times if there's anything she's interested in doing, like piano or art lessons, you name it. So far, all she's wanted to do is go to your camp and ride horses. Granted, there's a pretty brunette counselor there that she absolutely adores," he added with a squeeze of her shoulders. "But it's only been a month since she's come to live with me. I don't want to pressure her into doing something she's not ready for."

The pad of his thumb brushed her collarbone, making small circles. He seemed so casual sitting next to her, his long legs spread wide with one foot propped on the coffee table. He was talking to her like, well, like a husband would talk to a wife. At least that's how she'd always pictured a loving couple, snuggling together at the end of a long day, sitting on the couch in the dark and discussing their kids. She felt completely at ease with Seth. No sexual come-ons, no pressures. Just two adults discussing their children.

She rested her head on his shoulder. "I'm still wondering when you're going to come out and take that trail ride with her."

He pinched the bridge of his nose then looked down at her from the corner of his eye. "I've got a confession to make, but you have to promise not to make fun of me."

CHAPTER TWELVE

Hearing the apprehension in his voice, Heather peered up at him through her one good eye. "Of course, I won't make fun of you. What is it?"

"Well," he hedged. "I kind of got bucked off a horse at my uncle's ranch when I was in high school."

She brought her hand over her mouth and didn't know whether to laugh or sympathize. "I'm sorry. You must have been very scared."

"To be honest," he said, trailing a finger over the skin of her arm, going back and forth from her elbow to her wrist, "I was at that cocky teenager stage and tried to impress my uncle's ranch hands by riding one of their greenest horses. I'd barely thrown my butt into the saddle before I was tossed several yards on my head. I've never been on a horse since. I told myself it was because of college and not having enough time away from work. But I think deep down, I've been avoiding the whole horse scene."

She couldn't help but smile at his innocent blush. "What was that about getting back in the saddle, dear Seth?"

"I was afraid you were going to say something like that. Why do you think I've been putting off coming out and watching Nicole?"

"Well, we're just going to have to get you over that little fear, won't we?"

He arched his brows with a hint of mischief. "Maybe we'll

just have to cut a deal."

"A deal? Do you always turn everything into a negotiation, Mr. Roberts?"

"When it's effective, and in this case, leverage. Yes. If I get my butt back in a saddle, you have to go flying with me."

She could literally feel the blood drain from her head. "I thought I told you I'm never—"

He pressed two fingers to her lips. "I know you're scared, honey, but let me take you up once. That's all I'm asking. If you still hate it after that, I won't bring it up again."

"Why are you so adamant about me flying?"

"I don't know. I guess I just don't want to see you deny yourself something you once had a passion for. Just think about it, okay?"

Without answering, she lowered her head to his chest and gave a heavy sigh, fiddling with the buttons of his shirt. His breathing was slow and deep, his heart a gentle cadence calming her frazzled state of mind. She'd thought about flying a lot since he'd brought it up, but then she'd always talked herself out of it, convinced it was too dangerous.

She closed her eyes and just listened to the rhythm of Seth's heart, reveling in the warmth of his arms, languishing in the security of his strength. Little by little, she was learning to trust this man. Maybe he could show her how to fly again.

As she snuggled closer, she knew that if she was really honest with herself, it wasn't just learning to fly again that had her scared. Little by little she was also learning to love again, and that scared her more than anything. Being held like this, never wanting to let him go.

But eventually he would leave. Men like Seth Roberts couldn't be tied down to a family for very long before they needed more. More than anything she'd ever be able to give him. A perfect home. Gourmet meals. Well-disciplined and highly talented children.

Great sex. She gave a heavy swallow, remembering how she'd failed in that arena with Eric.

She realized she'd slid her fingers in between the buttons of Seth's shirt, stroking the soft mat of curly chest hair. Eric used to hate being touched like this, said he was ticklish and it ruined the mood. She quickly tugged her fingers away and curled them into her lap.

"That felt nice," Seth murmured in her hair, next to her ear.

"I didn't mean to be so forward." She looked down, avoiding his gaze.

He unbuttoned the third button and took her hand in his. "It's okay, honey. You can touch me." He proceeded to splay her hand over his chest, gently rubbing her knuckles. "Can you feel what you do to my heart?"

She gave a shy laugh and burrowed into the crook of his shoulder. "That was totally corny."

His chest rumbled under her fingertips when he laughed. "I'm trying to be romantic here."

"Romantic, huh? It's been so long, I guess I didn't recognize it." Building courage, she unbuttoned the next two buttons of Seth's shirt and tunneled her fingers beneath the fabric, stroking the skin of his belly. His muscles tightened. His breathing grew deeper, his warm cinnamon breath fanning the side of her face.

"Now, back to our discussion," she said, flattening her palm over his heart, wondering if it was beating just as hard as hers. It was. She looked up at him and smiled. "If I decide to go flying with you, will you promise to come out and ride with Nicole?"

He grabbed her wrist with one hand, and gently gripped her hair with the other, tugging her head back so she was looking up at him. "Honey, if you keep that up, I'll promise to ride the world's toughest bull if you want." Then he kissed her square on the mouth, squelching any further conversation about flying, riding horses, his niece, kids. . . .

She gave a sensual moan and relaxed under his tight hold. At his simple touch, her earlier arguments about not being enough for this man ejected right out of her mind. All that was left now was a surge of passionate energy that had lain dormant for so many years.

She parted her lips, suddenly hungry for more. Hungry to be loved for who she was, just once in her life.

Cradling her in the crook of his arm, he pressed her down to the end of the couch. In one swift movement, he swept her long legs underneath him compressing her entire body into the thickness of the cushion. She was completely paralyzed, unable to push him away under his deep searching kisses. Not that she wanted to push him away as his kisses became more urgent. His tongue slipped between her lips, tantalizing her even further.

She didn't know a tongue could feel so soft and smooth, and taste so good. He didn't poke or prod to see how far back he could reach the way Eric had always done. Instead, Seth swirled his tongue with hers like a slow waltz, sucking on the tip gently, then bringing it back into the warmth of his mouth.

Almost timidly, she drew his tongue into her mouth the way he'd done to hers, unsure if it would turn him off. Eric had always been the one in control, taking, but never letting her receive any of the pleasure. But this . . . Seth gave foreplay a whole new meaning. He hadn't even touched her breasts and she was burning in places that had never been so on fire.

As he tormented her with his tongue, she couldn't help but wonder if Seth was the dominant type when it came to sex, always the one in control, the one on top. She suddenly found it hard to breathe. She rolled her head away from his mouth and tugged her hands up to his chest. "Please, stop," she whispered.

He rolled off to his side, pressing her against the back of the couch. "I'm sorry. I didn't mean to get carried away like that. Are you all right?"

She had trouble catching her breath and sounded winded when she spoke. "Yeah, it's just. . . ." She paused, covering her face with her hands.

"It's just what?" he asked, sweeping a strand of hair from her forehead. "Was I that bad of a kisser?"

She laughed and lowered her hands, peering up at him as he loomed over her head. "You were a great kisser. In fact, I didn't know kissing could be so . . . erotic," she panted. "I think I had more pleasure with that one kiss than with anything that I've ever done in my life."

He brushed the backs of his fingers across her cheeks, down the side of her neck, up and down the bare skin of her arm. "Is anything wrong?"

She may as well let him know now, before they got in too deep. "Well, um, to put it bluntly, I've been told on numerous occasions that I'm not exactly the world's greatest lover."

His lips did that little twitch in the corners of his mouth, as if he were trying to suppress a grin. "I take it your ex didn't give you a whole lot of compliments when you were making love?"

Making love? Was that what they were doing? She gave a nervous laugh. "Uh, no, not exactly. Love wasn't even part of the equation. It was just plain, mechanical sex. I'm afraid foreplay with Eric consisted of thirty seconds of kissing, an occasional tweak of a nipple—usually more of a yank—then wham bam, he was done, and without so much as a 'thank you, ma'am,' he'd roll off, panting like a dog. Sometimes, he'd be asleep within a minute."

Seth leaned forward and kissed her brow, then spoke through a husky murmur. "I'm sorry, Heather. That's not how it's supposed to be."

She tipped her face up, pressing her cheek into his neck. "He was always the one in control. I guess that's why I pulled away just now. I felt—"

"Dominated?" he filled in for her, as if reading her mind.

Closing her eyes, she only nodded.

His hand splayed over her stomach. "So, does that mean," he hesitated, narrowing his eyes slightly. "You know, did you ever get to where you could, um, you know. . . ."

She let out a small laugh, embarrassed at where this conversation was headed, but at the same time, extremely touched that he cared enough to ask. "Well, let's see, I can probably count on one hand the number of times I've come . . . and that was during our first year of marriage. After that, I felt like a drive-up window at a fast-food restaurant. A twenty-four-hour fast-food restaurant," she clarified. "He wanted it quick and didn't like to wait on me. It didn't matter what time of day it was or what I was doing. If he wanted it, I had no choice in the matter."

He drew his head back, eyes widening. "God, Heather. Did he ever . . . force himself on you?"

She shook her head, lowering her eyes away from his pitying gaze. "Oh, no. It was never anything like that. It was more of the guilt factor. If I resisted or acted like I didn't want it, he'd remind me how I'd failed him with Kyle, like sex was some kind of a consolation prize." She looked up and gave a shrug of her shoulders. "Toward the end, though, I think he must have been getting it somewhere else. He never even touched me during the last two years of our marriage."

"Rotten bastard," Seth growled through gritted teeth. Sliding his arms clear underneath her, he pulled her into a tight embrace. "You deserve so much more, honey."

A thick lump formed in the back of her throat, making her voice sound choked when she spoke again. "I'm sorry. I don't know why I told you all that."

"I'm glad you did." He drew apart and kissed her injured brow bone before staring down into her eyes. "I'd like to show you how much you've been missing, but I don't think doing it on the living-room couch with your daughter in the next room would be such a good idea."

She gave a short laugh. "Like, I totally agree," she said, hoping to lighten the mood. "I should probably go check on Katie, anyway."

"You sure you're okay?"

Drowning in the depths of his compassionate blue eyes, she nodded. "Promise you won't leave yet?"

"You could probably persuade me to stick around a few more minutes." He sat up and helped her stand.

"Thanks, Seth. For everything."

He gently gripped her shoulders and leaned in for another kiss. "Believe me, it was my pleasure."

"I'll be right back," she said with a long sigh. Her head felt extremely light as she checked in on her daughter. Katie was still snuggled under Heather's thick comforter, her cast resting on a pillow to keep it elevated. Her fingers were pink and there was no swelling. Satisfied she was okay, Heather placed a kiss on her forehead, then headed back out to the living room.

"How is she?" Seth asked, sounding genuinely concerned.

"Still zonked, thank goodness. Sleep is the best thing for her right now."

He opened his arms, inviting her back into the circle of his embrace.

She crawled onto the couch next to him, lying side by side with her body wedged between him and the cushions. Snuggling into the crook of his shoulder, she fed her fingers through his hair and lifted her leg, allowing him to slide his thigh into the apex of her jeans. She pressed in hard and squeezed him tight, snuggling her face into his neck, breathing in his scent, his strength, his essence. This felt good. It felt right. How had she ever made it through life without this man beside her every day?

Then he just held her, stroking his hands over her back, caressing her skin, running his fingertips up and down her arm. "This feels nice just holding you," he said, lowering and kissing her cheek. "I didn't realize parenting could be so exhausting."

She spoke through a heavy yawn. "It's not so bad if there's someone there to help you. Thanks for being here tonight. I appreciate it more than you'll ever know."

"I'd like to be here more if you'd let me."

She wanted to let him, but she knew he'd be leaving by the end of the summer. Then what? She'd been on her own for nearly two years now and had finally started feeling she was on solid ground. Should she risk another heartache only to watch yet another man waltz out of her life to pursue his career?

His arms tightened their hold around her, and she suddenly realized it didn't matter right now. Tonight, she was a desirable woman being held by an incredibly compassionate, sexy, handsome man. She'd worry about the end of the summer when that time came. It was only June.

"Mommy?"

Heather opened her eyes, trying to focus in the darkness. She didn't know where she was, but more to the point, who was snoring softly in her ear? She made out the television across the room and realized she was on the couch.

"I can't find my dolly, Mommy." Katie's tiny voice sounded from down the hall.

Then she remembered the hospital. Katie's arm.

"Seth?" She lifted her head, grimacing when her hair got caught under his arm. "Seth, wake up."

"Wh-what?" Seth jerked his head up, cracking his forehead square onto her chin.

"Oomph," Heather grunted.

Seth rolled backwards off the couch, bringing her along with him. They both let out a low groan as she landed smack on top of him.

"Shhh," she whispered loudly, rubbing her chin. "I heard Katie. I forgot to put her doll in bed with her."

"Jeez, I thought the place was on fire or something."

He lifted his head, slower this time, and spoke in a husky whisper. "I can't believe I fell asleep on you. I'm sorry."

"I think I'm the one who fell asleep on you."

When she tried to push away, he cupped his palms over her bottom, pressing her into his hips, the growing hardness behind his zipper a good indication he'd gotten plenty of rest. "Hurry back."

She laughed and shoved off Seth, holding out her hand. "I don't think that would be such a good idea."

He grabbed her hand and stood. They both swayed from the head rush and about lost their balance.

She laughed and pushed him down onto the couch. "Stay. I'll go take care of Katie." She grabbed a blanket from a corner rocker and fluffed a pillow on the couch. She stood over him a moment then swept back a lock of disheveled black hair curling onto his forehead.

He smiled and gripped her waist, tugging her closer. An exhilarating shiver raced over her skin as he pressed his face into her stomach and kissed her belly through her shirt. "I'll wait up if you want to come back to the . . . negotiation couch." He looked up and smiled. Even in the darkness, a dangerous gleam sparkled behind his offer.

She stepped away and shook her head. "As tempting as that offer sounds, something tells me your negotiation tactics wouldn't be fair, Mr. Roberts. I'd better get some distance. It's been a long night. See you in the morning."

"Good night, then. Oh, which door is the bathroom? I'd hate to stumble into the wrong room."

She gave a nervous laugh. "The only door on the left. Mine will be locked."

Heather set the alarm clock for early Saturday morning, thinking Seth probably had a whole day planned out. She didn't want to impose on him any more than she already had. When the buzzer went off, she felt like she'd just fallen asleep. She stumbled out of bed and strolled to the kitchen in her long T-shirt to start a pot of coffee.

Peeking around the corner, she stopped and stared at the large man lying on her couch. He'd taken off his shirt. The morning sunlight filtered through a crack in the curtains, glinting off a sparse mat of dark hair covering his broad chest. She found herself shamelessly following a thin line of hair down his torso, ending at the rim of his unsnapped trousers. His long legs seemed to go on forever till she got to his bare feet dangling off the end of the couch.

Her heart fluttered as she remembered the closeness she'd felt for this man just hours before. Some of the things she'd told him made her blush even now, but that's what he did to her whenever he came near. Her pulse skittered; her stomach tightened. Every nerve ending on her body came alive. He made her feel like a vibrant, sexy woman. He didn't see her as just a mommy, or a counselor, or a sister.

She tipped her head against the doorframe and sighed. When she'd first met him, she was certain he'd be just like Eric, measuring happiness by how much money was in the bank account. But Seth continued to do things that totally contradicted anything that Eric would have done.

For one thing, Eric had never canceled a meeting to be with her and the kids, the way Seth had done last night. Even when

Katie was a baby and they'd all had the flu, Eric had just handed Heather an antacid tablet and headed out the door.

The way Seth had cradled Katie in his arms made her feelings for this man grow into something she'd never expected to feel in her life again. Had she ever felt this way with Eric?

"The light from the kitchen shines right through your T-shirt." Seth's low voice startled her from her thoughts.

Heather gasped and pulled her shirt down. When she looked up, his grin told her he was only teasing. She warily strode over toward him. "You don't look very comfortable. This is probably a far cry from what you're used to."

He draped his long legs over the edge of the couch, sat up and scratched his stubbled chin. "What time is it?" he asked with a yawn.

"Almost seven. Do you have to be anywhere right away? I'm just going to take a quick shower and then we'll be ready to go. That should give you enough time to swing by your place, take a shower, and change."

He lazily rolled his head to the side and gazed up at her through slitted lids. "Or, we could kill two birds with one stone, so to speak." His eyebrows lifted as he slid her an adolescent grin. "I'll wash your back, you wash mine?" His voice was groggy, his blue eyes tired and dreamy.

She gave a nervous laugh, a part of her wishing she could take him up on his offer. "My back is fine, thank you for the offer anyway." She motioned her head to the kitchen. "Coffee's ready, and there's a package of rolls on the counter. Help yourself. I'll be quick."

"No rush. Today's Nicole's birthday and I didn't schedule any meetings." He reached up and took her hand. "Is Katie still asleep?" He slid his bare feet over hers, rubbing the tops of her toes.

She licked her lips. "Yeah."

"I feel bad for falling asleep on you last night."

"I guess we were both exhausted."

He rubbed his hand over the outside of her leg, inching upwards under her T-shirt. "I didn't think it was possible, but you're even sexier first thing in the morning. Now that I'm all rested, maybe we could go over a few more details about the deal we made last night. You know, flying in exchange for riding a horse . . . or anything else we may have discussed."

For a minute, those hypnotic blue eyes almost pulled her into his charm, that and the fact that his hand was now splayed over the roundness of her bottom, his searing touch separated by only a thin pair of silk panties.

She scooted away from him and grabbed his hand. "I think we'd better . . . I mean, *I'd* better take a shower. I'd hate for Katie to walk in on her mom and Uncle Seth doing the horizontal mambo on the couch."

"Mommy?" Katie cried from the bedroom.

Heather bent and placed a soft kiss on his cheek, wishing with all her soul she could stay with him. "I won't be long," she whispered.

"Mommy! Mommy!"

Seth almost groaned as Heather pulled away and trotted down the hallway. Her long legs seemed to go on forever underneath her T-shirt. When he'd found her standing there in the kitchen doorway, watching him, something dangerously sensual had washed through his system. After only a few weeks of knowing this incredibly beautiful woman, he knew there was so much more to learn. He'd only scratched the surface.

He closed his eyes, envisioning her skin and how soft and supple she felt in his arms last night. He'd almost hoped she'd have taken him up on his offer to come back to the couch. But she was right, sleep had been the farthest thing from his mind.

Besides, if they ever did find themselves alone together, he sure as hell wasn't going to rush it. If her sex life had been anything like she'd hinted at last night, he wanted to be sure she knew the difference between mechanical sex and making mad, passionate love.

He suddenly realized how long it had been since he'd actually been with a woman, felt a woman lying next to him. Ages ago. And even then, his heart hadn't pounded the way it had done last night. Remembering how he'd fallen asleep on Heather didn't help matters either.

He scrubbed at his whiskery chin. "Coffee," he said out loud. "I need a cup of strong black coffee." He strode to the kitchen, grabbed a glazed cinnamon Danish then headed back out to the couch.

A stack of notebooks lay strewn on the coffee table. The top notebook was open, the pages filled with bullet points and scribbled notes. With the roll shoved halfway into his mouth, he cocked his head to the side and read a few lines. He remembered seeing her scribbling in a notebook on the plane back from Los Angeles. Was this what she'd been writing?

He shoved the rest of the pastry into his mouth and sat down, licking his fingers to keep from getting any of the icing on the pages. He'd just turned the first page when Heather strolled out to the living room, dressed in a pair of low-rise, hip-hugging jeans and a white, low-scooped tank top that accentuated her perfectly rounded breasts. Her sore eye was a dark shade of purple, a stark contrast to the whites surrounding her chocolate-brown irises. Her hair fell around her shoulders in long wet ringlets as water dripped down the sides of her freshly scrubbed face.

He sipped another long drink of his coffee, the hot liquid only making his desires for this woman reach the boiling point.

She walked over, her brows arching. "What are you doing?"

He quickly flipped the cover closed. "Sorry. They were sitting open and I couldn't help myself. I didn't mean to invade your privacy."

Giving a slight shrug of her shoulders, she wrinkled her nose. "What did you think?"

He patted the couch for her to sit next to him. He wasn't in any rush to leave. "It's fascinating," he said, setting his coffee on the table. "Are you writing a book about autistic children?"

With a towel in her hand, she slouched down beside him with a leg crooked beneath her. Fresh-showered scents of lilac and body soap made him think twice about what he'd told himself about waiting for the perfect time when they were alone.

She dabbed the towel at her face. "Over the years I've compiled a lot of notes on raising an autistic child. I'd like to write a series of child-development books for parents. Maybe I can help instill hope in a marriage where mine failed. I've been working with a few other mothers over the Internet, and have even created my own Web site. I answer a lot of people's concerns."

"Wow, you're ambitious. What kinds of concerns?"

"Just everyday matters like how to get them dressed in the morning, to finally breaking through and getting a smile. It sounds simple, but having the support of others is crucial in raising a child with so many challenges." She took her journal and flipped it closed. "Maybe someday I'll get serious about writing, but with the ranch and teaching Kyle and Katie full-time, it's kind of hard to find the time."

He took the notebook and flipped it to the back cover. "I noticed some drawings of buildings at the back. What's this?"

She cocked her head to the side to get a better glimpse then gave a timid laugh. "I'm afraid my stepfather has put some wild ideas into my head."

"Like what?"

"Like developing a place that can accommodate physically challenged or mentally challenged adults."

"Don't they have homes like that?"

"Yeah, but they're usually located in the lower-income neighborhoods where crime rates are high, and with their limited income potential, autistic people have few other options unless they were born into a wealthy family."

"So, what are you proposing?"

She rolled her eyes. "It's just a dream. It could never happen. For one thing, it would take an inordinate amount of money."

He patted her thigh. "Why don't you just tell me your ideas and quit worrying about the money."

"Okay, but don't laugh."

"You mean the way you didn't laugh last night when I told you about me being afraid of horses? I saw the little snicker you were trying to hold back."

She giggled. "I'm sorry."

"That's okay. I'm still holding you to our deal. We'll get into that another time. For now, I want to hear your ideas."

"Well, I've been searching the Internet and have found several five-star retirement communities where the tenants live independently, but they aren't responsible for maintenance or upkeep. There's also an on-site physician and twenty-four-hour nursing care available, as well as a cafeteria that will monitor and cater to an individual's dietetic and nutritional needs."

"Sounds like your typical snow-bird resort in Arizona or Florida."

"Yeah, but I kind of had another idea in addition to the retirees."

"Go, ahead. You've piqued my curiosity."

"Well, what if a separate cluster of condos was constructed for adults who were mildly disabled in either a physical or a mental capacity, but could still function independently? I've researched independent living homes, where a caregiver lives on-site with these kinds of people, but the tenants still hold down jobs and are free to come and go. They could have the same situation here, where the caregiver, like a registered nurse or a therapist, lives in one of the units, supervising their comings and goings. Their meds would be monitored as well as their diet and anything else each individual would need."

"Like you said, a lot of these people you're talking about can't afford to live in this kind of a resort community."

"That's the best part of my idea. They'd get to live there practically for free."

"Free?" he almost choked on his Danish.

"Let me finish. We're talking about an eighteen-hole golf course, an indoor swimming and lap pool, tennis and racquetball courts, maybe even horse stables, not to mention a dining facility and acres and acres of grounds to keep. Am I right?"

He licked icing off his thumb. "Yeah, keep going."

"Well, the owners of the resort would hire those people with disabilities to do a lot of the work in exchange for room and board. The resort has to hire someone anyway. Most of those people can learn to caddy on the golf course. They can handle administrative and janitorial duties, cafeteria work, even keep most of the grounds, like gardening and maintenance of the lawns."

"Sounds like you've put a lot of thought into this place."

"On the Internet, I heard about a place like this in Iowa, and now that Saint Anthony's is closing, I've become a little more desperate. Kyle would be an ideal candidate for this someday and there are lots of kids just like him at Saint Anthony's."

"A place like that would take some pretty big backers."

She let out a huge sigh and closed her eyes. "I know. I mentioned it to Eric a few years ago. He almost laughed in my face. I guess it's just a pipe dream."

Seth rubbed his chin, his mind already churning out ideas. Grinning, he wrapped his arm around her waist. "The greatest accomplishments in life start with a dream, Heather. Never give up your dreams. They might just come true."

He took the towel and gently wiped a drip from the side of her face. "You're an amazing woman. I can't believe how much you've taken on yourself, opening your heart to all those people and raising two great kids alone. The more I'm around you, the more you amaze me."

"There's nothing amazing about it. It's very fulfilling to reach out to people and let them know they're not alone in the world. I want them to know that someone out there is going through the exact same thing, day in and day out. It's tough on parents, caregivers, and friends, but with patience, family and an iron spirit, even the toughest times don't seem so bad."

"You're definitely surrounded by all your family."

"I know. J.D. and Jared have been wonderful father figures over the years. I don't know what I'd do without them."

Seth watched her a moment as she combed her fingers through her long, wavy tresses. He wanted so much to be with her, but was unsure how to even approach her. He cupped her hand and squeezed. "Your family can't give you everything you need, Heather."

She stopped combing and returned his gaze. "And what else do I need?"

"You need someone to show you how sensual and desirous you are." He leaned closer, smelling the mint from her mouthwash, then brushed a whispery kiss over her black eye, sliding around to her ear. "You're an incredibly sexy woman."

She turned her head and met his lips, her mouth opening in invitation. He deepened their kiss, curling his hand around her ribcage. "Mmmmm," she moaned, tracing her tongue over his lips. "You taste like icing from the cinnamon rolls." She tasted him again, devouring his lips like she hadn't eaten in years.

Sweet God, in heaven. He pulled her onto his lap, fully covering her breast with his palm, feeling the hardened tip clear through her bra. When she arched her head back, he trailed his mouth down her throat and tugged her shirt out of her jeans, wanting to sample just a little, even if he couldn't have all of her right now.

He slipped his hand under her shirt, his thumb brushing the lower swells of her breasts. He swept around to her back and searched for the clasp to her bra.

"I need to go check on Katie," she said, not making any attempt to leave.

"Did she sleep through the night?" He ran his finger all along her bra strap, but he still couldn't find the darned clasp. Maybe this was one of those pullover jobbies.

"Yeah," she said, arching her neck, giving him access to her throat. "I gave her some medicine around five."

"So, she'll be asleep for a couple more hours then?" He kissed down her neck, tracing his tongue along the rim of her shirt, dipping in between the swells of her breasts. "You always smell so good, do you know that?"

She pressed her hands against his bare chest. "I feel like a teenager making out like this." She looked down the hall and gave a shy laugh, her fresh washed face turning as pretty as the early-morning sunrise.

Feeling about as horny as a teenager, but knowing the difference, he watched as she sat up and tucked her shirt back into her jeans. Before he could object, she shoved off his lap and trotted down the hall on tiptoes. She was back in an instant, her face still flushed, her lips shiny and full. "You're probably right," she whispered, sounding far too sexy. "As late as we were up last night, she'll be out for at least another hour."

Hoping to spend more time with this incredible lady, he

reached out and took her fingers, rubbing his thumb over her nails. "So, what have you got planned for today?"

"Actually, I was going to take Kyle to the baseball game this afternoon. J.D. was supposed to take him, but he has to go to a sale in Boulder. As far as the baseball game today, though, I don't think I should leave Katie. She probably wouldn't be too comfortable sitting in the hot sun with a throbbing arm."

Seth rubbed his stubbled jaw, remembering his plans to take Marty and his roommate to the Pizza Palace this evening for Nicole's birthday party. He also knew how much Marty loved baseball. "Tell you what. How about I take Kyle and Nicole to the game this afternoon?"

He hoped he wasn't opening a can of worms but knew he had to tell her eventually. "I was going to take my brother out for his birthday this evening anyway. I'll just pick him up early, go to the game, then swing back by here and take you and Katie out for pizza with us."

Heather gave a slight shake of her head. "Back up a minute. Your brother? I didn't even know you had a brother."

"His name is Marty, and he'll be twenty-six next week."

"Why haven't you mentioned him before?"

"I guess because I know how you feel about institutions."

She arched her brows. "I'm not following."

"Marty's been living at Pine Tree Family Services Center since he was a baby. He was born with Down syndrome, and after Mom died, Pop could barely handle Shelli and me, much less a baby like Marty. He's the main reason I settled down here in the Springs."

She sat down beside him. "I had no idea."

"I assure you," he quickly added, "sending him to Pine Tree was probably the best thing for him. He's made good friends and gets individualized help from all his tutors. Maybe you could meet him and we could celebrate Marty and Nicole's birthday together."

"Of course, I'd love to meet your brother." Then she looked guiltily down at her fingernails. "I'm sorry if you thought I was badmouthing these facilities, Seth. I know there are a lot of good places out there, and Kyle would probably do well, it's just that—"

"It wouldn't be home," he finished for her. "I agree. Kyle needs you and he needs his sister. Shelli and I weren't so lucky. To be honest, I think we'd have been better off in a place with Marty. Pop could barely afford to keep a gallon of milk in the house, and after Mom died, I had to pretty much take care of Shelli all by myself."

She turned toward him and stroked her hand over his thigh. "Sounds like you've had it kind of tough. Is that why you're so set on making millions of dollars?"

"I don't know about millions." He chuckled and rubbed his jaw. "But I guess I'd like to know my future is secure. Now that I'm responsible for Nicole, it's even more important."

She turned away and started stacking her notebooks together, her pretty smile fading into a contemplative frown. "Seth, can I ask you something?"

He splayed his palm on her back giving her a soft caress. "Sure. What's on your mind?"

"I can't seem to figure you out." She tapped the tablets into a pile. "I mean I can understand you wanting to fulfill your obligations after the charity auction and everything, but now that you know the kind of responsibilities I have, I guess I'm left wondering."

She turned and looked at him. "Why are you still here? For someone who wants to avoid complications, I'm about as complicated as they get. What is it, exactly, that you want from me?"

CHAPTER THIRTEEN

What did he want?

Seth looked around her living room. It was filled with clutter. But, he had to admit, he felt at home. It felt right. He could feel Heather's touch in every country knickknack on the walls to all the kids' drawings on the refrigerator. This was what he'd missed growing up. This was a home. This was a family.

But was this what he wanted?

She started fidgeting with the notebooks again, a definite sign she was nervous. "Don't get me wrong or anything. You're an incredible kisser, and I'm extremely flattered that a guy like you would take an interest in someone like me. And if Katie wasn't here, I'm pretty sure we'd be doing more than a horizontal tango right now."

He gave a seductive chuckle and wrapped his arm clear around her waist, drawing her closer. "Someone like me, huh? Sounds like you're making me into something I'm not."

She shoved a hand against his chest. "You know what I mean. The fact remains, Katie is here, and soon Kyle will be back, and now there's Nicole to consider, too. She's extremely vulnerable right now. As much as I'd like to be with you, I just can't have an affair, and then watch you leave for Dallas at the end of the summer."

He sat back, surprised. "Who told you about Dallas?"

"Jillie mentioned it yesterday. She said Nicole told her you were up for a big promotion. Is it true, then?"

He nodded and rubbed the back of his neck. "Yeah, the vice presidency of the southern division is pretty much a sure thing if I take it."

"What do you mean, if you take it? Isn't that what you've planned for all your life?" She made quotation marks in the air, her voice taking on a slight edge.

Sensing a little tension, he arched his brows and nodded. "I'll admit, getting the promotion and moving to Dallas has definite advantages. Nicole will certainly be taken care of the rest of her life."

"Does that include shipping her off to a preppy boarding school in the fall? Is that all part of this big plan you have?" Again with the quotation marks.

"I don't know what Nicole told you," he said, feeling on the defensive all of a sudden. "But I'm not doing anything that she doesn't want to do. Her parents didn't have a lot of money, and I was just thinking about her future, trying to help her set some goals and prepare her for college."

Without answering, Heather got down on the floor and started packing up a Barbie mobile home, jabbing dolls and clothes inside. At least Katie still liked Barbie. Maybe he'd give her the new suitcases he'd bought for Nicole.

He reached over and touched Heather's shoulder, getting her to stop picking up Katie's toys and forcing her to look up at him. "Just so you know, I've already talked this over with Nicole and made it very clear that it's her decision, not mine. I'm not going to make her do anything she doesn't want to do."

After jamming the last doll away, she sat back on her haunches and gave a heavy sigh, swiping strands of hair from her face. "I'm going to ask you again, Seth. Why are you here? What do you want from me? Am I just a convenience? A counselor for Nicole? A fling for you this summer? Hello-o-o. I can't be one of your girlfriends that you've got strung out all over the world."

He shook his head, irritated that she kept pegging him as a jet-set playboy. What did he have to do or say to prove himself? "I told you, I don't have any other girlfriends. I don't know what else I can do to convince you—"

"You know what?" she said, standing and shoving a hand on her hip. "It doesn't matter. This has all just been a huge mistake. I've been letting my fantasies interfere with my thinking lately. I never should have let you get involved last night. I should have just let J.D. drive me into the hospital."

"Of course," he mumbled, dragging his fingers through his hair, frustrated. "The brother who can do no wrong."

"What's that supposed to mean?"

He grabbed his shirt from the back of the couch. "It means, you've got your brothers so high up on these pedestals, like they're gods or something. What is it they actually do for you?" He struggled to keep his voice level, shoving one arm through a sleeve. "I see J.D. working long hours, keeping his ranch going, heading off to sales, taking care of his own family, leaving you to give riding lessons and tend to all the campers." He reached around and shoved his other arm in the sleeve. "Soon, there'll be a new baby in the picture, and they'll be even busier. Where does that leave you? Are they getting someone to replace Debra?"

"I don't know. We haven't really discussed replacing her."

"What about Jared? Will he be helping you once the baby arrives?"

She picked up a laundry basket filled with folded clothes and propped it against her hip. "He's very busy right now with his new vet clinic."

Shirt unbuttoned and hanging open, he shoved his hands on his waist. "That's my point. They've all got their own lives. Megan only comes home a couple of times a year. Probably less, now that she's doing her residency. Hell, your mother isn't even around because she's off pursuing her own career."

"It's just a busy time for everyone. It's not always like this."

"Isn't it?" He knew he should probably shut up, but he kept venting his own frustrations at the whole situation. "All I see is you reaching out to everyone else, running around giving speeches at fundraisers, leading support groups, all the while you're trying to home school your two kids and work full time at J.D.'s ranch, counseling these kids. How much does he pay you, anyway?"

"Typical. It always comes back to money."

"That's what I thought," he said with a slight shake of his head. "You're doing it all for nothing."

"It's not for nothing," she retorted, dropping the laundry basket at her feet. A couple of towels on the top bounced out on the floor. "Money doesn't matter to me. I love being with the children and helping them through their problems."

"I know you do, honey, and that's what makes you such a compassionate and caring woman. But you're so busy jumping through hoops of fire for everyone else's cause, that you don't see the flame that's about to nip you right in the ass."

"Stop!" She pressed her hands over her ears. "I've heard enough."

"I don't think you have." He lined up the buttons of his shirt and started fastening the third one down. "Maybe I do put a lot of focus on money, but I've seen the lack of it, and I don't want that for my kids or Nicole. I don't want my children sharing their beds with rodents and cockroaches, or being mocked and made fun of at school because they couldn't afford a new pair of tennis shoes. You wondered how I knew so much about black eyes? I've had the shit beat out of me more times than I can count because I was so poor."

He jammed his shirttails into the back of his slacks. "So if planning my future and setting goals seems self-important to you, then I'm sorry. I guess I shouldn't be here. Maybe it would be best for all of us if I just took Nicole out of the camp the rest of the summer before she gets any more attached."

He slouched down on the edge of the couch and yanked on his socks. "Life is ironic, isn't it? I grew up in poverty and people ridiculed me. Now I have wealth, and I'm still being ridiculed. No matter how hard I try, it'll never be good enough."

She turned away from him, but didn't say anything, just stood there with her head bowed between her shoulders. She had her arms crossed in front of her, rubbing them, as if she were cold.

He let out a loud exhausted sigh, angered at how things had turned out between them. But he also knew she was right. He couldn't just have an affair with her and leave at the end of the summer. She and her kids had come to mean too much to him. "Heather?" He lowered his voice, not sure what he was going to say, but he didn't want to leave things like this between them, either. "You wanted to know why I'm here?"

When she wouldn't answer or even look at him, he stood and warily approached her from behind. "I'm here because from the moment you stared up at me on the plane with your big brown eyes, I haven't been able to think about anyone or anything else since. Contrary to what you believe, I can count on one hand all the women I've been with over the years, and that includes Dottie Snodgrass in the eleventh grade."

She let out a small snort of laughter that was soon muffled by a gut-wrenching sob that tore right through his heart. He reached up and cupped her shoulders, dragging her back against his chest. "God, Heather. I'm sorry. I didn't mean to get so angry. Please don't cry." He pressed a kiss to the back of her head.

"No, I'm the one who's sorry," she murmured barely over a whisper. "I don't know why I flew off the handle like that." She dabbed the tip of her nose then cleared her throat before she turned in his arms and looked up at him. "You've been nothing but a good friend to my kids and me since I met you." She curled her fingers into his shirt and closed her eyes. "Please don't go away mad and take Nicole out of our camp this summer."

He leaned in and kissed her forehead. "I'm not mad at you, honey. I just want you to take a good look in the mirror sometime. There's a passionate, fun-loving woman in there desperately trying to get out. I felt her last night in my arms." He framed her face with his palms, lowering his voice. "I felt her in your kiss. She's been locked away a long time. Let her out. Let her enjoy life again."

Her lips trembled when she spoke. "What am I supposed to do? Drop all my responsibilities? I tried that for three days and look where it got me. I'm doing the best that I can."

"I know you are, sweetheart. Don't get me wrong. I think you're one of the most loving mothers I've ever met, but sometimes I think you're clinging a little too tightly to your kids. Kyle's almost ten, but you barely let him wipe his own nose. He's a bright, smart kid. Give him a chance to grow up and do things on his own. I think that's why he idolizes J.D. and Jared so much. He wants to be just like them."

"I know, but it's hard to let go. His behavior is so unpredictable. Just when I think I can trust him, something happens, and I feel like I have to start all over."

"I'm not a therapist, but I don't think his behavior change has anything to do with you. Even I can see why Kyle might be acting out at times."

"What do you mean?"

"Well, take J.D. for instance. With the new baby coming, he's spending all his spare time with his wife, taking her to doctors' appointments, shopping for baby things. And when he's not with her, he's busy with ranch responsibilities and giving riding lessons to the campers. And look at Jared. You said yourself he's busy with his vet clinic. Maybe Kyle's feeling a little jealous."

"Jealous? That's ridiculous. He gets plenty of attention."

"Does he? If Katie so much as whimpers about a spider or something, you're there coddling her. You need to tether your apron strings and let them both have some slack so they can discover the world on their own."

"Mommy?" Katie called from the bedroom.

Her gaze darted over his shoulder, her eyes tearing over. "I don't know what to tell you, Seth. I don't have my life all mapped out like you do. And I won't just ship my kids away because they don't fit into some master plan."

Feeling desperate, he gripped her shoulders. "Maybe I do have things all mapped out. But look around, Heather. Is this the life you really want? Is this condo where you want to be the rest of your life? I saw something in your eyes earlier. I could hear it in your voice when you spoke about writing those books and reaching out to all those people experiencing the kinds of trials you've endured. After only reading a few pages of your notes, I can see what a talented writer you are. You've got a gift. Don't let it go to waste."

"Mommy, my arm hurts." Katie's voice grew more insistent.

"Maybe this doesn't look like much to you, but my kids are my life right now. They are my dreams. So, if you'll excuse me," she snapped, pulling from his touch. "I need to go coddle my daughter. And don't bother taking Kyle to the baseball game. He's got to learn that everything in life doesn't always go as planned." Then she jogged out of the room and down the hall to the master bedroom.

Gritting his teeth, Seth stared up at the ceiling, blowing out an exasperated gust of air. What the hell was he doing? Why was he getting so emotionally involved with this woman?

He grabbed his coffee mug, strode into the kitchen and set it firmly in the sink. He braced his hands on the counter, his chest rising and falling in angry breaths. If everything went as well as he expected, the hospital project would go off without a hitch. Saint Anthony's would be demolished, and they would break ground on the new resort by next summer. It shouldn't matter what realtor he was dealing with for the conversion of Saint Anthony's.

It shouldn't matter that Heather had such an emotional attachment to the hospital.

It shouldn't matter that Seth was taking Nicole and moving to Dallas.

He closed his eyes and clenched his teeth. None of it should matter . . . but it did. Everything about this woman mattered.

His heart pounded hard, but he knew his ragged breathing was more than just anger, it was more like desperation, thinking of the possibility of never seeing her again. He suddenly realized that his feelings for Heather ran deeper than he'd ever imagined possible.

Dear God. This was it. He'd been struck down without a warning.

He was in love with Heather.

Shit. Now what? He paced back and forth across the kitchen floor, reviewing all his options. The most obvious being that he would ask her to marry him, and they'd all move to Dallas.

Obvious, but not possible. There was no way Heather would move that far away from her family, especially now that she was about to become an aunt for the first time.

Seth stopped pacing and braced his hands on the counter, staring out the kitchen window toward the playground in the middle of the atrium. Okay, option two. If he truly wanted to make this work, he would have to turn down that promotion and remain in Colorado Springs. Although Joe Ferguson had made it more than clear he would be out on his ass if he did, it still wouldn't be all that bad.

How many times had he thought about going out on his own? Maybe this was his chance to become an independent financial advisor. He'd thought about investing in Davison's new aero-park subdivision where homeowners lived right next to their own private runway. He could build a house and keep his plane right there on his property.

Then he remembered Heather's aversion to airplanes.

Okay, scratch that. They could all just live here in her condo, or better yet, in his fifth-floor-penthouse suite. Hell, maybe he could just buy some land near the Garrison acreage and make it all one big happy village! That would certainly make Heather and everyone else happy.

To hell with all his dreams, all his so-called plans. He made angry quotes in the air the way Heather had done earlier. She thought he couldn't change midstream? That he was a carbon copy of Eric? She was wrong and somehow he was determined to prove it.

He strode down the hallway and found her lying next to Katie in the middle of the bed. She was reading a story out of a children's Bible about Daniel and the lion's den. All his anger—all his bitter resentment about this whole predicament—puddled at his feet.

At that moment, he knew nothing else mattered but being with Heather and becoming a father to her children, as well as making a family for Nicole. Watching Heather hold Katie, he leaned a shoulder against the doorframe and crossed his ankles in front of him. Truth be told, maybe he was the jealous one. After feeling Heather's arms wrapped around him all night, he could use a little coddling himself right about now.

"How's my little Katie-did this morning?" he asked, bringing both their heads up at the same time.

Katie curled her bottom lip into a pout. "It hurts really bad, Uncle Seth."

He moved swiftly to the end of the bed and picked up her doll to keep from sitting on it. He recognized the doll with the missing eye and chopped haircut as the one he'd found in the horse stall the day Jared had toured him around the ranch. He snuggled it up next to Katie and crawled in beside her, placing a quick kiss on her forehead. "I know it hurts, punkin'. But in a few days you'll be swinging that thing around like a baseball bat. Can I be the first one to sign your cast?"

She squeezed the doll under her arm. "I guess so. Can you draw me something?"

He rubbed his jaw and gazed up at Heather who hadn't said a word. Her eyes were bloodshot and her nose was puffy from crying. She reached behind her and grabbed a brown Sharpie from the end table, then handed it to him.

Tugging the cap off, he drew a lion's head with a bushy mane all around it. "Remember how brave Daniel was when he went into the lion's den?"

She sniffed and nodded.

"Well, this is to remind you how brave you have to be right now. Daniel was very brave and so are lions." When he drew the whiskers and finishing touches, he signed, "Uncle Seth." He tapped her nose. "What do you think? Are you going to be a brave girl for your momma?"

Katie smiled and nodded her head. "Even if it hurts, I'll just grit my teeth and growl like a lion."

He chuckled. "That's a big girl." Now that she was calmed down, he reached up and swept a strand of hair away from her big brown eyes. "So, what happened last night on the swing set? You said Kyle pushed you?"

"Well," she hedged, looking guiltily up at her mother out of the corner of her eye. "He didn't exactly push me."

"What do you mean, Katie?" Heather wedged up on an elbow. "You said Kyle pushed you out of the swing."

Katie started picking at the doll's hair. "Well, he did give me a push, but then I pumped real hard and sort of jumped. But I didn't know I'd gotten so high," she finished, trying to defend her mistake. She lowered her gaze, tracing a finger over the doll's one good eye. "Did I get Kyle in trouble?"

Seth looked up and found Heather's eyes glossing over in unshed tears. Hoping to ease the tension, he reached across Katie and gave Heather's leg a reassuring squeeze. "No, Katie. Kyle didn't get into trouble, but maybe you could talk to him about it. You said some things that I bet you didn't mean."

"I know. I promise to apologize when he gets home." She squeezed her doll and looked up at Heather. "Mommy?" she asked, her eyes tearing over.

"Yes, sweetie, what is it?"

She let out a little sob. "Kyle didn't start the fire."

"What?" Heather's eyes widened. "What do you mean?"

She glanced up at Seth, biting her lower lip. He gave a reassuring nod. "Go on, Katie. Tell us what happened."

She looked back up at her mom. "It was me. I found the matches in Auntie Debra's end table. I started the papers on fire. It all happened so fast I didn't know what to do. Kyle came in and shoved me outside." She kept talking through her tears. "I ran and found Uncle J.D., and Kyle tried to put out the fire with water from the sink. It was all my fault he got hurt, Mommy. I'm so sorry," she cried, burying her face into Heather's chest.

A tear dripped down Heather's cheek as she closed her eyes and stroked Katie's hair. "Shhh, it's okay, now," she soothed in a choked whisper. "Kyle's going to be fine. I'm just glad you told me the truth."

Glancing down at the tattered doll still clutched in Katie's hand, Seth thought back to that first day when Kyle and Katie about got trampled by one of the stallions in the barn. Seth had a sneaking suspicion that Kyle had been protecting Katie from being hurt by the stallion. Seems Kyle was turning out to be Katie's unsung hero. Seth reached over and touched Heather's hand, offering solace, offering strength. Without opening her eyes, she accepted his gesture, immediately squeezing his hand.

He had to swallow several times to keep his own emotions in check. He pushed himself up and leaned over Katie, placing a kiss over Heather's trembly lips, sealing his commitment to make this all work out. Somehow, somewhere, they would all be a family someday.

He rested his cheek against hers and spoke softly next to her ear. "I'm going to spend some time with my brother this morning, then I'll get Kyle and Nicole and take them to the baseball game this afternoon." He drew apart just enough to see Heather's face. "Sound okay?"

She gave a tremulous smile, her eyes shimmering with tears. "Are you sure? I'd hate to impose."

"Impose. I wouldn't have asked if I didn't want to. Will you need your van this afternoon?"

"No. Go and ahead and take it. Sounds like you'll need it anyway. I think I'll just stay here and cuddle with Katie." She gave him a timid smile. "And I said cuddle, not coddle. There's a difference."

"You can coddle or cuddle all you want, just as long as I get some of that later, okay?" He grinned and snuck another kiss, drinking in her tears, wanting to be beside her the rest of his life. "We'll be back after the game. Maybe Katie will feel better later, and we can all go to the Pizza Palace for a big birthday celebration."

Heather nodded, smiling through glossy brown eyes.

He pressed another kiss to her sore eye. "Get some sleep. I'll

Jacquie Greenfield

have my phone if you need to get hold of me."

When he went to pull away, she held tight to his hand and mouthed, "I'm sorry . . . about everything."

"Don't be. We've got a lot to talk about, but right now, I'd better get a move on." He pressed his lips over hers, lingering for an extra moment before dipping down and placing a kiss on Katie's head. "See you later, my little Katie-did."

She gave a sleepy yawn and wrapped her good arm around his neck. "Bye, Uncle Seth. Love you."

He swallowed a thick lump at the back of his throat and murmured, "Love you, too, sweetie." With Katie's arm around his neck, he slowly raised his lids and met Heather's gaze. For a moment, neither of them moved and he couldn't be sure what she was thinking. Was this real? Did Heather love him, too?

Regretful, he shoved off the bed and strode toward the door. He looked back and found Heather curled down into the pillows and blankets with Katie. Both already looked sound asleep. Leaving their embrace had to be about the hardest thing he'd ever had to do in his life. If this was what he had to look forward to, then no job in the world would ever come between them.

Heading out to the living room, he picked up the van keys sitting next to Heather's notebooks.

He grabbed the tablet with all her ideas she'd drawn on the back and stepped across the living room. He had a lot of work ahead of him. Maybe he could figure a way to work with this Eric Thomas after all.

Heather pulled out a tray of chocolate chip cookies from the oven and set them on the stove. She slid the last tray into the oven, shut the door and gave herself a silent pat on the back. Only one more tray and she'd completed the whole batch without burning a single cookie.

Usually the phone rang, or someone came to the door, or she

had to help one of the kids with something, and she'd inevitably wind up with a few scorched cookies. She sunk her teeth into one and sighed. They'd turned out soft and chewy and perfect, just the way Kyle liked them.

With the rim of his Rockies T-shirt in his mouth, Kyle tapped his pencil against the table in a steady rhythmic pattern. His legs were swinging back and forth under the kitchen chair. Since she'd left for California and he'd burned his hands, they'd neglected their school assignments, falling out of their normal routine.

His hands were a little sore from riding Evening Star yesterday, so Heather had wrapped bandages around his palms to keep from irritating them further. At least he could hold onto a pencil and work on his assignments. He was supposed to be writing about his baseball excursion with Seth yesterday and the pizza party last night. She was using this writing exercise as a way to get him back into the swing of school.

Across the table, Katie was coloring a picture, using various markers and an array of crayons. Other than her skin itching beneath her cast, her arm didn't seem to be bothering her as much today.

"Kyle?" Heather noticed he'd only written one sentence. "Keep writing. You'll get a warm cookie when you're through. I even put in extra chocolate chips just the way you like them," she bribed.

Without answering, he curled his fingers around the end and slowly began printing another word. While she waited for the last tray, she wiped her hands on a kitchen towel and watched Kyle.

He'd had a good time at the Rockies game with Seth yesterday afternoon. She'd sent along his earphones to help muffle the loud cheering so it wouldn't hurt his ears. Fortunately, Seth said he hadn't thrown any tantrums and had behaved all day.

She'd enjoyed meeting Seth's younger brother, Marty, after the game. He wasn't near as tall as Seth, but he had the same thick black hair. He'd talked nonstop about his home at Pine Tree, how he loved to plant flowers and the fun games they all played every day. He had the cutest dimple in his rounded cheeks, and his expressive blue eyes sparkled with a childlike innocence.

Between Seth, Marty and Nicole, Heather, Kyle and Katie, they all scarfed down five jumbo-sized pizzas. Before the night was out, they'd blown several rolls of quarters on arcade games, and listened to the animated big bear band play the happy birthday song about a thousand times.

Even though it was probably a little juvenile for a teenager, Nicole seemed to have had a good time, too. After they'd cut the cake, Seth had handed them each several gifts to open and had even thought to add Heather's name to the tags. Without her van all day, she hadn't had a chance to do any shopping for Nicole.

Heather had caught his little wink and smiled her approval when Nicole had opened two pairs of earrings and a new music CD. But it was the gift Seth had put his name on that still made her eyes sting with tears.

He'd bought Nicole a paint-and-palette set, complete with sketching paper, an easel and all the different paintbrushes known to man. At first, Nicole had just stared, but then her eyes spilled over with tears, and she'd wrapped her arms clear around her uncle's shoulders.

Heather put a hand to her throat, still feeling an emotional tug, remembering how Seth's eyes had watered over, his face flushing red with embarrassment. He'd been just as thoughtful with Marty, giving him a brand-new baseball glove and batting helmet and had even given small tokens to Kyle and Katie. Seth was just one big surprise after another.

They hadn't talked about their conversation from yesterday morning, but he almost seemed smitten the rest of the day, his eyes alight with something similar to puppy love.

Or was it the real thing?

A panicky feeling struck her in the pit of her stomach. Was this love? Did she love Seth Roberts?

Her heart shuddered every time she thought it could be a possibility, but then the rational side of her brain always seemed to dismiss his sensual glances and his lazy smiles from across the room as something more akin to friendship. That was all the farther they could take their relationship, anyway.

She had her kids to think about now, and Nicole's well-being was at stake, as well. Besides, she couldn't sleep with this man, give him her whole heart, knowing he was leaving for Dallas at the end of the summer.

And he would. The draw of the vice presidency would be too hard for a man like Seth to resist.

"All done, Mommy," Katie beamed, holding up the picture she'd drawn.

Heather set her spatula on the counter and came around behind Katie. "Wow, it's beautiful."

"I drew it for Kyle," she said, looking over at her brother. "I know you like raccoons. See? There's a momma coon curled up next to the big tree."

Without lifting his head, Kyle glanced over at Katie's picture from the corner of his eye.

Heather nudged Katie's shoulder. "This would be a good time to tell him you're sorry, honey."

"Sorry, Kyle," she said, staring down at her picture.

"Do you know what you're sorry for?" Heather prodded.

Katie looked down at her cast, tracing her finger around the lion Seth had drawn. "I'm sorry I lied 'bout the fire and about

271

what happened to my arm." She looked up at Kyle with tear-filled, brown eyes. "I hope you're not mad at me. I didn't mean to get you in trouble."

Kyle kept glancing at the picture Katie had drawn. "They eat eggs," he mumbled through his shirt.

Katie looked down at her picture and blinked, clearing her vision. "Do you like it? I made it for your room."

Without answer, Kyle took the picture and ran down the hallway toward his bedroom. Heather and Katie both followed and found him tacking the picture to his bulletin board above his desk.

Heather's heart swelled with pride as she realized that Kyle had probably saved Katie's life that day of the fire, not to mention J.D.'s house. Kyle was the real hero, and somehow, Heather was determined to let him know how proud she was of him. If he would just let her get close.

She nudged Katie toward her brother. "I think he likes it. Why don't you give him a big hug?"

Katie wrapped her good arm around Kyle. "I'm glad you got the fire out at Uncle J.D.'s house. Maybe you could be a fireman someday."

Kyle didn't move, but he didn't pull away either.

"Do you want to put your name on my cast?" she asked.

Kyle pulled away from Katie and opened the top drawer to his desk and began rummaging through an array of colorful markers. He settled on a bright purple one and tugged off the lid. When he finished writing his name, he threw the pen in the drawer and barreled out the door.

Katie laughed and looked down at her cast. "He's funny, isn't he, Mommy?"

Heather smiled and knelt down next to her daughter. "Kyle's very special, honey. He does things just a little differently from other kids. But we love him no matter what, right?"

"Yep. He's my favorite brother," she beamed.

"Remember, you promised to make his bed every day for two weeks for lying about the fire, okay?"

"Okay, and I promise I won't lie again."

"Good. You know I love you very much. No matter what happens, you can always tell me the truth. Now, I need to finish up with his school lessons this morning. Does your arm hurt?"

"Not too bad."

"Maybe you could go out to the playground and build a sand castle. Kyle can come out and play in a little bit."

"Okay. I'll go build one for Kyle."

"I bet he'd like that."

As Katie skipped outside, Heather breathed a sigh of relief, feeling like she'd just gotten over another hurdle. Maybe Seth had been right. She'd been coddling both kids too much and hanging on too tight. Now that Saint Anthony's was shutting their doors, she had some decisions to make. She'd been thinking about mainstreaming Kyle gradually into the public school system. She'd even called the school counselor and had asked about the various programs offered for special needs children just like Kyle. She was impressed with some of the programs offered, including being assigned an aide to help him throughout the school day.

The couple of times Heather had mentioned school to Katie, the girl's expression had turned exuberant. And with them both in school, Heather would have more time to herself, allowing her to take on that writing project she'd been dreaming about for years. Maybe now was the perfect time to start letting out her apron strings.

With a new resolved lease on life, she found herself smiling and headed for the kitchen. Then she caught a whiff of something burning.

The cookies!

CHAPTER FOURTEEN

The loud shrill of the smoke alarm pierced the air. She raced into the kitchen into a cloud of smoke roiling from the oven. Kyle yelled and clamped his hands over his ears.

"It's okay, honey, it's just the smoke detector. It'll go off in a minute." She donned an oven mitt and yanked the oven door down. Smoke billowed into the room.

Grabbing the tray, she jerked it out of the oven and in her haste, bumped the edge of the tray on the counter, dropping the entire cookie sheet on the floor with a loud clatter.

"Oh, shoot!" Crispy, black cookies crumbled and splattered all over the floor.

Kyle was moaning loudly still covering his ears.

"The alarm will stop in a minute, Kyle," she tried to reassure him.

She reached up and turned off the oven and ran over to the sliding doors to get the smoke to filter outside.

The front doorbell sounded over the smoke alarm. Probably one of the neighbors. "Hold on! It's just a false alarm," she called out, trotting to the door. As soon as she opened it, her mouth gaped open.

"What the hell's going on in here?" Eric bellowed and brushed past her. "Are you burning the place down, for god-sakes? Where are the kids?"

"It's nothing. A tray of cookies got burned, that's all." She followed her ex-husband into the kitchen and about rammed into his backside when he halted at the kitchen threshold. The smoke alarm finally ceased, but Kyle remained in a stupor, clamping his hands over his ears.

Eric coughed and waved his hand. "Kyle? Son? Are you okay?" He stepped through several smashed cookies and crouched closer to Kyle. Eric's eyes widened as he took Kyle's hands away from his ears. "My God. What happened to his hands?"

"No!" Kyle screamed.

Heather bolted to the other side of the table and curled her arms around Kyle's shoulder. "It's okay, honey. It's Daddy. Do you remember Daddy?"

Kyle didn't answer, but continued to rock back and forth.

"What the hell happened to his hands? Looks like he's been burned!"

Rubbing Kyle's shoulders, she tried to keep her voice level. "Some newspapers caught on fire a few weeks ago. The doctor said he'll be fine. It probably won't even leave a scar."

"How did it happen? Weren't you watching him?"

There was no way she'd let him know she'd been a thousand miles away at the time. "I'm not going to defend myself to you. It was no one's fault. He's fine now, so let's just drop it."

"Maybe this time he's fine, but what about the next time? He might not be so lucky, or worse, what if Katie gets hurt? Don't you know he needs constant supervision?"

"Don't you dare walk in here and presume to tell me how to raise our son! You have no idea what he needs."

"Apparently you don't either!"

"No!" Kyle yelled.

She narrowed her eyes and patted Kyle's back, lowering her voice. "You need to calm down, Eric. You're upsetting Kyle."

"*I'm* upsetting Kyle? I walk in here with the fire alarm going full blast and smoke billowing from the room, my son is covered in burns, and you say I'm upsetting him?"

She gripped the back of Kyle's chair, raising her chin. "What do you want? Why are you here?"

He reached over and touched her chin. "What the hell happened to your eye?"

She'd completely forgotten. The swelling had gone down, but a dark purple stain surrounded the socket. Avoiding his scrutiny, she pulled away from his touch and squatted to the floor, scooping the cookies off the tile and onto the tray. "It's nothing. I was playing baseball, and it just got away from me."

She stared up at this huge man towering over her. As always, he was dressed in the finest suit money could buy, a hand-tailored, dark-gray business suit, crème-colored shirt and a beautiful maroon silk tie. She forced a cynical laugh. "Don't tell me you're here because you miss your kids."

He slouched against the counter and crossed his ankles in front of him, grabbing a cookie from the good pile. "I was going over some last-minute changes on the conversion of Saint Anthony's. We got done early, so I decided to check in on the kids before I headed back to Telluride." He took a bite of the cookie, made a face, and then dumped it back with the others. "Looks like it's a good thing I did. Where's Katie?"

A high-pitched giggle diverted their attention to the patio doors where Katie had run up. "Daddy! Daddy!"

Eric's expression only hardened as he gazed through the glass doors at his daughter. "My God! What happened to her arm?" He slid the door wide and hunkered down in front of her.

Katie threw her arms around Eric, cast and all. "I didn't know you were here."

"Hi, puddin'. What did you do to your arm?"

"Kyle pushed me, and I fell off the swing. Look," she said pointing to her cast. "Uncle Seth drew a lion for me because I was so brave."

"Who's Uncle Seth?"

Heather hurried over and quickly intervened. "He's just one of our clients at the ranch. His niece is attending the camp this summer." Wanting to clarify how Katie broke her arm, Heather gave her daughter a stern glance. "Katie, tell Daddy what really happened on the swings."

"Are you accusing her of lying? Has anything else happened that I'm not aware of?" Eric set Katie down and took her fingers, holding her out to appraise his daughter. "Wow, I think you've grown a whole foot since I saw you last."

"I get to be in second grade next year. Mommy said I get to go to a real school and everything!"

"That's great. You'll get so much smarter with a real teacher. Now you'll get to play with lots of other little girls your age."

"Can you stay and play with me? Please?"

"Sorry, darlin', not this trip, but I have something for you." He reached into the breast pocket of his jacket and pulled out a little box. He opened it, displaying a gold necklace with a heart-shaped pendant. "Happy birthday, sweetheart."

"Wow, it's so pretty. Can I put it on?"

"Sure. Turn around." Eric carefully undid the clasp with his large fingers and draped it around Katie's petite neck.

Her smile spanned from ear to ear as she touched the pretty gold heart. "I love it, Daddy. Guess what? Mommy said I could get my ears pierced for my birthday. I can't wait."

Eric's lips formed a straight line as he glared at Heather. "Isn't she a little young?"

"For earrings?" Heather arched her brows. "Hardly. Some girls have it done when they're babies. All her friends have them, and besides, I was eight when I got mine pierced. She's very responsible. But then, I guess you wouldn't know that, would you?"

He shoved his hands on his thighs and stood. "Responsible?

Let's talk about responsible, Heather. Like why Kyle's hands are burned, and Katie's arm is broken. Now I have to wonder how exactly you got that black eye. Maybe I overestimated your ability at raising our kids."

Feeling a burning flush work its way over her face, Heather strode to the counter and grabbed two cookies. With her teeth gritted together, she handed one to Katie and the other to Kyle. "You two run outside and play. Your daddy and I have to talk a little bit more."

As soon as Eric closed the door, Heather swung around and glowered. "How dare you put me down in front of my kids! You have no right to waltz in here and criticize me after only five minutes." She flung her hand toward the front door. "Just get out!"

Eric only stared at her, shaking his head. "Look at this place. I had no idea things had gotten so out of control around here."

"Things aren't out of control." She swallowed and tried to keep a rational tone of voice. "They're kids. Accidents happen. I'm doing the best that I can."

"That's my point. Your best obviously isn't good enough. After what I've seen today, it's pretty obvious Kyle needs more than what you've been giving him. If I have my way, Kyle will be at Pine Tree before the end of the summer, and Katie will be attending a private school in Telluride this fall."

"Don't you dare threaten to take my kids away from me."

"Oh, it's not a threat." He looked around her condo, cluttered with toys and a laundry basket full of clothes to be folded. Giving an arrogant chuckle, he said, "Don't take it personally, sweetheart. Some women just aren't cut out to be wives or mothers."

A deafening silence engulfed the condo the moment Eric slammed the door. For several moments, Heather didn't know if she could even breathe. Blood rushed from her head. Feeling dizzy, she fumbled her way to a kitchen chair and sat down before she collapsed in the middle of the floor.

She blinked several times, hoping she'd been in some kind of nightmare and just needed to wake up. It was as if she was having an out-of-body experience and any moment she would float back to safety and everything would be fine.

But she wasn't fine, and in fact, had never felt this desperate in her life.

With trembling hands, she reached for the portable phone and hit the number-one speed-dial number. "Hello, you've reached the home of J.D. and Debra. We're away from the phone right now, but leave your name and numb—"

She clicked off the phone and punched in J.D.'s cell number. Her shaky fingers made her hit the wrong button and she had to redial. Clenching the receiver, she listened to several rings before she got J.D.'s voice mail. Tears blurred her vision as she punched the END button and dialed her mom's number at the ranch house. On the fifth ring, she got their machine, too. She hung up and dialed Jared's number and got the after-hours answering service to his clinic. They told her he was out on an emergency call and probably wouldn't be available for another hour. Heather didn't want to pull him off his call and just told them to have Jared call at his earliest convenience.

Desperation seized her heart. She clicked the phone off and held the receiver against her chest. "Where is everybody?"

Making a quick glance through the sliding glass doors, she was relieved that the kids were playing nicely in the sandbox, making castles. She scrolled through the memory of her telephone number bank and stopped at her attorney's office. It was a Sunday night and the odds of getting her would be a miracle, but Heather dialed anyway. She left a message with the night answering service, but knew that she probably wouldn't get a call back until tomorrow sometime.

Going back through her address book, she stopped on Seth's cell phone number, biting her lower lip, wanting to call him. But then she remembered how he'd told her about his breakup with his ex-fiancée last summer, and how her ex-husband had been at the root of all their problems. Dragging Seth into her problems now would only prove his fears of getting involved with a woman with so much baggage. She had to handle this on her own.

With all her resources exhausted, she closed her eyes and slumped her head between her shoulders, swallowing deeply to keep the tears from falling. She couldn't let Eric beat her down like this. She'd worked too hard, too long to let him take all her dreams away from her now.

But dammit, she was tired. Tired of fighting for what was hers, what was right. She had no doubt that Eric would follow through with his threat. She'd seen that look in his eyes before. She'd seen it the night he'd walked out for the last time. She'd seen it that night at the hospital, when he'd told her about his involvement with the demolition of Saint Anthony's. He wasn't bluffing.

He was going to take her kids away.

Heather's stomach tightened. Her head spun. The phone slipped from her hands and clanked to the kitchen floor, land-ing amongst charred cookie crumbs. Pressing her fingers to her mouth, she bowed her head between her knees and let out a muffled cry. She had to do something. She couldn't just sit back and wait for Eric to make the next move.

The first thought was to grab both kids, pack a suitcase and run as far away as possible. She'd been putting away money for the kids' future since they were born. They could probably live on that for a while. But where? Where would she go? And how long would she have to stay away? Till Katie graduated high school?

Heather only shook her head. She couldn't run away. She wouldn't run away. She had to face Eric and pray that the judge would see how well adjusted Kyle was, and that Katie was better off living with her mother, and that he should be denied custody. Hopefully, everything would go back to normal.

She almost laughed. What was normal anyway?

"Mommy? Are you okay?" Katie's feet crunched through the cookie crumbs before she patted Heather on the back. "Don't you feel good?"

Heather breathed deeply and swiped the pads of her fingers under her eyes. "I'm fine. Just a little hot, is all." She forced a smile for Katie. "Why don't you get a couple of juice boxes and take one out to Kyle. I need to clean up this mess before it gets all over the house."

"Where did Daddy go? I wanted to give him a picture I drew."

Heather stood and opened the refrigerator door, grabbing out two juice boxes. "I'm sorry, honey. He had to leave."

"Awe. He never plays with me anymore. When's he coming back?"

Heather stabbed a straw into a juice box. The day hell froze over would be too soon.

The following Friday, Heather had just seen the last camper off before the weekend when Jillie met her at the office door, looking frazzled. "Heather, got a minute?"

Pressing two fingers to her temple, Heather tried to soothe a pounding headache. "Sure, what's up?"

Jillie motioned her head toward the bathroom facilities down by the cabins. "Nicole has been in the bathroom for over an hour. I've tried talking to her, but she only wants to talk to you."

"Is she sick?"

"I don't think so. Her bunkmate, Chloe, said Nicole's been acting strange all week. I thought maybe you'd talked to her today."

Heather shook her head. "I've been manning the office since lunch. Debra's back was bothering her so she's been lying down in the other room." Heather had been glad for the reprieve from her counseling duties for the afternoon after a courier had hand-delivered a package from Eric's lawyers, shortly after lunch. True to his word, he'd begun procedures to gain full custody of both kids, which would allow him to control Kyle's future, as well. She'd called her lawyer immediately, but all she could do now was wait. Wait for someone to contact her. Wait for her whole world to shatter all around her.

"Is Debra okay?" Jillie asked, breaking into her thoughts.

"Yeah, just extremely hot and tired. She's only got two weeks left before the baby's due, so she's pretty uncomfortable. Katie's been reading to her and keeping her company." As she rubbed her temples, Heather's thoughts drifted back to Nicole and she wondered if she was having troubles with the other campers. "Did she or any of the other girls have an argument?"

Jillie shook her head. "Nothing that I'm aware of."

Heather flicked a glance at her watch. It was almost five-forty. "Seth called this morning and arranged to go trail riding with Nicole at six. I hope she's not getting sick. Hard telling when he'll be able to schedule another time." Seth's call had been brief and strictly business. He hadn't mentioned last weekend at all, and definitely hadn't sounded like a man who was in love.

Maybe he'd finally seen the light and had had enough of her and her kids. Between Katie's broken arm and all the confusion at the Pizza Palace, any single man in his right mind would be running for the hills. It just took Seth a few days to come to his senses. And now with Eric back in the picture, it was probably all for the best.

Disillusioned with life once again, she squared her shoulders and stepped around her desk, pulled out a set of keys, and then followed Jillie out the door. Right now she had to focus on Nicole. As they headed down the ranch yard, she asked, "Did she say if she had a stomachache or anything?"

"No, she was fine when we fed the goats after lunch."

When they arrived at the restroom facilities situated among the cabins, Heather jiggled the doorknob. "Nicole?" She knocked and spoke at the same time. "Are you okay? It's Heather."

Her heart beat faster when Nicole didn't answer. Was something wrong? Had something happened between her and Seth?

With more urgency, she banged on the door. "Nicole, please answer me. I'm coming in if you don't open up."

She flipped through several keys on her key ring then heard the tumbler on the door click, but the door remained closed.

Heather looked over her shoulder toward Jillie. "You can go ahead and leave. Everyone else has already been picked up for the day."

"Are you sure? I'd be glad to wait in case you need any help."

"I'll be fine. Katie is with Debra, and Kyle is helping J.D. in the barn. So you're free to go."

"Okay. I'll see you Monday then."

As Jillie hurried off toward the camp office, Heather warily entered the bathroom and was relieved to find Nicole standing inside next to the sink. She didn't look up, but kept her fingers tucked into the front pockets of her jeans.

Heather shut the door, stepping inside. The fresh scent of pine and potpourri from the air freshener filled her senses. The bright fluorescent lights emphasized Nicole's sun-kissed cheeks, her freckles seeming to jump right off her face. She had on a pair of flared designer jeans with several hearts embroidered along the length of her thin legs. She wore a baseball cap and had a yellow tank top with more sequined hearts across the chest. Noting the fullness of her developing breasts, she looked more and more like a young woman every day.

"Nicole?" Heather stepped closer. "Are you okay, honey? Are you sick?"

Nicole shook her head but didn't answer.

Heather approached and put her hands on her shoulders. "What is it? Did you have a fight with one of the girls?"

"No, nothing like that."

Worried, Heather slouched down to get at eye level. "Is it your uncle? Did you two have a fight?"

"No. It's not that . . . exactly."

"What is it then . . . exactly?"

Nicole rolled her eyes. "It's kind of embarrassing."

Heather gave her shoulders a squeeze. "Don't be embarrassed, honey. You can come to me for anything."

Nicole turned her back, facing the sink. "I think I may have started."

Glancing at Nicole's reflection in the mirror, Heather narrowed her eyes, not sure what she meant. "Started what?"

"You know. My period. My monthly curse."

Heather couldn't keep the smile from spreading across her face. She was shocked, excited, relieved. Her heart swelled, knowing Nicole had just entered a new phase of becoming a woman. She only hoped she'd be there for Katie someday.

"That's wonderful. Congratulations. This is an exciting moment in your life."

Heather caught Nicole rolling her eyes in the mirror.

"Ugh. What's so wonderful about it?"

Understanding completely, Heather approached Nicole from

behind and put her arms around her shoulders, talking to Nicole's reflection in the mirror. "It means you're one of us now. You're almost a woman." Heather shrank down and pressed her cheek against Nicole's and smiled. "This is a very important day. You'll remember it the rest of your life." She pulled back and asked, "Are you okay? Do you have any questions?"

"No, we talked about it in the fourth grade, and I remember my mom going through it. I just . . . I don't have any. . . ." She arched her brows, fidgeting back and forth between feet.

Realization dawned and Heather held up her hand. "Say no more. I'll run up and get everything you need. There's no reason to be embarrassed."

"Oh, I'm not embarrassed—around you, anyway. It's just that. . . ." She trailed off and bit her bottom lip. "What about you-know-who?"

Nicole's apprehensions all started to make sense. "You mean Uncle Seth?"

"Uh, yeah? Like, who else? He doesn't have to know, does he? Ugh. I could just die."

Trying to stifle a laugh, Heather turned Nicole around and took her hands. "Your uncle's a pretty cool guy, Nicole. I think he should know what's going on, but if you'd like, I could tell him for you."

"Whewww!" Nicole sighed. "I was afraid I'd have to tell him. Can you imagine?" Her mouth gaped open as if she'd rather die than go to Seth. "I mean, that'd be like, totally mortifying."

"Like, totally," Heather agreed with a laugh. "Do you need anything else? Clean panties or anything?"

"No. I caught it before that happened."

"Well, if you're cramping or feeling bloated, let me know. I've got stuff for that, too."

Shifting between legs, Nicole gave what sounded like an irritated grunt. "And this is supposed to be a good thing?"

Heather laughed and wrapped her arms around Nicole's shoulders. "Believe me. Someday when you're holding your newborn baby, it'll all be worth it. Do you want to postpone your trail ride with your uncle?"

"No way. I'll probably never get him to reschedule if we don't do it tonight. He's been working like every night this week. I'd kind of hoped that after last weekend things would be different. It felt like. . . ." She paused, her eyes watering over. "It felt like I was part of a real family again." She dabbed at her nose and sniffed through her tears. "I don't know why I'm crying. It was just a pizza party."

Remembering how'd they'd laughed, sung off-key and played silly games, Heather had to admit it had been a wonderful feeling. That Saturday, which had begun with an argument with Seth in the morning, had turned out to be one of the best days she'd had in months.

After Eric's surprise visit the next day, Sunday had turned out to be one of her worst.

Knowing her kids could be ripped away from her with one stroke of a judge's pen had her panicking again. Her lawyer had reassured her that it would take some pretty extreme circumstances to take children away from their biological mother and award them to a single father with an adulterous track record.

That's when Heather had informed her that Eric had remarried and had a daughter around Katie's age, and that Eric's new wife was the daughter of a Colorado congressman. Heather's lawyer didn't sound as confident as she had before she'd heard that bit of information.

Trying to keep her mind off her problems, Heather handed Nicole a tissue. "Remember Nicole, this is all going to take time. Don't lose faith."

"It's just so hard sometimes." Nicole wiped her nose and threw the tissue in the trashcan. "It's like, when you're around, everything seems happier. Uncle Seth forgets all about work, and it makes me not miss my mom so much."

"I know it's hard, sweetie. You've had to adjust to lots of changes in the last few months. But you have to believe that everything is going to work out. Let's just take one day at a time and enjoy the time we have together." She told herself the same thing and just prayed she had the rest of the summer to be with Kyle and Katie.

"What about after summer? Then what?" Nicole asked with a choked voice. "I don't want to leave you, Heather. You're like, such a good mom."

Remembering Eric's hurtful words, Heather had to keep herself from tearing over. "I don't feel like a very good mom sometimes."

"Are you kidding? You're like this totally perfect super mom. Kyle and Katie are so lucky."

Heather didn't feel so lucky. Not wanting to let Nicole see how much turmoil her life was in at the moment, she tapped Nicole's nose and smiled. "Thanks. If I ever need you to vouch for me in front of a judge, I'll give you a call." She said it half-joking, but wondered if it would come down to that. "Now let's mop up these tears and clean our faces. We wouldn't want Uncle Seth to think we're PMSing or anything." Although Heather almost wished she could blame her foul mood on PMS.

"Is that why I've been like such a total crank lately? I think I've cried more in the last two weeks than when I lost my parents back in March. Uncle Seth probably wishes I'd never moved in."

"Awe, honey." Heather sighed, tucking a strand of hair behind Nicole's ear. "You've kept everything pent up inside you for so long, it's like a gusher now that you've finally opened up. All it took was a tiny pin prick, and the whole dam came flooding over. It's good to cry now and then. It's kind of like cleansing the soul."

Too bad crying wouldn't help Heather. "I'm sure when I tell Seth everything, he'll understand. It just takes time for you to adjust to your maturing body. I'll be back in a second." She opened the door and looked back. "Maybe we can get J.D. to watch Kyle some afternoon and we women will go out shopping. We still need to do a birthday shopping trip."

"Awesome. Maybe I could get some new clothes for school."

"Have you thought any more about the Nantucket Girls School?"

"I read through the brochures." Nicole lifted her shoulders. "I gotta admit, it looks kind of fun. It's like a big resort, only there's teachers and principals and tests. Yuck."

Heather laughed and checked the time. "I'd better hurry. Your uncle will be here any minute. I'm so proud of you, Nicole. This has been a big day. I'm glad I could be a part of it with you."

"I don't think I like it so far."

Heather wrinkled her nose and nodded. "I turn thirty next month and I still don't like it, but that's what makes us women so mysterious to guys. It's part of our chemistry."

Nicole's eyes widened. "Hey, Uncle Seth turns thirty next month, but I'm not sure which day. The first part of August, I think."

"Hmmmm, he's turning thirty, huh? Maybe we could surprise him with a party or something. You think about it, and I'll be right back." She headed up to the main house and got a few necessities for Nicole. After Nicole was settled into her cabin, Heather strode up to the main house, her heart swelling with joy about what had transpired today.

Now the real fun. Telling Uncle Seth. Her heart rate skittered when Seth's Corvette rumbled into the drive. He had the top down. Dark aviator sunglasses shaded his eyes. She smoothed her palms over her thighs and tucked her red tank top into the rim of her jeans. Hoping to appear relaxed and unfazed by his visit, she casually leaned against a wooden column on the front porch. She wasn't sure what she was more nervous about: knowing how much she'd fallen for him, or telling him about Nicole's big day, and how she'd taken her first step into womanhood.

The temperatures were in the eighties, the sky a crystal blue, reminding her of Seth's vibrant blue eyes. She breathed deep, taking in all the earthy scents of pine and spruce, reminding her of their hiking excursion into the mountains. What she would do to be there now, in his arms, tucked safely away in nature where no one could find her.

Seth's car engine shut off. He whipped off his sunglasses and flashed her one of those killer, sexy grins. Even through the windshield, his penetrating blue gaze practically hypnotized her into a state of paralysis. Fortunately, her wobbly knees reminded her she was, in fact, still standing—at least for the moment.

The first thing she noticed as he swung his long legs out of his vehicle was a set of shiny, lizard-skinned cowboy boots. She felt a slight tug at her lips, trying to keep from grinning. When he pulled his tall, lean body to standing, a warm shudder raced all the way down to her toes. He wore a crisp teal-and-black, Western-cut shirt that still had the crease down the sleeves. He'd even worn a shiny silver belt buckle and what looked like a pair of brand new Wrangler jeans. Darned if he didn't take her breath away with that fresh-shaven, sexy cowboy look.

Before he shut the door, he reached in for something off the front seat, stood and settled a black cowboy hat over his head. He touched the brim in greeting. "Howdy, ma'am," he drawled, his voice sounding low and smooth. Holding up a finger, he unhooked his cell phone and threw it in his car.

When he shut his door, she wasn't sure whether to laugh or just pretend he hadn't walked right off the movie set of *Urban Cowboy.* "I'm shocked. You've turned off your cell phone. You're wearing jeans and cowboy boots. Will miracles never cease?"

He gave a low, easy chuckle, shoved his hands on his thighs and did a half-squat. "I hope I can swing my leg over a horse. There's not a whole lot of room in these jeans."

She let out a hoot of laughter that echoed throughout the acreage. Putting two fingers to her lips, she whistled. "Turn around, cowboy. I want to see those tight buns of yours in them brand-spankin'-new jeans."

With an overexaggerated swagger, he walked around in a circle, turned back and hooked his thumbs in his belt loops. Adding to his mystique, he slipped his dark, wire-rimmed sunglasses back on and held out his arms to the sides. "What do you think? Do I look like a real cowboy now?"

"Define 'real cowboy,' " she said, ready to tie him down right here in the middle of the ranch yard. Standing on the top step of the porch, she remained entranced in his gaze as he sauntered up to the house. Even through his sunglasses, something thick sizzled between them.

He propped his booted foot on the bottom step and leaned an elbow on the railing. "Do ya'll know where I might find me a pretty little trail guide?" He actually had a halfway decent Southern drawl.

She tilted her head to the side and gave him a tentative grin. "Nicole's coming. She'll be up in a minute."

He hauled himself up to the step just below hers, moving closer. "Well, now, I'd kinda had my heart set on someone a might older. Say, around twenty-one-ish or so, and someone with legs that stretched from here to Texas."

She laughed. "Sorry. Jillie's already left for the day."

"I ain't talking about Jillie." He scanned her length and

whistled, his sunglasses sliding to the tip of his nose. "I almost wish I were a horse. I wouldn't mind having those wrapped around me right about now." He slid her a wink before shoving his sunglasses back on his nose.

She smacked him on the chest. "You're incorrigible. You've ignored me all week, and now you think you can just saunter up here with that little grin of yours and flatter me into your arms? Just remember, we'll have a chaperone on this trail ride, so don't get any ideas."

He touched her waist and leaned close. "I'm just chock full of ideas, darlin'. Come away with me this weekend, and I'll share a few with you."

"I think those jeans must have cut off the circulation to your brain. You've forgotten who you're talking to."

He gave a husky chuckle. "It ain't my brain having circulation problems right now. My jeans seemed to have gotten tighter since I came near you." He moved up a step, his face becoming level with hers.

Still leaning against the column with her hands tucked behind her, she lowered her lashes, gazing longingly at his lips. God, she'd missed him this week. As hard as she'd been fighting it, she couldn't deny this unquenchable desire to be near him.

As if reading her thoughts, he smiled and pressed his mouth over hers, thoroughly kissing her till her head dropped back, weightless.

She gave a moan of unabashed desire and brought her hands from behind her back and wrapped her arms around his firm, trim waist, tucking her fingers into his back pockets, cupping those adorable tight buns.

He trailed soft wet kisses along her jaw back to her ear. "If you expect me to be able to get on a horse, you'd better back off now. These jeans don't have much more room, for, uh . . . expansion."

291

Heather broke out laughing. "I hate to give you the satisfaction, but I actually missed your charming personality this week." Throwing all rationalization to the wind, she wrapped her arms around his shoulders and planted another wet kiss on that adorable sexy mouth.

"Wow," he moaned through her kisses. "If I'd have known a tight pair of jeans would get this kind of reaction, I'd have bought me a closet full of Wranglers a month ago."

Ashamed at throwing herself at him, she hopped down from his tight embrace. "Sorry, I shouldn't have—"

"Yes, you should have, and don't be sorry. I kinda missed you, too." Stroking his hands up and down her back, he tugged her into his arms. "I didn't mean to ignore you. Work's been crazy."

Disappointed that she still ranked behind business, she looked down at her boots, absently wiping her mouth.

He bent slightly, catching her gaze. "To be honest, I wasn't sure if you wanted to be more than friends. We haven't really talked since last Saturday. Everything okay with Kyle this week?"

Not wanting to mention Eric's visit, she toed the point of her boot into the dirt. "I had a little discussion with J.D. and Jared— you know, about what you said about Kyle maybe feeling a little jealous."

"I hope I didn't stir anything up."

"Not at all. In fact, they completely agreed with you about Kyle missing their attention these last few months. J.D.'s taking Kyle fishing this evening, and Jared said he'd pick him up sometime this weekend and let him go on a routine vet call. They may not be able to be around as much as they used to, but at least they're aware."

"That's good to hear. I had a great time at the game. He and Marty really hit it off. I told them I'd take them to another game, if that's okay with you."

"Of course, it's okay. I mean, if you're sure?"

"I'm positive. And since I'm holding up my end of the deal by getting on a horse and going on this trail ride, how 'bout I take you up flying tomorrow night? Not too late, say around six. We can watch the sun set over the horizon from the cockpit in the sky."

She slipped her arms around his waist, tugging him firmly against her hips. "I suppose this means I need to find a babysitter?"

His hands lowered to the curve of her jeans. "Why don't we arrange to have the kids stay over with J.D. and Debra tomorrow night? Give us the evening to figure out what this is between us." Before she could answer, he lowered his mouth to hers, pressing more than just his lips against her.

She nudged her palms against his chest, feeling the strong beat of his heart, but knew if she let him kiss her much longer, it would lead to more than just a kiss. That would have to wait . . . till tomorrow night. "Okay," she whispered, breaking the kiss. "I'll go flying with you, but I think we'd better cool it before Nicole sees us."

She made a quick glance over his shoulder toward the cabins. "And speaking of Nicole. There've been a few interesting developments today. Come up to the porch and sit down. We need to have a little chat."

CHAPTER FIFTEEN

Seth's gut tightened at the sudden serious change in Heather's mood. He'd hoped after his conversation with Nicole about her parents a couple of weeks ago, things would start to get better between them. On the contrary, she'd been even more grouchy and argumentative. Once she'd learned to trust that he would never hurt her, she'd pretty much said whatever was on her mind. She hated his music. All his DVDs were boring. When he'd walked into her room last night to check on her, he'd found her painting on the new easel he'd bought her for her birthday. He'd asked what she was painting, and she'd flipped out on him and had started crying.

This morning he'd made the mistake of telling her he liked her hair in the pretty barrettes. She'd immediately pulled them all out and swept everything back into a short little ponytail. No matter what he said or did, the slightest thing seemed to set her off. Maybe Heather was having the same trouble and didn't want Nicole in the camp anymore.

Whatever it was, Heather's fingers trembled in his hand as she tugged him up to the front porch, leading him over to the hanging porch swing. "You might want to sit down for this," she warned.

"Uh-oh. This doesn't sound good. What'd she do?"

"Nothing, at least not the way you think."

He sat down on the swing, his long legs spreading wide as he pushed back with the heels of his boots. Tugging off his sunglasses, he slid them into his shirt pocket. "Okay. I'm sitting. What happened?"

"Hmmm, how to word this?" She paced back and forth in front of him, tapping a finger to her chin. "You might say she's officially joined our sorority of sisterhood."

What the hell was that supposed to mean? He swung forward slightly and stopped. "Okay? I give. What are you talking about?"

Heather stopped pacing and propped her hands on her hips. "It means, dear Seth, that she's taken that first step into womanhood." Her mouth curved into a wide, knowing smile.

It suddenly all clicked into place. The mood swings. Crying over nothing. Oversensitivity. He remembered when Shelli had gone through it. He and Pop as much as looked at her wrong and she'd flown off the handle.

He stopped swinging. Closed his eyes. Groaned. "Oh, God. Does that mean what I think it means?"

"It means, she got her per—"

"For Pete's sake, woman. Don't say it out loud." He glanced around, looking for any bystanders and lowered his voice. "Isn't she a little young?"

"Not really," she whispered back, mocking his voice. "Most girls start between the ages of nine and fourteen, and with the emotional stress she's been under this year, it's a wonder she hasn't started before now." She smiled. "I got mine when I was thirteen."

He held up his hand. "That's more information about you than I needed to know."

"Come on," she teased with a laugh. "You do know where babies come from, right?"

"Babies are one thing." He peered up at her from under the rim of his hat. "Their mothers are a totally different picture." Rubbing the pads of his fingers over his eyes, he asked, "So, what exactly does this mean? What do I do?"

"Well, the most important thing is to be supportive. Don't embarrass her. Remember, you're the adult. She's the adolescent going through several life changes."

That didn't sound so bad. "Is that it?"

"Well, I gave her what she'll need to get by for a couple of days. But. . . ." She paused and reached into her pocket, tugging out a piece of paper. "I've made a list of a few supplies you'll need to keep stocked in her bathroom."

"Supplies?" he repeated, looking at the paper. He slowly rolled his gaze up to meet her eyes, which at the moment held a hint of amusement in their depths.

"Yeah, supplies. You know, sanitary—"

"There you go again," he interrupted, holding up his hand. "I don't even want to hear the word."

"What? You mean sanitary napkins?" she finished, trying to contain her laughter.

He sat back and whipped off his hat, flicking her hand away with the paper. "You can just keep that little list. I'm not going anywhere near that stuff."

"It's a perfectly normal body function, Seth. It dates clear back to Eve. There's nothing to be embarrassed about."

"Easy for you to say. You're one of them."

"Excuse me?" She crossed her arms over her chest. "One of them?"

"You know what I mean. I'll bet Adam never had to make a trek to the drugstore for. . . ."

"Tampons?" she filled in for him.

"God. Just shoot me now." He dramatically placed a hand over his heart.

"Remember, Seth, she's nervous about this, too. Have you set her up with her own room yet?"

"Yeah. I moved all my stuff out of my office. She's even got her own bathroom, thank God."

In the next instant, Seth dropped to the porch on his knees and grabbed Heather's hand. "Please, Heather, I'll pay you a thousand bucks if you'll handle this one little area for me."

Looking down at him, she tapped her chin. "As much as that offer tempts me, I would pay a thousand bucks to be able to watch you buy a box of maxi pads." She laughed and squatted down in front of him, bringing her to eye level. "But in all seriousness, I think I might have a solution. Nicole said she's been helping you out around the place, why not give her an allowance and she can get the things she needs. That might save you both from a little embarrassment."

"Now that's the best idea I've heard all day." He blew out a gust of relief and shook his head. "Man, I need a drink. I don't suppose. . . ."

"No," she laughed, shaking her head. "Alcohol at a children's camp wouldn't be too cool." She placed a palm on the side of his face. "I know you can do this, Seth. It's all part of what makes us females so mysterious to you males." Tucking the list inside his shirt pocket, she splayed her palm over his heart. "I've experienced firsthand how sensitive you are to a woman's needs. This is no different."

He looked down at his pocket then back to her. "You're enjoying this, aren't you?"

"More than you know," she said with a giggle.

More than anything, he wanted to wipe that smug smile right off her cute little mouth. "Are we alone?"

She lazily rolled her head to the side and peered over her shoulder. "For the time being, anyway. Why? What'd you have in mind?"

"This," he said, gripping her bottom and tugging her onto his lap. She gave a little squeal as she straddled his waist. He pressed his lips firmly over hers, devouring her mouth, wanting to taste every inch of her body. His cowboy hat dropped to the floor behind them.

"My, my," she panted, wrapping her arms around his neck. "All this woman talk sure has you all fired up. Must be the hormones."

Digging his fingers into her jeans, he groaned into the side of her neck. "It's hormones, all right, and they're just achin' to solve one of those little mysteries you were talking about earlier."

"Like, I'm totally sure, Uncle Seth."

Nicole's sarcasm jerked his attention away from Heather. He shoved to standing, inadvertently dumping Heather on her backside with a thud. Feeling like he'd just been caught making out with the boss's daughter, he growled a greeting through gritted teeth. "Nicole."

"Uncle Seth," she mocked in a low voice, climbing the steps, seemingly unfazed at their predicament.

How did parents ever find privacy to have sex? It was a wonder there were so many kids in the world.

"Gee, nice duds," Nicole added, picking up his cowboy hat from the floor. "Was there a sale at Cowboys 'R' Us?" She propped the hat on her head, stepped around them then slumped down onto the porch swing, blowing a bubble, swaying back and forth.

Catching Heather's amused grin as she remained on the porch, staring up at him, Seth extended his hand. She was obviously just as embarrassed as he at being caught. Her face was as bright as her low-scooped red tank top. She took his hand and stood next to him.

The office door swung open and Debra waddled out, holding her back. Her belly had to be the size of a basketball. Katie galloped onto the front porch, her cast not hindering her at all as she did circles all around them before she came to a halt next to Heather.

Debra glanced back and forth between Seth and Nicole with

a knowing smile. "Did you tell him yet?"

Heather simply said, "Yep."

All in unison, four sets of female eyes focused on him. The porch became silent except for the creek of a rusty hinge on the swing. A brisk warm wind blew from the south, not helping his state of embarrassment any. Was he supposed to say something to Nicole? Congratulate her? Buy her a present?

When they all broke out into a fit of laughter, he suddenly felt like he was on the outside of a very private inside joke. This was it. He'd died and gone to hormone hell.

He grabbed his cowboy hat from Nicole, shoved it on his head then shuffled backwards down the steps. "I think I'll go find J.D. This is one sorority I have no intentions of joining." He touched his hat. "Ladies? If you'll excuse me? I'll be out with the stallions rejuvenating my testosterone levels."

Walking with a slight discomfort from the tightness of his jeans, he ignored the girls' laughter and strode down the ranch yard toward the paddock. Not exactly the kind of news most men celebrated, he thought with a little chagrin.

He'd hoped to be celebrating another kind of news with Heather tonight, but his meeting with Eric Thomas this afternoon had turned out to be a total waste of time. After he'd left Heather's last weekend, he'd spent the entire week preparing a new pitch to Eric Thomas and his Telluride investors. He'd even gone to Heather's stepfather's firm of Dalton & Jones Architects. Brad had taken Heather's drawings, and with his grandson's interest at heart, had worked several late nights with Seth, converting the original resort plans into what Seth now affectionately called the Golden Springs Retirement Village and Independent Living Complex.

This afternoon, he had shown Thomas the numbers. And though the rate of return was lower than in his original proposal, this new resort still held a huge potential for growth and expansion down the road. But Eric Thomas refused to even present it to his investors. He'd made it clear he wanted nothing to do with a place where a bunch of misfits could be running around free, causing havoc and mayhem amongst the tenants and guests.

Idiot. Why wouldn't this man want to do what was right for his own son?

A horse nickered from inside the barn as Seth approached. He strode around to the wide barn door and casually leaned his shoulder against the frame, watching J.D. throw a saddle over the back of a buckskin quarter horse. Seth breathed deep, the smell of horse manure and hay a sharp contrast to all those female concoctions that had turned his brain into pudding. He smiled when he found Kyle sitting with a fishing pole and an opened tackle box, sorting through various worms and lures. Looked like he was getting ready to go fishing with J.D.

Standing behind the horse, J.D. looked up and nodded. "How's it goin', Seth?"

He scratched his chin. "Pretty good, I guess."

"Did you hear about Nicole?"

"Oh, no," he groaned. "Don't tell me you're in on this, too."

"Sorry, man. When you live with a pregnant woman, there's nothing they don't discuss. Nicole's news is a walk in the park, buddy." He tightened the leather girth around the horse's belly. "You ready to ride? Nicole's a natural around horses. We may have to hire her on next summer."

Seth couldn't help but wonder where he'd be living next summer.

J.D. took the reins and led the mare over to a hitching post, then brought back a big sorrel quarter horse. "This here's Ol' Roy."

"Ol' Roy, huh?" Seth patted the horse on the neck. "How're ya doin', buddy?"

"He shouldn't give you any problems. He knows our ranch

inside and out."

Seth cleared his throat. "I suppose Heather mentioned my aversion to the equine species."

"She may have mentioned it," J.D. answered with a chuckle, draping a worn Western saddle over the horse's back. "So, how's work going? I hear you're moving to Dallas."

"Is there anything they don't tell you around here?"

"Nope," J.D. said matter-of-factly. He stopped saddling and peered over the horse. "It's true, then?"

Seth picked up a piece of straw and gave a shrug of his shoulders. "I'm pretty much guaranteed VP of the southern region, if I want it."

"If?" J.D. repeated, grabbing a bridle and slipping the bit into the gelding's jaw.

Seth propped a booted foot on a fence beside him. "I've kind of been having second thoughts about leaving Colorado. You know, Nicole and all. She just got settled in here, and I'd hate to pull her away from everything again."

"Nicole, huh?" J.D. strode to the tack room and lugged a children's saddle off a barrel then walked over to a palomino mare crunching on a mound of sweet oats. "She mentioned she might be going to a prep school out east."

Seth scratched the back of his neck. "I threw the idea out there, but like I told Nicole and Heather, I won't do anything she doesn't want to do. I only want what's best for Nicole."

J.D. spoke with a disbelieving grunt. "So you said."

Feeling on the defensive, Seth added, "I don't know if Heather told you, but my brother's in the area, too. He lives over at Pine Tree Family Services Center. Now that my sister's gone, I kind of feel like I should stay close to him, you know, so Nicole can grow up around her uncle."

"Right. Nicole." J.D. repeated, giving the cinch a tug with a jerk. Blowing out a heavy sigh, he perched his elbows on the mare's rump, his expression turning serious. "Look, man, thinking about Nicole's needs is all well and good, but I think there's more to your sudden change of heart than the welfare of your niece." He rubbed his bearded chin. "What you do with your life is none of my business, except when it involves someone as dear to my heart as Heather."

Seth opened his mouth to defend himself to what was obviously going to be a lecture about dating his sister, but J.D. held up his hand and cut him off. "I've seen what's been going on around here this summer, and I just want to give you a word of caution. Think about what you really want. She's had a lot of disappointments in her life. Eric has pulled a lot of low punches, and I'd hate to see her make the same mistake twice."

Seth's jaw tightened. A stabbing pain shot right down between his shoulder blades. Why did he feel like he would always be walking in Eric's shadow?

"I don't mean to sound presumptuous," J.D. continued, talking more like a father than a brother. "But I'd take a good hard look at where your priorities are right now, and where you really want to be in life. I'd hate for you to give up something you've worked so hard for. Heather's a great gal, but she's got a heavy load. It's going to take a lot more than an occasional pizza party to keep it all together."

Before he could answer, Heather's cheerful voice cut the tension that had suddenly engulfed the barn. "Okay, we're here. Are the horses all ready to go?"

"Just about," J.D. answered, giving the cinch one last tug.

Nicole trotted by and sneaked him a sideways grin. "You get to ride Ol' Roy."

Her expression didn't make him feel any better. "Yeah, we've already met." He tugged the brim of his cowboy hat low over his forehead.

Heather strode over and hooked her arm into the crook of

Seth's elbow, tugging him toward Ol' Roy. "Come on. Let's go for that trail ride."

The simple touch of Heather's hands around his arm, her sparkling big brown eyes and her pretty vibrant smile relieved any apprehensions he may have had about where his priorities were at this moment. Smelling her sweet fragrance, touching her silky smooth skin and gazing at her heart-shaped lips, all seemed to deepen his desires to be with this woman. He knew everything J.D. had said was true. She had a helluva heavy load, but that didn't change the way he felt about her. One way or another, he was determined to figure out a way to make things work between them.

Nicole mounted the palomino and followed J.D. out into the ranch yard.

Heather easily hoisted her long supple legs into the saddle. "Are you ready for this, city boy?"

He patted Ol' Roy on the neck. "As ready as I'll ever be, I guess."

"Do you think you can get your butt up onto that horse?" Her lips curled into that sweet, delectable smile that he'd come to know was meant just for him.

He grinned and wiped his hands over his backside and squatted, performing a quick stretch. "We'll know here in a second."

He grabbed Ol' Roy's reins and patted his neck. "Okay, boy. Make me look good." With more effort than he thought, he slung his legs over the horse's rump, landing square in the saddle.

Ol' Roy didn't budge. Seth grabbed the reins and noticed the big guy hadn't even twitched a muscle. Seth leaned over and checked his eyes. "Is he asleep?"

"I thought you might appreciate a more seasoned horse. He shouldn't pull any punches."

Seth scratched the back of his neck. "Exactly how many

seasons has this old boy seen?"

Heather laughed and nudged her horse out of the barn. "Just give him a swift kick with the heel of your boot."

If this ride hadn't meant so much to Nicole and the fact that every part of him wanted to impress her gorgeous counselor, he'd dismount right now. Hiking, flying; that's where he felt in control. This was downright humiliating.

He squared his shoulders and dug the heel of his boots into Ol' Roy's flanks. The horse pulled his head back and snorted, confirming that he was indeed alive. Seth nudged him again, this time harder. The horse raised his head and lunged forward.

"Come on, boy. You're not doing me any favors."

Several barn swallows took flight, making a fluttery sound as they exited the wide steel doors. The sun beat down hot this early Friday evening. The horse picked up to a trot and fell in behind Nicole and Heather. "That's the way. Good boy."

He sidled up next to Heather as they trotted through the brush side by side. Nicole loped on ahead, her face covered in the biggest smile he'd seen since she'd moved here. Her form, the way she bounced up and down with the horses' steady gait really impressed him.

"Good job, Nicole," he called out. "J.D. said you were a natural."

She actually returned his smile with a genuine heartfelt smile of her own. "Thanks!"

"Well, I'll be darned," he said, resting a hand on his thigh. "She didn't even roll her eyes." Something unusual swelled deep inside his heart. It was the same feeling he'd had last weekend at the pizza party. He couldn't explain the feeling. Was it pride? He was definitely proud of the way she'd learned to ride. But he knew it was something deeper, something almost paternal that filled his heart to overflowing.

He looked over at Heather and motioned his head toward

Nicole. "She looks pretty good out there. I've never seen her so happy."

"I know. J.D.'s been a great teacher."

"Don't be so modest. If it weren't for you, we wouldn't be here in the first place. You've helped her get through a pretty emotional time."

Heather stared ahead toward Nicole and nodded. "She'll still hit some rough spots, but I'm glad I could be here for her this summer."

They wound their way around the acreage, keeping to a gentle trot. Seth had relaxed into the saddle and was actually having a great time on Ol' Roy. Nicole shared stories of some of the happier times spent with her parents, like the year she'd turned nine, and they'd surprised her with a trip to Disney World. Then there was the trip to the San Diego Zoo where she got to feed the giraffes. It was good to know she had some good memories.

Nicole trotted ahead a few horse lengths. Seth reached over and took Heather's hand. "Thank you for being patient and giving Nicole what she needs."

"Don't thank me. She's doing all the work. I'm just here to lend an ear and smooth out the rough spots. She's really a good kid once you get to know her."

"Yeah, I know," he agreed, watching Nicole. "I'm finding that out the more time I spend with her. Shelli deserves all the credit. She was a great mom."

When he looked back at Heather, he found her gazing off at the distant peaks of Cheyenne Mountain. But she wasn't smiling anymore. In fact, her eyes seemed to be shiny, as if she were trying to keep from crying. He gave her hand a squeeze. "Hey, are you all right? You look sad all of a sudden."

She let go of his hand and made a quick dab at her nose. "I'm fine. My mind just wandered off for a moment."

"Was it me? Did I say something?"

She quickly looked over and shook her head. "No. Of course not. It has nothing to do with you."

"Can you tell me, then? What's got you so upset?"

"I really don't want to drag you into my problems. Let's just forget it and catch up with Nicole." She clicked her tongue and urged her horse into a trot.

He nudged Ol' Roy and actually got the old boy to lope. He caught up with Heather and reached over and touched her arm. "I want you to drag me into it, honey. Is it Kyle? Is he giving you problems again?"

She pulled back to a walking gait and sighed. "No, it's not Kyle . . . exactly." She bit her lower lip, looking deeply troubled about something.

"Exactly, what is it, then? Please, honey. You can tell me anything."

Without looking at him, she narrowed her eyes, squinting into the lowering sun. "Guess who paid me a visit last Sunday?"

From the sound of her voice, he knew it had to have been Eric. Seth suspected that Eric would be spending more time here until they closed on the resort. Unfortunately, there wasn't much Seth could do to prevent it. "I'm going to take a wild guess and say it was Eric."

She gave a barely perceptible nod and swiped at her eyes again.

His gut tightened. "What happened?"

"He went ballistic, that's what happened."

"What do you mean? Did he hurt you? I'll kill the bastard."

"No, he didn't hurt me, at least not physically. That's not Eric's style." She gave a frustrated shake of her head. "He just started ranting and raving when he saw Kyle's burns and Katie's arm. Oh, and my black eye only fueled his anger more. He's going forward with his plans to take Kyle and Katie away from me. I got the papers from his lawyers today."

Seth clenched his fingers around the reins, wishing he could cinch the leather straps around Eric's neck. "I'm sorry, honey. Why didn't you call me?"

"Right. What was that you said about ex-husbands and all the complications of a divorced mom?"

He remembered telling her about Brenda and why he'd broken up with her last summer. No wonder Heather was so afraid to confide in him now. "Look, that was different. I was different," he clarified. "I'm a different person now. I want to help you. What else did he say?"

"He thinks Katie needs a more stable home life with two parents, and that Kyle's a threat to her well-being. Eric thinks he needs more structured care."

"Have you talked to your lawyer yet?"

"Yeah, but until someone contacts us, there's really nothing we can do. I swear, Eric's doing this just to prove he still has control over me." She reined her horse to a halt beside a small stream. A large, white two-story Colonial house sat some fifty feet away. He assumed this was J.D. and Debra's house.

The back screen door swung wide and Katie galloped out onto the porch. "Hi, Mommy! Auntie Debra wants to know if you guys want some lemonade."

Nicole jumped off her horse and waved back. "Can we, Uncle Seth?"

"I don't see why not. Why don't you go on up and help. We'll be up in a minute. I want to talk to Heather for a little bit, okay?"

Nicole glanced toward Heather, who now stood next to the stream, swiping at her eyes. "Is she okay?" Nicole asked, keeping her voice to a whisper. "Did you say something stupid?"

He choked out a laugh. "No. At least not that I'm aware of. I think she's just had a long day. Tell Debra lemonade sounds great."

"Okay. There's a hitching post near the house. I'll tie my horse over there and wait for you."

"Sounds good, and Nicole," he added, reaching out and cupping her shoulder, "you looked great out there. I'm proud of you. I may have to get us a couple of these guys so we can trail ride anytime. How's that sound?"

"Really? My own horse?"

He laughed at the exuberance he saw in her eyes. "Sure. We may have to figure out a way to get them up the elevator without Freddy seeing 'em, but leave the small details to me." He winked.

Nicole laughed and shook her head. "You can be so lame, sometimes. I'm going to tell Debra."

As Nicole trotted to the back porch, Seth dismounted and led his horse to the stream next to Heather and her horse. When she looked up at him through watery brown eyes, he took off his cowboy hat and set it on the saddle horn. "He's not going to take your kids away, honey."

"He scares me, Seth. He's got a lot of power and money. He won't be afraid to use it."

Seth tunneled his fingers under her hair, tracing his thumb in circles over the nape of her neck. "I'm no expert, but I think you're doing a fantastic job with both your kids. I'm sure Kyle's evaluation will prove he's doing great. No judge worth his salt is going to take them away from you."

She tipped her head back and closed her eyes. "Oh, God. I would absolutely die if that happened."

"It won't happen. Trust me on this. I know Eric's kind. I've seen how they operate. They like to manipulate people. It makes him feel powerful, but it's all a game. He'll get distracted by some big deal and forget about you again."

She grunted. "I don't know how I ever loved that man."

Seth blew out a heavy sigh. "People change. Sometimes it's not for the better, but then again," he added, gazing deeply into her eyes, "sometimes a person enters someone's life and their whole world turns upside down."

"You mean like Nicole?"

He leaned close and whispered, "Yeah, her, too."

Her shoulders relaxed. Her face brightened with a small smile. He knew right then he'd completely lost his whole heart to this woman. He wanted to protect her. Raise her kids. Make her smile every day for the rest of her life. He wanted her . . . all of her.

A sliver of moonlight shone among the first few stars in the early evening dusk. A cool summer breeze brushed against his skin. He wrapped his arm around her waist, her body molding perfectly against his. He guided her over to a giant oak tree situated near the stream, pressing her back against the trunk. Her sweet scent of flowers, baby powder and leather only heightened his urge to be near her.

She looked up at him through worried brown eyes, a trace of sadness still buried in the depths. Somehow, he wanted to give her comfort and security . . . tell her how much he loved her. The way she responded to him every time he kissed her, he knew she had strong feelings for him. Did she love him, too?

When a fresh tear rolled down her cheek, he reached up and stroked a thumb gently under her eye. "Everything's going to be okay, honey. You're not going to lose your kids. Trust me. There's nothing to be afraid of."

"You don't understand. I am afraid, but it's more than just Eric taking the kids."

He narrowed his eyes, not understanding. "What is it then? What else are you afraid of?"

"You. This. Us," she said, waving her hand between them.

309

He suddenly had a sinking sensation that she was about to brush him off again. He didn't think he had it in him to just drive away this time. Or in this case, ride off into the sunset . . . alone.

"What, exactly, are you trying to tell me, Heather?" He rolled his head around on his shoulders, steeling himself for the worst.

She licked her tears that had dripped onto her lips, her voice barely heard over the stream rushing behind them. "It's silly. I know there's no way for us to be together. I mean, we're at different crossroads in life. You're on a career path to the vice presidency. I'm a stay-at-home mom raising two young kids. I've told myself over and over we could never work. But no matter how hard I fight this . . . this feeling, it happened anyway, and now I'm afraid that you're going to leave for Dallas in another month, and I'll never see you again."

He couldn't keep the smile from making its way across his face. The tension he'd felt a moment before was quickly replaced with exhilaration. He moved closer and touched her waist, bending slightly to get at eye level. "When you say *it* happened. Exactly, what happened, Heather? What are you afraid to tell me?"

She tipped her head back and stared up toward the sky. "I don't even want to say it out loud, because you're leaving in a few weeks and I may never see you again."

He closed his eyes and pressed his forehead to hers. "Would you say it if I told you I'm not going to Dallas?"

Her eyes widened. "What do you mean? You said it was a done deal. Why aren't you going?"

"Because of you. Because of Kyle and Katie and Nicole. Because I feel the same way about you." He gripped her shoulders. "I can't go to Dallas. You need me, and I don't want to leave you, either."

"But . . . but . . . but what about your big promotion?"

"It doesn't mean anything if you're not with me. I can't stand the thought of never seeing you again. If I stayed, we could get married and give your kids a stable, secure home life with a mother and a father to take care of them. The chances of Eric getting custody of your kids would pretty much be zilch. And think about Nicole. She needs a mother in her life now more than ever. And I know she loves you like a mother already, anyway."

"And I love her, too, but you'd be willing to give up all your dreams, all your plans, to stay here and marry me?"

"In a heartbeat."

She gave an adamant shake of her head and stepped away. "I can't let you do that. I won't let you do that."

He squared his shoulders. "I've already made up my mind. I'm staying. I've been wanting to cut back and open my own business anyway."

"What do you mean? Wouldn't you still work for Ferguson and Tate?"

He scratched his head, wondering how he could tell her he'd be out of a job. "Well, see, it's like this. They've pretty much said it's all or nothing. Either I go to Dallas or I'm out."

"Are you nuts?" She gave a short hysterical burst of laughter. "That's it. You're crazy." She flung her hands and yelled up through the trees. "He's gone berserk!" Several birds took flight, making loud fluttery sounds.

He chuckled and took both her hands, hoping to convince her he was as sane as the next guy. "If I'm crazy about anything, it's about you and your kids, Heather. You need me, and Nicole needs you."

"Why haven't you asked me?"

"To marry you? I thought I just did." Damn, he should have bought her a ring. "Guess I'm not very good at this proposing stuff."

"No, that's not what I meant. Why don't you ask me if I'd go to Dallas with you?" Before he could answer, she started to pace back and forth in the yard, her voice sounding on the brink of hysteria. "Is it because you're afraid I won't fit in with all the other executives' wives? Would you be embarrassed to tell them you married a divorcée with two kids? Or is it because of Kyle? Would you be embarrassed to admit you had an autistic stepson? Is that it?"

"Don't be ridiculous." Seth shook his head, wondering where the hell she got those ideas. Her steps were brisk and wide, and he had a hard time keeping up with her. "I can't wait to be a real father to Kyle and Katie. I love both your kids. I'm not embarrassed at all—" He stopped short, his brain just now registering what she'd been telling him. "Wait a minute. What are you saying?" He snaked a hand out and gently grabbed her arm to get her to stop pacing. "Back up a sec. Are you telling me you'd consider moving to Dallas?"

She didn't answer. She just stood there, breathing heavy, staring deeply into his eyes. He stepped closer and touched her waist. "Heather? Would you go to Dallas with me?"

She still didn't answer, but she lowered her lashes, her lips curling into a little grin as if she were trying to keep from smiling.

He brushed full length against her, his adrenaline surging through his veins. "Am I reading you right? Will you marry me and move to Dallas?"

"Well," she hedged, fiddling with the snaps of his shirt. "Do you want to marry me? I mean, I can't cook, I'm a lousy housekeeper, and I always leave the lights on—"

"And your coffee is too strong, and you snore in your sleep."

"I snore in my sleep?" she gasped.

He laughed and shook his head. "No. Just thought I'd throw that one in for good measure."

"Oh, you!" She smacked him on the chest then tried to wriggle away from him. He clasped his arms tighter around her waist and lowered to her face, getting serious. "Heather, I think you're the most perfect woman I've ever met. I've been going out of my mind trying to figure out a way to tell you. Yes, I want to marry you. I want to be a father to your kids, and I want you to be a mother for Nicole. I want us all to be a family."

He set her apart and got down on one knee. Corny maybe, but he wanted to do this right. "Heather? Wait, what's your middle name?"

She gave a short laugh. "Marie."

He resituated and took her hand, his fingers trembling just about as much as hers. "Heather Marie Garrison Thomas, will you do me the honor of becoming my wife and moving to Dallas with me?"

"Yes, Seth. I would love to be your wife and move anywhere with you!"

"Yee-haw!" he hollered, jumping to his feet. Then he wrapped his arms around her waist, twirling her in his arms. "As soon as I get back to town, I'm going to have Nicole help me pick out the prettiest diamond you've ever seen so we can make it official."

"Uncle Seth! Heather!" Nicole bolted out the back door of the house. "Come quick! It's Debra! I think she's having a baby!"

Heather gasped and pushed out of Seth's arms. "Now? She's not due for two more weeks!"

"Tell that to her baby!" Nicole hollered. "Debra said she's been having real bad back pains all day and now she's having contractions." She whirled around and disappeared inside the house.

"Oh, my gosh. Oh, my gosh!" Heather gasped. "I should have noticed the signs. Debra's been in labor all day! She's going to have a baby!" She whirled around toward the stream. "The horses. What should I do about the horses?"

Seth laughed and framed her face with his hands, his emotions flying on an out-of-control roller coaster. "Take a deep breath, honey. Debra's having the baby, not you."

"I need to be with her, Seth. She needs me. J.D. needs me."

"Okay, okay, listen. Go tell Nicole to come back out. She and I can walk these guys back to the barn. It's only what, twenty miles?"

Heather laughed and shook her head. "Maybe two at the most, but you should be okay riding. Just hold onto Lightning's lead rope. She'll follow right along."

"I think we can handle that. If you want, I'll take Kyle and Katie home with Nicole and me tonight. Nicole would probably love having a sleepover. We'll watch movies and eat popcorn and ice cream till we get sick."

She smiled and wrapped her arms clear around his neck. "You are the most wonderful man in the world. Have I ever told you that before?"

He pressed his face into her hair. "Actually, no." She had also never said she loved him.

"Heather, hurry!" Nicole hollered from the porch. "She just had another contraction!"

"I'll be right there." She started trotting backwards toward the house. "Oh, God, Seth. J.D.'s going to be a daddy!" Her voice choked, and her eyes filled with tears. "Do you know how long we've waited for this? I don't think I've ever told you, but it was miracle that Debra became pregnant in the first place. Now she's going to have a little baby! I'll call you as soon as I know anything."

Chapter Sixteen

"Oh, J.D.," Heather cooed, holding J.D.'s newborn son. "He's perfect. I'm so proud of you." Sitting in a rocking chair near a window in Debra's hospital room of Saint Anthony's Children's Hospital, she placed a kiss on the newest Garrison member to join their clan.

After they'd arrived Friday night, Debra's labor had slowed to a crawl, and by five o'clock the following Saturday evening she'd only dilated to five centimeters. Then her blood pressure had escalated to dangerously high levels, and at eleven-thirty, the baby's heart rate had dropped from one hundred fifty-five beats a minute to thirty-five.

Within minutes, they'd performed an emergency caesarean section, bringing young Daniel Jeremiah Garrison into the world shortly after midnight, Sunday morning. Now, thank the good Lord and the wonderful doctors and nurses here at Saint Anthony's, Daniel and his mother were both doing fine.

With tears of joy in his eyes, J.D. knelt down beside Heather and lovingly stroked his thumb over his son's forehead. "I thought I'd lost them both for a while there. I'm just thankful it's all over and they're going to be fine."

"Looks like Debra's finally getting some rest. How long before they'll let her go home?"

J.D. looked over at his wife, his eyes turning misty. "Her blood pressure is still a little high. They want to keep her here at least another forty-eight hours. Probably Tuesday if everything looks good."

Heather snuggled little Daniel closer, remembering like it was yesterday when she'd nursed her kids. Now Debra would be continuing the Garrison traditions with her own family. She looked up at J.D. and smiled. "Daddy would be proud. You've kept the Garrison name going through to the next generation. And weighing in at a whopping nine pounds, five ounces, it looks like he'll definitely carry on the Garrison height and size."

J.D. chuckled and slid his arms under the mound of baby blankets. "Come here, big guy," he said as he scooped young Daniel into his arms. "Daddy wants to hold you for a while. From that look in your auntie's eyes, I'm afraid she might take you home with her. Yes, she's got a little boy and a little girl who are going to teach you all about horses and play with you all the time. Yes, she does," he murmured. "You're going to learn so much from them."

Heather's heart swelled with joy as she watched J.D. talk with his son. Still wearing his green hospital scrubs, J.D. strode across the room and cuddled Daniel to his chest, humming what sounded like the song, "Baby of Mine," the song their mother used to sing to them as kids. Heather tipped her head back against the rocker and closed her eyes. It wasn't that long ago that she'd been here in this very room holding little Kyle, singing that very same song.

She hugged her arms to her stomach as a maternal tug of her heartstrings made her yearn for another child. Maybe it was just being around Daniel and smelling all the wonderful scents of a newborn, but she couldn't help but envy J.D. and Debra's new-found happiness.

Would Seth ever want to have a child of his own? Now that he had Nicole, and soon her two kids, maybe another child would be too much to ask. Getting married was a pretty big step in itself without adding another child to the mix.

She still hadn't told anyone about Seth's proposal. After she'd left him Friday night, she'd been with J.D. and Debra while they delivered their baby. There'd been a few brief phone calls to make sure Kyle and Katie were all right, but she hadn't even seen Seth.

He'd kept Kyle and Katie both Friday night and last night, and she knew it was time to give him some relief. But, right now, all she wanted to do was go home and sleep for about twenty-four hours. She was exhausted, and she wasn't even the one who'd had the baby.

But she was glad she'd been here for J.D. When the doctors had told him how serious Debra's situation had become, he'd about come unglued. Mom and Brad and Megan had shown up around midnight Friday and had also stayed most of the weekend. Among them all, they'd managed to keep J.D. calm and collected.

Now, here they were, father and son bonding together while Momma slept peacefully beside them. Their journey as a family had just begun.

And hers, it would seem, had just taken a new path, as well. She'd always thought she'd be around to watch J.D.'s children grow up, and that her own kids would stay close to their little cousins. But in only a few short weeks, she'd be off on a new adventure in a state that she'd only ever read about or had seen on television.

Texas. The Lone Star state.

She should be excited. She'd only ever heard good things about Dallas. But now that J.D. had his baby, could she just up and leave him and the rest of her family? How could they stay close if she was off in another state a thousand miles away? Seeing them at holidays a couple times a year wasn't the same. Yet, there was no way she'd ask Seth to give up the vice presidency and stay here in Colorado. He'd worked too hard for his dreams.

Then she began to wonder why Seth had asked her to marry him in the first place. He'd never really come out and said he loved her. He thought she was a great mom, and that she was a beautiful, sexy, and a desirable woman, but he'd never once actually said those three little words that she'd yearned to hear for so many years.

In the beginning of her marriage to Eric, he'd told her he loved her. But as soon as they'd said their vows, he said words were senseless, that it was a waste of breath once they were married. Said he was a man of action and that words weren't necessary. He'd bought her expensive jewelry, designer clothes, and even a dozen roses when Kyle and Katie were born. But other than their wedding vows, he'd never used the word love to her.

Was Seth the same way? Did he really love her as a husband should love his wife? Or was he marrying her to give Nicole a mother, and a stable home life to Kyle and Katie?

The more she thought about it, the more convinced she became that Seth had only proposed out of concern for the kids. Even though she loved Seth with all her heart, and she loved Nicole, there was no way she would let Seth marry her out of a sense of obligation. He deserved to fall in love with the right woman, without so many complications.

A light tap sounded at the door. She lifted her head from the back of the rocker and found her eyes locked with the man who'd stolen her heart.

"Is it okay if I come in?" Seth asked barely over a whisper.

Heather smiled and nodded. He walked in carrying a beautiful bouquet of flowers in a bootie-shaped, baby-blue planter with a round Mylar balloon with *It's a Boy* printed on the side. He was dressed in a pair of faded Levis, Nike sneakers, and a short-sleeved, bright-red golf shirt stretched taut over his broad chest muscles. All her earlier thoughts of backing out suddenly vanished as she drifted into the depths of his iridescent blue eyes. The heck with sleep; she just wanted to go home and curl up in his arms and never leave.

He stepped lightly across the room and set the flower arrangement on a nightstand near the window, slid her a private wink then walked over beside J.D., patting him on the shoulder. "Congratulations, man. Looks like you got yourself a fine young cowboy in the making."

"Thanks. I appreciate you helping out with Heather's kids. She's been a lifesaver. I don't know how these women can go through so much and stay so calm." He brought Daniel to his face and kissed his forehead.

Seth chuckled and picked up Daniel's tiny fingers. "I've always known we were the weaker sex," he said, then got down close to Daniel. "We just can't let them know that, can we, little guy? We can't let them think they got the upper hand, even if they do."

J.D. settled back on the couch and propped his stocking feet on the table, expertly tipping his son up on his shoulder. He closed his eyes and started patting Daniel's back.

Seth stepped toward Heather and knelt down in front of the rocking chair, sliding his hands over her thighs. "Would you like to join the kids and me for breakfast? I promised them pancakes and sausage. Then I thought I'd take them to the zoo this afternoon, and give you a chance to get some sleep."

"Sounds like a pretty good offer," J.D. answered for her. "I've got things under control here. I'm already an expert at changing diapers. I've done three all by myself." He gave a proud smile and kissed Daniel again.

Seth held out his hand, helping her stand. With their fingers intertwined, she glanced over her shoulder at J.D. "Tell Debra I'll be back in a little while."

"No rush. We'll be here for a couple of days. Oh, and Seth,

be forewarned. I saw something very maternal flicker in Heather's eyes when she was holding Daniel a minute ago."

Seth grinned, gazing down at her with arched brows. "Is that so? Maybe we'll have to see about bringing in another little cousin for young Daniel." He looked over at J.D. and pulled out a maroon velvet box from his pocket. Her heart slammed against her chest. Did he already get her a ring?

"I was going to do this later, but I really wanted to get J.D.'s blessing first." He stared down at the box and swallowed several times, as if garnering strength to say the words. He cleared his throat and looked J.D. in the eyes. "I took to heart what you said the other day, and I've done a lot of soul searching. I know it's going to take a lot more than pizza parties and Disney videos to make a relationship work."

What exactly had J.D. and Seth talked about?

"I know there'll be tough times ahead," he continued. "But together, I hope I can be the kind of husband she deserves and a good father to her kids. I've asked Heather to marry me and become my wife. What do you say? Have I got your blessing?"

With arched brows, J.D. rubbed his stubbled jaw and met Heather's gaze across the room. She bit her lower lip and practically held her breath, not sure what kind of reaction J.D. would have. Then his lips formed into his characteristic crooked grin. "I'd say you've got my blessings tenfold." Then with one arm supporting Daniel, he extended his free hand. "Welcome to the family, man."

Seth walked over and accepted J.D.'s outstretched hand. "I only hope I make her as happy as you've made Debra. And it wouldn't bother me one bit if Heather wanted a half dozen more of these little guys."

"A half dozen!" Heather gasped, eyes and mouth wide open.

"Better get that ring on her finger fast," J.D. added with a chuckle. "She's not getting any younger. She turns thirty in a month."

"Is that so?" Seth said, reaching down and taking her left hand. "Maybe we'll have to have a little wedding birthday bash." The maroon velvet box creaked as he slowly opened the lid, revealing the most stunning diamond solitaire she'd ever seen. It had to have been at least three carats.

"I took the kids to the mall yesterday afternoon, and Nicole and Katie helped me pick it out. I hope you like it. Your mom got us one of your other rings from your dresser to get the right size. I hope it fits."

"Oh, Seth," she whispered, placing two fingers over her lips. So, the kids knew. Her mom and Brad knew. And now with J.D.'s blessing, it was just a matter of making it all official. She just had to slip it on her finger and her future would change forever. "I didn't expect this. I don't know what to say. It's absolutely breathtaking."

"Well, I can't very well let you get married without an engagement ring." He carefully lifted the large diamond solitaire from the box. Tears filled her eyes, making the ensemble smear into an array of rainbow colors as it reflected the sunlight from the window. "All you have to say is yes, and we can get on with the wedding plans. Though I should warn you, Nicole and Katie bought a bridal magazine at least two inches thick, and they've already got your dress picked out."

She heard herself laugh, though she knew tears were dripping down her cheeks. "Okay, yes," she finally cried. "Yes, Seth. I'll marry you."

Seth slid the ring lovingly onto her finger, then kissed her hand and smiled up at her. "You've made me the happiest man on earth, Heather."

"Make that the second happiest," J.D. chimed in, holding his newborn son with pride.

Heather stared down at the ring, her fingers trembling slightly still in Seth's gentle grip. The ring fit perfectly. The man was perfect. It was the icing on an already perfect day. So, why didn't she feel ecstatic?

"The kids are out in the waiting room with Grampa Brad," Seth said, cupping her shoulder. "I think they've missed you."

Holding her ring up in the sunlight, she let out a little sob. "I've missed them, too. Thank you so much for stepping in and taking care of them for me."

"I was glad to be there," he said, sliding his arms around her waist. "They weren't a problem at all. It's been good practice. In fact, I've got good news. Kyle doesn't care what shirt he wears anymore."

She swiped her eyes to clear her head. "How'd you manage that?"

"Bought him a new baseball cap," he answered with a proud grin. "There's only one thing."

"What's that?" she asked, a little wary of his crooked smile.

"He won't take it off his head. I had to bribe him with an ice cream shake last night to take a shower."

Heather laughed. "I'm amazed you got him to take a shower. He hates to get water in his ears. Sounds like you've kind of gotten the hang of this parenting stuff."

"Can you believe it? Me? A once-confirmed bachelor?"

"Oh, Seth," she gushed, wrapping her arms clear around his neck. "You're such a wonderful man."

"Shucks, you're making me blush now."

She gave a short laugh and landed a kiss smack on his mouth, reconfirming her original commitment to marry this man. Right now, she'd move to Timbuktu if he asked her.

Sitting at the bar of the Royal Rock Lounge, Seth took an anxious glance at his wristwatch, hoping his four-o'clock meet-

ing didn't run too late. Heather had finally agreed to go up flying with him this evening, and he didn't want to show up late.

He motioned for the bartender to bring him a rum and Coke,
hoping to take the edge off his nerves. Not only for his meeting,
but for his upcoming nuptials to Heather. Since he'd placed the
ring on her finger two weeks ago, he'd sensed more than once
her hesitance at accepting his proposal. Whenever he'd
mentioned setting a date, she'd quickly changed the subject,
avoiding the whole conversation. Her mother had even offered
to have the ceremony out at the ranch, but until they set a firm
date, he couldn't make any definite plans.

Other than a polite kiss goodnight on the porch of her condo,
they'd never really been alone together since he'd proposed,
either. They'd spent every free moment either at the ranch with
Debra and the new baby, or taking trail rides with Nicole, or attending baseball games with Marty and Kyle. Every moment
made him fall harder and deeper in love. Not only with Heather,
but with Kyle and Katie, and their whole family dynamics with
Nicole. He'd come to love them all as if they were his own flesh
and blood. He wanted so much to have a child with Heather,
maybe even two more if she was willing. He'd never been so
happy.

But there'd also been an annoying cockroach that kept creep-
ing into their happiness. True to his threats, Eric had arranged
for Kyle to be put through several physical and mental evalua-
tions, leaving Kyle exhausted and pulling back into himself with
every day that passed. A social worker had even been assigned
to the case, doing impromptu drop-ins at the condo and the
ranch, making Heather jumpy and irritable. There were times
he wondered if she were only marrying him to secure her
children. But if that were the case, wouldn't she have already
agreed to set a date? Even be married already?

So, why was she hesitating?

Did she still want to marry him? And more to point, did she even love him? He knew without a doubt she had strong feelings for him. But was that enough to give up her family and the only home she'd ever known, to move to a state a thousand miles away?

He shook his head, absently rubbing a hand over his heart. Rather than losing her, he'd gladly quit his job in a heartbeat. He had more than enough money set aside to start his own business right here in the Springs. He'd already told her as much several times. So, to see her build up this emotional wall was tearing him apart. He tossed the rest of the drink to the back of his throat, swallowing, wishing he had some answers.

The bartender set him up with another drink just as John Wilson of Wilson Electronics strode through the lounge doors. Seth broke into a grin and stood. "Hey, John," he said, approaching him with his hand extended. "How's it going?"

"Sorry, I'm late. I just finished up a meeting with my corporate accountant. With all the upheaval in the Middle East, our profits are shooting sky high."

"Congratulations," Seth said, motioning his hand to the corner booth. "I guess it's true what they say. Good things come from bad situations." He flagged the waiter over to get John's order, then slid into the booth across from him, loosening his tie. "Thanks for taking time to meet with me. I know your schedule is pretty tight."

"No problem. I never got a chance to thank you for taking Jennifer to the Ice Capades. She hasn't stopped talking about it. For the first time in her life I think she felt like a full-fledged woman. I should warn you, though," he added with a chuckle. "She's got a crush on a younger man."

Seth pressed a hand over his heart, feigning hurt. "I knew it was too good to be true. Who is he?"

"Actually, it's your brother, Marty."

Seth gave a proud smile. "No kidding? I knew they were good friends. Guess I never thought about them having feelings like that: romantically, I mean. This is going to take a little getting used to. How do you feel about it?"

"I think it's wonderful. I just wish there was some way those two could survive on their own, you know, as a couple."

Seth arched his brows. That was exactly why he'd arranged this meeting in the first place. If he could entice John to invest in his revised Golden Springs resort project, Seth might have a fleeting chance at making this thing fly. "I think you may want to hear what I have to say, then. I've been working on a project all summer you might be interested in, and I wanted to throw some ideas by you."

John accepted the drink from the waiter and sat forward. "You've got my full attention."

Seth pitched the presentation he'd given to the Telluride investors, along with several new ideas that had John asking so many questions, it was twenty after six before they came up for air and checked the time.

"Sounds like it's got a lot of potential. Count me in," John said with enthusiasm. "It's about time this community recognized these individuals as dependable, trustworthy adults. I'd like to stop over at your office next week and take a closer look at the numbers."

"That'd be great. I'll have my secretary set up a time."

John stood and extended his hand. "It'll be good doing business with you again, Seth. You've made me a lot of money over the years. I'll spread the word, maybe come up with a few other names for you to call."

"Appreciate it. They're welcome to join us at our meeting next week."

Seth walked John to the door then headed back to the bar to pay the tab. A familiar low voice drew his attention to the opposite corner in the dimly lit lounge. He blinked, thinking he must have been mistaken. But the close-set eyes and the arrogant chuckle left no doubt it was none other than Eric Thomas. He was turned slightly toward a young woman sitting next to him, practically in his lap.

Remembering the picture of Eric's new wife with long blonde hair, this woman with her short vibrant red hair was in serious contrast to the picture. Was this bastard already cheating on his new wife?

Seth's gut tightened as he watched Eric plant a kiss over the woman's mouth, making no qualms about being seen in public with another woman. With all the hell Eric was putting Heather through, Seth clenched the glass in his hands, adrenaline surging through his veins. He had half a mind to go over there and give him a piece of what was due him, but knew he couldn't jeopardize his relationship with the rat. Whether Seth liked it or not, the future of Heather's resort hinged on whether Eric would sway his investors to sign.

Seth felt a small smile tug at his lips and ordered another round of what Eric and his newest girlfriend were drinking. Hitting a guy like Eric Thomas with his fist would be counterproductive. Instead, Seth needed to aim a little lower where it would hurt the most . . . his pocketbook.

Hoping to have a little blackmail material, Seth flipped open his cell phone and casually clicked several pictures of the twosome kissing, Eric's meaty hands pawing all over the woman. With just a simple push of a button, he could send these out to anyone over the Internet.

After the waitress delivered the drinks, Eric looked up to the bar. Seth held up his drink in a toast. The barstool scraped across the floor as he shoved away from the bar and strode over to their table.

"Well, well, well. If it isn't Mr. Eric Thomas. What a surprise to find you here. Your wife at home tonight?"

"I, uh, well," he stammered with a conceited chuckle, taking a guilty glance toward the redhead. "She's off shopping with her mother this weekend. You know how it is. We'll just keep this between you and me . . . right, buddy?"

"Buddy. R-i-ght." Seth drew out the word in one long breath. He looked over at the lady. "Miss, would mind if Mr. Thomas and I had a private discussion? It'll only take a moment."

Eric stood and let the woman out, watching as she hurried off to the ladies' room. "Quite a body, isn't it? You can tell she hasn't had kids, if you know what I mean."

"No!" Seth slammed his glass on the table. "I don't know what you mean."

Eric glanced around and tugged his trousers up over his bulging middle. "Now, Seth, let's not make a scene. Please, sit down."

"I think you'd better sit down. We have a little negotiation to complete."

"What are you talking about?"

"I'm talking about Heather, your first wife."

"What about her?"

"I want you to drop this ridiculous notion of suing for custody of Katie and sending Kyle away to an institute."

"How do you know anything about that?" Then he narrowed his beady eyes to a slit. "Wait a minute, you're not the guy she's planning on marrying?"

"As a matter of fact, we're getting married at the end of the summer."

Eric only shook his head. "Let me save you some headaches. She may be a looker, but she's as dumb as a doorknob and about as responsive in bed. And don't even get me started on her cooking abilities. That woman can't even boil water."

Seth had heard enough. "You arrogant bastard. She may not

meet up to your so-called high standards, but she's one of the most dedicated and compassionate women I've ever met. How could you even threaten to take the two beings that mean the most in this world away from a woman who's done nothing but give her heart and soul to those kids?"

Eric jutted his chin out. "If you know so much about her, then why are they getting hurt? Why did my baby suffer from a broken arm? Kyle's hands are scarred because she isn't giving him enough supervision. She's incompetent!"

"The only one who's incompetent is you, Mr. Thomas. I've spent the last couple of months with Heather and her kids, and I've seen firsthand how well they've thrived under her care. Kyle is reading at an eighth-grade-comprehension level, all because of the extra time she's spent homeschooling him. He's responsible and cares for his sister better than a so-called normal kid."

"I don't have to listen to this. She can deal with my lawyer." Eric flipped a twenty on the table and shoved past Seth, heading toward the door.

Sensing the confrontation was about to get ugly, Seth followed Eric out the door where they wouldn't make such a scene inside the lounge. "I suggest you rethink that notion if you don't want your millionaire wife and her congressman father to find out what I witnessed here tonight."

"You don't have the balls, Roberts. You need me, and you won't do anything to jeopardize this project."

Seth angled his shoulders in front of Eric, stopping him in the middle of the parking lot. Only a few cars were parked nearby, leaving them nearly alone. "The only reason I need this project to go through is because I'm doing it for Heather and for Kyle and for kids just like him. If it weren't for them, I would have backed out of this deal weeks ago."

"This is absolutely ludicrous. You obviously don't know who

you're dealing with." Then the bastard actually took a swing a Seth, connecting with his lower jaw.

Son of a bitch! Thomas obviously didn't know who *he* was dealing with. When the bastard took another swing, Seth ducked and instinctively brought up his right fist, connecting with Eric's nose. The power behind the blow knocked him square on his ass.

For a split second, he felt like he was back behind the high school again, only this time he wasn't a spineless wimp. He'd taken several self-defense courses in college and had even joined the boxing club. Since graduating, he'd worked out at the company's private club several times a week. He swore he'd never find himself vulnerable to bullies like Eric again.

Before the bastard had a chance to get back on his feet, Seth planted a foot on his chest and stared down at him. "I think you'd better rethink your position, asshole." Panting, Seth flipped his cell phone open and began scrolling through the incriminating photos, giving Eric front-row viewing. "These pictures are already sitting in my in-box at home, as well as my e-mail at work. Just one click and your congressman father-in-law will have your balls for breakfast in divorce court!"

Eric struggled to grab the phone, but Seth shoved his foot harder against his chest. "First of all, you're going to drop this insane notion of taking those children away from Heather. You and I both know you don't want the girl. It's just your way of hurting Heather because you see what you've given up. She's gone on with her life without you, and it galls you to see her so happy."

Seth leaned closer. "Second, you and your new wife are going to personally invest every last dime you have in this resort to see that it's funded."

"Wait right there," Eric protested.

"No, you wait right there. You haven't heard the best part."

Seth shoved Eric's shoulder down. "You, Mr. Thomas, will convince each and every investor to back this resort. I'll arrange a meeting for next week to go over the final plans, and I expect every last one of your people to sign." He gave Eric a smile of satisfaction. "You should be happy. After all, it is in the best interest of your son that this resort be built."

Beads of sweat dripped down the side of Eric's pudgy face. "Okay, okay. There might be something I can do."

"I want your word, Thomas. Drop the suit against Heather and agree to this new resort, and your millionaire wife will never have to know what a two-timing rotten bastard you really are."

"Okay, just don't do anything hasty with those pictures. I'll make some calls tonight."

Seth gave one last dig of his foot before stepping back. "I never thought I'd say this, but I'm looking forward to your call, Mr. Thomas."

"It's not too late. You can still back out if you want."

"No. I can do this. Just give me a minute to get my bearings."

Standing outside Seth's hangar at the Prairie Park Airport, Heather stared up at the majestic clear blue sky. Several jet streams had colored into an orange-pink hue as the sun edged lower into the Colorado horizon. Just before dusk was her father's favorite time of evening to fly.

All was still. The birds had quieted. Just a whisper of air came from the gods as they jiggled the windsock. She breathed in the warm July air. Hard to believe it was almost August. Two weeks had passed since the birth of J.D. and Debra's baby. Two weeks since Seth had proposed and she'd said yes. Two weeks of hell while she'd watched her family be dissected by the so-called "system."

She closed her eyes, wishing she could just wake up from this nightmare and all her problems would magically disappear. Of course, she knew if she married Seth tonight, the chances of Eric taking the kids would be slim at best.

So, why was she hedging? Why didn't she just marry Seth and live happily ever after? Was it Dallas? Was her hesitance because she didn't want to move away from her family? Or was it more than leaving Colorado that had her so tense?

She gulped, coming to the real conclusion that it was the happily ever after part that scared her to death. No matter how much she loved Seth, how could she allow him to commit the rest of his life to a woman just for the sake of the kids? Once the so-called honeymoon was over, then what? Would he be content eating chicken nuggets and macaroni-and-cheese on plastic Superman plates?

She almost laughed, imagining Seth calling home and telling her to have dinner ready by six o'clock for eight of his colleagues and their wives. What would she do? Serve them pizza bites and corn dogs? She couldn't even get through a stupid batch of cookies without burning them. How could she possibly become a wife to a successful executive? She'd already failed at being Eric's wife. What made her think she'd be any better at being Seth's? Even thinking the "W" word terrified her to death.

The low hum of an aircraft dragged her back to the present. She blinked and looked up to the sky as a small plane flew off into the lowering sun. Glancing down an asphalted runway of the private airport just north of Colorado Springs, she realized she was about to embark on yet another terrifying journey that would take her soaring into the heavens and beyond.

She wasn't sure which terrified her more: flying or marriage. Both had the potential of crashing and destroying her life.

Her stomach in knots, she strode a few feet ahead of Seth. Various hangars housed dozens of planes, protecting them from the Colorado elements of snow, hail and wind. Several small planes were tied to the ground outside.

How many times had she come here alone with Daddy when she was a girl? After every flight, he'd always stopped at the Dairy Crème to get them each a double-thick, blueberry malt. She could almost taste the blueberries and feel the cool ice cream slide down her throat. He used to call it their "date" night.

She surveyed an array of Cessnas, Piper Cubs, and different experimental aircraft. "Which one's yours?" she asked.

He took her hand and motioned with his head toward the tarmac. "The blue-and-white Cessna. I pulled it out of the hangar this afternoon."

She stopped mid-stride. Her breath caught in her throat. A soft breeze whispered in her ears, and she could almost hear her daddy saying, "Everything's okay. I'll be right here."

She forced herself to continue toward the aircraft, expecting her heart to start racing, her stomach to start churning. Instead, she felt a peace wash over her like a gentle summer breeze. She let go of Seth's hand and strode around the plane, slowly pondering all the angles and lines of symmetry. As he began his preflight inspection, she trailed her finger along the wing, touching each rivet, moving the ailerons up and down. Walking around to the tail, she touched the rudder, delicately running her fingertips over the edge.

Seth had pulled out a glass fuel checker and drained a little gas from the tank. She remembered Daddy doing this every time before he flew, checking for contamination to the fuel tank and to see if air was in the lines. He continued his inspection of the flap settings and the rudder pedals. Moving the ailerons, he made sure they were controlled correctly by the yoke.

Gaining courage, she stepped around to the passenger side of the cockpit. Walking under the fixed, high wing of the aircraft, she stared through a Plexiglas window, looking in at the instrument panel that consisted of dozens of circular gauges and switches. She turned the metal latch and opened the door. The smell of the cockpit whooshed into her senses. Traces of gas and oil were combined with an old musty car smell. She breathed deeply, feeling lightheaded, but only because it was as if she'd been transported back to when she was a little girl, climbing into the passenger seat to take a flight with her father.

Seth pushed the door all the way open, standing close behind her, one hand gently holding her waist. She reached in and ran her hand over the leather passenger seat, then traced her hands over the yoke. Suddenly, her heart beat faster. An adrenaline rush made her chest rise and fall in short fast breaths. She wanted to get in. She wanted to fly.

"What do you think?" he asked, gently brushing her hair from her neck. "Think you're ready to get in?"

Wiping her palms on her denim skirt, she nodded and raised her sandaled foot to the stepping pad on the fixed landing gear of the plane. When Seth braced his hand on her lower back to help her in, she turned and looked into his eyes. "I think Daddy's here, Seth." She closed her eyes as another gentle breeze rustled wisps of hair out of her face. "I can feel him."

She pulled herself up and carefully climbed into the cockpit of the four-passenger plane. Her body trembled as she lowered to the seat and adjusted her skirt. She reached over and stroked her hand over the pilot's seat, a place where her father had sat so many times, so many years ago.

A set of headphones hung over the yoke in front of her. She pulled them slightly apart and slipped them over her ears. There wasn't a sound coming from them, but she could still hear her father talking to her as if he were sitting right beside her.

"Okay, my little navigator," he'd said a thousand times. "Radio us in for takeoff."

"Prairie Park traffic. This is two-eight-three-one-Bravo clearing for takeoff," she'd call out his plane's call letters to other planes in the area.

"Let's go fly with the angels," he'd always say, before lifting them safely into the vast expanse of heaven.

Warm, loving hands massaged her shoulders bringing her back to the present. She slipped off the headphones and turned to Seth who'd ducked close in front of her. "What do you think?" he asked. "Do you want to go up?" He dragged his hands down her bare arms, stopping at her fingertips.

"I think so."

When his lips pressed tenderly against hers, her head floated back against the headrest, and she drank in all his strength, all his tender compassion. Yes, she was definitely ready to soar with the angels.

He pulled away, strode around and climbed into the cockpit next to Heather. He reminded her so much of her father: tall, strong, handsome prominent facial features, and thick, dark hair. Seth had worn his faded Levis and a crisp white golf shirt, exposing his muscular forearms and his shiny gold Rolex. He slipped on a pair of dark-green aviator sunglasses.

Their shoulders nudged together in the small space, his warmth the reassurance she needed for this monumental occasion. She pulled the seat belt over her lap and tried to buckle it, but her fingers trembled, almost quaked, making it difficult to perform such an easy task.

Seth reached over, clicked it together for her, then cupped her hand in his. "Do you trust me?"

She swallowed and spoke barely over a whisper. "Yes, completely."

He slid his headphones on, adjusting the microphone near his mouth, plugged two cords into the instrument panel then switched on the radio. Heather slipped on her wire-rimmed sunglasses and adjusted her headset over her ears.

"Testing, testing. Can you hear me?" His voice sounded deep in her ears.

Holding the microphone close to her mouth, she smiled. "Yes. Loud and clear."

After an internal preflight inspection, he yelled out his opened window. "Clear prop!" Then he reached down and turned the master key. The familiar whir of the gyro as it fired up sent her heart into overdrive. Her chest rose and fell in shallow breaths. He pulled his window shut and cinched everything tight.

Looking for traffic in the air and on the ground, he slowly taxied out to the end of the runway. As he lined the nose up with the white dots down the airstrip, vibrations from the engines and the prop shook the plane, along with every fiber of her being. He did a final run-up test, revving the engine and checking the duel ignition systems.

Pressing the button on the yoke, he alerted area planes of his status. "Prairie Park traffic. This is Cessna seven-seven-three-three-Romeo. We're departing runway three-six and will be flying locally." He reached over and took her hand, waiting for any response from other planes in the area. When all was clear, he glanced toward the windsock, still barely moving. He gave the plane full throttle, forcing the aircraft down the runway.

She nervously bit her lip, watching the airspeed indicator. The needle moved around the gauge till it was almost at eighty knots. As their plane rolled down the asphalt runway, maintaining a straight path down the middle, the roar of the engine and prop shook her to the core. Her eyes widened, she wanted to stop. She reached for his arm and held her breath just as he pulled back on the yoke for liftoff.

An immediate calm engulfed the aircraft as they floated into a pillow of air, climbing slowly into the horizon. Now there was only the buzz of the engine and the whir of the prop as he climbed to a thousand feet above ground level. He patted her hand, which still clenched the skin of his forearm. She loosened her grip and cringed when she found she'd left fingernail indentations.

She rubbed his arm gently and smiled. "Sorry about that."

"No problem. I'm just going to level off and do a few circles around the airport. Nothing fancy. If you're up for more, just let me know. We're not far from J.D.'s ranch if you want to make a flyby."

She nodded and sat up, getting her bearings on the horizon. "I'd forgotten how beautiful it is up here. It's like we're the only ones in the universe."

"I know. That's why I love it." He did a steady climb, banking at an angle.

"This is so smooth compared to the seven-twenty-seven we flew on from California."

"The air is pretty calm tonight. Remember, back then we flew right through a thunderstorm."

She rolled her eyes and held her stomach. "You don't have to remind me. I want to enjoy this."

She rested her head back on the seat, letting the weightless feeling carry her away from all her anxieties back home, Eric's custody suit, her impending marriage to Seth, their relocation to Dallas and leaving her family. All of it slipped to the back of her mind as she allowed this extraordinary man to take her on a flight of a lifetime.

She felt like a piece of her had been put back together, as if Daddy had never really left. She could feel him . . . here . . . in the oceans of clear blue sky.

Seth nudged her shoulder and motioned with his head to look down. She peered out her window and let out a gasp of awe as they flew over the J Bar D Outreach Camp for Kids. The horses were tiny dots as they grazed in various paddocks surrounding the barn, now on a tenth-scale version. It reminded her of Katie's farmhouse play set. Only this was real; this was the legacy their father had started so many years ago.

"That's where our runway used to be," she said, pointing to a hayfield behind one of the barns. "It's all pasture now. I remember waking up my father at five in the morning so we could go flying to watch the sun rise. The sunset was just as spectacular. Sometimes we'd be out till it was almost too dark to land safely. Daddy had always wanted to light up the airstrip." She smiled and intertwined her fingers with Seth's. "Now that I'm up here, I don't want to go back down."

His smile turned lazy as he leaned closer. "I've got a full tank of gas. We could just fly on down to Vegas and get hitched tonight."

Her heart kicked up several notches, realizing how serious he sounded. She was having a hard enough time trying to accept the idea of getting married in the first place. The practical side of her answered for her. "Between my mom, Megan and Debra, they'd all hang us if we didn't have a traditional wedding at the ranch. Besides, I really want the kids to be there. This is as much their wedding as it is ours."

He brought her hand to his mouth and kissed her ring finger. "You're right. I was just hoping I'd caught you at a weak moment."

She felt weak, but she wasn't sure if it was because of Seth's devastating smile and confidence he exuded as a pilot, or because she literally felt weightless as they journeyed toward the horizon. When they were within a few miles of the Prairie Park airstrip, his voice sounded over the headset. "Prairie Park traffic. This is seven-seven-three-three-Romeo. We're approaching from the north at eighty-eight hundred feet. We'll be entering the left downward pattern for runway three-six."

When the pattern was clear, he lined up with the runway and

eased back on the throttle, decreasing the airspeed. The plane drifted downward, floating almost effortlessly as he gently pushed the yoke forward. When they were within twenty feet of the runway, there was that instant before they touched down when the ground effect gently lifted the nose and they flared, floating just inches above the asphalt runway.

Daddy had always said landing was like a balancing act with the nose and the pull back of the yoke. Seth expertly set the plane down, the aircraft quickly slowing as he pushed on the rudder pedals, applying the brakes. He taxied down the runway and came to a complete stop in front of his hangar. He pulled the throttle out and turned off the master key. Heather took off her headset then just sat there, complete tranquility replacing the roar of the engine.

With her head resting on the seat, she lazily looked over at Seth. "Was I dreaming, or did we just fly to heaven and back?"

He chuckled and took her hand. "I take it you enjoyed the flight?"

"Yes. More than you'll ever know. Thank you. I feel like I'm still floating." She looked into his iridescent blue eyes and smiled. "I'm glad you could get tonight off." Since Daniel was born, Seth had been putting in late nights and long weekends at the office. Nicole had even stayed with Heather and the kids a couple nights. He'd managed to get away a few times to take them to a Rockies game, or to trail ride with Nicole, and he promised things would go back to normal in only a few more days.

She was beginning to wonder what normal meant to a guy like Seth.

He unfastened his seat belt. "I'm glad you came flying with me. When things slow down at work, I'd like to take Nicole up."

"I'm sure she'd love it."

He turned and draped his arm behind her shoulder. "How's

everything with Kyle and Katie?"

"As well as can be expected. All these extra sessions are wearing Kyle out, though. He hasn't been sleeping well since Eric started these interrogations into our lives. I've even had a couple impromptu visits from the social workers, disturbing our routines and writing down everything they see. You should see my condo, not a toy out of place."

"It's going to get better, Heather. I can almost guarantee you that Eric will not take your kids."

"I wish I had your confidence." Still sitting in the cockpit, she traced a finger around the yoke, not in any hurry to get out. "Kyle asked about you. I think he wants to go to another baseball game. He won't take off the hat you gave him."

Seth smiled. "He's a good boy. I can't wait to take him to a game every weekend. The Texas Rangers are based in Dallas–Fort Worth. Maybe I can get season tickets, and we can all go as a family."

"Hmmmm, family," she sighed, even though it was a thousand miles away. "I like the sound of that."

He reached down and unbuckled her seat belt. "Are you ready to go?"

"Yeah, I guess. Now that I'm here, I don't want to leave."

"That's the beauty of owning your own plane. We can go flying every night if the weather's good. I'll even make you my official navigator. What do you think? Would your father mind?"

Tears stinging her eyes, she laid a palm on the side of Seth's face. "I think he would definitely approve."

After he climbed out, he strode around to her side and opened her door. She took his hand and stepped down onto the landing gear, wrapped her hands around his neck, sliding downward against the length of his body, surging with enough energy to fuel three planes. No words were needed as their lips sought a release that soared them into their own flight pattern.

They swayed into one another, only the sound of crickets waning between soft and loud in the dusky night air.

He lovingly touched her cheeks. "I'm proud of you."

"Why? You did all the work. You're a very good pilot."

He cocked her a sly grin. "Was there ever any doubt?"

"Seth?"

"What?"

She slipped her fingers into his belt loops and tugged him closer. "What are your plans the rest of the evening?"

He stepped closer, boxing her against the plane. "Nothing. What did you have in mind?"

"Will you take me flying?"

"We just set down." He chuckled. "It'll be dark soon."

She stood on tiptoes, wrapped her arms around his shoulders and spoke as she kissed his ear. "I'm not talking about flying in your Cessna."

He drew back and squinted his eyes, as if contemplating what she meant. "I think I might just be able to file a flight plan at the last minute. What about your kids?"

"Oh, you mean Kyle and Katie? The ones who are staying at Grandma Kara's and Grandpa Brad's the rest of the weekend?"

He slid his hands down her back, easing under her summer blouse, his palm covering her skin. "Yeah, those kids." He gave a low, sultry chuckle and pressed her back against the plane. "When's your birthday, anyway?"

"In two weeks, August thirteenth."

"You're kidding."

She arched her brows. "Nope, why?"

"Mine's August thirteenth."

"Get out of town," she jested. "Are you telling me we're both turning thirty on the same day?"

"It would appear that way, now, wouldn't it? Tell you what. How about we make it an anniversary? We could get married at the ranch and start our next thirty years together. Fifty, if I have any say in the matter."

"Two weeks?" she repeated, gulping heavily. She'd purposely been avoiding this discussion for the past two weeks for just this reason. If she officially set a date, there would be no turning back. Was she ready for this? Was she ready to marry Seth Roberts? "Don't you think it's kind of sudden? I mean, what about the kids? My mom will need time to get things planned."

"It's plenty of time. We're just having immediate family. We'll call the pastor of your church and see if he can fit us into his schedule. And if we hurry," he murmured, lowering his voice, snuggling his face into the side of her neck. "Maybe we'll get in a little flying practice before we say good-bye to our twenties. And I promise," he said, nibbling on her earlobe, "you're going to be begging me to land before I'm through with you."

The implication, along with the tingling sensations running up and down her body, made her shudder. "Is that a threat or a promise?" she teased, quickly twirling from his arms. All previous doubts of this union flitted right from her mind. This was good. She loved Seth. And even though neither of them had actually said it to one another, she knew in her heart Seth loved her, too. Suddenly giddy with anticipation of what the rest of the evening held, she trotted toward his Corvette.

"Heather," Seth called out from behind.

She turned just as he tossed her his keys.

"You drive." A crooked grin crossed his face.

She caught the keys midair, almost stumbling over her feet. "You want me to drive your car?"

"Sure. Why not?"

"Are you positive?" she verified, practically skipping toward the driver's-side door.

"I've seen how you drool every time I drive in at the ranch. I'd like to think it was because of me, but I've got this sneaking suspicion that Goldi has something to do with it."

"Goldi?" she repeated, slipping behind the wheel.

"Short for Goldilocks. She knows how to treat a man just right," he said, caressing the dash with his palm.

"Well, hold on, Papa Bear, because Mama Bear's going to take Goldilocks out for the ride of her life!"

CHAPTER SEVENTEEN

They'd barely shut the door to his penthouse before they'd kicked off their shoes, leaving a trail of tennis shoes and sandals through the living room. She dropped her purse on the floor, spilling her cell phone, compact, and billfold all over the carpet. His lips had a way of distracting her thoughts as they stumbled up two steps to the landing that lead to the master suite.

He backed her down the hallway, while his clever hands started unbuttoning her summer blouse. Still kissing, she peeked through slitted lids, taking in the surroundings. Only one picture hung in the hallway, a black-and-white photo of an old Corsair fighter plane from World War II.

They passed a room and she pulled apart, speaking through heavy breaths. "Is this Nicole's room?"

"Hmmm-huh," he moaned while looking down at her shirt, still working the buttons.

She giggled and turned in his arms, self-consciously tugging her shirt back together, gazing into Nicole's room. She stared at all the posters of pop stars taped on the walls. "I can definitely see a generation gap. I've never even heard of these groups."

He swayed into her from behind and swept her hair off the back of her neck. "Don't tell her I said this, but most of them are pretty good."

She smiled at his admission and glanced down into Spike's tank. Empty. "Where's Spike?"

"Spike?" he asked, his hands sneaking up her back, trailing

along the back strap of her bra.

"Yeah," she sighed and tipped her head against his chest, reveling in the wonderful new sensations his fingertips aroused. "You know, the four-legged little creature with beady eyes and a tongue, who reminds me so much of a certain man I used to know."

He chuckled and kissed the side of her neck while looking over toward Spike's cage. Seth stopped moving, lifted his head, his brows arching in confusion. "I fed him right before I left this afternoon."

She stepped next to the tank and picked up a screen. "Uh, Seth? I think you forgot to put the lid back on."

In the next instant, he jumped up on Nicole's bed, his head almost bumping the ceiling. "You mean he's out running loose?"

Heather tipped her head back and cracked up laughing. "Don't tell me you're afraid of a lizard, Uncle Seth?"

"Lizard, hell, that thing's the size of a small alligator!"

Kneeling down on the floor, she flipped the covers up and looked under the bed. "He's harmless. Just think of him as a little puppy."

"A puppy? I don't know where you grew up, but I've never petted a beagle with spikes growing out of its back."

"Are you sure Nicole didn't take him down to Maggie's with her?"

"Not unless she came back up and got him."

"Does she have her own key?"

"Yes. Maybe I should call her just to make sure."

Heather stood and rested her hands on her hips, unabashedly letting her blouse hang open as she stared up at this big strong man and mighty protector. "I had no idea you were such a big chicken shit." She laughed and began backing up when his gaze lowered to her opened blouse.

"Found it," he said, his eyes hazing over with desire.

She clutched her shirt together and gave a nervous glance behind her. "You found Spike?"

"Nope. The clasp to your bra. I thought I'd lost my touch." He stepped down from the bed and took one long stride toward her, lowered to her mouth, then gently took her hands in his. "Let's get out of here before I find Spike the hard way."

Without breaking his kiss, he scooped her into his arms, stepped out into the hallway and lowered so she could shut the door behind them. "Spike's on his own. I have no intention of ever sharing you with another male."

As she arched back to grab the doorknob, he dipped his head down to her chest, tracing his tongue over the swells of her breasts. A shiver raced over her moist skin as she grabbed hold of his neck.

He whisked her across the threshold of his bedroom and set her gently on the side of his king-size bed covered with a thick blue comforter. The room was darkened except for a light from an adjoining bathroom that created a romantic yellow glow.

She let out a trembly breath, trying to calm her rising heart rate. His blue eyes practically sparkled in the dim light, his perfect white teeth glimmering through a smile. She scooted back into the middle of the bed, luxuriating in the rich manly scents that was uniquely Seth.

He yanked the tails of his golf shirt out of his jeans and whipped it off, flinging it across the room. His muscular chest and biceps rippled as he emptied the contents of his jeans pockets onto the nightstand beside the bed.

This was so new, so romantic. The airplane ride was perfect. The night was perfect. The man was perfect. She closed her eyes and buried deeper into the comforter, breathing deep. "Mmmm, this is so comfortable, I could just fall asleep right now."

A low sensual chuckle made her shudder. "Honey, if you

want to sleep through the most incredible night of your life, be my guest. But in all actuality, the odds of you falling asleep anytime before dawn will be slim to none."

She gave a loud mocking laugh and leaned up on her elbows, rubbing her bare feet together. "This coming from my big bwave warrior afwaid of a wittle old weptile?"

"Okay, you found my Achilles heel. Now it's time for me to find yours." With his vibrant blue gaze fixed on hers, he knelt down on the floor in front of her and smiled. "Come here," he said, grabbing her ankles. "Time for my preflight inspection before I take you flying."

She fell back on the bed as he tugged her to the edge till her bare legs straddled his firm naked waist. She was very aware that her skirt had inched up over her thighs, and leveraged herself to sitting, wrapping her arms around his neck. He kissed under her chin, tilting her head back.

She sighed as his fingertips threaded under her blouse, lifting the garment off her shoulders, dropping it on the bed behind her. His fingers trembled slightly as he unhooked the front clasp on her bra, slipping it off till her breasts were bared for his viewing pleasure.

He sat back on his haunches and smiled, his gaze firmly fixed below her neck. "Just as I suspected. The symmetry is perfect."

"Really?" she said, sitting taller and staring down at her breasts. "Eric always thought my right side was too small."

He cocked his head slightly to the side, his lips creasing together as he contemplated each breast. He cupped them both in each hand, lifting one then the other, like an old-fashioned scale. "I'm no expert here, but from my initial observation, they're absolutely perfect. And from the little I know about Eric, he's the one who's too small."

Sliding his hands around her back, he added, "And if you don't mind, I don't even want you to think that man's name the rest of the night—or ever, if I have my way." He reached behind her and unzipped her skirt, slipping it down her legs till she was sitting in only a pair of lacy white panties.

Kneeling between her legs, he pressed his naked chest against her breasts. His matt of soft dark hair stimulated the tips as she pressed against his firm pectoral muscles. He met her mouth, her tongue seeking his, seeking release. His hands cupped both breasts, his fingers teasing the hardened tips, sending lightning heat to the area between her legs. She squeezed her knees against Seth's side, getting absolutely no relief. She'd never had this achy impatient feeling before in her life. She couldn't seem to get close enough.

"Seth," she panted, drawing away from his mouth. "Please."

"Please, what?" he murmured, dragging his mouth from the underside of her chin, lower to the peaks of one breast where he circled his tongue around the areola without ever quite taking hold.

"Make love to me," she pleaded.

"Patience, sweetheart." He leisurely kissed over to the other breast, following the same tormenting path avoiding her nipple.

"You're determined to drive me crazy, aren't you?" She clutched his hair between her fingers, steering him to the tip of one breast.

He finally, almost painfully nibbled the sensitive nub, only making the region between her thighs explode into a lake of fire. She clamped her legs together, but remained hindered by his broad chest as he knelt in front of her on the floor.

When he switched to the other breast, she braced both hands on the bed behind her and arched her head back, her hair sweeping into a pile behind her. Her whole body writhed against him. The friction of his jeans through her lace panties made her whimper. "Oh, Seth. I've never felt like this. Ever. It's like . . . oh . . . ," she moaned, not able to have any coherent thought in her mind. It was all about sensations and feelings and wanting to get as close to this man as she possibly could. Dragging kisses down her stomach, he went lower, his hands cupping the roundness of her bottom.

Cool air drifted over her thighs when he drew apart and picked up one foot, kissing the top, making his way up her calf to her thigh. Lowering that leg, he picked up the other, following the same sensual path from the arch of her foot to the sensitive area behind her knee. His wet kisses left a cool trail of moisture on both legs and she gave a slight shiver.

He started kissing the inside of her thighs, one leg then the other, till he was a whisper's length from driving her over the edge. Panting, she clenched the comforter in her fingers at her sides.

He chuckled, looking up at her. "Relax, honey. We haven't even left the runway, yet."

"It's been so long. I don't know if I can—" But she didn't even finish before he slid the lace of her panties aside and found the release she was hoping for, suckling the most intimate part of her sex. She fell back on her elbows and arched her neck, reveling in all the wonderful feelings that seemed to be exploding throughout her body.

She found herself rocking against his chin, the sensations she'd missed out on all these years hitting her with the force so deep, so primal she had to bite her lip to keep from yelling out.

"Don't hold back," he murmured against her. "Let it go."

He was all hands and mouth and tongue. She scooted closer, pressing into him harder, her knees gripping his shoulders as he worked his magic. His fingers rolled one of her nipples into a tight little bud, and she felt herself slipping over the edge, slowly, effortlessly, till her whole body fell backwards onto the bed. He only suckled harder, harder till she soared into the next universe, floating and drifting, then free-falling back to earth. All she could hear was her heart thrumming inside her head. Her arms went limp. Her whole body melted into the bed like warm honey.

As her lungs heaved for air and her heart hammered inside her chest, he pressed kisses all the way up her stomach, between her breasts, and up the underside of her chin, ending with a devouring kiss on her mouth. He tasted of passion and cinnamon, and the love she had for this man just grew ten times more.

Slipping his hands under her shoulders, he lifted her up and laid her back in the middle of the bed. She didn't even have the strength to move her legs as he straightened them, running his fingertips up and down her thighs. She peered up at him through slitted lids. "Hi," she murmured through a contented whisper.

"Hi, yourself." His crooked grin was sexy and way too sure of himself.

Her body still limp, she could only smile. "Don't look so cocky, Roberts. As long as it's been for me, anyone could have done it that fast."

He chuckled. "Is that so?"

"Actually, no, but I didn't want you to get a big head."

Rubbing his arousal against her thigh, he laughed. "Sorry, too late."

She found the strength to wrap her arms around his neck. "Are you going to use that thing, or are you just going to tease me all night long?"

He chuckled and kissed her brow. "You know what they say about good things coming to those who wait." Leveraging himself up on one elbow, he continued to kiss her as he dragged the backside of his fingers down her neck, brushing her collarbone.

"I want you," she whispered, writhing against him. "If you don't hurry up and make love to me I'll. . . ."

"You'll what?" he teased, sliding his arms under her back till he cupped the crown of her head, the bulging mass in his jeans now positioned directly over her hips.

She squeezed him tight and laughed. "I'll sick Spike on you, that's what."

He laughed huskily and rolled to his side, dragging her with him. "God, you feel so good." His voice rumbled in her ear as he rocked against her, bringing her close to shattering again.

She reached down and unfastened the top button of his jeans. "Now," she urged, staring through a haze into the dusky dimness of his room. Eager, she bravely slid her hand over his bulging zipper.

He hissed, sucking air through his teeth, reaching down and grabbing her hand. "Easy, darlin'. It's been a while for me, too. I want to at least make it out of the chutes, if you know what I mean."

A dark shadow moved across the bed behind Seth.

She blinked. Froze as the shadow continued to creep slowly across the bed.

She swallowed and tapped Seth's back. "Seth? Don't be alarmed or anything."

"Alarmed?" he repeated, kissing the underside of her jaw.

"Whatever you do, don't roll backwards."

He spoke as he kissed down her neck. "Why? What are you talking about?"

"I found Spike."

He jerked backwards!

A low guttural moan escaped his throat, crescendoing into an earsplitting yell. He swooped back on top of her just as she heard a loud slap.

He gave a hard jerk as if he'd just been electrocuted, shouting a profanity at the top of his lungs.

His tail! Seth must have gotten whipped by Spike's tail!

Scrambling backwards off the bed, Seth flipped on the wall switch and craned his neck around to his backside. A huge red welt had already risen on his lower right side.

Suddenly afraid for her own vulnerability, she bounded off the bed and hurried around the end toward Seth. "Oh, my gosh. Are you all right?"

"Do I fucking look all right? Where the hell is it? I'll kill the little dragon!"

"No! You can't kill it," she said, grabbing hold of his arms. "Just calm down. I'll catch it. Go to the bathroom and put a cold washcloth over the welt."

With his fingers clenched into a fist, he stared over at the bed. Spike was nowhere to be seen. This didn't look good.

She quickly grabbed her blouse and slipped it over her shoulders, fastening two buttons in the middle. "I'll go get his leash and see if I can catch him." She splayed her palms over Seth's naked chest, his pectorals flexing as he tightened his fingers. She edged him away from the bed toward the bathroom. "Go get a cold compress and don't do anything you're going to regret."

"Too late. I already regret the day I allowed that creature to live here!" He stormed into the bathroom, mumbling another expletive under his breath. Now she was sorry she'd ever chided him about Spike. She had no idea a tail could cause so much pain.

She found Spike's leash and peeked under the bed. Two beady eyes stared right back at her. She almost flinched, but didn't want to scare him further. She started talking softly like she'd heard Nicole do so many times. When he didn't back up, she reached out and cringed, gripping the little guy behind the neck, carefully coaxing it out from under the bed.

"Got you," she said, easing the leash over its head. She stood, holding his tail away from her. "I got him, Seth. I'll put him

351

back in his tank."

Just as she left the room, the phone rang. His footsteps sounded as he crossed the bedroom and answered on the third ring. "Hello?" he grumbled into the phone.

Heather peered back through the doorway and found him with his back toward her, slouched on one side, holding a washcloth over the welt that Spike had made. "Hell, no. It's eight-thirty, for crying out loud. There's no way I can meet tonight. It has to be tomorrow." He rubbed the pads of his fingers over his eyes and lowered his voice. "Yeah, I'm interested. Just don't go anywhere near her." He scribbled something down on a notepad on the end table and groaned. "Fine. I'll be there in thirty minutes."

Heather's heart lunged to her stomach. She backed away from his bedroom and could only shake her head. She wasn't even married, and he was already ditching her to go to a meeting? Or worse . . . another woman?

Her fingers trembled as she carefully set Spike in his cage. She actually found herself rubbing her fingers over his scales, stroking his neck with affection. Her heart raced. What had she been thinking? This would never work. The fact that he was dumping her tonight should be warning enough. She couldn't even entice the man to stay and have sex with her!

She closed her eyes, trying to remain calm, but everything inside her said to run. Run now before it was too late. She gulped. She couldn't marry Seth Roberts. She would never make it as an executive wife. She couldn't let Seth throw his life away and be saddled with an old ball and chain and her two demanding children, not to mention being stuck with a teenager whose hormones were whacked out from here to Pluto. The man had to be certifiably nuts!

Through tear-clouded vision, she set the lid on the tank and turned around.

Seth was standing there in his jeans, the top button still undone, his torso bare. "Spike okay?" he asked.

She cleared the lump from her throat. "Yeah. I'm afraid you got the worst end of it . . . or should I say, tail end of it?" She tried to joke, but her voice choked on her words. "You gonna be okay?"

His gaze bore into hers with a look that said, "I'm sorry, but business awaits." He pushed off the wall and stepped toward her, slouching on the end of Nicole's bed. He reached out and touched her fingertips. "This isn't exactly how I'd pictured tonight."

She pulled her hand away and started buttoning her blouse. "Good thing I met you here earlier. I'll just get my things so you can go on to work." She turned and padded barefoot into his bedroom, grabbing her skirt from the floor.

"Heather? Please, wait. I don't want you to leave."

She zipped her skirt and brushed by him and headed toward the living room. A tear dripped from her eye as she scooped up a sandal, hopped on one foot trying to slip it on, then bent to get the other.

"Honey, please don't go. I'll only be about an hour. We've got the whole rest of the night to be together."

She hobbled across the floor as she jammed on her other sandal then knelt down to pick up all the belongings from her purse. "No, really. I should go. I know how these meetings go. An hour usually turns into three or four. I don't want you to feel like you have to hurry."

He hunkered down beside her and picked up her compact and lipstick then handed them to her. She closed her eyes when he gently wrapped his fingers around her wrists, stopping her from any more movements. "I'm sorry, Heather. I know this is bad timing, but I promise. It'll never happen again, I swear." He brushed a feathery kiss over her forehead then drew apart.

"Heather? Look at me."

She slowly lifted her heavy lids till she met his incredible blue eyes. Eyes that she'd fallen madly in love with.

"I have to go this one more time. After tomorrow it will be all over. I'll never leave you again. I promise."

Till the next big project came along. She straightened and stared over his shoulder. She couldn't look at him, knowing she had to end this now before it was too late. It would never work in the long run. He'd get tired of her just like Eric.

Something in Seth's briefcase caught her eye. A document on top had two words across the front. She slowly turned to face Seth, who still held her wrists captive. She tried to speak, but her voice came out barely over a strangled whisper. "Is Saint Anthony's the resort you've been working on all summer?"

He slowly turned his head and looked over at his opened briefcase. "Heather? Give me a chance to explain."

Then it all started to click. "Are you working with Eric?"

"I know this looks bad, but just hear me out."

His avoidance to answer had her panicking. "Have you or have you not been dealing with Eric this whole summer?"

"Yes, but it's not what you think."

Still kneeling in front of him, she jerked away from his touch. "What I think is that you've been lying to me this whole time! That's what I think! Was that Eric on the phone? Are you dumping me to go meet with him?"

"I know it sounds bad, but please, just give me a second, and I'll explain everything."

"Explain?" she repeated, throwing her hands in the air. "Explain why you're dumping me in the middle of making love to go to your office and deal with my ex-husband?" She spotted her keys on the floor and scrambled over to retrieve them.

He grabbed an ankle to keep her from leaving. "Heather, wait. It's not as bad as it sounds. Please, we have to talk."

She yanked away from him, crawling toward the door, trying to stand, but her knees quaked, making her stumble. She hobbled toward the door, determined to flee. Her chest hurt trying to get air into her lungs. Or was it her heart? She wondered if she might be having a heart attack, the way her heart hurt so badly.

Struggling to her feet, she grabbed the doorknob and flung the door wide. Then she whirled around and faced him, meeting his gaze head on. "Yes or no, Seth: are you behind the demolition of Saint Anthony's?"

"Heather," he panted, reaching for her shoulders. "Please. You have to listen."

"I'll take that as a yes. Is Eric the realtor you've been dealing with?"

"Yes, but—"

"But what?" she snapped, flinging his hands away from her. "There are no buts. You've lied to me. You've used me this whole summer! All you've ever wanted was an easy drop-off for Nicole so you could go off and make your stupid deals and become vice president of your precious firm! You don't need a wife. You need a nanny for Nicole so you don't have to deal with a teenage girl!"

"It's not like that, honey. Please, you have to—"

"No. I don't have to do anything! You have no control over me. I'll never let anyone control me again. Do you hear me? I'm not going to be left home alone night after night so you can be off with your colleagues screwing the locals." She tipped her head to the ceiling and shook her head. "I guess I pegged you right all along. There's not enough money in this world to make guys like you and Eric happy. I don't know why I ever thought you'd be any different."

She raced out the door and punched the elevator buttons, feeling betrayed and used. He'd known the entire summer how she felt about Saint Anthony's, yet he'd gone through with his plans anyway, just so he could secure some big promotion in his firm.

She'd been right all along. He couldn't turn down the vice presidency. It was what he'd planned for his entire life.

She gasped when his hand gripped her arm, spinning her around, almost abruptly. "You've pegged me all wrong, Heather. I'm not like Eric. I would never cheat on you with anyone. I *do* care about family. I love Nicole like she was my own daughter. I've never said that about anyone, but I love her, and I love Kyle and Katie, too. They're why I've been working so hard all summer. I'm doing this so we can all be together as a family. I wanted to tell you all about it tomorrow, but—"

"Don't you get it? I don't want your stupid resort or your money. All I want, all I've ever wanted—" She hiccupped and closed her eyes, shaking her head. "You know what? It doesn't matter what I want. God, I can't do this anymore. I never should have let myself get so attached to Nicole." She jerked her arm away. "Go to your stupid meeting, Seth. Close the deal and go to Dallas. Ship Nicole off to a boarding school and find yourself some pretty young thing without so many problems."

She headed to the stairwell and flung the door open. "You should be relieved," she said, glaring back at him. "You and I never would have worked. Guys like you can't be strapped down with so much responsibility." Before he could answer, she took the stairs by twos, her sandals echoing in the metal stairwell.

He gripped the railing and yelled down after her. "Guys like me? You mean like Eric?" He took off down the stairs, following her in hot pursuit. "From the moment we met on that plane, you've been trying to typecast me into his shadow. Time and time again I've tried to prove how much you mean to me. Dammit! Would you stop and listen to me?"

At the bottom landing, she pressed her hands against the wall and leaned her forehead against the cool painted cement. He approached from behind and leaned his arms on the wall above her shoulders, speaking in heavy breaths near her ear. "I'm sorry, Heather. I should have been honest with you from the start about Saint Anthony's, but you know what? I think you were just waiting for the other shoe to drop. I think you were just looking for any excuse you could find, to get out of marrying me."

"How can you say that?" She whirled around and jerked her head back. "Do you have any idea what it feels like, knowing that I can't even keep a man interested long enough to have sex with me? That he'd rather be off at the office closing some deal or maybe even screwing his secretary?"

"Oh, God, Heather." He groaned and cupped her face with his hands. "My leaving has nothing to do with you, at least not physically. I love you so much. I would never cheat on you with another woman. I've never wanted to be with anyone more than I do with you. You're on my mind night and day. I can't eat. I can't sleep. These last two weeks have been the longest two weeks of my life because I didn't want to spend even one more day without you as my wife. I'm sorry about Spike. I'm sorry that I've lied to you about Saint Anthony's, but just hear me out. I know you'll understand. I did it all for you. I love you."

She closed her eyes, his words echoing in her head. He'd said it. He actually said he loved her, but was it real? Or just something he felt he should say out of guilt, considering he was ditching her to go to work. She fluttered her wet lashes up and met his gaze. "I don't want your pity, Seth. I'm a big girl. My family is all I need right now. You'd be better off going to Dallas without me, without so many burdens. You shouldn't be saddled with so many responsibilities in the prime of your life."

Knowing it was better this way, she pulled away from him and pushed through the metal exit door. She spoke over her shoulder as she headed toward her van. "Like Eric said, some women just aren't cut out to be wives or mothers."

He shoved through the door behind her. "That's it, isn't it?" His voice grew stern. Dressed only in his jeans, still barefoot, he followed her across the lobby, getting a concerned glance from the doorman. "Admit it, Heather. Your not marrying me has nothing to do with this resort, does it? I already told you I'd give up Dallas and stay here to be near your family. But that's not what's keeping you from marrying me, is it?"

Not sure where he was headed with this, she hurried through the lobby doors and approached her van, parked in the front parking stall.

"You say you don't want anyone controlling your life, but look at you, running scared the minute you fall in love with someone."

She flung her van door open and tossed her purse on the floor. "Scared? Hell yes, I'm scared." She turned and shoved her hands on her waist. "I'm afraid I won't meet up to what you expect out of a wife, that after a while I'm going to disappoint you just like I disappointed Eric."

"Oh, baby," he said, stepping closer, cupping her shoulders. His bare feet slid to the outside of her sandals. "You'll never disappoint me. You've let Eric cast you into this unfit-mother role, and he's got you brainwashed into thinking you've failed at producing less than a perfect son. But Eric's wrong. Kyle's as perfect as the next kid, and I love him as if he were my own son. You've poured your heart and soul into both your children, and it shows in their eyes and in their smiles. But all you can see is Eric judging you, castigating you for every little problem that comes up."

She couldn't keep her chin from wobbling and had to force a heavy swallow to keep from breaking down in a pathetic sob. As if sensing her distress, he touched her chin, forcing her to look him in the eyes. "It kills me to see what he's done to you, honey. You say you don't want anyone to control your life, but you're doing it. You're letting Eric beat you down. Ever since I met you, you've done nothing but put yourself down and tell yourself what a bad mother you are, what a liability you'd be to me . . . or—I'm assuming—to any other man. But I'm not any other man, and I'm not Eric."

Sliding his warm, comforting hands around her face, he closed his eyes and rested his chin on her forehead. "I love you, Heather. I want you to be my wife more than anything in this world. I don't give a rat's ass where we live, or what I do for a living. I don't care if you can cook or clean or boil a pot of water. You're perfect just the way you are, and I know you'll make a wonderful wife."

A lump in her throat blocked her airway and she found it hard to breathe, much less speak. It was so good to hear those wonderful three little words. He loved her. He really loved her. "I'm sorry," she finally squeaked out.

He shook his head. "I don't want you to be sorry. I want you to be happy. You've kept the real Heather locked away for so many years, it's time to let her out, honey. Let her live. Let her learn to trust. Let her learn to love again." He pressed his mouth tenderly over hers, whispering through his kiss. "I love you so much, Heather." Then he drew apart and looked down at her. "But until you figure out what you really want, who you really are, I think you're right. We shouldn't get married."

Then he turned and left her standing there in the parking lot. Her heart almost shattered, watching Seth walk away. She wanted to run after him, tell him how much she loved him, too. But he was right. She had to learn to love herself again. Find out who she was and what made her happy. And until she could do that, there was no way she would be able to make Seth or anyone else happy.

So, how was she supposed to do that? And would Seth wait for her?

CHAPTER EIGHTEEN

"Happy Birthday, Mommy." Katie's voice sounded softly in her ear.

Heather raised her head and squinted through slitted lids at the clock on the table. "It's only six o'clock in the morning, sweetie. I still have a couple of more hours till I'm thirty. Now go back to bed." Heather dragged the pillow over her head.

"Mommy," Katie whined, jiggling her back. "Open my present. Please?"

"You're not leaving my bed till I do, are you?" Her voice sounded muffled.

"Nope. So you might as well open it."

"Is Kyle up yet?"

"No, he's still sleeping."

"Lucky him," Heather grumbled and shoved her pillows back against the headboard. A sliver of orange sunlight filtered through the Venetian blinds hanging over the window. She spoke through a loud yawn. "The sun's barely even up. I hope this is worth it," she teased, tickling Katie's tummy.

"Oh, it is, Mommy. Hurry!"

"Why? Is it going to explode?"

"No, of course not," Katie giggled and started ripping the paper for her.

"Don't I even get to guess?"

"Okay." She sat back, almost looking dejected.

Heather shook the rectangular object, its contours obviously a picture frame. "Um, it's an elephant."

"Mo-mm-y," she dragged it out into three long syllables.

"Okay, it's a horse."

"Just open it."

The plumbing from the bathroom indicated Kyle was up. He peered in from the hallway yawning and rubbing his eyes. Heather had to smile at the fact that he'd already donned the new baseball cap Seth had given him. He'd sleep in it if Heather would let him.

"Morning, Kyle."

"Hurry, Kyle. Come and watch Mommy open her present." She looked over at Heather and smiled. "Kyle helped make it, too."

"He did? Wow, I can't imagine what you two could have made."

Kyle shuffled his way around the other side of Heather and crawled up onto the bed beside her. "Hungry," he mumbled, tugging the rim of his shirt into his mouth.

"I'll fix something special in a few minutes. Will you help me open my present?"

Heather slouched against the pillows, smiling, wondering what pretty picture they'd made this time. Heather loved all of Kyle and Katie's drawings and already had a huge box full of their pictures she'd collected over the years.

She pulled down the gold foil wrapping paper and tilted her head to the side. It was a drawing of a two-story house with a swing set and even had a huge pool in the backyard. "It's lovely. Did you both draw this all by yourself?"

"We had a little help from Uncle Seth."

"Uncle Seth?" she repeated, surprised. "When did he help you with this?"

"When Auntie Debra had her baby. See?" Katie said, pointing to a second-story window. "This is my room."

"My room," Kyle added, pointing to another window on the second floor.

Katie pointed to another window in the middle. "This is where the new baby will sleep."

Heather's eyes widened. "New baby? What are you talking about, honey?"

"Seth said that we might be having a new baby someday, and he wanted to make sure she had her very own room."

Heather couldn't help but feel a sting of tears behind her eyes. He must have helped the kids draw this before they'd broken off their engagement. Did Seth want a baby as badly as she did?

Hoping to let them down easily, Heather wrapped her arm around both Kyle and Katie, tugging them to her side. "This is a beautiful drawing, guys, but Seth and I aren't going to get married. Remember? I told you about this last week. I know it's hard to understand, but we aren't going to be together anymore. It's all for the best."

Katie's eyes started tearing over. "But I thought since he sent you a birthday present, everything was okay again."

"Seth sent me a birthday present?"

"Uh-huh. I'll go get it." Katie jumped off the bed and skipped out of the room. Her tiny pitter-patters could be heard all the way down the hall into the living room.

"Hungry," Kyle mumbled again. Obviously, he wasn't as affected as Katie by his mother's breakup with Seth. Maybe he didn't understand. He bounded out of bed and jogged out of the room toward the kitchen.

Heather closed her eyes, forcing the well of tears to remain locked inside her heart. She hadn't heard from Seth since he'd walked away from her in the parking lot of his penthouse suite two weeks ago. Yet she couldn't seem to get his eyes and his perfect smile out of her head.

And those three little words. The way he'd held her so tenderly and professed his love and devotion to her, she'd wanted to go running back into his arms, screaming at the top of her lungs how much she loved him, too. She dabbed at a tear and took in a deep breath. She didn't know if her heart would ever be whole again.

"Here it is, Mommy." Katie galloped into the room and jumped up on the bed with a brown drafting tube in her hand.

Heather cleared her throat and reached for a tissue. Then she took the tube and realized it was from Dalton & Jones Architects, her stepfather's firm. She pulled off a small card attached under a pretty pink bow. It simply read, "Happy birthday, with all my love, Seth."

Sliding what looked like a set of blueprints from the tube, she unrolled it to display the top page. The title read, "The Golden Springs Retirement Village and Independent Living Complex."

Heather's heart completely stopped beating. "Oh, my gosh, Katie. What has he done?"

"Look, Mommy. There's a picture."

Flattening the parchment out on her bed, Heather knelt in front of it with her hand splayed over the edges to keep the sides from curling. The top page was a full-color layout of the future site of the resort Seth had been working on all summer.

Fountains and lush green lawns surrounded two-story condos, with the foothills of Cheyenne Mountain off in the distance. An eighteen-hole golf course was creatively designed, snaking its way in and around all the condos throughout the resort. A clubhouse was positioned in the middle, next to a health spa that would be fully equipped with therapeutic equipment, including three whirlpool therapy pools, an Olympic-sized swimming pool, as well as a weight room and a separate aerobics studio. The administrative buildings included a special section for a medical clinic where an on-site physician and pharmacy would be available twenty-four hours a day.

Heather carefully flipped through page after page, suddenly realizing what it all meant. This was more than just another golf course and country club. It was her dream. It was everything she'd ever imagined and ten times more. Seth had made it possible for Kyle and others like him to have a promising and secure future.

She couldn't have been more wrong about Seth. All these weeks, he'd been working late to make her dream a reality. She couldn't even begin to fathom the selfless hours he'd spent on creating a community this complex, this dedicated to catering to people with special needs, and still make it a place for folks who wanted to enjoy their golden years in luxury.

It was perfect.

He was perfect.

Closing her eyes, she held her hand over her heart. "Oh, God," she whispered. "I've made a huge mistake. What should I do?"

"What's the matter, Mommy? Aren't you happy?"

She nodded, trying to find her voice. "Oh, yes, honey. I'm very happy." But was it too late? If she went to him now, would he still want her?

The front doorbell rang. Heather's heart skipped a beat. Maybe that was him now. She quickly rolled up the blueprints and crawled out of bed. Combing her fingers through her hair, she headed out to the living room and had barely unlocked the front door before Jared stepped inside carrying what looked like a baker's box.

Although disappointed, she couldn't help but smile when she caught his ornery grin. "What's this?" she asked, peeking inside the lid.

"Tradition." He bent over and gave her a kiss on the cheek. "Happy birthday, sis. One donut for every year."

"I think we'd better rethink this tradition. I'm not going to fit into my jeans by my next birthday." She breathed in the yummy aroma of warm doughnuts covered with glaze, sprinkles, nuts, whipped cream, every kind of confection ever made, she guessed.

"How's it feel to be thirty?" he asked, stuffing a chocolate crème donut into his mouth.

"Honestly? I feel like I'm turning fifty."

"I think there's someone here that might perk you up."

Heather made a hopeful glance out the living-room window toward the parking lot, hoping for a glimpse of a cute yellow Corvette, but felt a little deflated when all she saw was Jared's truck.

Putting on a forced smile, she turned back to Jared and took the box of doughnuts. "Oh, yeah? Who?"

"Come on in, Nicole," he hollered over his shoulder and opened the front door.

Shuffling into her condo was a petite strawberry blonde teenager. Heather set the box of doughnuts on the counter, wanting to run over and give Nicole a hug. She didn't realize till this instant just how much she'd missed her in the last two weeks.

"Nicole!" She wrapped her arms around her shoulders. "What a wonderful surprise."

"I hope it's okay I came here. Uncle Seth dropped me off at Jared's so I could come over and wish you a happy birthday."

Heather drew apart. "Of course, it's okay, sweetie. No matter what happened between your uncle and me, you can always come and talk to me."

"I thought maybe since you hadn't been out to the ranch, that maybe you didn't want to see—"

"Oh, no, Nicole. My not coming to the ranch had nothing to do with you." Heather took Nicole's hands. "I should have explained things to you, but everything kind of came down on me at once. I just needed to take some time off, kind of rethink where my priorities were. I'm sorry if you thought it had anything to do with you." Heather gave Nicole another hug, pressing a kiss to her temple.

"Uncle Seth has been like a total grump. He's miserable without you."

"He is?" Heather asked, her voice sounding hopeful. "I'm sorry you got caught in the middle of all this. It seems kind of unfair, huh?"

Nicole shrugged. "I'm just bummed, is all. Maggie's mom asked if I'd go camping with them. So, I jumped at the chance."

"You're going camping?"

"Yeah. We're going to Yellowstone for two weeks. We're leaving this morning as soon as Jared drops me off. I just wanted to say good-bye."

"I know you and Maggie will have a great time. I bet your uncle will miss you, though."

"Nah, he's flying to Dallas this morning anyway."

"Dallas? He's leaving this morning?" Heather's voice took a sudden rise in pitch, almost sounding hysterical. Was there any way she could catch him before he left? "What time does his flight leave?"

"Oh, he's not flying commercial. He's taking his Cessna. Maybe when I get back from Yellowstone he'll be in a better mood."

Heather had to swallow the lump of disappointment in her throat. He was going to Dallas without her. It was too late. He didn't wait for her. "I suppose he's going to do some house hunting while he's down there?"

"House hunting? What do you mean?"

"If he's taking the promotion, that means he'll have to live in Dallas."

"Uncle Seth is moving to Dallas?"

"Didn't he tell you?"

She took a step back and shook her head. "He just said he had to sign a bunch of paperwork. He didn't say anything to me about moving to Dallas." Her eyes teared over as she bit her lower lip.

"What about the Nantucket Girls School? Won't you be going to the east coast after your camping trip?"

Nicole's eyes widened. "Is that what he told you? I told him I didn't want to go."

Not sure what Seth had or hadn't told Nicole, Heather forced a reassuring smile. "I'm sure he won't do anything without your approval first. You'll love Dallas. It's a beautiful city."

"I can't believe he didn't say anything. Won't you go with us? Please?" she begged. Her lower lip quivered as she gave a little sniff.

"Oh, honey." Heather's voice cracked. She squeezed Nicole's shoulders.

Heather knew without a doubt that she loved Seth. The question was, did he still love her? There was only one way to find out.

She had to go to Dallas.

She looked down at Nicole and tucked a strand of hair behind her ear. "Why don't you watch cartoons with Kyle and Katie? I'll get you a donut and some milk."

Nicole swiped at her tears and sat down in between Katie and Kyle on the floor.

Not sure what to do, Heather shuffled into the kitchen with the box of donuts, then grabbed a coffeepot and started filling it with water.

Jared grunted and leaned his shoulder against the kitchen doorframe. "You love him, don't you?"

She poured the water into the coffeemaker and gave a heavy sigh. "Yeah, I love him," she confirmed out loud, as much for herself as for Jared. She put a scoop of coffee grounds in the filter, backing off by a few tablespoons, remembering Seth's remark about her coffee being too strong.

"Did you see the plans for the new resort?" he asked.

"I just saw them this morning."

"Did you know he convinced Eric into dropping all his threats about taking your kids?"

Surprised, she turned around and perched her hands on the counter behind her. "I had no idea. How did he manage that?"

"Maybe you should ask Seth."

She wiped her hand on a towel and squeezed by Jared, heading back to her bedroom, but didn't answer.

Jared quickly followed. "Aren't you being a little unfair to the guy?" He followed her into her bedroom. "What's this really about, Heather? You love the guy. He loves you. It's that simple."

"Is it? Is marrying me and taking on all my problems that simple?"

"What problems? You're a divorced mother with two great kids who deserves to find happiness. You've found it. Don't let it slip away. You may never get another chance. The guy's in love with you. You should go with him. Everything has a way of working out."

She wiped her face, suddenly realizing that Jared was right. In her attempt to prove Eric couldn't control her, she'd done just that. She'd allowed his lies, his verbal abuse to beat her down and allow her insecurities to run her life. That's exactly what Eric would have wanted. She couldn't let him win. She couldn't lose the only man she'd ever truly loved.

She squared her shoulders. "Do you think it's too late? Do you think he would still take me back?"

"There's only one way to find out. Why don't you go get showered and dressed, then pack a suitcase for Kyle and Katie. I think between Mom, J.D., and me, we'll find a place for them to bunk for a few days, you know, in case you find yourself on a honeymoon in Dallas or something." He winked.

"Oh, Jared," she almost squealed, wrapping her arms around his shoulders, suddenly feeling like the whole world was back on its axis again. She could do this. She could marry Seth and move to Dallas. "I'm going to miss you guys so much. Promise me you'll come down and visit all the time? Maybe there'll be some cute little cowgirl I could fix you up with."

He kissed her on the cheek and winked. "Count on it. Now go get dressed."

CHAPTER NINETEEN

It was already after nine when she drove into the Prairie Park Airport where Seth stored his plane. She drove up to his hangar, but the door was closed and she didn't see any signs of Seth or his car anywhere. Maybe she'd missed him. Maybe he'd already taken off.

With her heart thudding hard in disappointment, she drove over to the office and put her van in park, then shut off the engine. She just sat there, wondering what to do next. Was it too late? Had he already left?

She got out and shut the door, breathing in the warm August sunshine. The sky was crystal blue, and the birds were calling out to one another, chirping and singing in unison. She smoothed her hands over her white linen skirt, hitting several inches above her knees. She rarely wore heels, but had bought these three-inch strappy sandals for Easter. In fact, her whole outfit was from Easter. A sheer, long-sleeved silk blouse hung loosely over a spaghetti-strap white camisole made of the same soft satin. She'd fully intended to wear it to the wedding.

The wedding that had never happened because she'd been too stubborn and too blind to see love when it had stared her right in the face.

She caught her reflection in the office window and adjusted a hair comb decorated with tiny white rosebuds that she'd used to hold one side of her hair back. She clutched her white handbag, suddenly feeling foolish for dressing as if she were going to get married. As if he'd just rush into her arms and take her back.

The sound of a plane engine revved to full power, sounding like it was preparing for takeoff. With her heart in her throat, she hurried around the terminal building. She shielded her eyes from the bright morning sun, glimpsing the windsock standing almost motionless.

A blue-and-white Cessna started down the runway full throttle. Her feet suddenly froze. She couldn't breathe. She couldn't move. She just stood there as the plane sped toward her and lifted into the air, climbing rapidly higher. She pressed trembling fingers over her lips, watching as it disappeared into the horizon, out of sight, forever out of her life.

He was gone. She'd missed him.

She covered her face with her hands, ashamed for letting him go. Not getting to say good-bye. Not thanking him for all he'd done for her and her kids this summer.

Not telling him how much she loved him.

She'd never told him. She'd never said those three little words back to him. Now it was too late.

"Oh, Daddy," she cried in a whisper. "I lost him. He's gone."

She hugged her arms to her chest and stared off toward the horizon as if expecting Seth to come back for her. She stood there for what seemed like an eternity. What had she been thinking? Of course, Seth hadn't waited for her.

With a heart so heavy it was hard to walk, she finally made her way back around the office to her van. A couple of men emerged from the building, and before the door swung shut, she heard Seth's deep baritone over the field office airport radio.

The radio.

Her heart revved into overdrive. Maybe she could reach him on the radio. If she could just talk to him. Tell him how she truly felt. Maybe he would turn back.

She hurried inside and found one of the airport personnel just coming out of the men's restroom. He was an older balding gentleman who looked to be retirement age. She flagged him over to the counter.

"Can I help you, miss?"

Breathing heavy, she nodded. "Yes. Can you tell me if that was Seth Roberts that just took off in the blue-and-white Cessna?"

"Yes, ma'am. I believe it was."

She reached out and touched the man's forearm. "You have to help me. Can you get on the radio and give him a message?"

"What kind of a message?"

"Tell him, um. . . ." She paused, biting her lower lip, wondering exactly what to say that would convince him to turn around. "Tell him he needs to come back. That he forgot his navigator."

The man scratched the back of his head. "Traffic's kind of slow. I'll see what I can do." He shuffled over to the airport radio and picked up the microphone. "Seven-seven-three-three-Romeo, this is Prairie Park Airport. Do you copy?"

A few seconds passed before Seth's deep baritone sounded over the radio. "Copy that, Prairie Park. This is seven-seven-three-three-Romeo. What's up, Ned?"

Ned chuckled and looked back at Heather. "Hey, Seth. I'm supposed to give you a message. Seems you need to come back and pick up your navigator." Ned said it with a hint of a question at the end, staring over at Heather to make sure he'd said it right.

She nodded and clenched her fingers tighter around her purse. Her heart thudded so hard it was difficult to breathe. Several more seconds ticked by, and when Seth didn't reply, Ned squeezed the mic and spoke louder. "Seven-seven-three-three-Romeo, do you copy?"

Only silence filled the airways. Ned rubbed his chubby chin

and hung the mic on the wall. "Maybe he's out of range. I can contact the Dallas airport if you want to leave him a message when he lands."

She swallowed heavily, knowing Ned was just glossing over the fact that Seth had more than likely heard everything, but had chosen not to answer. She pressed a trembling hand over her heart and shook her head. "Um, no. That won't be necessary. But I appreciate your help. Thank—"

The roar of an engine took the words right out of her mouth. A small aircraft buzzed the airport office. She whipped her head around and stared out the full-length glass window. A blue-and-white Cessna made a hard climb into the setting sun, but the letters 7733R on the tail were as clear as day.

Seth. He'd come back for her!

A small squeal escaped the back of her throat as she shoved through the office doors. Her spiked sandals made it difficult for her to run across the asphalted parking lot, past all the hangars, across a grassy median, till she was at a cross section in the middle of the runway. She looked up just as Seth's plane effortlessly drifted to the ground, skidding its wheels on the far end of the runway, safely landing with Seth in the pilot's seat.

Nerves overcame her jubilation, and she quickly halted in her tracks. He'd come back, but did that mean he would take her back? After everything she'd put him through this summer, did he still love her enough to make her his wife?

The whir of the prop grew louder as Seth approached and shut off the engine. Then all was silent, except the heavy pounding of her pulse. She raised her hand and shielded her eyes, squinting toward the cockpit. He slipped off his headset and unfastened his seat belt, before he opened the door of his plane.

She could only stare as his backside emerged, stepping carefully down on the fixed landing gear then down to the ground. Just the sight of him nearly took her breath away. Dressed in tan trousers and a short-sleeved maroon-colored golf shirt, he turned around and whipped off his aviator sunglasses. His brows were furrowed slightly together, and she wasn't sure what his expression meant. She wanted to call out his name, but her voice had temporarily been blocked by a huge lump in her throat.

For a moment in time, her whole world stopped spinning. She didn't know whether to approach him, or turn around and run. Was it too late? Would he still take her back?

Seth had to blink several times to make sure the vision before him was real. But it was real. Heather was real. His heart swelled ten times bigger than his chest at the sight of her standing before him.

He didn't know whether to run up and wrap his arms around her and never let her go or wait until she approached him. He couldn't tell by her widened eyes and stiffened figure what she was thinking. It was as if she were frozen to the ground.

Was she here to take him back? Or was she here just to say good-bye for good?

Seth warily took one step toward Heather, then another till she finally took a step in his direction. She was an angel, dressed in white from head to toe. Her long, suntanned legs were accentuated by a pair of white strappy sandals with heels that boosted her well over six feet tall.

When he was within a plane's length away, he slowed his steps and stopped, not sure what he should do. Noticing she hadn't taken another step, he gave her a cautious smile. "I heard I forgot my navigator. I don't suppose you'd be up for the position?"

Her eyes glossed over before she gave a slow nod. "If you have room, I'd sure like to try."

He had to blink back the tears that threatened his own eyes. "Job's open, if you still want it."

"Oh, Seth," she whispered in a trembling voice. "I want it. I want you." Her voice choked and he didn't think he'd ever heard anything so sweet in his life.

He held out his arms, and that was all it took.

She dropped her purse and rushed to him, sobbing, but her face had a smile that spread from ear to ear. The moment her arms wrapped around his neck, he picked her up and swung her around, pressing his face into her neck. "God, I can't believe you're here. You feel so good."

Crying, she drew apart and smiled through her tears. "I love you, Seth. I love you so much it hurts."

"I know the feeling. I think I love you more every time I see you." He pressed his mouth over hers and spun slowly in a circle, never wanting to let her go again. Walking away from her two weeks ago had been the hardest thing he'd ever done in his life. Now, here she was, back in his arms, and he was never letting her out of his sight again. He set her gently on the ground and rubbed his palms on her shoulders. "So, does this mean you're going to marry me, after all?"

She framed his face with her hands. "Will you still take me after everything I've put you through?"

"Oh, baby, you haven't put me through anything. I love you so much, and I want you to be my wife more than anything in this universe and beyond."

"Then, yes. I want to marry you and be your navigator." She threw her arms back around him, laughing and crying and squeezing him so hard he grunted through his own laughter.

"Take it easy, honey. I still need to use these lungs for the next sixty years or so."

"Oh, I missed you so much. I saw all the wonderful plans for the resort. Everything's perfect. I'm sorry I ever doubted you. Thank you so much for making my dreams come true. For believing in me."

"The important thing is that you believe in yourself."

"Yes, Seth. I've never been happier in my life. I can't wait to start our new life together in Dallas."

"Dallas?"

"Yes, it'll be a wonderful place to raise a family. I love the home you and the kids drew for my birthday. And just as soon as the new resort is finished, we can come back for the ribbon-cutting ceremony."

He shook his head, not sure he was following her. "Honey, I'm not going to Dallas."

She stepped back, her mouth gaped open. "But Nicole said you were flying down there this morning."

He reached down and squeezed her hands. "I am, but it's to sign off on a few unfinished contracts."

"Wait a minute. You're not taking the promotion?"

"No."

"But why? It's what you've worked so hard for."

"No, honey. I've worked hard so I can enjoy my new family. If I'd taken that position, I'd be gone more than ever. That's not what I want anymore. You're what I want now."

"So, did they fire you?"

"No. They didn't fire me."

She blew out a huge breath. "That's a relief. At least you still have a—"

"I quit." He winked.

"You what?"

"You heard me. I'm going to be too busy with my new family, overseeing the future resort, playing Mr. Mom to three great kids, and getting to be the brother I've always wanted to be to Marty." He tapped her nose. "And my beautiful, wonderful wife will be busy writing those Pulitzers she's been dreaming about."

She lazily draped her arms back around his neck. "It all sounds like a fantasy."

He smiled and wrapped his arms around her waist. "I promise, Heather, every day from now on will be a fantasy."

She looked down and fiddled with the collar of his shirt. "How soon do you have to be in Dallas?"

"There's no rush. I just thought while Nicole was with Maggie, I'd slip down and get everything squared away. Why? What'd you have in mind?"

"Well, how would you feel about going to Vegas? If we leave now, we could officially start our next sixty years together."

"Vegas, huh?" He chuckled and rubbed his jaw. "You want to go to Vegas . . . today?"

"Unless you don't. . . ."

He laughed and kissed her pretty mouth till she couldn't say another word. He dragged his lips around to her ear and spoke with husky emotion. "Give me a minute to file a new flight plan, and we can leave right now if you want."

"Oh, Seth. Have I told you how much I love you?"

With tears in his eyes, he spoke through his own choked voice, "Not nearly enough, sweetheart." He snuggled his face into the side of her neck and breathed deep, relishing her sweet perfume. "Do you need to go back to your condo and get a suitcase packed?"

She giggled and sidestepped over to where her purse lay on the ground. She picked it up and tucked it under her arm. "I'm already packed. I even packed for you." She reached in her purse and pulled out two toothbrushes. "Red or blue?"

He gave a knowing chuckle and rubbed his palms together. "Blue."

"Did I forget anything?"

"Nope. I think that just about covers it."

Her pretty smile turned almost sad as she wrapped her arms around his waist, her big honey-brown eyes bearing deeply into his. "I'm sorry, Seth," she whispered in a choked voice. "So sorry I ever doubted you."

"Don't be," he murmured. "You're here now, and that's all that matters. From now on we're a family. You and me, Kyle, Katie, Nicole, and Marty, we're all in this together for the long haul."

"You forgot someone," she said with a muffled laugh.

"Oh, you mean the green-spiked monster that's really to blame for this whole mess? Yes. Spike, too."

She curled her fingers over his rump, giving it a slight squeeze. "How is your little ouchee?"

He feigned a grimace, and pressed in closer. "I don't know. I may need some extra coddling tonight."

Arching her brows, she smiled seductively. "If you'll cuddle, I'll coddle."

"Lady?" He tunneled his fingers through her hair and landed a warm, wet kiss square on her mouth. "You got yourself a deal."

PERMISSIONS

ABOUT THE AUTHOR

Jacquie Greenfield resides with her husband on a small acreage in a little piece of Heaven known as Iowa. She has four children who are her biggest fans and who are a constant source of inspiration and much-needed comic relief. She has been writing since 2001 and has won many awards in the romance genre. Stop by and visit her website to read excerpts from her novels at www.jacquiegreenfield.com. Be sure to click on the horseshoe and drop her a line. She loves to hear from her fans!